RAZE

Book Four of
THE COMPLETIONIST CHRONICLES
Series
Written by DAKOTA KROUT

TABLE OF CONTENTS

ACKNOWLEDGMENTS

As always, the first among the acknowledgments is my *amazing* wife, who works harder than anyone I know.

A special thank you to all of my patrons, who not only help me make better stories, but are great friends and people. An extra special thanks to: Justin Williams, Samuel Landrie, William Merrick, Brayden Wallach, John Grover, Dominic Q Roddan, and Keifer Gibbs.

To the deer that are tearing up my apple trees, I will find you.

Lastly, a heartfelt thanks to you, the reader! I could not do this without you, and I hope to keep you entertained for years to come!

PROLOGUE

"Good morning, America and, of course, the rest of the world." President Musk stood on a stage with flags flying behind him and fanfare still dying down. The most beloved President in American history spoke in a firm tone, "I am here today to tell you all some very *serious* news. Over the next few weeks, it is imperative that everyone goes to a government building and is issued a data core."

Holding up a small, shining gem, he continued speaking; doing his level best not to let his fingers tremble too much, "Within the next month, this world is going to become a *very dangerous place*. For that reason, we—and the world at large—have prepared a refuge, a safe haven for humanity to weather the impending storm. Until we can tame the dangers of this new reality, it will be *impossible* for us as a people to survive on earth."

The media erupted, shouting questions at him so loudly that not a single voice could be distinguished. He shouted over them, hoping that everyone would hear his message, "*All* of our troops, all government employees, *all people who hope to survive longer than one month*, please go to your nearest government building and get a Core. They are free, and I will now demonstrate their purpose."

He held up the gem so that everyone could see it. "These gems act as a key, a storage device, and a path to safety. Already, tens of *thousands* of people are in this new world, not knowing that they are fighting to save literally all of us. None of them are coming back. At the time of this broadcast, all people connected to the game 'Eternium' are living their true life *there*. As the man who sent them, it is my duty to join them as well.

Take the Core, and hold it to your head. That is all you need to do. Good luck... and Godspeed."

Finishing his speech, he held the Core to his head and vanished without a trace. The gem went with him. Utter silence filled all media outlets in America at the same time, a feat that had never before been accomplished.

Then the world went mad.

CHAPTER ONE

A burst of noise nearly knocked Joe from his kneeling position as the crowd of gathered Nobles and various factions burst into applause. King Henry wrapped an arm around Joe's shoulder as much to steady him as to show his favor. "A little strange, isn't it?"

Joe looked at the King in wonder. *Everything* sounded different, everything reverberated with different tones than he was used to hearing. "What... what was that? Wait, is that *my* voice?"

"Ah." The King bobbed his head in understanding, every slight motion seeming to suck the air from the room. "By your expression and the way you are clutching at your ears, the gift you have been granted must be Magical Synesthesia. I was wondering what you would earn. I know you are keeping your eyes off of your notifications out of politeness, but I would look into that more closely when you leave here. As a secondary gift, let me increase the land allotment that you earned from the part you played in that little war."

Joe heard a *ding* but again refrained from looking over at the blinking notification. The King spoke to the room at large after sitting down, his motion calculated to force clapping to a halt so that his words would have maximum impact on the gathering. "My people, we are here today to honor a man that not only played a large part in ending the Wolfman uprising, but also saved my very life."

"This man, Joe," here the King motioned at Joe and silenced the excited whispering that had broken out, "has earned my favor and the favor of my people by extension. I deem the first of his steps toward Nobility as complete."

"Should he complete two more tasks of such aid to the Kingdom, he will be granted the rights of full Nobility." The room exploded into furious noise, and Joe could have *sworn* that he somehow saw a smug look on the King's face through the armor that blocked all sight. "Of course, this is easier said than done. How many times can one man save a King... who has only ever needed to be saved *once*?"

Polite laughter broke out, but the smiles were cut with calculated staring that felt anything *except* excited or happy. "Let the feast begin!"

Joe sat to the right of the King, only two seats away from the man himself. The Queen sat next to Joe, but both of the Regents remained as still as cut stone the entire meal. The Prince, sitting on the left of the King, kept glancing at Joe in confusion, as if he had seen him before but could not remember where. *Joe* remembered *quite* clearly. It was one of the most unexpected deaths he had experienced in the game, and if he hadn't been nearly immediately given recompense, Joe may have held a grudge. As it stood, it was likely better *not* to point out errors perpetrated by the Crown Prince at dinner.

"Joe, thank you again for what you did to save my husband." The Queen was speaking in a low tone and hadn't turned her head to address him. That would have instantly drawn attention since the movement would have caused all the gathered people to choke. "I thought all was lost. Also, how is the wildebeest?"

"Is that what this is?" Joe inspected the haunch of meat, and sure enough he got the expected result.

Perception check + knowledge check success! This is a perfectly seared slice of meat from a wildebeest. Stamina +10 for the next two hours.

"Wow." Joe allowed his excitement to show through. "I've never seen normal food cooked well enough to give bonuses by itself! Oh, um. It's delicious, ma'am. That is, Your Majesty. As for the King, as happy as I am to have saved him, I truly can't take much credit. At the end of the day, it was an incredibly self-serving act."

"You refer to the penalties imposed on males of our race?" The Queen shifted a *tiny* amount, and Joe assumed she had needed to hold in a shrug. "It would have been far worse for me and mine, Joe. We would have lost *Henry*. As for being self-serving, I disagree. While there was sure to be the benefits of having a King, I was told that you crossed the battlefield not only with terrible burns but also missing a leg. No one would have faulted you for *not* making the journey."

"Ugh, I'm so hungry." The words were *not* what Joe expected to hear coming from her next. "Our battle prowess makes more... *regular* aspects of life somewhat more difficult. If I wanted to tear into that meat with you, no one else but Henry could eat at the same time. I *told* him we should have eaten before the ceremony. I *do* have one more question for you, and it may seem a little strange."

"Um. Right, please." Joe nodded slightly as an indication for her to continue and refrained from taking another bite of food while he waited for her to speak.

"*How* did you revive Henry?" Seeing Joe's confused expression, she tried again, "Please don't misunderstand, but I know how the abilities you wield work, and there is no way that you should have been able to bring him back to life. Did you somehow have a divine favor to use?"

"I didn't." Joe hadn't even *considered* his actions. He had gone into the battlefield *knowing* that he could save the King. Now that he thought about it, he could only resurrect people his own level or *lower*. There was *no way* that 'King Henry the Battle Tyrant' was a lower level than him. "I'm... I guess I have no idea *how* I did it. I just... did it."

"Hmm." The Queen paused. "I would like you to ignore propriety and take a moment to look at your notifications. Please, let me know if you see anything different, at least, in a negative manner."

Joe nodded gravely and intentionally let his notifications flow over him.

Skill gained: Magical Synesthesia (Novice I). One of the four magical senses that can be granted by the King or Queen of Ardania. From now on, all items holding magic within them will hum softly to your senses. As a consequence of your hearing being enhanced, all sounds will be interpreted differently than before, even voices. Higher levels of this skill will allow for more robust sounds to be heard. Masters of this skill are rumored to weave magic by the sound of their mana alone. Effect: 1n% increased mana-auditory sensation, where n = skill level.

The King of Ardania has doubled the amount of land that you have been authorized to claim! All land must be contiguous and cannot have a current landowner in place.

You are at a Royal Feast in your honor! Reputation gains with factions friendly to the Crown are doubled for the duration!

You are seated at the Royal table! Reputation gains with factions friendly to the Crown are doubled for the duration!

"I'm not seeing any issues, and I had read through all my notifications before coming here," Joe quietly informed the Queen. "Would you please thank the King for me again if I don't get the chance? Magical Synesthesia seems amazing."

"You don't know the half of it." She snorted softly. "Just wait until it hits the upper ranks! No change in stats then, everything is good? I am glad to hear that you have not had any blowback for helping us so much."

"Stats? I don't think so..." He hastily opened his status sheet and looked over his stats, wincing as he realized that there was *indeed* an issue; and a rather devastating one at that.

Name: Joe '*Tatum's Chosen Legend*' Class: Mage (Actual: Rituarchitect)
Profession: Tenured Scholar (Actual: Arcanologist)
Character Level: 15 Exp: 125,993 Exp to next level: 10,007
Rituarchitect Level: 2 Exp: 2,190 Exp to next level: 810
Hit Points: 220/220
Mana: 963/963
Mana regen: 19.97/sec
Stamina: 195

Characteristic: Raw score (Modifier)

Strength: 22 (1.22)
Dexterity: 31 (1.31)
Constitution: 27 (1.27)
Intelligence: 72 (2.22)
Wisdom: 66 (2.16)
Charisma: 26 (1.26)
Perception: 51 (2.01)
Luck: 29 (1.29)
Karmic Luck: +3

"I'm pretty sure I should have *twice* the amount of mana that I do right now," Joe confessed to the Queen as quietly as possible. "It's normally doubled by my deity."

"That could indeed be a problem." She took in a deep breath. "I'll arrange transport to the temples as soon as our meal is complete. You should find the issue at the source, after all. Unfortunately, if you leave right now, there will be the issue of breaking protocol and many people will hold a grudge against you."

"I'd rather that didn't happen." Joe groaned as he looked over his stats once more. There was only one thing that he could do to mitigate the loss, and that was to pour a hefty amount of characteristic points into the intelligence stat. He had fifteen points remaining from his sudden level increase, as well as eighteen skill points, but he was unsure if using them was the best course of action. He reluctantly decided instead to wait until meeting with Tatum.

As the feast slowed and people started loosening their belts, individuals began to wander around the area. Small social groups were forming, and some intrepid people began approaching the Monarchs. To Joe's surprise, a few even came to speak with *him*! None of them really had much to say to each other, but Joe realized that by appearing friendly with him, they were also able to stand directly in front of the Monarchs and have themselves noticed.

Only one person really stood out from the others, and it was only by his actions. The man in question was dressed in colors just as garish as the other Nobles in the room, but instead of speaking to Joe, the man simply looked at him like he was an interesting bug. This wouldn't have been a *terrible* issue, but he was leaning across the table and had even slid Joe's plate to the side in order to get closer.

"Humph." This was the only 'word' the man spoke, but a notification scrolled across Joe's vision that made his pulse race.

Reputation increased! Your reputation with the Grand Zoo of Ardania has increased from 'Loathed' to 'Hated'! Only 1000 more points to reach 'Hostile'!

Reputation increased! Your reputation with the Grand Zoo of Ardania has increased from 'Hated' to 'Hostile'! Only 300 more points to reach 'Cautious'!

After that gruff sound, the man simply turned and walked away. Joe managed to close his mouth, just now realizing that it had dropped during that uncomfortable exchange. "What in the world was *that*?"

"Hmm?" The Queen was staring at a plate of still-steaming bread, and Joe could feel his breath catch as she twitched toward it. "Oh, him. That's 'The Ringleader'. Pff. His name is *Robert*. He runs one of the most popular forms of entertainment for Nobility, a zoo that boasts the most unique creatures known to Eternium. I have no idea *why* people like the menagerie and clowns so much. For now, at least. I'll figure it out soon, I'm certain."

"He didn't seem to like *me* very much," Joe blandly stated, taking a sip of wine and committing the man's face to memory. Whatever had happened in the past to get him to this point, the fact remained that he had somehow just gained a thousand and seven hundred reputation points at a minimum. "Did I do something to upset him?"

"It's highly unlikely. He doesn't get out much." The Queen sighed as a server took the bread basket away. "Drat. Ah, well. They'll save some for me. As for *Robert*, he just doesn't like many people."

Joe watched as the dance floor started to be populated. Feeling a tickle of dread, he saw several people eyeing him carefully. The King chuckled and spoke just loud enough for Joe to hear, "I think it's time to sneak you out of here. That mark on your head will always get you access to the throne room if you need it, but do your best not to abuse the privilege. Good luck, Joe. How I *envy* you getting to leave early!"

"We should have eaten before this started."

"I know, I *know*." King Henry sounded exasperated, and Joe smiled. It was nice to see that some things were the same regardless of social strata.

CHAPTER TWO

The unassuming carriage rolled to a stop in front of the temple district. Joe popped out and waved at the driver, who nodded and got the horses moving once more. The Rituarchitect looked up at the imposing building and frowned. Normally, he would be happy to be here, but right now he had a sneaking suspicion that something had gone *very* wrong.

Walking through the temple, he heard an odd ringing in his ears that just barely *tickled* at his senses. Oddly enough, covering his ears did nothing to stop the ringing, and he realized that this must have something to do with his new hearing skill. Obviously, this place was highly enchanted or just stuffed full of mana; which would make sense at a giant hub of divine energy like this.

"Let's see... neutral, dark, water." Joe followed the path to Tatum's altar just as he had before, but was surprised to find that it was closer to the center and more ornate than it had been previously. He touched it, expecting to find himself away on a mountaintop temple in the next instant, but was instead given a notification.

System message: Hello, Joe. You are the Chosen of Tatum, which is why you are being shown this message at all. The Deity Occultatum is under review for his actions to this point. He has spent too much divine energy in too short an amount of time. Not only that, but he directly resurrected King Henry of Ardania using you as a medium.

As such, certain passive bonuses will be unavailable to you. Specifically, you cannot be granted an extended mana pool, though your ability to resurrect others will remain. You are free

to choose another deity to serve during this time, or you can
work to pay off Occultatum's debt of 13,000,000 divine energy.

"Good *lord*, Tatum!" Joe muttered to himself, shocked at the vast deficit. He continued reading through the message. "What did you *do*?"

As you know, each place of power connected to a deity
generates divine energy for them. There are five different
standard *types of divine sources as buildings. In order: Altar,*
Shrine, Temple (small), Temple, and Temple (Grand). Followers
will also generate divine energy at a lower rate, and less
consistently as they may shift allegiance. The choice is yours to
make!

"Well, obviously I'm not gonna turn my back on a guy who destroyed himself to get me to this point." Joe sighed and rubbed his bald head. "Hold on, Tatum. I'll figure out a way to help you out or else I'll see you whenever the current temples pay out enough."

Quest Gained: Paying a Great Debt. By choosing to
remain faithful to your chosen deity, you have agreed to take on
their debt. Find a way to pay off 13,000,000 divine energy.
Followers generate up to 25 DE a day. Altars generate 50 DE a
day. Shrines generate 100 DE a day. Temples generate 250, 500,
and 1000 DE daily in order of rank. There may be other places
of power that can be converted to your deity, but you will need
to find that information yourself. Reward: Interaction with Tatum
unlocked, Unknown. Failure: Tatum remains locked away.

"Sheesh, they are not making it easy on me." Joe patted the altar, "Sorry, big guy. Even if I make this my mission for a good long time, I think you are stuck for a while. See ya when I see ya."

Joe found that the fast-travel system was still in place and that the altar had a built-in connection. Excellent, he had been worried that he would need to go to the town square in order to teleport back to the Wanderer's Guild. With a tiny clap of air being displaced, he vanished from Ardania and appeared in the unnamed town that had been taken over by the Noble Guild. Instantly, he felt slightly queasy. "What in the...?"

He looked at his stats and noticed that the teleport had taken a full eighth of his mana. Normally, that was such a small amount that he wouldn't even notice it happening! Heck, by the time he noticed the loss even now, his mana was already regenerating. Just one more limiting factor he hadn't even needed to *observe* until now.

"Are you Joe?" A man came running up to him wearing light clothing and winged sandals. "Looks like they were right! Just wait in the egg-shaped Pathfinder's Hall, and ol' Joe will pop out of nowhere. Neat trick! I have a message for you. There is a guild leadership meeting starting in about twenty minutes. I know it's late, but I wasn't the one who set it up."

The messenger handed over a small missive, gave the guild salute of a fist banging on his chest, and ran off once more. Joe hadn't even gotten a chance to respond! Some people's kids. Joe turned over the letter and pondered it momentarily. "At least they gave me warning. Not like I have anything else to do right now. Sleep would be nice, though."

After regrowing his leg—and attending to Reggie, the traitor mage—Joe had left for the capital right away in order to claim whatever reward the King wanted to give him. No need to put that off for a rainy day; rewards from a Royal were best taken right away... just in case you lost their favor in the future. Plus, gaining a new sense that *leveled?* Definitely worth making the trip. Joe looked around at the mid-sized temple he was in and sighed. At least there was five hundred divine energy guaranteed to go off to Tatum each day. At this rate, he would see the deity in... twenty-six thousand days, or a bit more than seventy-one years.

"Well, that just won't work for me." Joe started walking toward the newly built guild hall. It wasn't hard to find; in fact, it was one of the only buildings currently standing. Everything else, even if it had survived the initial blast of the detonating... whatever that *thing* was... had been so unsafe that the guild had ripped it apart. There were very few survivors from the original town; most of them had been shuffled to the side to be taken care of by healers when the nuke-like object went off. There had been no sign of them respawning.

Through all the tragedy, the benefit to the guild was obvious. They now had a clean section of land to build and expand upon, but the downside was that they were going to need to import labor. That was rough. At least there was plenty of wood around! Whatever hadn't burned right away had simply been knocked over, and this made it a simple matter to collect a few tons of trees to be cut into lumber. People in the guild with the carpenter class were *ecstatic*. Lumberjacks less so.

The doors in front of Joe opened, and he was ushered over to sit at a large, oval table. He wasn't the last to arrive, but it was pretty close. Aten stepped into the room as soon as the final person was present and charged straight into conversation, "Hey, guys! Just popped over from the front lines and have a really short window to make it back before the Gate spell collapses. I'll get straight to the agenda. First up, we're having a lot of issues with leadership abusing their positions."

"If you are suspected of doing this, there will be an investigation. If it is found that you are doing things you shouldn't be, like putting someone into the position of attention or messing with them when they *aren't* breaking our rules, your position is *gone*. No argument, no appeal. You might even get kicked from the guild." Aten was speaking in a deep voice and trying to make eye contact with the whole table at once. "Now, look around. All the people here are guild leadership. Become friends. It matters."

"Lastly, with Sir Bearington's permission, I was officially able to claim the entire town and about one square mile of land with this building at the exact center. We need to make this place into a *fortress*, but first, we need to get people out of tents and into barracks at the minimum. There are a *lot* of support and logistics issues that need to be addressed, so work together to make it happen. If you have a skillset that could help us here, *please* use it to help us all out." Aten was practically staring holes in Joe as he was speaking. "Alright, that's all. I gotta go!"

Aten ran out of the building, and the other people just sort of... sat there with information overload. They started chatting, but Joe had been having a *very* long day and left after the eighth person introduced themselves. He was doing his best to be friendly, but *Celestial Feces* some of these people were boring. Joe was pretty sure that at least half the staff were there as stand-ins for some corporation that was funding this guild. The other half seemed... *zealous* about treating this purely as a game. Not really Joe's scene when he was so tired.

After escaping the clutches of polite small-talk for the second time in one night, Joe finally made it back to the Pathfinder's Hall. He was looking forward to a bed in one of the most defended places he could manage. The last time he had slept out in the open, an assassin had tried to lay a terrifying curse on him. It had failed, sure, but it had also made Joe *far* more wary.

Just as he was closing the door behind him, someone out in the darkness screamed, "*I can't log out!*"

Silence followed this proclamation for only as long as it took *other* people to try logging out as well. Then the night erupted into screams and shouts, rage and fear.

"Nope." Joe *firmly* closed the door behind him. "Not dealing with that right now. *Bed.* Most of that'll be sorted by morning anyway."

CHAPTER THREE

"Ahh. Nothing like a well-rested bonus to get you going in the morning!" Joe stepped out of the massive, egg-shaped building and looked around. There were a lot of sleepless faces around, eyes ringed with the purple and black bruises that showed up after a long and trying night. "Though maybe I'll go ahead and keep that to myself..."

Joe had a very standard routine in the morning: wake up, cast Cleanse on himself, find coffee, and *drink* said coffee. His body and clothing were cleaner than if he had spent fifteen minutes in the shower and used a modern washing machine, and now he was ready for the second half of the morning *ritual*. Heh. No one ever said his jokes were *good* before coffee, but that one came close.

While walking over to the dining hall, Joe kept an eye on his fellow guild members. A good chunk of them seemed distraught, but an even larger number of them seemed hyper-manic and happy with this outcome. Joe wasn't sure where the discrepancy lay; perhaps they were simply hardcore gamers that had been chasing after this fantasy from the start? Where was the coffee?

Joe got in the back of a long line and not-exactly patiently waited for his chance at the anthracite ambrosia. When he finally got around to the front, he realized why this process was taking so long today and cursed whoever had brought this tradition to Eternium. "Grande half-caf double whip toffee nut latte with an extra shot."

People turned and stared at him as he screamed, but he didn't care. "*No~o~o*! Why, you monster? In the first place, why would you get a shot of espresso and put that delicious liquid in *half-caf mud*? Move! *You*! Coffee! Black! Large!"

The server... no, the *barista* smiled at him and poured a long stream of coffee into a mug for him. "Can I get a name for this?"

"Joe."

"Thanks, Elbow! That'll be five copper." The barista hadn't changed his plastered-on facial expression the entire time. Joe had to do his best not to slap him, grab the mug, and run away screaming.

"Here's the *copper*." Joe slapped the coins on the table and snatched the mug away. "I can't even tell you how upset I am about this situation."

"New policy! Coffee is expensive to get out here, so we can't just give it away for free. Have a great day, Elbow!" The barista was already back to helping other customers, and Joe could only walk stiffly away while sipping his drink. *Anger* sipping.

"Okay, I can do this, this is fine." Joe laughed in a slightly too-high pitched tone. "Since everyone else is out on quests and stuff, I guess I'll just go–"

"Excuse me, Joe?" A glasses-wearing man stepped toward him with a too-friendly expression on his face. The glasses had to be an affectation as everyone had perfect eyesight here. That, or they offered some bonus similar to Joe's scholarly spectacles. "I don't think we've had a chance to meet. I am the Vice-Guild leader. My name is Michael. My friends call me Mike, and I hope you will as well."

"Oh, good morning, Mike." Joe switched his coffee mug to his left hand and shook Mike's outstretched appendage. "How can I help you today?"

"I have a few problems that I am told you might be willing to help with, especially in light of our most recent meeting and subsequent lack of being able to log off." Mike saw the coffee in Joe's hand and smiled widely. "Oh, you found our newest coffee shop! That was my idea. Did you find something that you liked?"

"*Blasphemy.*"

"I'm... sorry, I didn't catch that?" Mike frowned at Joe's whispered word but decided to just launch into his reason for being there, "I'm told that you can raise buildings *very* quickly, and I know that you are the one who made the Pathfinder's Hall. Can I ask what you would need from us to get a few housing developments going? Since no one can log off, we are finding that having rooms would be very beneficial."

"You want me to make... housing." Joe tried not to crack his knuckles, a bad habit from his past life. "I can create war-starting-and-ending structures, and you want me to magic *houses* into existence."

Joe's flat tone wasn't lost on Mike, who gestured at the massive, black marble building. "I do. I know that this isn't as glorious as something like *that*, but this is something that may actually be more important in the short term. It'll take a week for our people to put up a house, *two* for an apartment building or barracks, but you... you can do it in under a day, I'm told. We'll supply whatever you need, within reason, and this is a great way to earn contribution points!"

"Contribution... points." Joe wasn't dumb; he was just surprised by the blatant attempt to get him to do a lot of work on what was essentially credit. An 'I owe you' didn't help much when a wolf was tearing out your throat. He'd found that out firsthand.

"Right! We took the concept from the Wolfman war," Mike jovially informed Joe. "When we go on raids or clear dungeons, there will be gear and items that everyone wants. Those will go into the guild's storage, and people will be able to buy that sort of thing *only* with contribution points. I swear it'll be a useful currency."

"*Will* be." Joe sighed and drank his now-cool coffee in one long pull. "Ahh. Alright. Listen, Mike, there is a *reason* that buildings take a long time to build. What you are doing is having a bunch of people share the energy cost and potentially cutting down on the resources needed to put a building together properly. If I were to do it, I could get a building up in ten minutes after the process got going. There is *still* a *cost*, both in mana and resources. It's a *lot* cheaper to just build the building."

"How high of a cost are we talking?" Before Joe could answer, Mike held up a hand and continued, "Is the cost so high that it would be worth about a hundred people—who just lost *everything*—sleeping outside? *My* job is morale. Even that coffee you were looking so sour over a moment ago? The intentionally-insulting treatment is something familiar to a lot of people. The options they get to choose from? Those make them feel less powerless in a place they just found out they *can't leave*. I'm telling you that if it will help the people relying on us, I'll happily foot the bill."

Joe's opinion of the man in front of him just *soared*. "Ex-military?"

"Lieutenant-Colonel, retired." Mike showed him a real smile and pushed his glasses up his nose. "But you never *really* retire."

"Huh." Joe rubbed the back of his bald head. "It's good to see that there are some people in upper management thinking about the low-level people. Alright, *Sir*, first thing I'm gonna need is a blueprint of whatever building you want made. I need it to be perfect because *whatever is on that blueprint* is what is being built."

"I'll make it happen, and don't call me 'Sir', that life is over." Mike smiled and shook Joe's hand again.

"You never *really* retire though, do you?" Joe grinned back at the expression on Mike's face as he repeated the words Mike had used. "Plus, this makes it really easy for me to get back at you for tainting my morning coffee run."

Mike growled a deep, meaningful growl that only people with military experience can make, and Joe laughed at him. "Alright, Sir, I'm going to be occupied over at the mess hall for the next two hours. Don't let people interrupt me. Just have 'em leave the blueprints in front of me."

"Hmm. Mess hall, *indeed*. It's a double row of picnic tables, and you abyss-well know it." Mike nodded at him and marched off. Now that Joe knew what to look for, the military bearing was plain. Joe turned and went over to the wooden tables, having decided to work on his puzzle cube. Since Joe had three of the four stats in the second tier, it took an hour and forty-five minutes for a notification to appear. Still, that was better than the seven hours it *should* have taken.

Characteristic point training completed! +1 to intelligence, wisdom, perception, and dexterity! These stats cannot be increased further by any means other than system rewards, study, or practice for twenty-four hours game time.

Joe blinked away the question that the puzzle cube had given him today: 'Why do we have emotions?'. He had been caught in an odd loop there. Was the cube saying that *it* had emotions? He assumed that it was talking about humans, but this thing had some really non-standard questions on it, so he couldn't discount the possibility that it was using him to justify its existence. Still, the training had paid off.

In front of Joe—actually tucked under his left elbow—was a small stack of papers. Blueprints. Excellent. Joe picked up the first one, took a look, and set it aside. He was going to be building a few of the larger housing complexes like a barracks or an apartment to maximize the housing efficiency first. Small, well-appointed houses could wait.

A pot of ink, a quill, some low-grade scroll paper, and Joe's ritual reference book all appeared on the table in front of him. Joe smiled as he pulled the items directly from his Codpiece of Holding to his hand without needing to make a seemingly obscene action. He already had people looking at him strangely on the regular, no need for them to think that he kept a pot of ink and a quill in his undies.

"Step one, surround a copy of the magical blueprint with the Architect's Fury ritual." Joe placed his scroll of paper under the blueprint after putting a thin layer of the darkest shadow he could make over the lines on the ritual template he had already drawn up. Then he used the quill to deftly make a tracing of the dark lines, finishing within about half an hour. He dropped the quill into the inkwell and sat back to let the paper dry. "Ugh, that's so much easier than making all of this from scratch. Or, wait, I'm not actually sure. Easier than coming up with the design, at least."

Skill increase: Drawing (Novice VI). Go you, dirty tracer.

"Looks like even the drawing skill is as picky about real art as *artists* are." Joe snorted at the notification, deciding it was time to get back to work. "This is going to be a tier-one building, but with this great of a blueprint and if I add on a second spell circle, I should be able to get this to be at least a Common-ranked building."

After working out the spell circle on a separate piece of paper and validating it thanks to his Occultist bonus, he started the process of infusing the ritual with mana and linking the blueprint. This was always the most delicate part, but he had faith in his success even though this was a student-ranked diagram. His copy of the blueprint appeared in the ritual circle and seemed to struggle to escape. As the mana-infused ink dried on to the paper, the entire thing shuddered slightly once more... but stabilized. Whew!

It was already lunchtime, and Joe had only been able to create a single ritual diagram to create a single building. Actually, now that he thought about it, that wasn't a terrible amount of time to make something that would become a permanent fixture. He smacked himself in the face when he remembered that there was a bonus to creation speed he could have gotten from the ritual room of the Pathfinder's Hall, but instead of falling into despair, he sighed and decided lunch needed to come before his mood. Actually, his mood was likely being affected by hunger and thirst.

"Cleanse." Joe watched as his mana appeared on his fingers and turned into water. That water found a vein on his arm and poured in, hydrating him better than an IV could have ever hoped to do. "Food next."

After getting a quick bite to eat, Joe decided to do the calculations for the building before seeking out Mike again. He was muttering aloud without realizing it, "Reducing the cost by a flat fifty percent, down another twenty-three percent from the ritual magic skill... Coalescence, so another twenty-one percent... looks like this is going to come out to about seven hundred mana for initial investment, then fifty mana per second for about thirty seconds. I have... ugh... nine seventy-six."

"That means I'll need at least one other mage on this with me. More if I want to keep my Mage Armor active. I wonder if... heh... let's see if we have a magic Mike."

Chapter Four

"You want *me* to participate in making the building?" Mike didn't even look up from the forms he was signing rapid-fire, getting through a massive stack of documents in only a few minutes. "Why?"

"Multiple reasons, one of which is to allow people to see one of their top guys going out to help them directly. It's a public relations win, a morale booster, you know it would be." Joe smiled winningly, but Mike just waved his hand for the next reason. "Alright, the other reason I want this so much is so that you realize *exactly* what's going on when I pull magic out of my butt and create a building. It's really cool but very draining. I can't do it constantly, and I want you to see why I *won't* do this sort of thing all the time. Also, here is a list of extra components I need beyond the building materials. Also, what are the... *contribution points* I'll get for this?"

"Two thousand, the same amount that will be given to a logistics group that supplies raids on dungeons in the near future. We can negotiate future rates after this first building goes up." Mike took the list, looked it over, and looked up at Joe with raised brows. "*Why* do you need some of these things? Termite spoor... for instance?"

"That'll do for the time being. Now, the odd items on the list. Lots of reasons, but that one *specifically* because this area has a huge termite problem, and this will automatically add anti-infestation protections to the building. The rest of it is the cost of building a Common-ranked barracks in a day from the ground up. Also, I added in extra room to each building so that they can be upgraded if we ever find better designs for them."

Mike looked over the list once more, signed it into a requisition order, and handed it to one of his aides. "How important is it that I participate?"

"You join in, or I won't." Joe's smile showed teeth.

Mike nodded slowly, his eyes narrowing a fraction. "I see. Let's make it happen. Where should we deliver all these... goods?"

"Wherever you want the building." Joe paused and raised a hand to his chin. "Also, it might be better to do this on a spot already cleared and prepared. The mana cost especially will jump if we need to tear up the ground and knock over trees. Having a foundation in place *would* be best, but it won't work for my modified plans. In the future, we can work that out ahead of time."

"Alright, when are we doing this?"

"As soon as you can get all the supplies in place." Joe turned toward the door. "Everything else is already built into this ritual blueprint. All we need to do is power and activate it."

"Is it reusable?" Mike leaned forward interestedly.

"No. Since I made the ritual by using a blueprint instead of scanning an already-built structure, we only get to use it once, then I have to make the whole thing again. Also, word of warning: anyone else activating it would need to pay the full cost of all materials and mana." Joe smiled at Mike and opened the door. "Let me know when you are ready for me. I'll be working on my skills over at the training grounds."

Joe went over to the mid-range spell practice area and worked to familiarize himself with his newest powers. Effortless Shaping, contrary to its name, required an exact picture in mind when working to make something out of darkness. It was intense mental work but was such an *insignificant* drain on mana that Joe had to assume that was where the 'effortless' portion of the skill name came from. Beyond that, getting details too close to each other tended to make them blend, which could really only be fixed by gaining skill levels. Sadly, the lack of needed mana was quickly made up for when Joe solidified the shadows into... anything.

He could invest ten points of mana per skill level and had found that larger amounts of mana would let him do more damage or stabilize the structure for longer periods of time. Right now, shadows would 'bleed' and slowly vanish when they were exposed to bright light. Joe had found this out when he was running mana through a ritual and one of the lines snapped. If he had been doing anything important with it, he would have been in a *lot* of trouble. Joe had gotten *very* lucky in the past, especially during the war when his basic enchanting ritual was stuffed under a tent. That could have gone *very* badly.

So, training. Perfecting his shadowy shapes and holding them under the sun to find ways to make them last longer and hold more detail was the only thing he could think to do for training himself in this regard. Also, solidifying the shadows required him to pour mana into the shape, and he wanted to be able to do that *faster*. Over the course of a few hours—and thanks to the boost from proximity to the Pathfinder's Hall—he gained a few skill levels.

Skill increase: Effortless (Darkness) Shaping (Apprentice VII). Boo! Did I scare you?

Skill increase: Solidified Shadows. (Apprentice VII). You looked scared.

Skill increase: Cleanse (Apprentice VII). Strange that you increased three skills and they all became the same rank and level. +1 Luck.

"Alright. I'll take it." Multiple hours of hydrating people around him upon request had also paid off, it seemed. Joe looked at the shadow skills almost *greedily*. They were the only Legendary and Mythical skills he had, and he couldn't wait to see what kind of bonuses he would gain from them as they ranked up.

"Joe, ready to get this over with?" Mike came trotting up, a few of his aides in tow. "Let's get some people housed before darkness sets in. Whoa, what happened *here*?"

The ground was torn up all over the place, and a few of the targets had brutal scarring on them. Joe looked at his handiwork and winced; he hadn't been thinking about what others would see when they watched his spells going off or what they would think when they saw the torn-up landscape.

"Miss a lot, don't ya?" Mike commented dryly as he took a look around. He smirked and started walking away, Joe following after with a bright red face. "I can see why you wanted to practice."

"*No*, I don't *miss* a lot. I was trying new spell effects!" Joe's defensiveness caused the small group to snicker, and he realized that he was being intentionally baited. "Laugh it up, big guy."

Mike's lips twitched, but Joe couldn't see it happening. By the time they got to a cleared lot, he had his face under control once again. "Here we are. All of the normal material needed for building this barracks are over here, and here are the items you... requested."

"Great!" Joe grabbed the bag, looking through it and inspecting the quality of each of the items in it. "Alright... good. Yeah, we should be all set. Let me place this... how do you want the building oriented?"

"Lengthwise, like this," one of the aides spoke up, gesturing with his hands, "with the doors placed here and here."

"Right." Joe took a deep breath at the order that was inconsistent with the blueprint they had already agreed upon. He took another, just so that he didn't say anything he would regret. "Hey, Mike, interesting issue here. You wanted the doors shifted around? To be different than what was on the *blueprint*?"

"It was more of a last-minute judgment call." The aide waved his hands flippantly. "It isn't *that* important... if you can't *do* it."

"Good, because it isn't happening," Joe responded bluntly, shocking the aide into red-faced anger. "I told you, Mike, whatever is on the blueprint is what is made. There *are no* alterations that I can make right now unless you want to wait until tomorrow. I would need to make this ritual diagram from scratch, from blueprints that are *correct*, and that took me... oh, about five-ish hours today?"

"As he mentioned, it wasn't that important." Mike stared at the now-wilting aide. "Frankly, I'm not sure *why* it came up."

"Because you are trying to test me, Mike." Joe sighed and cracked his neck. "Stupid power games and attempts to mess with me to see how far you can push me. Standard military fare, and it doesn't bother me much. But... it does bother me a *little*. Add on twenty-five percent to the contribution points we agreed on, or I'm out. Play stupid games, win stupid prizes."

The group around him went quiet at the direct challenge to Mike. The man in question sighed and nodded. "You drive a hard bargain, Joe."

"It's okay, Mike. You could triple what I'm earning. The currency is worthless right now." Joe didn't break eye contact.

"So was bitcoin a decade ago," Mike grumbled halfheartedly. "You got it, Joe. My bad. Look, it's just something pretty deeply ingrained in me."

"I've had my fill of military, Mike. As much as I respect all the people in it, my time there is done, and I'm very *happy* with that arrangement." Joe looked at the aides and made a motion at the edges of the property. "Can someone grab a stick and rough out where the building should be going? Gonna have to destroy it by hand if we get it wrong, and I don't know if a lot of people will be on board for that."

When all the preparations were complete and a drop of blood from both of them had been added to the silver focus chalice, Joe looked over at Mike and smiled darkly. "Ready? Here we go!"

With those words, the Rituarchitect poured mana into the ritual blueprint he had created, and a holographic double ring expanded away from the men and eclipsed the entire lot. "*In structuram, pulchra placent?*"

The two men running the ritual were lifted off their feet as wood, nails, and pipes began flying toward them and assembling themselves into barracks form. The ritual turned sideways, and as it passed over the area... it acted like a printer that left behind completed buildings. A massive three-D printer! Mike got a beautiful view of the entire process, and really seemed to be enjoying himself. Then Joe got down to twenty percent of his mana, and the draw switched over to the Vice Guild leader..

"Son of a...!" Mike exclaimed in sudden shock. Joe chuckled; his body was literally designed to move around massive flows of power like this, but he didn't need to let other people know that. Let them think that he got mana-sick like they did, and his work would be even more respected. Also less requested, if he made the person bothering him participate.

The ritual drained Mike down to ten mana before switching back to Joe. The Rituarchitect had been able to regenerate two-hundred and eighty mana over the intervening fourteen seconds. That, coupled with the almost two-hundred mana he had remaining from the first round, afforded him another ten seconds of mana input before it switched back to Mike. The man lasted three seconds, then the drain was back to Joe, but luckily, the ritual only lasted another second before finishing. Then the diagram burst into intense, blue flames and vanished.

They settled on the ground, both heaving great gulps of air and staring at the bright sky. Within a few moments, they were able to sit up and look at the building they had just erected. Mike was the first to speak, "It looks excellent. I... can see why you would attach a high price for your work, though."

"I'd get a carpenter to look at it, but it should be perfectly safe for people to sleep in there tonight," Joe informed the Vice-Guild leader.

No Class experience gained for buildings Common-ranked or below!

"Good show." Mike looked at the building once more. He squinted and pointed up. "No shingles on the roof?"

"Well, Mike," Joe stood up, brushed off his Robe of Liquid Darkness, and shrugged, "no shingles on the blueprint."

CHAPTER FIVE

"We're back, Joe!" Alexis ran over to Joe as he was leaving breakfast. Joe's bad mood over being interrupted halfway through his daily characteristic score training vanished like fog on a sunny day.

"Alexis!" Joe opened his arms, and his teammate gave him a hug. "It's so good to see you. How was your trip?"

"Pretty great!" Alexis smiled even as her eyes went flat. "We were able to improve our skills a lot, gain some good experience, and even prevent a few war crimes from occurring."

"War crimes...?" Joe almost didn't want to know. "As in?"

"The Wolfmen are sentient or close enough to it that slaughtering innocents is a *really bad thing*," she quietly informed him, even as she pulled him along to see the others in the party. "Thanks to Bard keeping people calm and Poppy stabbing a few of the most vicious people in the face, we stopped... a lot of things that shouldn't have even been considered."

"That's good. I'm proud of you guys," Joe told the three as the other two came into view. "When you went off to finish off that race, I was really worried that you would do some things you might eventually regret. I'm glad to be proven wrong."

"Ah, no' wi' ma pretty lass keepin' us in line!" Bard called over, causing Alexis to simultaneously roll her eyes and blush. "It's good ta see ya, Joe."

"Even better to be seen!" Joe smirked at the trio. "Hi, Poppy!"

"Ah, our fearless leader!" Poppy swept off his oversized, feathered hat and sketched a bow. "How it warms my heart to be in your presence once more!"

"Right." Joe snorted and slapped the man on the shoulder. "All we need now is Jaxon, and we'll be back to full strength!"

"I'd like to contend that we are at full strength whenever *I* am here." Poppy sniffed at the air haughtily. "I'd also–"

Joe splashed the duelist in the face with a Cleanse spell and then decided to make the most of it when he realized that the three of them actually stunk pretty badly. Water spun out from Joe and washed over the three, cleaning them and their clothes at the same time. "There we go. You guys should be losing that debuff right about... now. Much better!"

Poppy spat to the side. "Hey, thanks, but a bit of warning, yeah? That black water is *cold.*"

"Any plans for the day?" Joe looked around at the others and got shrugs in response. "Actually, weren't you all supposed to be gone for a few more days?"

"Ah. Yeah, but when no one could log out, food started vanishing *way* faster than we had plotted for. Not only that," Alexis took a swig of water from her canteen, "morale was pretty low at that point. We figured 'good enough' and got moving back here."

"Oh, well, good." Joe smiled around, but his happy look slowly faded. "I, unfortunately, seem to have been nerfed during our time apart."

"Wha' d'ya mean?" Bard questioned with a furrowed brow. "Ya doin' alright?"

"Yeah, but I lost my direct connection to my deity." Joe sighed softly. "Gonna need to do a lot of work to restore him, and I really need to test out my current combat ability."

"We caught a quest about cleaning out some caverns nearby that might connect to a deeper level of those mines we collapsed," Poppy offered quickly. "It looked *fun*, what with the total lack of information available and a dark, cramped space."

"Sounds just about perfect. You all okay to get going?" Joe looked around, and everyone nodded eagerly. He *really* hoped that they were eager to fight and get back together, not to see how weak he was. They started walking toward the gates, and Joe was *just* about to ask a question when he saw someone familiar.

"Jaxon! There you are!" Joe called happily. He had been the *most* concerned about Jaxon; the man had a tendency to break people accidentally or start fights accidentally or get warrants for his arrest accidentally... Joe had been worried. "Everyone just got back a short while ago. I was hoping that we could get up to date on our adventures. What do you think?"

"*Excuse* me, get *out* of the way." A pompous man Joe recognized from the late-night meeting a few days ago seemed to be nearly hyperventilating over Joe interrupting him, his fists clenched and pale as he continued shouting at Jaxon, "We told you what would happen if you came back, and you are–"

Joe stepped closer to Jaxon, still chatting happily to bait the youth into doing something stupid. The young leader seemed absolutely shocked that Joe had done so and decided to play right into Joe's hands. "Are you not in the Guild? I *said*, get out of the *way!*"

"Right, that's enough. I'm *Joe*. Who are you?" Joe turned to the other man and subtly pulled in shadows at strategic locations on his body. This combined with leaking his mana had the interesting effect of creating a seemingly powerful aura of magic that stifled those around him, and adding a point or three of mana to slightly solidify the shadows created an actual physical pressure that made it hard to breathe.

"I...I'm–"

"I don't actually care. Leave us alone." Joe turned back to Jaxon, suddenly all smiles again. "Jaxon, what happened to you? What are you *wearing*?"

"Oh, it's been an interesting few days!" Jaxon cheerfully stated, giving Joe an unwanted hug that left a thin film of blood and sweat behind. The bald man gave a weak smile, trying not to gag as he cast Cleanse on Jaxon and himself. A disk of water traveled up and down their bodies, followed by the woman with Jaxon as an afterthought. "Ah, I've missed your tricks. Oh! Before I go too far, I need to feed my hands a treat. Been too busy the last few days to really do so."

"Feed yer... hands?" Bard smiled uncomfortably. "Ah feel like ya have an interesting story fer me ta tell."

"One... moment." Jaxon ignored the others, including the pompous man's group who was still standing awkwardly near them. A box appeared in Jaxon's hands from which he pulled a brick of... meat? With a strange distortion, Jaxon's hands shifted into lizard-like heads and began tearing into the meat.

The people in the area all shouted, flinched, or took a step backward with two notable exceptions. The woman with Jaxon, as she appeared used to this, and Joe, who took a step closer with wonder filling his eyes. As the hands finished their snack, Jaxon held them aloft so they could roar their joy into the sky.

"Are those...?"

"T-Rex Head Hands," Jaxon cheerfully stated, pulling the now-placid creatures closer to his body. "They are a skill called Living Weapons."

"T-Rex Head Hands." Joe's eyes were burning with excitement, and as the other group took the chance to escape the situation, Joe wanted nothing more than to grab the miniature beasts and study them. "Long name. If they always come out together, could we call them something else?"

Jaxon smiled happily. Now *here* was a man who appreciated the finer things in life. "Sure, Joe. What did you have in mind?"

"How about 'Rexus'?"

"Interesting. Rexus." Jaxon rolled the word around in his mouth for a moment. "Rex, as in King, which is where T-rex comes from in the first place. Rexus as a whole, though... that means 'a mature, self-possessed, and responsible nature'. Absolutely *perfect,* Joe. That describes me perfectly."

"Glad to hear it, man!" Joe studied the head-hands intently until they shifted back into *regular* hands. "Oh, that might have been the coolest skill I've seen the entire time I've been here! I want some!"

"We can talk about it later. We're in a cornfield," Jaxon stated with a cautious smile. When there was no reaction, he snorted and looked around. "Ears everywhere? Come on, that expression can't be *that* outdated."

"Oh, yes it *can,* Jaxon." The woman standing next to Jaxon chimed in with a sigh. "Hi, everyone. I'm Jess since I *highly* doubt Jaxon was going to introduce me. He forgot I was *traveling with him* a few times over the last week."

"I've missed you, Jaxon." Poppy snickered, reaching out a hand to the lady. "Very nice to meet you, Jess. I'm Poppy, the leader of this team."

Alexis slapped his hand out of the air as Jess reached out. "He most certainly is *not.* Joe here is team leader. I'm Alexis, the second-in-command."

"Hi there! I feel like I've heard enough about you that we will be able to skip all the awkwardness!" Jess exclaimed happily.

Her smile cracked when Jaxon spoke up, "From who? I don't think I've talked about them to you at all."

The low-charisma Chiropractor waited impatiently for a response. "Was it those PvP assassins you used to hang out with? They don't seem like the sort of people to give happy information very often."

"Jaxon... I was *going* to make a joke where I said, 'not really, Jaxon is insane and can't hold a real conversation', but you are just the *worst*!" Jess turned and tried to stab Jaxon with an extra-shiny dagger that had appeared in her hand.

The man dodged easily and smiled. "Thank you, Jess! I was wondering how you planned to keep me battle ready while we were in a safe area, but I should have known you had something planned!"

Joe watched them go back-and-forth a few more times, but then he stepped in. "Alright, well, we're going to go attack a subterranean quest area right now. You interested in coming along?"

"I'd love to, but I am currently starving and dehydrated. Near death actually," Jaxon replied matter-of-factly. "I could really go for a–"

Joe had already set up an IV using Cleanse, and the lines on Jaxon's face started to ease. Guessing that Jess was likely in a similar situation, Joe set a spell on her as well. Now used to Joe's abilities thanks to the 'nice to meet you, have a cold shower', she dodged the spell and slashed the water out of the air, then glared at Joe with dangerous eyes. "Oh, shoot, I'm sorry. It's a buff that gets you hydrated. I'm a healer. Sometimes I forget that not everyone knows who I am."

"Got it," Jess slowly spoke the words, then watched Jaxon for a moment as more and more water flowed into him. When his face didn't change away from cheerful and he didn't attack the healer, she nodded at Joe. "Alright, that could really be helpful if you wouldn't mind."

"Not at all." Water wrapped up her arm in an instant and began flowing into her veins. She relaxed as the subtle debuffs began vanishing. "Let's get you guys some food, and then would you like to join us, Jaxon?"

"But of course!" Jaxon smiled and started walking toward the dining area. "Also, Jess here would like to join us as a strategist. Crawling through dark places seems to be what she is interested in."

Jess had an aggrieved expression on her face, and she ran her hands through her hair before blowing out a breath. "Ye*ah*. That wasn't the introduction that I had been hoping for, but it'll have to do... I'm Jess. I'm an aspiring strategist and team logistics manager. I'm here hoping for a job and a guild invite."

"You spent the last *week* with Jaxon?" Alexis narrowed her eyes at the woman. "How many times did you try to kill him?"

Jess looked stricken. "I... being honest... about six?"

"Not even once a *day*?" Alexis clapped and smiled. "She has really good self-control, Joe! I say we take her!"

Joe looked at Jess in a new light, a few cogs in his brain settling into place. "Alright, Jess. We don't have a position on the squad per se, but I think that we could find a great use for your talents. I don't know what class you have, but if you want a different one, one more specialized for what you really want to do... have you heard of the Pathfinder's Hall?"

Jess looked up at the black, egg-shaped building that Joe was gesturing at. "What is *that* used for?"

Joe just smiled at her.

CHAPTER SIX

After a trip to get rid of the near-starvation debuffs the two had returned with, Joe took Jess through the Pathfinder's Hall and found her a class more suited to her liking. The guild clerks running the place had insisted that they pay the fee for a non-guild member using the building's services, which had exasperated Joe to no end. He *owned* this place!

He calmed down after he realized that they were being more than fair. After all, it was Joe who had worked with the guild to find a good middle ground between ownership and management. Jess went into one of the stalls and came out a handful of minutes later, her face set and contemplative. The Pathfinder's Hall didn't *give* you a class, it only showed the way along paths that had already been tread by someone else. From the look on Jess's face, the path she had chosen required hard work but was manageable.

"We'll get you all set up with the guild after we've been able to work together for a while. Sound good?" Joe's question was mostly rhetorical, as he had no intention of bringing her in without testing her capabilities himself.

"It does." Jess sighed and ran her hand through her hair with a flick of her wrist. "Not being able to log out has definitely changed my *reasons* for doing what I'm doing, but it doesn't change the fact that I need to *want* to be doing what I do. Does that make sense?"

"If I think about it a little, yes. At face value, it seems all over the place," Joe bluntly replied, getting a grin from her.

"Oh, have you seen the news?" Jess met Joe's eyes with a dark look. "Looks like we aren't here because of a glitch or anything like that. This is a new reality, apparently. Somewhere in this place, President Musk is hanging out and walking among us. Showed it on live television."

Joe's steps faltered. "So... now we have *proof* that the beings in here aren't digital constructs? They are for sure... *real?*"

"What is *real?*" Jess flippantly turned the question back on him. "I guess it's best to treat everything like an actual living being, if that's what you are asking."

Joe nodded as they walked along, deep in thought. They found the rest of the team waiting for them, and Jess waved and headed off to find a place to get some sleep. Without needing to tell the others, the group got moving along the path. "Hey, someone want to actually share the quest with me?"

"Oh! Me as well, thank you!" Jaxon chimed in.

Quest gained: Salty Sensations. The Wanderer's Guild has been surveying the area in an attempt to find natural resources to exploit. One of these locations is a salt mine that may connect to a previously demolished ore mine. Search the area, defeat any creatures inhabiting the salt mine. Bonus objective: Find a way to access the ore mine from the salt mine. Reward: Based upon work completed. Failure: This quest is failed if abandoned or completed by another group first.

"Got it, thanks!" Joe called over to Poppy, who removed his hat with a flourish and bowed. "Shall we get going? Anyone need anything before we go?"

"You planning to go out and about with only what you're wearing right now?" Alexis looked critically at what Joe had equipped. Of course, she could only see his robe and staff, but that highlighted a point that Joe had been avoiding for quite a while. He was *very* under-equipped. In fact, he took a look at what he was wearing in his status screen to see the effects of the gear he had on.

Robe of Liquid Darkness (Rare). Wearing this robe makes you look a bit wet but increases the power of dark affinity magic by 10%.

Shoes and Socks. Reduces the penalty for walking over sharp objects, also keeps feet dry for up to three hours from standard wear.

Mystic Theurge Staff (Ironwood) (Special: Dual Class). Mystic Theurges place no boundaries on their magical abilities and find no irreconcilable paradox in devotion to the arcane as well as the divine. This staff helps to unite their power. Effect: Adds 10-20 blunt damage on strike. -12% cast time when casting either Cleric or Mage spells. Halves penalty for using cross-class (Mage or Cleric) skills. Note: This is a two-handed item, and only one spell may be cast at a time using it.

Spatial Codpiece (Legendary). This functional piece of armor also serves a greater purpose; it is able to store thirty cubic meters worth of items. Goods must come within two inches of the armor to be stored but can be retrieved directly on to the body or into the hand as long as the codpiece is touching your skin. Adds 5 points to overall armor class and prevents blows from damaging your genitals entirely. Let's just say your junk is safely stored.

Joe loved the descriptions of his useful items, but... yeah. He had equipment slots for underwear, shirts, pants, belts, robes, shoes, and socks. On top of the regular clothing, he could have armor, and he had dozens of possibilities for accessories even if he wouldn't use some of them such as nose piercings. When he looked at his current choices critically... he was grossly underdressed and frankly kinda *gross*. Going commando wasn't *supposed* to be a valid option, but he had been able to heal any chafing easily.

No! He couldn't think of the convenience of his mostly-nude self. Wait... he had been lifted into the air a lot recently... shake the thought off, shake it off! There *had* to be gear out there that could get his abilities boosted or protect him better than he could manage currently. Joe pulled a nasty expression and mumbled, "I'll gear up when we get back, alright?"

"Hmm." Alexis narrowed her eyes further, then stuck her tongue out at him. "Fine, but if you need help shopping–"

"We can go *together*!" Jaxon clapped his hands in delight, and Poppy snapped his mouth closed right before he offered to show Joe around the city's shopping area. "It'll be *fun*! The warrant for my arrest just timed out, so we can go have a *great* time!"

"Yeah, you can go with Jaxon." Alexis heartlessly laughed. There were chuckles all around, except for an excited squeal from Jaxon. They chatted for a bit as they traveled through what was left of the woods and felt nice and caught up after only the forty-minute walk to the quest location.

"Is it jus' me, or do tha' look like jus' a hole in ta ground?" Bard pointed at the entrance to the salt mine, which was *certainly* just a fissure in an otherwise rocky area. "Ah feel tha' Poppy should go first!"

"Wait, what, *why*?" Poppy whirled around with the question on his lips so quickly that he nearly lost his hat.

"Ya know, ta poker ya got." Bard mimicked stabbing straight forward. "No wind-up needed, ya get me?"

Poppy tried to argue, but the words kept failing to come out of his mouth. "Fine, you actually made sense. Lazy raggamuffin. Scoundrel."

Joe had been about to offer going first when he remembered that he was *much* more on par with a standard mage these days. With that thought in mind, he dumped nine hundred points of mana into his Exquisite Shell. Breathing heavily, he looked at his mana bar as it slowly refilled and stopped at eight-eighty-six, ninety points having been reserved for the upkeep of his protection. "Ugh. *Man*, that hurts the ego."

The group walked single-file into the darkness, the route worn down from use over time, though the footprints they left in the dust were showing that no one had been here for quite some time. Poppy cleared his throat, and the whole group went on high alert. "So, how do they know that this was a salt mine? It could have been anything, or nothing."

"The Mayor, Sir Bearington," Joe offered uncertainly. "He's been here a *long* time, and I think he would know a bunch of the resources in the area even if he hadn't been able to produce enough manpower to *get* at them."

"Sounds about right to me," Alexis offered. Then the group lapsed into silence once more as they got deep enough underground that it became hard to see. They pulled out various light sources, mostly torches; though Poppy activated a gem-like object on his hat that created a flashlight effect wherever his hat pointed.

"Look at tha', ye' another reason ya should be up front!" Bard proudly exclaimed, getting a dirty look from Poppy in return, though the flamboyant Duelist didn't say anything in reply.

They walked for a few more minutes before the group all flinched at the same time, a sign that all of them had gotten a system message.

You have entered a level five natural dungeon, the final resting place of the Legends of the League. This is one of the saltiest known places that can be found in the seven worlds. Keep an eye out for the naturally-occurring resources as well as the protectors! This dungeon will only remain until it is cleared, after which point the area can be claimed for incorporation into a guild or business venture!

"Interesting," Joe commented after reading through the entire message. "This place shouldn't be all that challenging for us then. Oh, hey, I have a progress bar!"

"What? What does it say?" Alexis stepped closer as if she would be able to read the information herself.

"Just 'zero out of question mark' right now," Joe responded after double checking. "I guess this is my dungeoneer title activating?"

"Not giving a ton of information though?" Alexis stepped away, following after the rest of the group as they continued. "If there isn't a point in keeping the title, at least you know which one to remove when you earn a better one!"

Joe frowned. So far, he had never seen a title that had such little effect, and he resolved to keep an eye on it. As they walked, he gained his answer. Another progress bar appeared, showing an 'area explored' title. "Got a fresh one! Looks like we have explored two-point-three percent of this place already."

"Now we're talking!" Poppy called back. "Everything seems a little easier when you know for sure how much you have left to do."

Then a third bar appeared, and Joe stared at it. No information appeared, and it stayed in place near the wall as they walked. "Odd, a new bar appeared, but I think it's connected to the wall. Let's take a look?"

They walked closer, but nothing about the wall seemed to explain the attached bar. Joe poked at the spot, and it *exploded* outward in a shower of salt. "Gah!"

"*Ree-he-he-he!*" A salty blade bounced off Joe's Exquisite Shell, taking a few dozen points of its durability away due to what had most likely been a critical hit. There was a monster in front of Joe, something that looked like a centaur with blades where its human hands should be. It had the lower body of a horse, the torso of a man, but the head of a horse again. Also, as far as Joe could tell, it was entirely made of salt.

An arrow slammed into the creature's chest, blowing a massive hole through the beast. It didn't seem to care and swung again at Joe just as Jaxon lashed out and obliterated the top half of its body. Jaxon looked at his fist with a snarling expression, then shook it to clear off the accumulated salt. "Nasty little things. Does a NaClydesdale mean anything to you guys? They're only worth ten experience, just so you know."

"I bet that any wound they give you is coated in salt," Alexis commented, getting a nod from Jaxon as he shook out his hand. "Looks painful. Joe, wanna wash that off for him?"

"Sure thing." Joe hadn't even thought of that! This was just one *more* reason he wanted to give Alexis the reins of leadership. He would have to get her alone and talk about it. A quick Cleanse got rid of the salt, and Jaxon instantly looked relieved. "Looks like what I was seeing on the wall was that thing's health bar."

Alexis gave Joe a thumbs-up. "I didn't see *anything*, so I think we found the usefulness of that little title. Looks like you're the scout!"

CHAPTER SEVEN

Pshhh

The sound of a huge creature devolving into a pile of salt was more fun to hear than Joe would ever admit to the general populace. He would still tell them that it *was* fun, but he wanted to keep this level of enjoyment confined to himself and the people in the know. He looked around with a wide smile on his face, only finding a matching expression on Jaxon's face. They high-fived and scooped the newly formed salt pile into a bag.

"Handy, tha'." Bard nodded at the resource they were collecting. "Think a' how many more people would be miners if tha' were the norm for collectin' ta goods!"

"No kidding!" Poppy agreed easily. "If I got to fight a metal contraption and it fell apart into bars of ore? I'd do that for sure! Fighting ability *and* nearly guaranteed profit?"

Jaxon licked his fingers with a grin. "Deadly *and* delicious! Excellent combination!"

"Like 'Lexis here." Bard drew a chuckle from the group as he pulled the Aromatic Artificer in for a kiss. When his words registered, Alexis punched him in the arm hard enough that he rubbed at the spot even while laughing.

Joe felt some salt raining on him, and he shouted even as he started to move, "From *above*!"

A pillar of salt crashed down where the group had stood only a few moments before, showering them in sharp particles even though they had avoided the main object. The group stood up, staring at the large cylinder in annoyance. Joe started to get closer, when his eyes widened and he fell back. "It has a *health bar*!"

The others scrambled further away as the edges of the pillar dropped to the sides like a discarded banana peel. They hit the ground hard enough to fall to chunks, and an enormous minotaur made entirely of salt took a step out of the object it had been entombed within. It bellowed at them; a dry, particle-laden shout. The sharp salt pinged off of Joe's shielding, knocking off four points of durability.

Poppy was the first to react, his rapier twirling outward and punching a perfectly round but *small* hole in the creature's side. "Bard, I think this guy is designed for you to hit!"

The axe-wielding man stomped forward and swung horizontally at the minotaur even as it sent a fist at Poppy. The axe hit and scored a deep line, even breaking apart the arm in multiple places. An arrow struck one of the fissures, breaking off the arm entirely and causing the minotaur to stumble. Jaxon took that chance to slam a fist into the off-balance monster's knee, taking it down to the ground. As it landed, cracks ran along the entirety of the salty creature, and a follow-up punch caused the entire thing to break apart into coarse salt.

"Why was that so easy?" Joe wondered out loud as he walked over to help with the salt collection. "That seemed like it should have been one of the stronger monsters in the entire cave."

"Look at your combat logs, Joe," Poppy called out. "Pretty obvious when you look at it objectively."

Joe pulled open the screen and took a look.

Exp: 18 (Saltataur x1)

"Oh, that was only worth eighteen experience?" Joe paused a moment and thought over that again. "If this is a level-five dungeon, that means we are *really* over leveled, then? I feel like that is actually a generous amount of experience."

"I bet it is because they are ambush creatures," Poppy offered before anyone else could react. "Since they *should* be harder to detect, as well as causing *overly* painful wounds, I bet the experience reward is balanced. We are a solid ten levels above them, right?"

Joe shrugged helplessly. "That must be it. Also, we have explored... twenty-three percent of this place. If we can clear it out, I say we claim it and get the guild to run it for us."

"Works for me!" Jaxon poked at the fallen body before shaking his head. "No bones in these beasts. Ah well, I suppose that would have been too much to ask for."

The group continued making their way through the dungeon, soon encountering small groups of the creatures they had fought until this point. There was one nerve-wracking moment at *just* about the seventy-five percent explored mark where seven pillars of salt rained down and released a small herd of Saltataurs, but having found that their weakness was simply blunt force trauma... well, that was enough for the group to easily dispatch the monsters.

The party continued onward, dedicated to clearing this place out on the first try. They got to the deepest passage of the cave system, finding that the naturally-pink walls were becoming ornamented and extravagantly carved. Joe consulted his progress meter and stopped the others, "Hey guys. I'm betting that we are closing in on the Boss of this dungeon, and I want to make sure we are all prepared to go in there. Anyone need food, water, or healing?"

Skill increased: Speech (Novice III). Sometimes asking the right questions matters.

"Feeling good over here, Joe!" Jaxon held his hands straight out in front of him and jogged in place, hitting his palms with his knees as he bounced. "Let's go get em!"

The group walked around the last bend and came in sight of the dungeon... Bosses. Two people made entirely of salt were waiting for them. The first was a huge humanoid that—were he not made of pink salt—looked like he had just stepped out of a bodybuilder magazine. The other was a thin man that looked at them hungrily and licked his dry lips, revealing needle-sharp canines.

"Aus, it seems that we have visitors," the thin man mentioned to the huge one.

"Indeed it *does*, Terry," the giant replied happily. "I was just mentioning how bored I was *yesterday!*"

"Aus, we haven't moved in over a decade," Terry commented sharply. "Let's just eat them and store the leftovers."

"Salted meat..." Aus seemed to be trying to drool, but as he had no liquid in his body, this was difficult to do. It was the thought that counted.

"I think they are trying to intimidate us?" Alexis leaned toward the others, who shrugged nonchalantly. "Yeah, right there with you, guys. Let's collect our *salt* and get back to the guild."

Aus glared at her, then charged across the room with a bellow of, "*Meat!*"

Alexis lifted her bow and fired just as the huge man twisted his charge and swung a blocky fist at Poppy, catching the Duelist off guard. The fist *slammed* into his face, sending the human to the floor as blood poured from multiple lacerations and a flattened nose.

"Poppy!" Joe called, watching the man bounce off the floor. Bard stepped in, his axes scoring deep lines on the salty arms of Aus. Joe tossed a Mend spell at Poppy, the water connecting and fixing the broken nose and fractured cheekbones. Still, the fighter didn't stir, and Joe realized that there must be an internal damage debuff.

The other Boss, Terry, jumped into the air and somehow morphed into a giant bat that swooped down at Jaxon. If Joe hadn't been convinced before that the man was a vampire, he was now. Jaxon crouched and deflected the attack, sending his elbow into what was normally a nerve cluster. The strike dealt damage, but as the Boss was entirely salt, there were no nerves to properly target.

Bard swung his axes again, but Aus clapped his hands and caught one of them between his palms while the other scored a deep line on his arm. Bard stumbled, his momentum thrown off by the unexpected maneuver. Aus took the opportunity to backhand the Skald, sending him flying with wounds on his face and neck that made falling into a grinder look pleasant. The huge salt-man was essentially a massive block of sandpaper, able to turn casual swipes into deep gouges.

Joe sent a globe of water at Bard, channeling mana into the spell to make it stay connected. This created a beautiful laminar flow between them—which was interrupted by Terry flying at Alexis through the unexpected obstacle and screaming. A red notification appeared in Joe's vision, showing that it was important enough to pass through his notification settings.

Critical critical! Terry takes 4x damage! (2x from water, 2x from holy attribute) Damage dealt: 620!

"Holy moley!" Joe whispered as Terry tried to get up. The Boss monster was struggling mightily, but his body was melting. Alexis pointed her crossbow and launched a bolt that took his head. The salty vampire fell into a puddle of goop, defeated in an instant.

"No! Terry!" Aus turned and charged at Alexis, but Joe already understood his role in this play, targeting the giant salt man and pouring water into him. Instead of healing the giant, the water caused him to start melting, slowing him considerably. He didn't take four times damage, but three hundred and ten water damage a second was enough to bring him down after only a few moments.

Exp: 110 (Aus Salt and Bat Terry). You have defeated two area Bosses in one fell swoop! Too bad you out leveled them so badly, else you would have gotten a great reward! Still, you fought against painful wounds! Constitution +1.

Quest complete: Salty Sensations. The Legends of League mines have been opened for capture by a guild or business venture! Calculating reward... 100% cleared by group. Area level greatly exceeded. Reward: Common class item box. Exp gained: 200.

Not bad! All told, Joe had gained five hundred thirty-three experience during their time in the mines. He stopped himself from digging into his stat sheet too far, knowing that his team needed his help. First off, he went over to Poppy and cast a Cleanse on him, focusing on his head. Joe grimaced as his mana began to plummet, growing more concerned by the second. He had never seen a debuff this severe, where it took nearly seven hundred mana to cure.

Status ailment cured: Brain damage, bleeding brain.

Skill increased: Mend (Student III). Finding new ways for the main branch of healing to be used results in great rewards!

Skill increased: Cleanse (Apprentice IX). You are almost great at this! Keep it up!

Woof. That explained it; seemed that Poppy was almost on his way to respawn. Yikes. His mending skill had likely been added into the attempt at healing the damage, but as it was still considered a status ailment, he had been able to fix the damage even without the proper knowledge of how to do so. Lucky.

Poppy hopped to his feet and looked around, and once more, Joe was reminded that this was a game, no matter how much it was all of their reality. "Ugh, I got penalized *real* hard there for not even attempting to block. I *cannot* believe he got the jump on me like that! A perfect critical, and I just stood there and took it to the face."

"Phrasing," Alexis muttered, making Bard giggle. Joe winced; the rugged Skald *giggling* was not in line with his mental image of the rugged, Scottish guy. "No worries, Pops, we got them."

"You had brain damage, just so you know," Joe mentioned casually. "Everything okay up there now?"

Poppy paused and looked at his status sheet. "Yeah... all set."

"Good." Joe checked their statuses and looked at the now-empty salt mine. "Shall we head back to the guild, then?"

CHAPTER EIGHT

"Welcome back, team!" Jessamyn waved at the group as they walked into the... town. Population center was a better term, as only the Pathfinder's Hall, Guild Hall, and buildings made after the explosion were currently standing. "I took the liberty of joining the guild using Joe's 'add one person to the guild no questions asked' ability as a party leader!"

"*Excuse* me?" Joe stopped short, his face thunderous and becoming red. "How did you even...? You had no right to...!"

Jess hurried to explain her other activities, "Also, Joe! Yes! I managed to file all the missing paperwork that the guild had been waiting on! I hope you all don't mind, but I signed the tax forms for you and got all the fines for non-payment taken care of with the explanation of the war. So, all of you got all the backpay you had been waiting on, a nice bonus from an award 'Joe' recommended you all for, and have a few offered quests pulled up for you all to look at!"

Joe waited a moment, gauging the proper reaction to this situation, and stepped close to her. "*Never* use my authority in the future for something I don't actually agree to, and where would you like your pay and a *very* large starting bonus to go?"

"Sorry, I just–wait." Jess smiled at him, and Joe allowed his expression to soften into a smile as well. "Nice. Well, you'll never have to worry about standard paperwork again."

"For that alone, your bonus is getting larger," Joe promised as they all started walking again. "What do you have for us in the way of quests?"

"Oh, about that. Aten wanted you to come and meet with him? Like, now." Jess pulled out a few other notes and carefully stacked one on top. "I'm pretty sure that he wants you to work on this one."

Reading the quest, Joe shook his head and grunted. The guild was looking for a way to rebuild the town, but the trouble was that they were paying for the work with contribution points. "I'm betting that they aren't getting many takers, are they? Alright, let's go see Aten. This should be a trip. Hey, team? If he tries to guilt us into doing work for free or reduced cost, what do we answer with?"

Alexis answered after a long moment of awkward silence, "I think the answer you're looking for is 'no'? Are you trying to get us to chant or something?"

"Forget it. Why is everyone so against chanting?" Joe rolled his eyes and continued skipping along at a walking pace. When they got near the new guild building, Joe smirked as he saw a team of people on the roof adding shingles to the structure. "Should have put those on the blueprint. Heh."

They walked to a large room people were running into and out of at speed. They entered with papers, left with papers, and all of them had a harried look on their face. Joe nearly got trampled twice, and only a timely intervention by Poppy kept him from being knocked over. When they finally got through the door, they all felt out of place in the organized chaos of the workspace. Mike, the Vice Guild Leader, was standing and orchestrating movement through the area. This was vastly different from a typical or conventional office, mainly due to things needing to be physical copies with a personal signature.

When Aten saw Joe, he called for a cessation of activities, and a line instantly began to form at the door. Aten waved them forward right away, near-panic on his face. "Conversation as short as possible! Huge, unfortunate issues. Ardania is getting swamped by new people joining the world, and there are already starting to be massive issues with any supply orders at all. Thanks to your advice on the matter, we had started buying up all the rare resources that we thought we would need, but I'm sorry to say that abyssal *economist* convinced our buyers to skimp, not really thinking that there would be supply issues for a long time."

"Now we are missing a bunch of basic supplies?" Joe guessed, getting a nod in reply. "What are we looking at here? Food, building material?"

"Yes," was the only answer. "We have all sorts of rare junk that people will need for advanced gear, but there aren't enough *basics* to even sustain our own people for two weeks without rationing. So, I wanted to offer a quest to our biggest problem solvers."

Aten made a gesture, and a notification appeared in front of Joe and his entire team.

Guild Quest offered: Feed the people! With the massive influx of travelers and even more on the way, there isn't nearly enough to go around. Find a way to sustain a population of at least 10,000 people, and put it in place. Reward: Guild contribution points. Accept? Yes / No

"Nope." Joe waved away the message and shook his head. "There is *no* way that I'm taking five people on a trip to who knows where looking for... what? Trade routes? Items? There isn't even a set... *what* would I be looking for? And *contribution* points as a reward? So, find a way to feed ten *thousand* people in return for something with no value? Or quantification? Why don't we just find a way into the next area?"

"The next area is still locked off, and I have it on good authority that we will be far too weak for that place." Aten's words brought a vision of a Goblin swinging a club at him into Joe's mind. "Frankly, Joe, we need to get this in place, and everyone else is still working out how to deal with their own issues. We need *sustainable resources*. Not everyone is taking being trapped here as well as you are. Do you really want our whole guild to starve to death over and over? Everyone is needed for their own tasks, and I think that this is something you are suited to doing."

Joe was already shaking his head. "Nope. I'm calling bull on this. I *also* have a clause in our contract that lets me refuse to do something that I think is unfair, and you know it. That's why we have this guilt trip going on. Make it worth our while, Aten. Give us details, a *specific* goal, and currency that matters. Otherwise, we're just going to keep doing our own thing and rocking it. Grabbed a salt mine, by the way. One of those *sustainable resource* centers that the guild needs, and we'd be happy to hand it over to the guild for a cut of the proceeds."

Aten narrowed his eyes. "I'll double the contribution points for this quest, and I can give you two percent of whatever we get out of the salt mine. We need to supply all the people for the work, and we still need to make a profit."

"Yes, to the salt mine, still no to the quest," Joe returned instantly. "Double the points? Multiplying two by zero is still zero. It doesn't even list how many points are offered, just 'contribution points'."

Aten rolled his eyes and seemed to be typing at thin air. "There. Ten thousand contribution points for the quest."

"So, *twenty* thousand when you double the fictitious currency?" Joe innocently asked.

Aten ground his teeth and growled, "I *suppose* that is what it will come out to, yes."

"Then *still* no, unless you have something that shows what the points are worth. Things that I could buy with them," Joe demanded on behalf of his group.

"Are you sure you want to play it this way, Joe?" Aten narrowed his eyes.

"Tell you what, Aten." Joe held his hands out to his sides. "I'll give you twenty thousand 'Joe points' if you build me a mansion and fill it with beautiful artwork."

Aten cocked his head and blinked. "What's the ratio of Joe points to contribution points?"

"The same ratio as leprechauns to unicorn poop," Joe returned serenely. "If you want work done, you need to offer something *real* in return. We all have our own game we want to play, Aten. Show me what these points are worth, and we'll talk."

"Alright, Joe. I guess it's time to bring in the big guns." Aten made a motion, and a small section of the room was unveiled. Joe paled and whirled on the guild leader.

"You brought my *mother* here?"

"Joe!" His mother stood up and shook her head. "I thought I raised you better than this. You have a chance to keep a *lot* of people from starving, and you should be jumping on the chance even if you won't get anything worthwhile out of the guild!"

"Mom! I thought I was–" Joe tried to defend himself, but a hand in the air made him stop speaking right away.

"Let me finish." His mom turned her glare on Aten. "Really? You used me visiting against my son? Are you *trying* to drive a wedge between us? Make him avoid me? I won't stand for it. Joe, as your mother, I want you to find a way to feed the people. As a businesswoman, make sure that the reward you get upon return is *worth* it, or else you make sure to hold on to the means of production and sell the food at a reasonable price. Outfit the operation yourself, and talk to me if you need a place to sell in the Kingdom. In a week or so, I'll be taking over Odds and Ends, and you can always sell through *me*."

Aten looked aggrieved and rubbed weary eyes. Then he locked eyes with Joe and said, "Thirty thousand contribution points."

"Thirty thousand upon completion, and Fifteen thousand points no matter what. I swear we'll put plenty of effort into this, and we need to be compensated for that amount of time no matter what. Also. Outfit us for the trip, Aten." Joe sighed and went over to give his mom a hug. "Give us two weeks' worth of gear. I can't imagine that this'll be a quick trip."

"Deal." Aten nodded his head, and the notification appeared in Joe's vision again. This time, the quest was accepted.

CHAPTER NINE

"Alright, guys." Joe and his team were sitting around a tiny table at the coffee shop, planning out their goals for the new quest. "What do we need to do to make this happen?"

Jess raised her hand, and Joe pointed at her. "Please don't do that. Just speak when you have something to say. High school is over."

"Gotcha." Jess grabbed a chunk of chalk from the table and started drawing on the wood. "There are more things to consider here than simply growing or importing food. There are the logistics of getting it here, having people to work with it, and places to store it if it isn't used right away. Here is what I think we need, in no particular order. Firstly, I think that it's important that we produce the food ourselves. If that means growing it, fine. If that means magical items, *whatever*, so long as they are able to make it happen long term."

"With that in mind, we need to make buildings to *store* food before we are producing large quantities of it. We can start with a little production, to keep from starving, but this is something to keep in mind. Food rots fast, and as this is a game, I expect that there will be other issues to take into account." Jess was making a long list, and the entire party was enraptured. "Warehouses, yes. Cold storage means good insulation on the building, which means high-quality materials used in the construction. Anyone know when winter is due in here? Is there winter?"

"Uh... I'll look into it." Poppy stood up and walked off at a brisk pace.

"Good." Jess looked back at the list with a furrowed brow. "Roads. We need good roads between our buildings if we want to be able to transport stuff. Walls, to keep out thieves and protect our workers. Workers! That means a place for them to sleep. So, an apartment at the minimum. Some form of entertainment so they don't need to go too far, and–"

"Winter is a thing, and the edge of it is about a month out, I think." Poppy popped back in with the information, making Bard jump and cuss softly at the scare.

"Good, perfect." Jess took a deep breath and looked Joe directly in the eyes. "In that case, in my professional opinion, I think that you need to find a way to make a greenhouse."

"Greenhouse," Joe parroted. He was in shock from having a full plan laid out like this. "I... wow. I was going to go on a quest for a magical cornucopia or something."

Jess shook her head. "This is far more likely to exist."

"Fair enough." Joe looked around. "All in favor of going searching for blueprints to a greenhouse?"

"Let's do it," Alexis put out into the group. Everyone else nodded, so Joe did so as well.

"Alright." He looked at Jess. "You've really proven yourself. I'm gonna give you a task while we're gone too, okay? Show that we can trust you when we aren't around, and we'll make sure it's worth your while. All of this?"

Joe motioned at the charts and list she was still making. "Get all the material you need for these. I'm going to give you a token to claim land for me as well. Find what you think will be a good spot, and start hiring people. Get the foundations set up. Make roads to where buildings *will* be. Don't worry about actually *building.* Just get everything else ready."

Jess hesitated, then nodded. "We should also work out my salary...?"

"Find what's fair, add twenty percent, and make it happen." Joe grinned at her. "I'll get you access to an account.

Make sure to keep receipts. I *highly* doubt that we are done paying taxes just because we are in a new world. All that changed was who collects them."

"It also lets you see what I buy," Jess sweetly added.

"Yes," Joe agreed bluntly.

"Consider it done, boss man." Jess mock saluted and looked around. "Don't forget to get geared up."

"Knew I was forgetting something." Joe blew a raspberry and stood up. "Alright, guys, I'm gonna pop over to the city for a shopping trip. Anyone want a ride?"

"Let's do it," Jaxon agreed winningly. Joe chuckled nervously. Everyone except Jess decided to go along, and the team walked into the temple and teleported into the main square of Ardania.

"Remember, Joe," Alexis stated sternly, "you are here for getting gear, not for researching. We'll do that too, just make sure that you get what you need for survival."

"On it!" Joe promised with crossed fingers.

"I see that." She glared. "If you die because you didn't do this right, I'm gonna be *so* mad."

Joe simply skipped off, headed for the market. He went for the Odds and Ends shop right away but also put Masterwork Metals on his list. As he walked into the first shop, he spied his mother and the current owner discussing stock over hot tea. He was confused for a moment as to how she had beat him here but remembered that she had access to the same transportation network that he did. "Hi there! I was hoping that I could get some help with upgrading my current gear?"

The owner looked at him and harrumphed. "Hello there, youngling! Here to run me out of business again? Tell everyone about outdated prices?"

"Nothing like that! Just the gear this time!" Joe responded to the curmudgeon as happily as possible.

"I see that you lost your little 'keep me alive' robe since I last saw you. Where did it get off to?" Her tone implied that she had better like the answer.

"I'm really sorry to say," Joe had to hold in his frustration, "I lost it in an instant dungeon to the Boss. He... I died right after, so I'm uncertain as to what happened."

"Hmmm. Not to be trusted with higher tier enchanted gear, huh?" the old woman muttered to herself.

"Nothing like that!" Joe shook his head vehemently.

"I'm pretty sure that I told you that all magical gear is alive, even if *just* barely, yes?" The ancient person stared at him with nearly mummified eyes. "The more *powerfully* made, the more alive it is. That building you made? I give it a year or two at *the most* until it is awake. What are you doing to protect that new, young mind?"

Joe thought about it and needed to make sure to choose his words carefully. "I am helping build a powerful Noble Guild around it. As we go forward, there will be powerful people and powerful protections in place. All of these will have a vested interest in keeping it strong and protected."

"Hmm." There was a pause. "I suppose that keeping you away from the good stuff will only weaken you in the long run and prevent you from keeping the building strong. I suppose that's a good enough reason to sell to you. Come here, let's find you something that suits you."

"Hi, Mom. Thanks for the help there." Joe only got a serene smile in reply, so he knew that she was in agreement with the old lady for some reason.

"What are you after?" the old lady demanded. "What do you *think* you need?"

"I need as much mana and mana regen as possible," Joe responded instantly. "I use lots and *lots*, and then even *more* mana."

"I see." She walked away and came back a few minutes later with a full set of luxurious, purple gear. "Here is my offer. I have a set of robes that will boost mana regen by one percent, shirt, pants, underwear, and socks that all do the same. Together, this becomes a set of gear called 'Wise Man's Wardrobe'. When worn all together, it grants a fifteen percent mana regen bonus, is self-cleaning, and does minor self-repair. Also, future note—all socks are set items. These ones just work with the rest of this gear."

"Got it." Joe looked at the gear, noting that the gear was only categorized as Rare. "Is this the best that I can get, or is this your highest recommendation for me?"

"Recommendation. Both," the cool answer came. "It doesn't add any armor, but it can take care of itself to a small degree, and I think that is going to be more important to any gear you purchase in the *future*."

"I see." Joe nodded and took the gear, paying a price of twelve hundred gold—or twelve platinum—that nearly made him gag, and that was *after* his discount. Attempts at haggling were met with a stony glare, and he had no choice but to accept the price tag that could be seen on large buildings for sale in town. "Is there... anything else you would recommend? Or do you have any of these items?"

He presented a list, and she shook her head. "That would all come from the Architect's Guild. Blueprints or blueprint paper, at least. Otherwise, you could always learn to make your own or buy from the Mage's College. The inks and such could be purchased from the Alchemist, or again, made yourself. Raw material from the alchemist as well."

Joe thought of the creepy alchemist, Jake, and winced. He'd rather not need to go in there, but if that was the best option going forward... Joe nodded, equipped his gear, and strolled out of the shop. Next on the list was Masterwork Metals, mostly just to see if he could find anything interesting. He had only been there a few times at the start of his time in this world, but he had a favorable impression of the owner. After browsing the shop and not seeing anything, Joe asked the owner if he could make weapon augments like his titanium taglock.

His wasn't in danger of breaking, but if you waited until you needed something, you were setting yourself up for failure. The smith wasn't impressed with his request. "Taglocks, huh? That's a nasty little implement you've got there. Yeah, I can make 'em. I just don't *like* to do so. I prefer making weapon and armor augments that help people protect themselves."

"*Armor* augments?" Joe greedily leaned forward. "Do tell!"

The smith looked Joe up and down. "Alright, well. You're creepin' me out, but yeah, you can take any type of armor or weapon and make an augment out of it. Essentially gives you boosted skill points for the type of gear it was. You can also try and make them yerself, but I gotta warn you, they are expensive for a reason. Now, you can also get basic augments like that taglock pretty easy, since it is actually just another, smaller weapon strapped to the first one. Same name, very different results."

"How do you make the skill-style augments?" Joe started recording the conversation on his personal notepad.

"Well, first ya take the class and learn how to do it," the smith grinned crookedly, "but the short version is that you take a chunk of gear and try to extract its 'meaning'. This destroys the gear, whether you succeed or fail and only gives you a fairly small boost even if you *do* get the augment. Better to pay the price, boyo."

"Gotcha." Joe already had plenty of skills to bring up, but he would get to this one eventually. There had to be some reason it existed. "Thanks! Can I get a few of these taglocks, though?"

"Sure, why not." The smith waved him away and told him they would be ready in a few days. Joe turned to leave, then stopped himself and got directions to a glassblower.

When he got to the glassblower, he put in a large order for hundreds of sheets of glass. They were all to be the same size and thickness, and he made sure to let the man know that he would come back every few days to get whatever had been made until that point. A quick stop at the alchemist and Joe felt that he was as ready for the next steps as he could be.

All ready for the trials ahead, Joe saw that he had a few hours until the assigned meeting time. So, naturally, he wandered over to the library and started researching mentions of greenhouses or other styles of easily growing large amounts of food in as short a time as possible.

CHAPTER TEN

"You're telling me that there is *no* lumber, nails, *anything* that I can purchase in bulk?" Joe was at the Architect's Guild, doing his best to get a deal while he could. He had found a good lead at the library, so he needed to take care of a few other issues if possible. "What if I paid a premium? Ten percent over asking price?"

"I'm *telling* you, Mr. Joe." The woman he was speaking with was adamantly shaking her head and holding her ground. "We are bought out for the next two months at the minimum. We honor our deals here. When we say you are next in line, you are, and, well, frankly you're not the first to try and get in good with us. You want lumber, you are going to either need to wait or get people to cut trees and make planks for you."

Joe thought on that for a moment and bobbed his head in understanding. "I see. Well, I can't say I don't like your honesty and the fact that you stick to your deals. Actually, it makes me want to work with you even more. Which is frustrating because I can't for now. This is a conundrum."

The lady seemed to relax a small amount and nodded. "Thank you for understanding. Not everyone has been so... anyway, is there anything else I can help you with?"

"Yes, well, while I am here, can I take a look at any blueprints that you have available for sale?" Joe asked hopefully.

"That's a no, sorry," she denied him instantly. "Blueprints are essentially the secret techniques of our guild. Mages have their spell books, alchemists have potion recipes, we have our blueprints. Now, you are welcome to *sell* blueprints to us, but we can't sell any to you."

"I see, I see." Joe knew right then and there that he would never sell *anything* to this organization. It might seem petty, but when a group refused to share the knowledge that they hoarded just so they could force people to work with or for them... Joe didn't ever want to get sucked into them. That was his real issue with guilds, unions, or colleges; a monopoly by any name was still hurtful to the overall progress of the world. Now people wouldn't even be able to build new homes without going through this group, and they were *busy* for the next several months? Despicable.

Well, he had his own method for creating blueprints and raising buildings, but he still needed supplies and a way to get blueprint paper. "Would your group be willing to sell *blank* blueprints so that I can attempt to create workable blueprints?"

"Oh, of course!" The seller gave him a charming smile, and he could practically *feel* his wisdom trying to fight against her obviously high charisma. "Each paper costs two gold, but that won't be an issue for an adventurer of your quality!"

"Or we could work out a deal where you *don't* rip me off." Joe chuckled at the pout that appeared on her face. "How about you let me take a look at the papers first?"

She walked out of the room and returned shortly with a stack of paper two feet high. The paper was a light blue, and she gestured for him to take a look. "Just so you know, any damage means that you have bought it."

"Understood." Joe carefully began going through the stack, separating the paper off and adding some to a pile on the side after staring at it, feeling it, and gently waving it through the air.

After he had gone through the entire stack, he turned to the paper he had set aside and made three piles. His Spellbinder skill was nagging at him, which was why he was taking his time to *really* look at the paper. He needed paper that could contain the magic that he would be putting through it, and there weren't many that made the cut. When he had gone through everything, he put away the paper that hadn't been up to the standard that he felt he needed. "I'll give you a gold each..."

"Highway robbery!" She gasped, putting both hands over her mouth.

"...or I can ask one of the other sellers if they could make a better deal," Joe finished his sentence.

"And *what* a good deal it is!" She shook his hand and looked at the paper he had set aside. "That'll be fifteen gold, then. Anything else I can get you?"

"On to your waiting list for supplies?" Joe added an extra gold to the pile he was counting out, and when he saw her raised eyebrow, he explained, "That's to fit me in right away if there is a cancellation. Not to jump into the current line. Here are the contact details for my assistant."

"I see." She nodded. Joe added the paper to his storage ring, and they parted ways.

Joe still had a half hour until he needed to meet the others in the town square, so he went into a restaurant and ordered a coffee. He had a good view of the square from here and was surprised to see that the place was *packed*. From all the starting gear, he could tell that this had to be a part of the influx of new people joining the world. Joe had taken a few minutes to watch the President's speech, but frankly, he was still shocked that so many people were taking it seriously, even though it *was* a serious situation. Most news channels had been screaming 'hoax'.

"A problem for future Joe," he said aloud, shaking his head and pulling out a blueprint. The paper was the lowest quality that he could find that would still be useful. He was going to try and see if his hunch about creating a magical blueprint was correct. As gently as he could manage, he began flooding the paper with mana. He felt it strain and press against his power and saw a few notifications appear in his view as the paper erupted into flames and burnt his hands and face.

Attempting to create magical blueprint... compiling data from all relevant skills. Spellbinder increases strength of paper by 63%. Magical Material Creation allows for a 9% increased density of mana matrix. Attempt to make blank magical blueprint... failed!

Exquisite Shell absorbs 129 mana and fire damage! Your Exquisite Shell has been destroyed! You have taken 24 magical fire damage!

Skill increase: Magical Material Creation (Apprentice 0). Congratulations!

Skill increase: Exquisite Shell (Novice V). Blow yourself up again! For... reasons! Great way to raise this skill!

You have healed 24 damage. Current health: 230/230

Joe shook his face to get the residual water off and tried to calm himself. He *knew* that he should have refreshed his shell after getting smacked around, but he hadn't thought it would matter so much in the city. Ignoring all the strange looks he was getting from the people around him eating lunch, he released his mana and formed a fresh shell around himself. Joe hadn't liked the snarky message, but there was a hint of good advice in there. Might as well use his failures to grow!

He sipped his now-tepid coffee and waited for his mana to regenerate. When he was back to full, he pulled out another paper and concentrated on it, ignoring the people scooting away from him at nearby tables. Joe kept a careful hold on his mana, smoothly applying a layer of the powerful energy to the paper and attempting to get it to sink into the blueprint. He felt something in his mind *click*, and he cut off the flow of power.

Attempting to create magical blueprint... compiling data from all relevant skills. Spellbinder increases strength of paper by 63%. Magical Material Creation allows for a 10% increased density of mana matrix. Attempt to make blank magical blueprint... Success!

Item gained: Blank Magical Blueprint (Uncommon). You have turned the mundane into the mystical by infusing this seemingly ordinary blueprint with mana! As an 'Uncommon' quality blueprint, it can store the information for a building at Uncommon quality or below!

"Nice!" Joe smiled and brought the paper to his lap, where it vanished into his codpiece. He tended to keep the rare and important things in there, as it was more likely that someone could steal his ring than his codpiece. Also, if they did steal his ring, they would think they got all of his valuables. A fresh paper appeared in his hands, and he started again. *Boom* Joe coughed a cloud of smoke, staring at his hands that should have been charred. His shell had taken the entirety of the damage, but he still had at least half of it remaining. He had gone into the process too excited, and the result spoke for itself.

Joe tried again, and once again, his shell took damage. As another paper appeared in his hand, the server came over and told him in no uncertain terms to leave. Joe checked the time, realized that he was already almost late, and agreed to go. Since he had already paid, he simply turned and hopped off the balcony. Joe landed perfectly in the square below... then fell to the ground. His stamina had failed him since he had needed to make so many adjustments as he fell so as to not crush someone. Whoops. He had forgotten about the new arrivals.

He got to his feet and brushed his butt off, then started walking to the agreed-upon spot to meet his friends. Joe found that moving through the crowd was difficult, and very few of the newbies seemed to know what they were doing or where to go. It was also *loud*, and a whole lot of people were calling for help or directions while the Kingdom's people tried to direct them. There were also less-than-scrupulous people recruiting for guilds, and Joe made sure to remember their guild name for later, just in case.

"There he is! Joe! Yoo-hoo! Follow the sounds of the screams!" Jaxon's voice called through the crowd, but Joe couldn't see from *where*. Then he heard the trumpeting of a T-rex, followed quickly by screams of fear from people who had T-rex head hands snapping at them. "Hi, Joe! Glad you found us! Nice new gear!"

"Hi, Jaxon." Joe tried *hard* not to laugh, but seeing his friend smiling at him while T-rex heads snapped at empty air was too much for him.

CHAPTER ELEVEN

"Now I'm wondering where our guild got that building blueprint that they had me use to build that building," Joe mumbled to himself. "Bleh, say that ten times fast. It was already on a magical blueprint, and I feel like that isn't something they just *found*. Hmm. Do we have a rogue architect?"

"Joe!" Poppy snapped his fingers in front of Joe and made the man jump. This resulted in a backflip and stylish landing, but it was still unwelcome. "What did you want to show us before we left the city? Having all these people around me all the time is *not* comfy. I feel like there have to be at least a few dozen people in here that are leveling up thieving skills, and I want to be gone before they practice on me."

"Right, sorry! We are almost there, promise!" Joe smiled and sped up, finding that the crowd thinned as they got closer to the guard's areas. Maybe Poppy had a point about thieves...? Joe walked over to the Captain's area and knocked on the door. It took a long moment, but then the door popped open, and a surprised face poked out.

"Joe? What is it? Is everything okay?" The Captain was concerned seeing a group waiting for him.

"Nothing new, *Dad*!" Joe responded with wide arms. "I just wanted to play catch with you, get a few hugs, and talk about when the wedding will be!"

Captain Blas went pale, and he started looking for an exit or a weapon to fend off the crazy man at his house. Joe chuckled and dropped his arms. "Just kidding. I wanted to ask permission to scan a barracks. I have a new spell that will allow me to make a copy of a building's blueprint, and we need sleeping areas pretty badly over at the guild."

The Captain dropped his arms and heaved a sigh of relief. "I can't see that being an issue, but I'll come with just to get ahead of any problems. This is a safe process?"

"Pretty sure," Joe promised, getting a *look* in return.

"Then I'm *definitely* coming along." Blas shut the door and followed them to a barracks, watching in fascination as Joe had his now-grumbling team stand around him in an odd spacing, the four of them in a square around where Joe stood in the center.

Joe pulled out a circular metal disk, the only magical blueprint he had managed to create, and a mid-grade Rare Core. "Alright everyone, I made the diagram for this ritual, Architect's Fury, ahead of time so we could hurry away here. You all ready? Here we go!"

He put a *touch* of mana into the disk to activate it, and lines of power wrapped around Joe and his team. Four magical circles appeared around them, but in a moment, two of the circles lifted off and joined together in midair. Then those two went to the building, ran along the walls, and seemed to swallow the entire structure. The power contained in the rings made it seem like the building was going to be burnt to a crisp, but there was no damage done as the rings drifted away from the barracks. The rings flew in front of Joe and shrank down and down... then into the blueprint paper he had supplied.

The paper shifted back and forth like a bear scratching its back on a tree, then settled on to Joe's open palm. He looked around, noting that his team was on the ground panting. His own mana had touched zero a couple times, but he had come prepared. Joe stored the empty mana potion bottle in his ring, hoping that he would be able to get some other usage out of the high-quality glass later. Reuse and all that.

"Good job, everyone. We got the blueprint of an Uncommon-ranked barracks, and this means we can get the people relying on us a whole lot of sleeping space." Joe pulled Bard to his feet, and the thick man swatted his hands away with a grumble. "Thank you all for your help, and *yes*, I am working on a way to keep you from *having* to do this again."

Blas looked at the barracks and saw no damage, so he waved the group away and went off to do his own thing. Joe smiled as he looked at the barracks ritual diagram, and his team all started walking back to the square to teleport to the guild area again. Alexis caught her breath and looked at Joe critically. "No armor?"

"No, but this gives me fifteen percent increased mana regen," Joe informed her. "That means that I can keep going in battle a lot longer and just get my shield back if it goes down. It also self-cleans and repairs over time."

"Hmm." Alexis kept walking, but Joe couldn't tell if she was approving or annoyed by his life and armor choices.

They teleported back to the demolished area the guild now owned and split up to take care of personal things before heading out. Joe went to find Aten, hoping to get some good brownie points in before asking for the next few things that he was going to need on his journey. After waiting in the line for a short while, he got into the main area where both Aten and Mike were slumped over their desks. Both were trying to focus on what was happening; both were trying to read the next thing that needed to be signed. Joe felt pity for them at that moment but reinforced his mindset while hardening his heart. There was a *reason* he hadn't wanted to start his own guild.

Joe slapped his hand on the desk, and both men jolted back. "Hey, guys! Listen, if you have the resources for it, I can get together with your people and get an Uncommon barracks set up *now*. I'm gonna need a lot of help, but we can get a few hundred people sleeping in shelter tonight if we work fast."

"Sleep?" Mike blearily called out.

"Mike, he's... Joe." Aten shook his head and giggled. "That's not a bed."

"Wow, you guys need sleep." Joe got the men on their feet and pulled them toward the quartermaster. "Here is a list. You need to get all these resources to wherever you want this monstrosity to go. Hop to it, people want to get inside."

Aten made motions at the quartermaster, who nodded and got a few teams of people running supplies. Massive amounts of strength or access to spatial storage devices made quick work of the needed components, and the man pulled a Core out of a small vault and handed it to Joe with a frown. That was the *real* downside to this process. A Core was needed to create the blueprint; a Core was required to build the building.

The cost of these two items was nearly equivalent to erecting a couple buildings, especially Common ones. At least, two Cores was the cost if anyone *else* were using the ritual, so Joe simply kept whatever remained after using a Core in his rituals as partial payment for services rendered. Still, in terms of convenience, the use of so many expensive Cores was the best possible trade that could be made. Zap! Whoosh! A building appears!

Joe followed the others to where the barracks would be built, and a town planner had already zoned off an area. There were a lot of tents that *had* been in the area, but since it was only late afternoon, they were largely unoccupied. Joe looked around at the gathering crowd and had an idea. "I need volunteers to help with a spell! Ten minutes of work, and you get a spot in the building that'll be built here!"

There were enough takers that Joe felt excited about his chances at keeping some mana. Twenty-nine people in total stood where Joe had directed them, and as he looked around for others, he saw Bard and Alexis laughing at the people that had stepped up. Hopefully, no one would notice them before it was too late. "Here we go!"

Joe held out the ritual that had inscribed itself on the blueprint, feeding mana into it and feeling the Core in his hand begin to drain. Since rituals cost sixty-seven percent less for him— thanks to his ritual magic skill—he only lost about a third of the Core and could make two more buildings if he needed to do so! Fun! The group of *almost* thirty lifted into the air on bands of power. The stacks of building material below them started to float alongside them, and then tiny bolts of power began dripping off the ritual and on to the material like rain falling on ruins.

The wood, stone, and metals began to arrange themselves, looking for all the world like a building being blown up in slow motion and in reverse. The building 'toppled' upward, the roof being built first, then the interior from the top down. Joe laughed when he saw that happen; it reminded him of old engineering jokes. As the foundation of the building settled in place, the group arrived on the ground with a swirl of air that tossed the surrounding dust and dirt into the air.

Ritual Blueprint loses 1 point of durability! Uses remaining: 2/3.

Class experience +100!

What? Did that mean that he could reuse this same ritual diagram two more times? It... yes, it looked like he could! Was that because he created the ritual by *using* a ritual? When he altered a blueprint directly, adding a ritual around it, the ritual was only single use. But... hmm. Then he could just scan it, right? Use a new building to make three more? Not a bad deal.

Joe started to congratulate the others, then realized that most of them were unconscious. Then he realized that the majority of them were fighter classes, and he had just forcefully unlocked their magic for them. Oops. Joe walked over to Aten and slapped him on the side. "Hey, Aten, all done here, buddy! Listen, there are a few things that I am going to need for my trip, and I was hoping you could help me out. Here's a list."

The two of them started to walk back to Aten's office, but Joe paused and smiled brightly at Mike. "Hey! Mike!"

"Yes, Joe?" Mike looked away from the immaculate new building and at the Rituarchitect.

Joe pointed upward at the roof of the building. "This one has shingles."

CHAPTER TWELVE

"Everyone!" the voice boomed over the area, and Joe recognized it as Aten's 'serious' voice. "I need you all to listen closely. If you can open your browser right now, I need you to do so. You are in a safe zone, so you should be able to do so. Look at the news. We will be having a meeting soon to discuss our next course of action."

Joe sat up and followed instructions, opening the first news channel he could find and pressing play on the current stream. He blanched as he recognized San Francisco, specifically when he saw that the city was under attack and burning. *Things* were coming out of the ocean, and Joe winced as he saw a massive tentacle lift out of the sea and wrap around the Golden Gate Bridge. In moments, the bridge was whisked away with a shriek of tearing metal.

The newscaster, pale and disheveled, replaced the view and held a paper in shaking hands. "Attacks like this are happening worldwide, with the coastal areas taking the most initial damage. The military is... *not* taking action, as they and their families have all apparently vanished in the same manner as President Musk. Government officials are just... they're *gone*! Police, medical... no one is coming. *No one* is out there to help or give instructions, and... I'm going too, as soon as I finish here. Reports are coming in now."

He gulped from a glass that was on the desk next to him, and the color suggested that it wasn't water. "These... *monsters* aren't moving all that quickly, and it is recommended that you move inland as fast as possible, running whenever the option presents itself. Just like Musk said, even with the slow pace, at this rate, there will be monsters *everywhere* within a month.

Personally, I recommend that you take this *Core*, slap it to your head, and flee to safety!"

The anchorman vanished as soon as he had followed his own instructions, and the stream cut off with a 'Technical Difficulties' message. Joe stared at the screen, mortified by what he had seen. How many people would think that this was still a hoax? Would ignore the warnings? Probably *too* many. Even still... what was the population of Ardania? A few million? What would happen if even *ten* percent of people made it into the game? The population would jump to nearly a billion people, all starting their journey in Ardania. He hopped out of bed and started jogging toward the guild meeting, knowing that he would need to hear what was said.

Joe didn't have to wait long after he arrived. Aten walked out with Mike and a few other officers and started shouting over the noise to get their attention, "Listen up! This changes *very* little for us! We need to continue fortifying our location, secure resources, and prepare to fend off raiders. Let's be realistic, people. We are in an enviable position right now, and there are going to be hungry people in the not-too-distant future. We are going to do everything that we can to help as many people as possible, but we all know that won't be enough for some of them. There *will* be people that want to take what you have, by force. Be prepared, do your duty. *Who comes for the Wanderers?*"

"The Strongest! The Best! We kill all the rest!" the crowd called back to him, some more enthusiastically than others. It was easy to be highly motivated when you were only doing this for fun, less so when it was your life, and you could see your civilization getting destroyed.

"As a side note, we are halting all guild invitations or requests to join." Aten's words were met with silence. "We need to be very careful who we take on from now on, to ensure that we have the infrastructure to support them. Good luck with everything you are all doing, people."

"Heh. The whole point is that we'd be overrun with *not* the strongest or the best, so that chant was really out of place. Maybe I should talk to him about rebranding the Guild?" Joe looked at the time and decided that it wasn't worth the effort of either discussing a point of semantics or trying to go back to bed.

Instead, he walked to the coffee shop and added his name to the growing list of people that were requesting the fragrant drink, then took his seat and pulled out his puzzle cube. Might as well get a jump on the day. Joe decided where he wanted to start, waited for his coffee, then downed it and got to puzzling. People around him came and went, but he didn't notice, too enthralled by the cube in front of him. An hour and forty-five minutes later, the sun was in the sky, and he was finished for the day.

Characteristic point training completed! +1 to intelligence, wisdom, perception, and dexterity! These stats cannot be increased further by any means other than system rewards, study, or practice for twenty-four hours game time.

Name: Joe '*Tatum's Chosen Legend*' Class: Mage (Actual: Rituarchitect)
Profession: Tenured Scholar (Actual: Arcanologist)
Character Level: 15 Exp: 125,993 Exp to next level: 10,007
Rituarchitect Level: 2 Exp: 2,290 Exp to next level: 710
Hit Points: 230/230
Mana: 963/963
Mana regen: 23.65/sec (Base 20.57/sec increased by gear)
Stamina: 200

<u>Characteristic:</u> <u>Raw score</u> <u>(Modifier)</u>

Strength: 22 (1.22)
Dexterity: 33 (1.33)
Constitution: 28 (1.28)
Intelligence: 74 (2.24)
Wisdom: 68 (2.18)
Charisma: 26 (1.26)
Perception: 53 (2.03)
Luck: 30 (1.30)
Karmic Luck: +3

Joe took a deep breath and let out a satisfied sigh. That was good stuff. "Here I go!"

He stood up and brushed off his new robe, then pulled his Mystic Theurge staff out of his ring and used it as a walking stick as he walked over to find his group. They needed to get a move on, daylight was burning! He found them in the usual places, training, crafting, and in Jaxon's case, a small stall that was offering buffs to passerby. Joe shook his head at the hand-painted sign, which featured sad-faced people crawling in, then walking out with smiles. They all joined together, and Joe laid out his plan.

"Here is what I found, guys. It isn't much, but it'll give us a starting point." Joe pulled out the only map he had been able to purchase, a sketchy drawing that he was *pretty* sure was of this continent. "Take a look at this. Here we are, about thirty miles north of Ardania. Here is Ardania. Here is the edge of the continent. If we continue north for about a hundred miles, we get to the northern edge. If we go *south* of Ardania, we have about two hundred miles until the edge."

"Now, as you get closer to the edges, the monsters get stronger." Joe waffled his hand back and forth. "At least that is what the guy who sold me this thinks. The point is, I found mention that there used to be people that could encourage plants to grow in any season. They *could* have been druids or the like, but from the book, I think they were Elves. We know for a fact that there are no Elves on this continent anymore, but if there was going to be a place with a greenhouse or similar technology, I think that is the spot to look, right... here. South and west of Ardania by about one hundred and thirty miles. It'll be fun!"

"One question," Alexis offered as soon as he finished speaking.

"Shoot."

"When did you do this research? *Yesterday?*" She stared him down, and Joe began to sweat. "You didn't just buy the first gear you found and then go gallivanting off to the library, right? That would be... *irresponsible.*"

"I got the best gear that I could from the most trustworthy source I know." Joe coughed into his hand and looked at anyone *but* Alexis. "Any other questions?"

"Are you Joe, the Chosen of Tatum?" a new voice asked him. Joe started to turn to answer the person asking and felt an impact on his Exquisite Shell. "Divine Shell, huh?"

Joe shouted an inarticulate cry that alerted his team, and the man that had just tried to assassinate him glowered. "Oh, I think not. I challenge you to a Duel of the Chosen!"

Duel of the Chosen instance initiated! You have been challenged by the chosen of ??? There is no way to refuse this duel, and no outside source can help or hinder either of you! Good luck, and fight well for your deity! Success: progress toward quest 'No, I'm right!' 100 favor points from your deity,

1000 divine energy for your deity! Failure: loss of 100 favor points from your deity, 1000 divine energy lost by your deity!

"What in the...?" Joe looked around, seeing that he was still in the same spot but that there were no other people present. Except, probably, the person that had challenged him to a duel. Joe was in a bad position; he had no anti-personnel rituals, no spell scrolls that would be useful here, and he had no idea what this other fighter would be capable of doing.

Ting. Joe felt an impact on his back and turned to find a wetly glistening dagger scraping against his shell and slowly sinking closer to him. He *jumped* back a few feet, crossing the distance like he was teleporting, thanks to his Master Jump skill. He couldn't let himself get pinned down; slow moving weapons sinking into his flesh would kill him just as much as fast moving weapons.

"You are slow and weak!" The mocking voice reached Joe's ears. "You serve a weak, pathetic deity, and I'm going to hunt you until he vanishes from the world!"

"Woo, you sure are driving the bus to crazy town, buddy," Joe called back, looking at the man that was still standing casually in front of him. "You realize that isn't a *thing*, right? That you're in a new world, sure, but also a *game* world?"

"Just die and let me collect my favor." The response was annoyed, no longer as if a role-player was getting his kicks. The man dashed forward, throwing knives at Joe's face to try and distract him. Joe ignored the blades, fully focused on the shadows he had been wrapping around the unknown man's ankles. Just one... more... *second.*

"*Solidified Shadows!*" Joe focused the mana through his Mystic Theurge staff and let the manacles he had created become tangible. The other guy tripped instantly, slamming to the ground and letting out an *oof* as the wind was knocked out of him. He rolled forward and sprang up, a mace in his hand that he whacked Joe across the face with before smashing the shadows around his legs. Joe reeled, the force of the blow forcing him to take a few steps backward. "How did you even know where to come after me?"

"You have a bounty!" the man informed him. "You keep showing up at the main temple and going toward the evil side of the place before vanishing for a few seconds, coming back, then turning around and leaving! We know you are whisked away by some dark power that is hiding your real affiliation! I'm only the *first* of the people that are going to try collecting! That I can grind some favor is only a fringe benefit! Down with the Dark Gods!"

A bottle was tossed at Joe, and in an instant, he was surrounded by blazing light that he couldn't see through. Was it a flashbang of some kind with an extra-long flash? Just before he was sent flying, Joe heard the words, "Holy Smite!"

He landed on the ground and bounced, his shield at a critical level. Joe got up, ready to *end* this guy. Enough was enough! "Acid Spray!"

Once more, power ran through his staff and changed forms, this time to a potent acid. He had caught the man running at him full in the face, and Joe decided to *channel* this spell! He could only cast a single spell at a time while using the staff, so it stood to reason that he kept hosing this creep down!

"My robe!" The man sputtered as his outer layer of clothing fell apart. "You *jerk*! For Ra-torian! *Holy Smite!*"

Joe was rocked back, tumbling across the ground again. This time, his shell shattered, and he took damage.

Holy Smite deals 300 light damage! 262 damage absorbed by Exquisite Shell! Hp -38 !

Joe popped back to his feet and whipped his staff around. This guy wanted to play with light? *Fine!* Joe started grabbing the shadows and spinning them into a whirling concertina wire. He stared at the other man, who had fallen to his knees and was just now struggling to his feet. Joe *almost* felt bad for the guy; the acid had done a number on his... everything. That was fine though, and Joe had needed a solid ten seconds to get the wire how he wanted it anyway.

He sent the darkness after his opponent, only at the last second activating Solidified Shadows and shredding the man into meat paste. Joe coughed and looked down, finding three daggers embedded in his chest. When had he thrown...?

Duel of the Chosen complete!

You have earned progress toward the ongoing quest: 'No, I'm right!' You have defeated your first opponent! Success! You gain 100 reputation points from your deity and 1000 divine energy for your deity!

You have died! Calculating... PvP, Chosen Duel, no experience lost. You will be respawned at your bind point in one hour!

CHAPTER THIRTEEN

Joe was furious about the interruption but had nothing to do and so used the short amount of time that he had remaining until respawn researching what was happening out in the 'real world'. While most of the news centers were slowly going off-air, especially since they were mainly coastal broadcasting stations, there were plenty of people streaming from their phones.

It looked like a nightmare come to life, and there didn't seem to be much anyone could do to stop what was happening. Bullets dealt some damage, but unless it was a perfect shot or *really* high caliber, not much happened at all to the monster getting shot. Not many people that were standing their ground were surviving for very long. High-powered weapons were hard to get ahold of. The government was gone, so there were no bombs, tanks, or missiles hitting. That was actually for the best most likely, as the issue was so widespread that there would have been as much loss of life and property damage from friendly fire either way.

The portal opened for Joe, and he stepped through and into the Pathfinder's Hall. He walked around and found his people again, then explained what had happened. "It's fine. It just seems to be something that's going to be happening from now on. Listen, it'll be easier for me if we got moving. The fewer people that know where I am at any given time would be *lovely*. Anyone need anything? No? Great."

They all went to the Temple section of the Pathfinder's Hall and teleported as far south as possible: Ardania. Joe felt sick looking around. The entire place was *stuffed*, and more people were arriving every second. "Quick, let's get out of here!"

Exiting the continuously growing crowd was *not* easy, and there was far more pushing and shoving than Joe wanted to use. He stood behind Bard, using the Skald as a tank that slowly drove the crowd. At one point, Joe heard a yelp, and Alexis suddenly was sporting a nasty smile. "Some thief just learned that it's a bad idea to pick my pocket. There was a nasty pain poison in there that will also turn his hand red for a few days."

Joe needed to stop in the shopping district to grab as many glass panes as had been completed, then they simply continued through the city on the main road until they came out the southern gates. Joe had never been this way before, or this far, and it took a little while to realize how *truly* massive this city was. Twenty-five million permanent residents had not made this a small space, and being a self-sustaining city meant that there were crops and places for animals to graze as well. The size and scope of the wall that surrounded the entire city made Joe's head spin.

They had already been traveling for *hours* by the time the southern gate came into view, and they were ready to abandon the city and get some fresh air and elbow room. They passed into the wildlands that were south of Ardania, and all of a sudden, there was practically *no one* around them. Most of the newbies were far too scared to go out and about, and none of them had signed up to be torn apart by monsters. In fact, they were *specifically* running from that. Joe's group started making good time at that point, and they were able to follow a basic dirt road that seemed to align with their destination pretty well.

"Joe!" Poppy startled the party leader out of his thoughts and pointed at a small building that was just off the path. "Is that one of those fast-travel points that you can use?"

The Rituarchitect took a closer look, and sure enough, there was a shrine next to the road. Like most of the other ones that he had seen to this point, the shrine was eroded and faded. Whatever it had once been dedicated to could be a fun debate, but Joe decided that he would rather just take it for himself and Tatum. "Thanks, Poppy! You guys want a break really quick?"

"Sounds nice to me!" Jaxon gave Joe a thumbs-up and started doing seemingly impossible stretches on the ground next to the shrine. The others sat *just* out of view and pulled out some food for a makeshift lunch.

Joe walked over to the shrine and put his hand on the small altar.

You have found an unguarded shrine! As you are not currently under attack, you have the option to rededicate this shrine to your deity. Would you like to do so now? Yes / No

After saying yes, the heavily eroded shrine simply collapsed inward as Joe's mana washed outward. More and more mana fell off, and Joe struggled to keep upright as the shrine sank away and was replaced by a small building; the patchwork roof turned into a stone book placed upside down, and the walls became books placed open and upright. All in all, a proper rest stop.

You have earned a reward from the continuous quest: Reclamation of the Lost. After making a new shrine for Tatum, you have been blessed! You have gained: +1 strength.

Quest update: Reclamation of the Lost: Daily Divine Energy generation has increased by 100!

"Looking good!" Alexis called over as the sun hit the white marble of the new shrine.

"Thanks!" Joe called back distractedly. He had his eyes closed and was listening for the nagging sensation that usually accompanied finding a waypoint. Something *else* was ringing in his ears though, and it stayed as constant as tinnitus. What *was* that? Joe focused in on it and suddenly realized that the entire shrine had a single note of music continuously coming off of it.

Skill increased: Magical Synesthesia (Novice II).
Realizing the directional angle of this skill was the important first step toward mastery! Or did you just so happen to look in the direction after hearing the sound?

"I suppose it makes sense that this is a magical building." Joe stared at the shrine and decided to look in all the standard places. He followed all the lines and checked each crevice. He only found the bind point after he almost gave up, then followed a hunch and pressed his finger into a page on the ceiling. He lost a point of health and a drop of blood, but a white ring of energy seemed to expand outward for about ten paces, and Joe knew that he had found what he was looking for. "Excellent."

"Hey, guys!" Joe called to the others. "Looks like we can make a trail of these and use them for fast travel if we can keep finding and converting them, so keep an eye out!"

"So, we could sleep every night in the guild and then just resume our trip in the morning?" Alexis perked up considerably at this happy news. "It shall be my first priority, party leader!"

Joe rolled his eyes even as Bard chuckled. Maybe being in a relationship made odd comments like that seem funny? Joe also decided not to mention the fact that if he had enough shrines, his deity would get unlocked in the future. They didn't need to know. "At least we won't need to go into Ardania if we don't want to."

The others pulled faces at the thought of going back there, and they decided to get on the road again. After they had been walking for another half hour, they found a large camp of people. The strangest thing was that they were this far out into the wildlands, and most of them were still level one and weaponless. Joe was concerned, but the people seemed happy enough. He went over to one of the people and asked where they were going. The man looked at him blankly, then took in his garb, weapon, and the similar state of the people with Joe.

"Oh! Hey there, I thought you had just gotten separated from us." The man smiled cheerfully and waved at Joe as he got closer. "We're going to our guild's area. There are so many people coming in with non-combat classes that some guilds are starting various divisions. We are going to be a part of the farming division. Plenty of work, food, shelter, protection from monsters."

"What do you get out of doing the work? I assume you are going to be feeding the guild?" Joe looked at the man quizzically.

"What do you mean?" The farmer seemed confused, then angry. "I just told you. Food, shelter, protection from monsters."

"You're willingly going off to be a *serf* in a feudalistic system?" Joe bluntly asked the guy. "For how long?"

"Until I can go back to my house in Iowa, dude." The soon-to-be farmer started to walk away, fists clenched. "Leave me alone."

Joe was flabbergasted. He had no idea how someone could so willingly and cheerfully... just give up? Did he even look into the guild that he had joined? Looked at options? Then he remembered that there were *so many* people joining right now that there was no realistic way for them to make demands of potential employers. With such a huge workforce arriving, there would always be someone *else* that would take *any* job—no questions asked. Joe was suddenly afraid for the future of this continent. Guilds would still be subject to the crown but would likely be making their own little kingdoms all over the place.

"Let's... let's get out of here, guys." Joe started walking past the giant camp full of refugees, only just now realizing that almost everyone that had come from Earth suddenly fit into that horrific category. He needed to do something, something that would help them all. All of humanity. He closed his eyes and took a deep breath. It would be a long journey.

They had gotten about a half mile away from the camp when Alexis suddenly spoke up, "Joe, I'm seeing a... is that a pride of lions? Are we in a different biome than our area or something? Anyway, I think they are going after that camp. Should we go after them?"

"Not even a question." Joe flicked his eyes in the direction she was indicating, only seeing long grass swaying against the wind from this distance. "*Anything* will tear through that group of level ones, and even if they have people that are guarding them, they can't be *everywhere*. Let's go."

They started on an interception course for the lions, and as they closed in, the grass stopped moving. Apparently, the ambush was set. "Alexis?"

"Oh, I'm all over this." She swept her cloak to the side, and her massive crossbow flipped over her shoulder and settled in front of her. Alexis pulled off the quarrel that was attached and slotted in a bolt that was more barrel than arrow. She fired the bolt into the area with the cats, and a huge nova of poison expanded from the impact zone.

A guttural roar destroyed any concern that the group had been wrong. A lioness bounded out toward them, then another... and another. Nine lionesses in total were coming after the humans, followed by a brute of a lion.

"*I like my skin intact, yes I do! I like my skin intact, how about you?*" Bard chanted into the air, and Joe was graced with a notification that he would take nine percent less slashing damage for thirty minutes.

"New song, Bard?" Jaxon beamed at the Skald, then went back to studying the cats running at them. "I *really* like it. I haven't had much luck with singing lately."

"Still workin' on this one." Bard's voice betrayed his embarrassment. Then the cats had arrived, and there was no more time for feelings like doubt or concern. There was only surviving and making sure that their opponent didn't.

CHAPTER FOURTEEN

Alexis was the first person to get off another attack, her hand-held crossbow's bolts zipping through the air to plunge into the leading lioness. The huge cat roared at her and leaped nearly thirty feet forward with outstretched claws. As fast as the cat moved, Joe was still able to send out and solidify a Shadow Spike. The leap was halted only feet away from Alexis, and the lioness scrabbled at her punctured chest in an attempt to destroy whatever it was that was causing pain.

Poppy glided forward and pulled his arm back, thrusting forward with a deadly *hiss* emanating from his rapier. The lioness he was targeting forced herself down, and the rapier missed her face and instead penetrated into her shoulder. The cat snarled and retaliated with an instant paw swipe that Poppy somehow moved *with*, removing his rapier with a twist that sent blood and gray fluid flying.

The third cat raced between the two that were injured, going through the open space to target Joe. The humans were in a bad position, and only the fact that Bard was standing next to Joe and was eager to get into the fight kept Joe from having claws scraping his shell. The Skald waded into combat with a whirl of his axes, the metal forcing the lioness to flatten herself to avoid losing more than just a few whiskers. Jaxon moved forward on Alexis's left, catching the next cat that was trying to attack the out-of-formation crossbow-user. He body-checked the cat, knocking it to the side and getting a slash across the ribcage for his trouble.

A second lioness reached Poppy and tried to take him to the ground, but only managed to knock the Duelist back a step. Poppy was using some kind of footwork pattern that allowed him to keep upright and mobile while he was in a fight, and it was showing its worth here. A second lioness hit Jaxon, then a third on Poppy. Another circled to Poppy's right and came after Bard as he fought off the first, and another piled into Alexis's area.

Now there were two lionesses on Bard, Alexis, and Jaxon; while there were three being fended off by Poppy. Joe targeted Jaxon with a healing spell, closing the gash in his side. Then he formed a Shadow Spike under the extremely poisoned lioness fighting Poppy, while at the same time, Alexis got off a shot at the lioness that had first attacked her. The bolt slamming into its head was enough to bring it down, though the bolt head only slightly penetrated the thick skull bone. The lioness had simply taken enough damage, lost enough blood, and the area poisoning had been particularly nasty.

The cost for Alexis to get her attack off was a paw to her chest that tore open her flesh to the bone as well as breaking a few of her ribs. She tumbled back, in total shock at the sudden pain. Joe's spike had impaled and held the damaged lioness that had been fighting Poppy, allowing the man to focus on the other two as the light went out of the first's eyes. He swiped back and forth with his wasp-stinger rapier, holding them back but dealing no damage.

"Alexis!" Joe called, realizing her predicament even as the lioness was jumping at her. Joe *jumped* first, covering her body with his own and using Lay on Hands to reverse the damage that had been done to her. The lioness landed on Joe, pressing him down with its body weight but clawing ineffectually at his shell. The reduction to slashing damage was showing its usefulness here, all the way until the cat got its mouth around Joe's arm and started trying to rip it off.

A bolt bounced off of Joe's Shell, reducing its durability further, and Alexis growled. "Can't get a shot, getting crushed!"

"Craw!"

"Nyah!"

The strange sounds reached Joe's ears just before he was showered with blood and tufts of fur. He sputtered as the huge weight of the cat suddenly vanished, looking up to see Jaxon gripping the lioness and *tearing* chunks of flesh off of it. No... *he* wasn't; his *hands* were! T-rex heads swallowed globs of meat, and Jaxon was tackled from the side by one of the cats he was still fighting with. The Chiropractor rolled with the blow and ended up on the lioness's back, riding her like a bucking bronco even as he continued to punch in one spot with his toothy, *hungry* hands.

Jaxon hopped off and seemed to concentrate, and the cat's spine just *twisted*. The animal fell, and Joe realized that he was neglecting his support duties to the rest of the team in order to watch a single fight. Joe turned to help Bard, who was bleeding from *several* nasty wounds. The Skald had apparently not been able to land a hit on the creatures he was fighting, and like the cats they were, Bard was being toyed with in preparation for a kill.

As Joe sent a stream of healing water to Bard, he saw that Poppy's health was dropping quickly as well, though he didn't seem to have any massive wounds. After the spell hit Bard, Joe slammed his staff to the ground with both hands and channeled a powerful group heal to all of his party members. At the cost of about fifty-five mana per second, he healed all of them for thirty-two point five health per second. This was enough to close the wound Poppy had in an opened artery and replenished his blood enough for him to continue moving at a fast pace.

Joe only managed to cast the spell for two seconds before being taken off his feet by the lion finally joining combat.

The huge creature clamped down on Joe with its teeth and shook back and forth even as it used its front paws to tear at his body. Joe could hear people shouting, but all he could do was try to form a spell to fight back against the lion. His staff fell from his hand after a particularly vicious shake, and Joe cast the only spell that he could think of. His muscle memory and the ease of the spell allowed him to dual cast Acid Spray. His extreme close range made it so that the lion was soaked by the spell, and he was able to continue channeling for a full second before he lost concentration.

Joe's shell broke, and instantly, there were teeth tearing into his arm while claws ripped at his side and acid dripping on to him. Joe screamed in pain, his low constitution and *high* perception allowing him to feel every second of this agony. The lion was hit from the side, and the weight was taken off of Joe. The pain didn't end though, and the addition of rolling allowed the multi-hundred-pound creature to *rip his arm off.*

Joe was bleeding horrifically, and only his total shock allowed him to cast Lay on Hands on himself. This spell was so powerful now that he could heal ten more damage than he had total health, bringing him up to maximum health in an instant. The main issue was that a thick layer of scar tissue formed over the hole in his side where his arm should be, and the limb was still in the *lion's mouth.*

The sudden lack of pain had set his mind whirling, and Joe could only stare as his team worked to finish off the lion. It had *way* more health than Joe thought that it should as only a basic creature. He slowly blinked, opening his eyes to Poppy sliding his rapier into the lion and having it roar at him while dropping a mangled arm to the ground. *Blink.* Jaxon was laughing maniacally as his hands bit off the lion's tail. *Blink.* Bard was under the lion, his axes crossed and holding the jaws back from clamping down.

Joe blinked again, and the lion was on its side. They had defeated it. Yay.

Bard came over with an odd-shaped stick. No, that was his arm. Joe watched as Bard lifted an axe and swung it at him, a light red glow appearing around him as his axe sliced off the scar tissue that had appeared over Joe's arm-hole. The pain shocked him again, out of whatever state of mind he had been in. Bard was speaking, "There ya goo, big guy. C'mon now, heal this up and then Cleanse yerself. I bet ye'll get a nasty bug otherwise."

Joe numbly cast Mend on himself and suddenly had feeling in his arm again. He screamed as new flesh formed on the demolished arm out of the healing water. Why would the *nerves* be the first thing to *heal?* The injustice of it made Joe come back to himself, and as his arm pain settled into a dull ache, he began healing his torn-to-shreds team. Strangely, it was Jaxon that had the most damage, not Bard. The bite marks... "Jaxon, what happened?"

"Oh, these?" Jaxon smiled nervously. "T-rex are good little babies. They just don't know how to show affection yet. We're working on training to nuzzle, but I only get a few seconds at a time to teach them not to bite me! At least it's only love nibbles!"

"Jaxon!" Joe was shocked at how long he needed to cast his healing for. "You took at least four *hundred* damage!"

"Nibbles," Jaxon petulantly asserted.

"How's the arm, Joe?" Alexis pointedly changed the conversation.

"Infected." He sighed and started casting Cleanse on himself. A few seconds later, the 'plague' marker vanished. "I'm *really* glad I didn't wait to cure that. I had the *plague* for a moment there. I can't even imagine what would have happened if these got loose in the camp back there."

"I can!" Jaxon raised a hand. "The humans would have likely died, a large chunk of them! Any survivors would have run to a population center and tried to find shelter, inadvertently spreading the plague to whoever was there!"

There was a long silence, and Joe shrugged. "Yeah, okay, I'm glad we killed them off. Anyone else infected? If not, let's destroy these bodies. Acid Spray!"

They got to work, and Joe was suddenly flooded with messages.

Exp: 360 (40 * Lioness x9).

Exp: 50 (50 * Lion x1)

Zone quest complete: Plague of Pride! You managed to stop an outbreak of plague before it managed to spread to the local population! Reward: 100 experience.

Skill increase: Channeling (Beginner III)

Skill increase: Acid Spray (Beginner II). You realize that this spell was designed for cleaning out landfills, right? How little do you think of your enemies?

Skill increase: Exquisite Shell (Novice VI). You're on your way to becoming a front-line fighter! Go you! Wait...

"Huh. Odd that there was no reward other than experience for the quest." Then Joe remembered that he hadn't even opened the Common-item reward he had gotten a while back, and he rubbed his hands together. "I guess I can open that and *pretend* it's a reward for this!"

CHAPTER FIFTEEN

Joe opened his reward box after melting the lions with Acid Spay. He had sat a little apart, hoping that it would be something cool enough that he didn't want to show it off right away. As the box popped open, Joe saw what appeared to be... he had no idea. At least, until he got the notification.

Item gained: Rituarchitect Survey Grid! (Artificially Rare) No more measuring out distances for buildings by hand; this item allows you to get exact measurements for the perimeter and area of any building you plan to build and displays a soft-light building to mark out exactly where it will be placed!

"Um." Joe looked at the item, which appeared to be a small solar light from Earth. It had a spike on the bottom—obviously designed to be pushed into the ground—and a mirrored panel on the top. All in all, a not-very-*impressive* tool but hopefully useful either way?

"Ready to get a move on, Joe?" Alexis called over to him. "It's already afternoon, and I want to see if we can find a shrine before dark. I know we all brought camping gear, but if we don't need to sleep outside, I'll be much happier in the morning!"

"Fair point!" Joe got to his feet and stood, pausing and frowning as he got a new notification.

Skill increase: Mental Manipulation Resistance (Novice V).

Where had that come from? Joe thought about his recent battle as well as searching the area. He was *pretty* sure he got that increase due to dwelling on his injury during combat and not shaking it off right away like he was *supposed* to do... but would that mean getting badly injured in the future would cause him to dwell on and remember *more* pain? How long would it take for this skill to break him? As much as Joe wanted to empower all of his skills, this one was certainly an exception.

Joe thought about this issue for a long while as they walked across the huge, savanna-style area they had recently entered. It was strange how suddenly and radically the landscape could shift in this world. At least they had found where the lions had come from, but Joe was finding that he preferred his spot in the northern forests. The heat was also slowly increasing, and as night came along... the area began to come alive. It seemed that most of the creatures in this area were going to end up being nocturnal, and–

"Hold up a moment." Alexis stopped them, then took a few steps off the path and pointed. "Can anyone tell me what that looks like?"

The group gathered around and looked. Sure enough, there was a recognizable track in the ground. Jaxon shrugged and shook his head. "Not a clue! Dirt? Mud that dried? Sand! Is there going to be a quiz on this later?"

"Jaxon..." Alexis cracked her neck, making Jaxon quiver with anticipation. "As much as I love a guessing game, look. That's the size and depth of an Elite Wolfman Warrior. What would they be doing around here?"

Bard offered his opinion, "Well, they ruled the majority of ta continent before we broke their spine. Likely they are gettin' together to regroup, repopulate, try again later, yea?"

"Oh, that makes sense." Jaxon nodded along. "They are such *nice* people too, when they aren't trying to tear your face off."

"You... know some of them?" Joe cocked his head to the side as he asked this. "*How* do you know them, I guess would be the better question."

"Helped a few of the young and elderly get out of the forest." Jaxon seemed to be in earnest, and Joe certainly wasn't going to condemn someone for helping others. "They seemed nice, gave me a free pass to visit. All the fun times."

The others exchanged a *look*, and Alexis asked the next question, "What way were they going when you helped them out?"

"Well, we started off going east, then we parted ways when I continued north," Jaxon explained amiably.

"So... did they go south?" Joe prodded him.

Jaxon scratched at his chin. "Maybe?"

There was nothing else for it, so the party continued onward. They would need to be on guard, but what else was new at this point? They moved across the open area as night began to fall, and soon, all of them were attempting to stave off yawns and grumpy attitudes. When they came to a tree, Joe called out to the others, "Alright, guys, I'm calling it. Let's set up here. I think we made it about forty miles today, and it looks like anything that's out here is going to be coming after us at night. We need to get some sleep and set a watch."

"Why don't you just set up one of those 'Predator Territory' spells?" Alexis demanded, already pulling out a sleeping bag.

"Mainly because I haven't been able to find the time to make one." Joe got a *look* at that and crossed his arms defensively across his chest. "Look, every single one of those rituals takes a lot of time and concentration to set up. You've seen what happens when it fails or goes wrong! Also, they are expensive to use, even *if* I can mitigate the cost of them. If you would like to step in and cover the mana cost or even just the components, we'll go make some of them right now!"

"Joe. Chill." Bard put an arm around Joe's shoulders and gave him a side-hug. "Ye need some sleep, bud. Go'on. I'll take first watch."

Was he getting too upset? Joe didn't think so, but from the looks of the people around him... perhaps Bard had the right idea. "I... sorry, guys. We'll talk after the inevitable attack tonight, alright?"

"Sounds good, sleep well!" Jaxon called from a hot pink, overstuffed sleeping bag that looked more like a beanbag chair than a sack. Joe decided that Jaxon must have some kind of storage device and tried not to think too hard about it. He closed his eyes and was asleep in moments. It wasn't meant to last, and it seemed that the game decided to punish him for his flippant remarks. *How* did it punish him?

With Giant Scorpions.

The poison-using, double-pincer-wielding bugs burrowed out of the sand around them, tossing huge geysers of sand into the night air. Joe wasted no time, grabbing his staff and releasing a spray of acid from the tip. There was some damage, but nothing like Joe expected. The acid rolled off the scorpion like it was just standard water, and Joe was forced to *jump* back as the stinger slithered through the air at him. His stamina reserves dropped by half, but he avoided the blow. "No soft flesh!"

"I *hate* these things!" Jaxon leaped at the bug in front of him, landing on it and riding the beast like a horse. His fists dropped like hammers, slamming into the weak points of the creatures' joints. A stinger plunged at him from behind, but Jaxon straight up ignored it and kept pummeling. The stinger dug into his back, and the scorpion pumped a load of poison into the Monk.

"Ge' up ya!" Bard joined in the fray, his axes coming down on to another of the creatures. A pincer took the blow, the bug retaliating with its other claw and tail near-simultaneously. Bard blocked the tail, but the pincer wrapped around his midsection and attempted to cut him in half.

Ssssit Poppy's rapier went right through his target, the armor-piercing effect of his class and weapon causing the otherwise frail creature to fall and spasm in its death throes after a single attack. Conversely, the first arrow that Alexis sent at one of the bugs skittered off and nearly damaged Bard. Seeing the issue, she switched over to a stiletto and prepared to defend herself if the creatures got too close.

"Hold them off while Poppy finishes them!" Joe spoke over the quiet scuffle happening on the sand, not needing to get anywhere near shouting.

"How abou' ya *focus*?" Bard growled at him, fending off another stinger. He had managed to smash the pincer that had gripped him, though he was heavily bruised under his armor. Jaxon rolled forward and to the left of the scorpion he had been straddling and collapsed on to the ground. The bug also fell, its head entirely caved in.

"That's... how it's done." Jaxon was breathing heavily, and black lines were tracing his veins. "*Entomologist*, baby! Down with bugs of all kinds!"

"Heal!" Joe sent an orb of healing water at Bard and then rushed to Jaxon's side. "Cleanse!"

Black water spun in Joe's hands, flooding out of him and into the gaping wound on Jaxon's back. Thick liquid started to pool out of the Monk's back, causing secondary damage as it touched his skin. "Corrosive poison? Now I get why my acid didn't even phase that nasty bug."

Poppy lunged forward again, creating a picture-perfect thrust with one arm extended behind him. Another scorpion down. Bard and Alexis worked together to fell the one that had been trying to re-establish a grip, and all of a sudden, they were alone amongst corpses. Jaxon shuddered as Joe's work continued. As the last of the poison left him and red blood began flowing from the deep stab wound, Joe used his Lay on Hands spell and fixed the damage.

"Looks like you're gonna need to get your gear fixed up, Jaxon." Joe touched the ragged hole in the Monk's robe. "Unless you know how to sew?"

"No, too expensive of a skill for me to learn." Jaxon sat up and smiled around at the group. "Anyone else not get experience yet?"

"Are we still in combat?" Poppy whipped around, looking for danger. The others, who had been relaxing after the event, went back on high-alert and grouped together. Since it was a very dark night around three in the morning, only Joe was able to see what was going on outside of the light provided by the campfire.

"I see nothing, but that only means that there might be something stalking us stealthily." Joe paused, feeling a tremble in the ground. "Or it might be right below us."

The group scattered as the sand split, and a tree-like tail pierced through where Poppy had been standing. From the amount of sand that was displaced, it seemed like a sandstorm was arriving. As the wind caught the dust and blew it away, a massive scorpion was revealed. Jaxon took a single look and seemed to fly into a rage. "*Kill it with fire!*"

CHAPTER SIXTEEN

The Monk was the first to charge, but the huge beast spun and sent him flying with a mere brushing of its gargantuan body. Joe readied a Shadow Spike, thinking about the terrible luck that had led to them fighting this monstrosity. Had it been here the entire time, or had it somehow dug to their location during the night?

"No one breathe this in!" Alexis called out, the only warning they got before a huge crossbow flipped up on to her shoulder and she launched a bolt that was more wine bottle than arrow. The bolt landed under the bug and released a cloud of gas that was sucked away by the steadily increasing wind. "That should disorient it. It's a hallucinogen that causes accuracy to drop by half!"

"Ya missed its face!" Bard informed her with an odd glance.

"Scorpions breath through 'book lungs' under their body. I got it good," she assured him. He nodded and charged forward, his axes landing and being just as effective as if he had struck a rock wall. Sparks flew as his axes chipped and turned, and Bard only *barely* managed to avoid hurting himself.

The Shadow Spike that Joe had cast was being channeled, and the dense armor of the bug was screeching under the strain of the continuous damage to its carapace. Still, the armor hadn't succumbed, and Joe hadn't managed to damage it yet. The stinger shot down toward Bard, slamming into the ground next to him and retracting in an instant. Bard gasped and looked at the fresh crater. "It missed?"

"You're welcome!" Alexis called to him.

Poppy dashed forward and sunk his rapier into an interlocking joint of the bug's leg, dealing the first damage to this massive beast since combat began. The bug squealed, turning and *clacking* its pincers at the Duelist in an attempt to not only damage but *threaten* the group. In the group—though it hadn't been tested—Poppy was currently thought to be unmatched in one-on-one combat. He flipped in the air, passing over the right pincer and dashing forward as soon as he landed. Just before he went under the scorpion, he forced himself to halt before jumping upward on to its body.

The bug, thinking that the human was attempting to get under and attack its less-armored underside, dropped downward to crush the foolish prey. Instead, Poppy was given a handy way to climb on top of the creature. He leaned back, aimed carefully at the space between segments, and focused all of his strength on the penetrative power of his rapier.

"Solidified Shadows!" Joe had been building an orb of shadow on the tip of the stinger and dumped mana into the shape just before it plunged downward.

A massive force dropped on to Poppy, firmly pressing him to the back of the scorpion. The tail retracted a moment later, and he stood and tried to skewer the creature's head. This time, he finished his attack and drove his rapier through the plating of the scorpion and into its brain. The creature spasmed, twisted, turned, bucked... then dropped and went limp. Poppy rolled off the bug and looked around. "What just happened?"

*Exp gained: 80 (20 * Giant Scorpion x4)*

Zone alert! Members of the guild The Wanderers have killed a local [animal] field boss! For the next twenty-four hours, all Scorpions in the zone—having lost their protector—will have their armor rating reduced by thirty percent! The Wanderer's Guild gains +50 fame with the city of Ardania!

The area alert faded, leaving only the reward for the battle in the group's view.

For being the first to vanquish the field boss [Sheila, The Fat-Tailed Mankiller] you gain +2 skill points and +100 personal and guild fame with Ardania. Exp: 450.

Title gained: Pierce the Earth. By being the first to defeat this Earth-attributed field boss, your party has gained a bonus to the type of damage used to defeat it! Effect: All damage dealt now includes 5% armor piercing.

"What in the actual fecal matter?" Poppy looked at his rapier and shook his head. "You all got the same reward as me? Do you guys even understand how difficult it is to gain armor piercing bonuses? You need special, *specific* weapons and tools! Now Jaxon can *punch* something, and he deals *piercing* damage?"

"What? I do?" Jaxon looked at his hands in awe. "*Nifty!*"

"All damage?" Alexis looked at her bolts. "How is that going to work with my poisons and such?"

"Maybe some kind of corrosion?" Joe offered, pulling up his status screen to take a look at his current bonuses, wincing as a new notification appeared.

Caution! All current title slots are filled! Either replace a title or the newest title gained will be lost! Time limit: 10 minutes.

Joe looked over his titles and tried to figure out a way to keep this new title as well as all his others. He currently had a broken title, but he wasn't sure if he wanted to use it up. Joe also had a cursed title, but that one wasn't going anywhere. He had a couple weaker titles from the start of the game, but if he could keep them, he would. The sign of a hoarder? Perhaps. "Combine title 'Pierce the Earth' and broken title 'in darkest night'."

You are attempting to combine titles! You may align them as you like, but be sure that titles with ellipses are placed in the correct position. After arranging them, you have the option to make small changes, such as adding the words 'an, a, the, of' or something similar to create a sentence. The fewer changes that need to be made, the more potent the effect! Good luck!

Title accepted! Calculating... Title condensed.

New title gained: Pierce the Darkest Night. You stand between your people and the darkness of the world, standing steadfast and potent where all others would flee in terror. Effect: 50% resistance to dark-aligned magic. All damage dealt now includes 5% armor piercing. The piercing bonus increases to 10% with dark-aligned spells and weapons.

"Well, now," Joe muttered as he read over the effects. "Oh, I like that. What... I have twenty skill points to spend?"

He tried to remember how he had gained so many and could only think that it was due to the leveling after the Wolfman War as well as the skill points that he had gained in situations like this. Joe swallowed, trying to think through his options. Right now, he had enough skill points to bring a single skill up by two entire tiers. Did he want to do that? Or should he hold off and learn as naturally as possible? Yikes.

That was a tough call. Did he want to get better now? His inner greed raven wanted to wrap its wings around the hoard of points and screech and peck at any attempts to use them. But... was that a realistic way of doing things? Maybe it was time to bring his Jump skill up to the Sage ranks. Joe nodded when he came to that decision—that was likely the best use of his skill points. He allocated the points and pressed accept.

Nope!

Joe stared at the system message, concerned and confused. "Nope? What in the...? No other information? That can't be right. Let me try again."

Nope. I see that you aren't stopping, so a tish more info for you. Getting into the Master ranks is possible by spending skill points, but moving through them requires you to form your own insight. All Masters have wildly varied techniques, even if those of a lower ranking have skills that are nearly identical. Let me condense this message: Get good.

"You're telling me that I am going to have to actually *jump* to get my skill levels up?" Joe started the sentence in a fury, but by the end, he had already accepted that this was fair. Drat. It *did* make sense; how could you be considered a Master at something if you only followed someone else's understanding of the issue? Well... at least he still had his twenty skill points. What should he use them on? Of all his abilities, Ritual Magic was his most used and useful... but he was having trouble powering his rituals. In that case...

"Add four points to Ritual Magic, seven points to Mana Manipulation, and nine points to Coalescence." Joe looked over his stat sheet, feeling pleased with himself. That had actually been the perfect amount of points! He was able to bring all three skills up to the next rank!

Skill increase: Mana Manipulation (Student 0). Congratulations! You have met the requirements to be considered a Student when controlling your Mana! By reaching the Student ranks, you no longer have your mana reduced! Current bonuses applied to this skill: 25% spell efficiency (Maxed). Steady Flow: Increases spell stability by 10% and reduces casting time of all mana-using skills and spells by 10%.

Skill increase: Coalescence (Student 0). Congratulations! Condensing your mana into a single point

allows you to create a denser and more potent mana source!
Current bonuses: +30% spell efficiency and +30% mana
regeneration. You will be pulled into your inner self to attempt
another breakthrough in 10... 9...

I think you forgot that you can't increase Ritual Magic
with skill points anymore. Sad day.

"Joe?" Poppy called over as the group settled back down, "you done talking to yourself? It's your turn to be on watch."

The Rituarchitect turned and nodded, taking a single step toward the fire before his eyes rolled up into his head and he dropped. Poppy saw him fall and sighed. Everyone else was already in their 'beds', pretending they didn't see what had just happened. Poppy started walking toward Joe, quickly rolling him over and checking on him. "Ugh. You did that on purpose. Somehow."

Joe not only couldn't hear the question, but there was also no way for him to respond. He was deep within himself at this very moment, staring at a howling hurricane; what was now an orb of power that represented all of his collected mana. "Alright, you. Time to *condense!*"

He exerted his willpower and forcefully worked to bring his orb of condensed mana back to the point it had been at the last time he had achieved a breakthrough. Back then, Joe had been able to condense all of his gaseous mana into a fingernail-sized orb. Obviously, his power had grown since then, even though he had since lost the ability to pull from the well of mana granted by Tatum. "Come... *on!*"

The mana shrank a small amount, but there wasn't enough of a change for Joe's liking. Why was this such a difficult process? It was just raw mana; he should be able to manipulate it freely! Joe tried to pull at the mana, but all that happened was a cloud of power drifting away from the core of it. The orb itself didn't change. "So *wild*. What if I need to make my mana undergo more of a *qualitative* change?"

Joe pushed at his raging power, attempting to convince the orb to be *calm*. To be *steady*. Then he remembered that he had gained the trait of '*Suppression* Resistance' when he was last here and made a small realization. What he was doing right now went against who he was as a person. He wanted to be free, to be able to move and do what he wanted without the restrictions that other people wanted to put on him. What if... what if his mana was a representation of *him*? Was that a thing?

"Alright, mana." Joe stared at the swirling orb. "You want to be free? I really hope this isn't a bad idea."

With a thought, the contained mana was released, all the mental pressure Joe had been using to shape it gone in an instant. The decompression of his power caused a thump like an artillery shell landing, and Joe was thrown out of his trance by the massive concussion.

CHAPTER SEVENTEEN

Skill increase: Coalescence (Student III).
Congratulations! You have achieved a breakthrough with your
ability! By understanding yourself, you have created a unique
understanding with your skill! Skill rarity has increased by a
rank! As a bonus, the mana regeneration provided by this skill
has increased by 50%! Casting time decreased by 10%. Caution:
as this skill has increased in rarity, it will be comparatively
difficult to grow naturally!

Joe's eyes popped open, and he was treated to the
nausea-inducing sight of Bard's kilt flapping right in front of his
face. He started struggling to move away, and Bard simply let
him flop to the ground. "Abou' time, ya great walnut! I though'
ya were gonna sleep ta day away!"

Quickly getting to his feet and brushing the dirt off his
robe, Joe looked around. It was already well into the morning,
and it was obvious that the group had been moving for quite a
while. "How long was I out?"

"Hours, friend." Poppy clapped him on the arm and
marched past. Joe did a double take when he saw that the stinger
from Sheila was strapped to the Duelist's back, but he realized
that the item could potentially be converted into a formidable
weapon. After all, a wasp's stinger had met the same fate to
create Poppy's current rapier.

"Ugh." Joe glanced inside himself and saw that there was
mana raging through his body, and his center was nearly empty.
That was... strange. Conventional wisdom demanded that mana
be tightly confined within a single space. Joe had studied enough
of the books that Journeyman Cel had recommended to
understand at least that much. He activated his Cleanse spell and

hydrated himself, narrowing his eyes at his arms as he felt the change in mana accessibility.

"Everything okay, Joe?" Alexis asked him as her path brought her past the team leader. "We couldn't figure out what was wrong with you, and since you're the healer..."

"Oh, no, I'm fine. Even had a breakthrough with a skill." Joe looked at his hands, where water was continuously flowing from his palms into the crook of his arms. "I'm... my mana feels strange now. My skill rarity increased, and my mana is now distributed through my body. I have no idea what that means, in terms of skills and such, but I can cast spells faster now."

"That's odd," Alexis agreed with him, giving him a push so that he would start walking. "Also, you're lacking a certain... sparkle that you normally have. What's up with that?"

"Sparkle?" Joe suddenly noticed that he no longer had Exquisite Shell active and winced at the realization that he had been unprotected for hours. He exerted his will, and mana seemed to seep out of each pore and into the air around him. "There we go."

"You look like someone dropped you in glitter! So pretty!" Jaxon clapped his hands and looked over Joe's body. "It is always the shiniest just after you cast this spell. Did you know that it tends to fade over time?"

"I did *not* know that!" Joe excitedly exclaimed. Maybe this spell wasn't so bad after all! "I *did* see that there was a serious difference with how fast I was able to cast the shell."

"Lovely!" Jaxon reached out and touched Joe's cheek, then looked at his finger. Joe was *pretty* sure that there was disappointment on the Chiropractor's face when none of the sparkly came over to him.

"Pardon me, I have business with your team leader." The entire group instantly went on edge when a voice reached them. On the path, not ten feet away, was a man dressed in garish colors. His face was hidden behind a Jester mask, and he tossed aside the myriad of cloth he had bundled over him to reveal a form-fitting Jester outfit. Brightly-colored, slightly creepy, but overall, he seemed to be non-threatening.

Joe looked around. There was nowhere for the man to have been hiding, there was no cover, and the ground was flat for hundreds of feet. How was it that this man had appeared without any of them seeing him coming? Joe decided that caution was going to be his watchword here. "I'm Joe. What can I help you with?"

"Hello." The colorful Jester took a step toward the group, somehow instantly crossing the distance and stabbing a knife into Joe's chest. "I was sent to assassinate you."

"While I admire your straightforwardness, I am not a fan of the task itself." Joe infused his mana on the assassin's shadow, and a Shadow Spike sliced into flesh.

"Hmm." The man looked at his knife, only to see that it had stopped just before penetrating Joe's chest. "I'm very sorry to tell you this, but I do have my orders."

"Any chance that you could tell me why I'm being attacked?" Joe wasn't sure where his calm clarity was coming from, but for some reason, he couldn't bring himself to muster fury or battle rage. "Also, why is my team not attacking you? I think that this is a situation where they should be screeching war cries, and there should be sharp metal flying at you."

"Ah, I can see the confusion." The stranger was mechanically stabbing his knife at Joe's chest, and the latter could feel the shell weakening. "Sorry to have to be the one to tell you this, but we are currently inside of a trap formation. Specifically, this is the formation 'Apathetic Advantage'. It is used to remove one's emotions and is usually used by my organization to capture powerful beasts. They tend to be arrogant and will refuse most bonds and such if they know about them. Truly, I'm not sure how you are able to keep functioning."

"I see. That would certainly explain why I am not sending constant streams of attacks at you as I normally would." Joe nodded at the other man, keeping his Shadow Spike channeled to increase the damage over time. "Again, might I know the reason behind the assault?"

"I suppose that there is no rush." The Jester skittered back, moving a distance that seemed impossible with a single movement. This also removed him from the effect of the spike, and it collapsed after a moment. His daggers vanished like a popping soap bubble, and he looked at a small scrap of paper. "Let me see... Joe. Ah, yes. Kill command ordered due to infringing upon the monopoly of the Zoo to contain, train, or sell Rare to Mythical creatures."

Joe stared blankly at the smiling-mask Jester to the point where it seemed that the formation had taken complete control. The colorful individual started to pull his knife out again, but Joe suddenly shook his head. "Thank you for the information, but I fear that there is nothing I can think of that would explain this situation."

"Oh? Did you not sell a Bunnicorn in the city?"

There was enough of a reaction on Joe's face that it was apparent he wanted to fly into a rage but physically couldn't. "I see. This is over such a small matter? Is there any way to resolve this peacefully?"

"I suppose that I could offer you a capture quest to complete as compensation," the man responded after a moment of contemplation. "I am authorized to do so, and it seems that you might create an issue if I attempt to slay you. Are you *certain* I can't simply check this off my to-do list? No? I see. In that case... let me see you. Hmm. Coffee addiction, level four? That must be an issue on long-distance missions. Here is my offer."

Quest gained: Too Many Zoos! The Zoo has offered you a chance to show that you aren't trying to compete with them! Capture a Rare or higher rarity animal and gift it to the Grand Zoo of Ardania within a month. Reward: Kill order rescinded. Small non-combat pet (Coffee Elemental). Failure: Kill order remains in place.

"A Coffee Elemental? I'm not even certain what that means." Joe remained fixed in place, no expression crossing his face.

"Allow me." The colorful man held out a hand, and after a moment, a coffee jug-sized creature appeared on his hand. In his other hand, a coffee cup appeared. The strangely liquid creature flowed into the cup until it was full, then vanished back into the man's many robes. A dash of sugar was added, and a spoon was placed in the cup. "Here you are."

"Thank you. Any poison in here?" Joe took the cup and looked down. Tiny liquid arms grasped the spoon and spun it around. A tiny voice came from the cup.

"Drink me! I'm delicious!"

"That's some strong coffee," Joe commented a moment later after the entire contents of the cup had literally poured itself down his throat.

"It really is. No, no poison. That would be rude to do mid-conversation." The man nodded. "The Elemental has no combat utility, sadly. Do we have a deal?"

"I couldn't possibly say no," Joe agreed easily. The man nodded, handed him a button to press when he was ready to speak with him again, and vanished. A moment later, Joe could feel his mental state evening out. "What in the craptacular abyss was *that?*"

"Ugh!" Alexis grabbed her head. "That was *horrible!* I felt like nothing mattered! I couldn't even be bothered when Joe was getting stabbed!"

The entire group seemed to agree with the assessment, though Joe was feeling something else at this moment.

Caffeinated! Temporary changes: Movement speed +10%! Charisma -2. Intelligence +1!

He smiled brilliantly at the others and started skipping along the path. "Oh well! New quest, awesome rewards to be had! You ready to go? I am! Let's ask questions later! I *really* wanna hear more about formations. Those seem useful!"

"You know that you nearly died there, right?" Jaxon called as Joe started to gain some distance from them.

"These things happen!" Joe called back happily. "In this case, I feel the threat was worthwhile!"

"Is he okay?" Poppy's questions only earned a shrug and a few chuckles when Joe tripped and popped back to his feet without a comment.

CHAPTER EIGHTEEN

"Hey. Look at that." Alexis pointed into the distance, and the group tried to see what she was pointing at. With her main characteristic being her high perception, she was able to see things that they couldn't as of yet.

It took a few more seconds of walking until Poppy spoke up, and the sight came into view for Joe at that moment. "Is that another group of people? Like that huge gathering of people going off to farm?"

"Looks like it, but how in the world did they get all the way out here without getting killed off?" Alexis shook her head. "We are a small group of people that are frankly a little overpowered for this area, and we were still having trouble! What kind of people do they have protecting that group?"

"Prolly the kind we don' wanna mess wit," Bard rumbled uneasily.

"It's fine. We aren't doing anything to make anyone else mad." Joe shook his head and continued onward. The coffee had evened out with his high hydration, and he was still feeling pretty good. "I doubt that anyone is going to attack us. They don't want to look bad in front of all their new recruits."

As they approached the mass of people who were standing in what seemed to be the middle of nowhere, shouts of alarm went up. The people shouting were still wearing the starter clothing, and the majority of them weren't even carrying a weapon of any kind. People in armor started appearing to block the small party's path. "Hold! What are you doing out here?"

"Walkin'?" Bard rolled his eyes and continued forward. "What kinda sot are ya? Get off the road if ya're *not* walkin'!"

This was obviously not the answer the man had been expecting, and it seemed that he was uncertain how to react. The crowd parted fearfully as Joe's team walked through, but when the group didn't do anything strange, the people began to calm down. Joe shook his head at the sight. "Poor suckers didn't know what they were getting into. Looks like they've been having some trouble."

His eyes lit up as he spied the reason this group must have chosen to stop and wait here. "A shrine! Nice! Here we go, Ardania! You guys ready to go take an *actual* shower instead of a cold-water Cleanse?"

"Absolutely!" Jaxon told him with a firm nod. "It is terrible when people don't have the self-awareness to realize that they are causing issue to the people around them. Showers are a must!"

There was a long silence, and the other members of the team decided to let the comment slide. They walked up to the shrine, getting stopped by people who were acting as guards. "Who are you? What do you want here?"

"Just trying to pop into the shrine." Joe was starting to get annoyed by this group. This was a *road*. "What's the issue?"

"Oh." The guy hadn't drawn a sword or anything so dramatic, but he still stood in their way. "Look, we are trying to use this shrine to keep our captain alive. The deity of this shrine keeps everyone who enters from dying but doesn't heal or remove the effects. We had to send someone to try and find an antidote for scorpion venom, and I gotta tell you, the building is pretty full right now."

At least this guy was being reasonable. Joe smiled gently and started walking past the man. "I don't mind helping out. Can you tell me who it is that you are trying to save?"

"You can't just–" The man's face darkened, and he reached for his weapon.

"Chill," Joe ordered. The word from normal society made the guard hesitate, and Joe took the chance to pop into the small shrine. There were people stacked up like logs in here, and it was obvious that there were more issues than a simple scorpion sting. "What in the heck happened here?"

"Got attacked," the frustrated guard told him, having followed Joe inside. "We were able to hold off the monsters, drove them off even, but a few of us got pretty messed up."

"Anyone just *hurt?*" Joe looked around, but there was no indication of who had status effects and who was simply injured.

"That section over there." The guard gestured at the closest pile of whining bodies.

"Mass Heal." Joe held out his Mystic Theurge staff, and a stream of water reached out to ten people at a time. They were mainly low-level, so the tendrils of water would break off and connect to another as the people reached full health. "If you are all healed up, please hurry out of here. I need to get to everyone."

People thanked him; many even seemed to want to kiss him. Luckily, he was involved in healing people, and the respect for doctors back on earth transferred over to this new world quite nicely. "What's next?"

The guard was staring at Joe like he was a mythical creature. "A healer?"

"Pretty much, yes," Joe conceded the point without quibbling. "Who should go next?"

"Uh... we have a few that are unconscious, but the people that are poisoned are in pain. So, them next?" The guard brought Joe over to a stack of people that were sweating and breathing heavily. Looking over the group, it was obvious who was in charge and who were people that were supposed to have been protected. Joe started with the newbies.

Cleansing water flowed out of his hands, and one person at a time, he started to remove the venom from their bodies. Then the unthinkable happened. Joe contorted in pain and fell to the ground twitching, his mind burning with confusion and blurry thinking. In a few moments, he groaned and sat up, clutching at his poor head. "I ran out of mana! You have got to be *kidding* me."

Blood flecked over Joe as the person he had half-healed coughed, once more suffering the effects of venom rushing through his body. Joe had no choice but to wait as his ability to Cleanse was reliant upon having an abundance of mana. The deadlier the poison—or venom in this case—the longer it took to clear out the various issues caused, not to mention the venom itself. This meant more mana, which was sadly a resource that he was back to 'standard' with. Boo.

Not that he didn't have an advantage. His skills afforded him a ten percent boost to clearing poisons in someone's body, and he was going to be relying on that pretty heavily today. Joe looked around at the literal stacks of people and shook his head. Drat. This was going to take quite a bit of time, and he couldn't convert the shrine while it was keeping all these people alive. Well... he *could*, but that would make him a terrible person.

As his mana approached full, he got back to work and healed the person in front of him, following up with a healing spell that brought the person back to full health. Joe saw that his mana had dropped by a quarter and knew that if he spaced out individual healings instead of trying to fix everyone instantly—as his ingrained instinct from the army demanded—he would be able to heal the group without suffering backlash. As he

Cleansed the next person, he watched his mana and worked on feeling out better ways to utilize his skill.

There was an interesting phenomenon at play. Some people were far more mana intensive to Cleanse, and the mana cost was adjusted accordingly. He asked the patients *why*, but none of them knew. No one had a special resistance to being healed, so he could only assume that a higher-leveled creature had injected them. Joe mused on this issue for quite a while, and near the end of his second hour at work, he finished with the last person.

Skill increase: Cleanse (Student 0) Congratulations! You have reached the student ranks! You have battled the effects of poison, disease, and other detrimental effects for so long that helping others has become second nature to you! This skill begins to hum and will alert you when you use another skill that resonates with it!

"Oh, that's awesome," Joe muttered as he finished reading over the notification. "Basically, it'll let me know when I can upgrade it with a high chance of success? Yes, please!"

"Pardon my interruption, I just wanted to personally thank you for healing my people and myself." Joe turned and saw a robed woman covered in dried blood and holding out a hand. Realizing that this must be the captain that he had originally come to heal, Joe shook the outstretched hand and smiled.

"It was the least I could do. You are trying to help such a massive group of people at the same time. I feel a little inadequate only being able to help them once." Joe's words caused the Captain to brighten, and Joe got a notification.

Reputation increase: You have reached 'Friend' status with the Guild Leader of 'Golden Greens'. (+3500).

"I'm just glad you came along!" The Captain chuckled. "I wish I had a way to repay you, but we just started this guild and pooled our money to buy a huge farmland."

"Interesting." Joe looked at the shrine and back to the guild leader. "Does your guild have any allegiance to an in-game deity? Mine could potentially help you all out quite a bit. Also, I'm Joe."

"Teddy. Also, not that I know of, though we were thinking about finding a nature-aligned deity. It just makes sense." She told Joe with a shrug. "I'm a mage, but I'm pretty bad at long-range stuff, so I thought maybe I'd go for plant growth and such."

"You're a rogue, and you know it!" One of her guildmates rolled his eyes as he walked past.

"I am *not*!" Teddy shouted back. Joe noticed a glint of light in her hand and thought that she was casting a spell. Nope. A knife. It vanished a moment later like it had never existed. "Sorry about that."

"How do you explain all the knife wounds on the creatures you killed on the way here?" the man persisted, ignoring the nasty glare he was getting. "No joke you're bad at long-range 'magic', you *stab* everything to death! Even the things that poisoned you were all stabbed to death, No signs of magic–"

"Alright, you can *go* now!" Teddy glared at the man until he complied. Joe tried not to laugh; this was way too familiar to him.

"Give me a moment, will you?" Joe walked over to the shrine and started the process of capturing it. There was no noticeable effect until just before it was captured. Then the shrine vanished into motes of light all at once, and a book-style shrine formed out of darkness and water before solidifying. Joe dropped to the ground, nearly wrung out of mana. "Oof. That was pretty. Teddy, could you do me a favor? Try out my deity. You will all find hidden things easier; you might even start plowing and find that your field is full of diamonds. If you don't like the bonuses you get, you can always switch away."

Teddy looked around at the new shrine, playing with a small knife that vanished into a pocket when she looked at him. "I guess... if they don't have a deity yet... sure. No promises that people will convert, but I'll do it and lead the charge."

"Nice!" Joe smiled; then his eyes took on a cunning gleam. "One more second..."

One minute later, the two of them returned to the shrine, having popped back to Ardania in an instant. Teddy shook Joe's hand firmly, a wide smile on her face. "Oh, I liked that. *Any* of us can use that as long as we are a 'follower' of Tatum?"

"Absolutely."

CHAPTER NINETEEN

Joe hummed happily as he walked down the path. One hundred and thirty new converts to his faction. That was how he was thinking of his deity affiliation: a faction. His small team had gone back to Ardania and slept at an inn, getting a good rest and a good if *very* small portioned and expensive meal. It appeared that rationing had taken effect, and if that wasn't enough to kick this quest into high gear, Joe didn't know what else would.

"A couple more days of travel, and we should be able to find whatever village might be in the forest!" Joe told the others as he looked over the quest information one more time. "The map is out of date, but there has to be *someone* living in the area still."

"That forest?" Jaxon pointed into the distance.

Joe looked up and saw trees ahead, but frowned and looked at his crude map. "That can't be right. The forest shouldn't start for at least another sixty miles."

"To be fair, whatever map you have is a couple hundred years out of date, isn't it?" Poppy offered a plausible explanation.

"Not *sixty miles of forest* out of date!" Joe countered with pure disbelief, slapping the paper in his hands.

"This is a different world, Joe," Alexis pointed out. "You gotta assume that there are a lot of things going on that wouldn't be happening in our world. If this is a *magical* forest, I am pretty sure sixty years is plenty of time to take over a huge amount of land."

"Ugh." Joe shook his head. "You guys are right. So, yeah, we should get ready to fight at all times now. From what I read; this place is going to be really hard to navigate. If it extends this much further than it used to, especially so."

The group continued walking, reaching the edge of the forest after another half hour. Alexis made odd motions with her hands, then pointed at the trees. "Look at this. The tree line is an actual *line*. Like... perfectly straight."

"Remember that we noticed that strange biome shift when we came south of the city?" Joe took a look at the trees and nodded. "Yup. Odd, do you think that the forest just took over the 'allotted area for forest' and can't extend anymore? If so, there is a lot more to this world that we really need to figure out the rules for."

They took a step into the forest, simultaneously getting a notification. More like a warning, to be honest.

Caution! Your level is below the recommendation for the Forest of Chlorophyll Chaos. You may want to consider leaving and returning at a later date when you are much *stronger. Level recommendation: 20.*

"Holy wombats," Poppy muttered as he read. "Level twenty? That could take... *months*."

"No joke!" Jaxon shook his head and looked at his status screen. "From level fifteen to level twenty requires ninety thousand experience. I don't think there are that many wars we can win for huge chunks of points like last time. I mean, do you guys know of another race we could shatter? Are there Elves? Do you guys like Elves? If not–"

"I think that we should get as much distance as we can from the edge of the forest," Alexis cut in before Jaxon could solidify his warmongering plans. "Anything that would be out this far might be weak for the area, but that also means that it would still be stronger than us as well as *hungry*. Joe, do you have a 'Predator's Territory' ready for when we go camping tonight?"

"I do, but..." Joe hesitated. "Looking at the level recommendation for the area, there is a possibility that there will be creatures here that are near the level thirty threshold of the ritual. If we draw them in, we would only know because of waking up at respawn."

"It's a risk I think is worth taking," Alexis told him after a moment of thought. "It'll keep us safe from anything below that, and there will also be a much greater chance of running into something at the lower levels than the higher ones, at least this far from the center of the forest."

"She makes a good point," Bard chimed in, looking up from a small book of chants he was reading out of. Then he went right back to ignoring everything around him. Joe was somewhat jealous of the man's ability to tune out the outside world, but perhaps that was a benefit of his class. 'Tuning' out. Heh. Bard certainly *sang* out of tune. Was that the way to say it? No. Drat. Can't carry a tune in a bucket? Yes!

Joe opened his mouth to tell the others his joke, then realized that the group had left him behind. He hurried to catch up and rejoined them just as they found the first enemy in the forest. His joke died on his lips as the team went totally silent. Joe tried to use his perception to inspect the creature but received an unsatisfying response.

Perception check + knowledge check failed!

"Any idea wa' tha' is?" Bard quietly questioned.

"What *what* is? Why are we all being so quiet?" Jaxon was just a *hair* too loud, and the small creature turned their way. It was flying, mottled green and brown, and screeched as it saw them.

"It's a Forest Imp," Poppy told them; his perception far higher than any but Alexis. "Level twenty."

"Imp? Like a demon?" Jaxon was perplexed. "Why is there a demon in a forest?"

"*Dodge!*" Bard bellowed, taking his own advice and diving to the side. A streak of green light left the Imp and traveled the distance between them in an instant. The light missed, thanks to Bard's warning and their own battle senses, but as it hit the ground, a series of roots popped out of the ground and whipped around. Not finding a target, the roots dropped below the ground once more. It didn't escape Joe's attention that the roots were *bladed.*

"That would have messed us *up.*" He swallowed hard and turned his attention more fully to the fight that they were in. Bard, Jaxon, and Poppy were rushing at the creature, and Alexis had already sent a bolt that was dodged by the small but speedy Imp. "Plenty of shadows to use here!"

He took a long moment and shaped a double spike out of shadows, solidifying the spell just as the melee fighters got into range. The spell impacted, cutting off retreat as the Imp attempted to dodge the weapons coming at it. Poppy's rapier slid through the small body, Jaxon's fist landed, and Bard's axe chopped in. Joe grinned a shark-smile, expecting to see the Imp dropping from the well-practiced combo.

It didn't. In fact, it seemed enraged more than anything. Joe let the information to his combat log seep in, frowning at what little he could see.

Double Shadow Spike hits for 198 shadow damage. (270*2, 360 shadow damage resisted, 18 piercing damage!)

Yikes. His most practiced spell only dealt a third of the damage that it should have? This type of creature must have a massive protection against darkness, being a 'devil' type creature. Would fire be effective? He needed to expand his spell list. A lot.

Another green bolt left the Imp, and the extreme close range ensured that Bard couldn't dodge. His entire body glowed green for an instant before roots shot out of the ground and wrapped around him, the bladed edges tearing into him and watering the ground with his blood. Alexis called out, "Seven seconds between casts!"

The Imp didn't seem to appreciate her efforts to help and responded to the words by slapping at Jaxon with its thorny hand. Jaxon wiggled out of the way in time, retaliating with a nasty jab of his own. "*Adjust!*"

The tiny arm twisted and the Imp hissed at the Monk, but the new angle of its arm didn't seem to impact the combat ability of the creature in the slightest. Poppy, thinking that the Imp was distracted, was hit by the root-like prehensile tail of the Imp and sent rolling. The creature was obviously able to use more power than its small form *imp*lied. Using his experience against the giant scorpions as a proof of concept, Joe spun up a new strand of darkness.

He wrapped shadows around the Imp's wings and solidified the binding after pumping mana into it for three seconds. Two hundred mana vanished in an instant, and Joe gasped for air as a void in his body appeared. He could feel the mana in his body rushing to even out, but perhaps this was an effect of his mana no longer being centralized.

A cocoon of darkness pulled the flapping wings back, and the Imp toppled from the air. The others started attacking as fast as possible, especially a still-bleeding Bard, whose axes seemed to be the perfect weapon to use against the root-and-vine-coated Imp. Everyone else's weapon seemed to be *imp*-erfect against it. *Gah*, not in a battle! Joe sent a healing spell into the Skald, and the filthy wounds closed up around gunk from the forest floor. He would need to remember to Cleanse the man after this battle.

The Imp wasn't done. In fact, once on the ground, it sprinted around in a small area. It wasn't a fast runner over long distances, but the small zone that it claimed for itself allowed the Imp to dodge nearly as well as Jaxon. The darkness its wings were encased in started to tear apart, and the others redoubled their attacks. It burst away from them as it freed itself, hopping into the air and flapping furiously at Alexis with a screech. Joe caught the Imp in a spray of acid, the corrosive liquid dealing reduced damage but still enough to finish it off.

Exp gained: 120 (120 * Forest Imp x1)

"This... might be a more difficult area than we planned for." Joe looked around for confirmation, and the others nodded at his words.

"My rapier hurt it, but it is like the whole body was made of roots," Poppy explained as he cleaned his blade. "I could put holes in that sucker, but it didn't seem to have any critical points."

"Couldn't find any bones." Jaxon spat to the side and kicked the fallen Imp.

Joe sighed and offered his own complaint, "Yeah... it was able to resist two-thirds of the shadow damage I could deal, and... looks like it only took half damage from acid."

"Well, dang." Bard shook his head. "Let's hope we don't run into any *groups* of those."

"We also know how the forest spread so far in the last few hundred years." Alexis pointed at the spot where the green energy had hit the ground, and the others looked over to see a small sapling that hadn't been there before.

Jaxon looked around at the massive forest full of tens of thousands of trees. "So, you're saying there are probably a *lot* more of those, then?"

CHAPTER TWENTY

Contrary to their concerns, Forest Imps seemed to be a fairly rare enemy. They weren't sure if that was due to the sheer size of the forest they were in or if there were only a few of them in the forest in total. Either way, after fighting the powerful Imp and winning, they had continued on and found creatures more in tune with the forest theme.

"Back, back, *back!*" Poppy shouted as he rolled under the bough of an enraged tree. The forest was alive, in both a figurative and literal sense. **Whomp** A spray of dirt and loam was forced into the air, leaving behind a crater that had *almost* contained the Duelist. "Looks like we've got another treant."

Bard grunted like a hog, twirling his axes in agitation. "Still naw way ta take em?"

"Nothing I can think of that is repeatable on a regular basis." Joe shuddered as eyes opened along the trunk of the 'tree' and a wide tongue licked vertically along a mouth that spanned the same distance. "I think I could come up with a single target ritual, but I don't have the kind of resources that we would need to kill off every one of them we find."

"I wonder if the trees back in the trial area were treants?" Jaxon mused aloud. "You think... nah, there's no way these have *bones*, right?"

"Alexis? How about you?" Poppy turned hopeful eyes on the Aromatic Artificer.

She shook her head as well. "Same issue on my end. If I made up a batch of poison to kill plants, which I could, it would require a *lot* to kill just one of these. I'd need a wagon full of barrels to make any kind of impression, and then what's the point?"

"Grr," Poppy trilled, a sound very out of character for him. "I feel like there should be an easy way to take these down! They *are* immobile, right?"

"Right, but it would be like pounding away at a tank." Joe motioned for them to start walking again. "You hit it, deal almost no damage, it hits you back, and you get demolished. Remember that we are really out leveled here, and we need to play it smart. A lot of the things in here can take us down nearly instantly if we get surprised by them."

"Stay alert, don't die. Good life advice." Jaxon nodded along heartily, then was yanked forward by Poppy, just managing not to get smashed by the treants he had wandered near yet again. "See? *Alert!*"

"I'm about to put you in time out," Poppy muttered as he got back to his normal position near the front of the group. "As in, I'll let the next one hit ya."

"I think that's my cue to call a halt for the evening," Joe called out as people started to grumble and get snippy at each other. "Who wants to make a fire, and who wants to cook? I can set up the campsite really quick."

"Good call." Alexis sighed and glanced sidelong at Joe. "How opposed are you to giving me a good Cleanse from a distance?"

"You know, I sometimes feel bad using a deity-granted power to help someone shower." Joe sighed as her gaze turned more pleading. "Fine. I did get it up to the Student ranks. So, I kinda wanna see what that looks like. Cleanse."

Alexis staggered as water washed over her from head to toe in an instant, removing all grime from her skin and equipment. "*Geez,* Joe!"

Joe was also surprised, and he looked at his hand in concern. "That took *so* much mana!"

"*And* it was basically a *firehose!*" Alexis had given him a second to make the connection and apology on his own, but he seemed distracted.

"Right, sorry about that." Joe shook off his confusion and explained himself, "I'm just worried that if I use that spell to hydrate someone, I might end up hurting them accidentally. Rupture some veins or some such."

She winced as her mental image meshed with his. "Oh, yeah, get some practice in first."

"Who wants a shower?"

Bard lifted a hand. "Protection ring fir– *glabuh**!"

Joe chuckled nervously as the soaked Skald glowered at him. "Ah, sorry, thought you were volunteering. Right, ritual. You're all sure about this?"

When they motioned for him to continue, he pulled a metal plate out of his spatial ring, set it in the center of the campsite and dripped a drop of blood on to it. He activated the ritual, which would now cause anything under level thirty to avoid them. "All set on this end. What do you guys want to do tonight?"

"Ooh!" Jaxon sat next to the tiny fire that had just been lit. "Ghost stories! Wait, no! S'mores! Are marshmallows a thing here? No? Stories, then? I see... watch rotation and logistical talk again?"

"There we go." Poppy nodded at the final statement.

Joe forestalled the conversation when he saw the resignation on Jaxon's face. "Actually, why don't we talk about things that are going on and what we want to do about them? We haven't really had much time to talk, and I know that a few of you weren't planning on being trapped in the game. I knew what I was getting into, but... some of you weren't even in pods. You guys doing okay?"

"Fantastic!" Jaxon enthusiastically responded, taking a moment to showcase his ability to bend around. "I could never do this back on earth, and now I have forever to do it and get even *better* at it! I was close to death back there, healthy and hale here!"

Joe grinned and looked at Poppy, who had a far different expression on his face. Resignation and regret were spelled out, and he wouldn't meet the eyes of the group. "I am not doing as well. I came here to earn enough to be able to take care of my daughter, using my actual trained skills as a Duelist to give us a comfortable life while only 'working' four hours a day."

He took a slow, steadying breathe. "I have been able to contact my parents, and luckily, they were able to come over and get little Amelia. She... she was still taking a nap. The time dilation ensured that she didn't suffer for my arrogance, at the very least. How many *didn't* get that? You know that my body wasn't even there? If I couldn't call, they woulda thought I ran and just *left* her to the monsters roaming the world."

He paused, taking a deep breath and looking up at the canopy above them. "But now what? The announcement to the world that they needed to come here to avoid danger is... what do I do with my girl, a *toddler* unable to wield a sword or magic? How do I bring her to a new place that even I don't understand? But monsters are walking our planet, and she isn't safe there! But beyond that... have any of you seen *any* children from our world?"

Joe was startled by the sudden turn. In fact, he could not remember a single instance of seeing any child, the youngest he had seen was a late-teen at the Mage's College. He was leery of this new thought and what it might mean. Poppy nodded upon seeing their realization. "Exactly. What happens to her when the data core is touched to her head? Does she get put in the trials? I do not wish that on my *enemies*."

"Terms and conditions," Joe softly muttered, a faded memory struggling to surface in his mind.

"What was that?" Poppy glared at Joe.

"The... at the start of the game, there was an option to read all the terms and conditions. One of them was about children below the age of majority, in this case, sixteen, I think. It said that all children would be placed in a different area, and they would... I can't remember exactly, but they are taken care of, and I think that you have the option to be with them. Or visit them. I'm sorry, I was less interested in that clause at the time." Joe's voice trailed off, but Poppy didn't seem to mind. The Duelist took a deep breath and sank into contemplative silence.

"Well, ahm havin' a grand ol' time," Bard cut in after a few beats of awkward silence. "Ah di'naw think ah'd enjoy this place half as much as ah do. Might be thanks to this lassy here."

A wink was sent at Alexis, who simply rolled her eyes and nodded at him. "Yes, you're lovely too, and in my mind, this is actually one of the best-case scenarios for me. I was drowning in debt and failure, and I am pretty sure that there's no way for people in that life to collect from me anymore. I can focus on making a *new* life here and live in the way I choose. How about you, Joe? More... crowded than you planned for?"

"A bit." Joe let a ghost of a smile play across his face. "I have an interesting goal now, which is nice. I am mostly concerned that there are going to be a lot of people that don't stick around this area when the next area opens up in a couple weeks."

"Why would that matter?" Jaxon cocked his head to the side. "They would be going elsewhere to get resources and such, right? Fewer people here means fewer people to take care of. Win-win."

"But what about the people here that have no money, food, shelter?" Joe shook his head and glanced around to see that he had their full attention. "We were told that the races that we eventually found and worked with would be important. That implies that we will have large-scale, *extinction* level fights. What would have happened if we became a shattered race?"

"I think that one of the most important things to do in this area, the starting area, is to power up as much of humanity as possible. Fix resource issues, create stable bases of power. I mean, look around. We are still in an area that outlevels us, and this is *still* the starter area!" Joe leaned against the wood of a tree, shaking his head. "How many people are actually going to be ready for the next area when they go there? I don't know that, but I do know I *will* be. Anyone with me will be as well. Why are you all looking at me like that?"

The faces of all the others were pale, washed out in the firelight. Alexis pointed up, her voice wavering and resigned, "That's not a tree behind you, Joe."

Joe looked back and up, meeting eyes with a treant that was double the size of any they had encountered thus far; well over a hundred feet tall at the crown. He rolled to his feet and managed to get off a blast of acid. A green and brown blur appeared in his vision, and the last thing that went through his mind... was a massive branch.

You have died! You were killed by: Trent the Treant, Guardian of The Northmost Zone of the Forest of Chlorophyll Chaos. Calculating... you lose 3,000 experience!

CHAPTER TWENTY-ONE

Joe stepped out of the respawn room eight in-game hours later, appearing at the shrine he had most recently converted. "Ick, it's a half day walk even to get back to the forest from here."

His rumination didn't last long. His team would likely appear shortly, and he wanted to see how things were going with his current quest to free Tatum. Joe pulled open the quest log and looked it over, the hope in his eyes quickly simmering away.

Quest update: Paying a Great Debt. 8,075/13,000,000 divine energy. Current sources of divine energy: 131 Followers, 1 Altar, 4 Shrines, 1 Temple (Mid-sized).

"It's not great, but it isn't *nothing*." He sighed and sat to wait for a moment. There was a flash of white light, then another, and soon his entire team was around him. "Hey, guys. You want to go back there right away or run back to the guild and train up a little? Maybe get more specialized stuff?"

"Yeah, let's take a couple days and train up." Poppy seemed much happier today, and it didn't take long to figure out why. "I found that my girl will be in what amounts to a daycare, and I can go there any time I wish. There is a second portal for me in my 'logout' room, and it leads to an island in the sky where the kids get the best education, care, and food possible. A little paradise that gets harder for them as they grow up until they need to go out into the world at sixteen. She will be more ready for this world than I ever was. Her grandma chose to stay with her in that area as well."

"I'm really glad to hear it." Jaxon went in for a hug, and for the first time, Poppy didn't dodge away from it.

"Me too." Poppy sighed softly. It was obvious that this had been a serious stressor for him.

"Joe, while we take a break, you should swing by the college and get some spells that are effective against plants. A classic fireball maybe?" Alexis nudged him into reacting, and Joe nodded right away.

"Will do. I'll see if I can find some other stuff for this specific area as well. Meet you all near the Pathfinder's Hall for skill training?" The others agreed, flashing away using the fast travel function of the shrines. Joe prepared himself for a crowd and, in an instant, appeared in Ardania. "Time to go get some spells!"

He started making his way through the crowd and was annoyed to the point of nearly lashing out within a few minutes. His Exquisite Shell had kept him from being crushed twice and had kept wandering hands out of his pockets at least three times that he could detect. Beyond that, he didn't have the raw physicality to push his way through the press of people milling about. In an attempt to work around this situation, Joe looked up, crouched, and *jumped.*

Joe left the ground like a bottle rocket, reaching the apex of his jump and flipping to land on the roof of a building. He caught the edge and pulled himself up the rest of the way. He laid there for a moment, gasping like a fish on land; he had only lost about half his stamina in one go to get here. "Okay. Effective and fun. But. Need. To boost. *Constitution!*"

After managing to get to his feet, Joe walked along the city-block-length rooftop and stood at the edge. For almost anyone else, the prospect of jumping to his next target would have been rejected; he needed to cross the street. Joe backed up a few feet, getting a running start, and *jumped* off the edge. His trajectory looked *very* unrealistic, almost against the laws of physics because he jumped in a nearly straight line. At the apex of his leap, he came down in another straight line to land on the building across the street, exactly where he had been aiming.

"Alright. I'm convinced," Joe spoke aloud, ignoring his current position on the hot stone shingles of the roof. "Gonna do some constitution and strength training. This is *way* too cool to not use it more often."

He looked over the edge at the position he had started in. There was a man in orange monk robes that had been right in front of him when he started, and now, that man was still only about halfway to Joe's current position. "Looks like I am still making good time, even with the resting in between."

Now back on his feet, he marched along the roof and hopped over to the next one; a much shorter distance. Joe continued this until he got near the merchant area, and the crowd started to thin. The guard presence here was much higher, and no one wanted to jostle them or get too close if they didn't need to do so. Now he was faced with another issue. How did he get down? If there were other buildings with handy ladders or roofing much closer to the ground, then this path would be more well-traveled, but he was twelve feet off the ground at the lowest point, and he needed to...

"Hold up. Did I jump twelve feet straight up from a standstill?" Joe questioned his own feats, trying to remember if the... "No, wait. The roof on that building was lower. This area is more affluent. Maybe there *are* a lot of people that use this 'skyway'. Still... ground..."

He looked down and decided to dangle off the edge to cut down the distance by about half. With twenty-three points in strength, he was about a fifth stronger than average humans from earth had been and was able to keep himself stable. Joe took a moment to wonder what the average stats for humanity were now... then got back to moving. He let go and landed well, the damage reduced to nothing thanks to his Jumping skill. "Now to the College, and I'll– Wait! No! To the *library!*"

The Mage's College had given the Library a large collection of 'useless' spells. These were all sorts of spells that either were so inefficient or difficult to use that they were deemed to be trash, even if a good chunk of them would have been useful and *powerful* if they were used. Joe decided to go through the trash heap; it would be better for him if the College didn't know every spell he could bring to bear. Not that they had an issue *currently*, but it was better to be safe than sorry with massive organizations that had nearly unlimited funds.

Joe nodded to Boris as he walked through the doors, and the head librarian nodded back and got back to reading. It seemed everyone had goals they wanted to accomplish. He tromped up the stairs, getting to floor three and a half and entering the room that had been dedicated to the College's donations. Just as the last time Joe had been here, he was surrounded by interesting titles. It really was too bad that most of these books shone a dull gray in his sight; he wanted to use *all* of them. Sadly, it would take *hours* to even get one of them to a useful state, and then he would still need to train that spell up to a point where it would be useful against the creatures he was now up against. So, he needed something specific.

"Instant Insect Repellant, no need. My shield already works for that," Joe was muttering as he perused the unorganized shelves. "Party Decoration version three, no thanks. What does that even...? No, focus! Wildfire? Put you in the 'maybe' bin. Yeesh, that's a dark book, though. Gonna take a lot of effort to make it work... Root Reducer? Sure, that might actually be something else, given that the title is dark. Plantomancy? Is this a primer on an entire field of magic?"

Joe looked at the most recent book he picked up; it was the size of a small, one-year-old child. There were so many gradations of correct and false statements that the book almost gave him a seizure when he looked at it from the side. "Would this turn into a class granting book if I corrected it? Good lord, how long would that take? Put that in the 'long term' section."

After a solid hour of selecting books, he narrowed his search to his top five. "Wildfire, Root Reducer, Weed-Be-Gone, Jack's Tree-Fell, Deadfall, Dale's Shattered Earth."

He looked at the strange, gimmicky names, and had to wonder if the College had a requirement of making a spell or something. He had no idea why a majority of these existed in the first place. "Let me think... Wildfire. I think you lose. My affinity is all about darkness and water, and you would be weaker than options I could get in that arena. Same deal with Tree-Fell, Deadfall, and Shattered Earth. So, either Root Reducer or Weed-Be-Gone."

After reading through both, he decided that Root Reducer was his best bet. The other was used to remove dandelions at *best*, and it was an over-time sort of spell. Root Reducer looked like a solid answer to Ents, as it would remove a foot of roots per five seconds. If they needed to take the Ents down, they would be able to do so when their roots were completely shriveled and the treant fell over. Maybe not a hugely useful spell outside of the forest, but who knew?

Joe decided that if this didn't look like it was going to work for him, he would come back and learn a spell from the College before they headed out. He left the library and Ardania entirely, getting back to his guild in a short half-hour thanks to his fast travel route. Joe went to the Pathfinder's Hall right away and descended into the truly potent area of this building. The building was *actually* a Grand Ritual Hall, but only a few people would ever be informed of this fact. In the deepest area was a room that allowed him to configure it to his needs on a whim.

A desk was waiting for him, along with plenty of light. He had stocked the area with paper and ink, and he was glad that he had set everything up on his last visit. He got to work, writing out all the important and true areas, then looking into areas of the slim spellbook that were gray but not black. Lots of 'required motions' went into the trash, but what *really* intrigued Joe was a small section of notes that detailed complaints the creator of the spell had. Apparently, the man felt that when he channeled the spell, he would feel invasive mana trying to enter him.

Joe tapped his chin. Did this spell have a feedback mechanism? He hadn't seen anything in the world so far that hinted at vampirism or life steal, only effects like mana burn or extra damage. He was sure they existed *somewhere*, but there was a strong possibility that more potent spells were used and controlled by more magical races. If they ever found Elves or Dwarves and were able to work with them... he was *certain* they would have access to better abilities, and Joe *wanted* them.

Until then... it was time to see if he could turn this spell into a potent new ability.

CHAPTER TWENTY-TWO

Joe stumbled out of the basement of the Grand Ritual Hall the next day, a taglock vanishing into his codpiece just as he opened the door to the town. He felt the need for coffee, but his sleep-deprivation had paid off. He had managed to create a clean spellform for the root reducing spell, and after putting it on a scroll, he had *learned* the spell. That wasn't even the best part; after creating another scroll, he had successfully integrated it into a ritual. That ritual had been activated and assigned to the taglock he just put away. If they found a treant or something similar that a channeled spell wasn't enough for, hopefully the ritual would be able to handle it. He had even gained a point in Ritual Magic after making it.

> *You have learned a spell: Wither Plant (Beginner V). Casting this spell on a plant will cause its roots to shrivel. By channeling the spell for at least ten seconds, mana from the plant will begin to flow back into the caster. Can only be cast on plants or plant-based lifeforms that have roots. Cost: 5n mana where n = skill level. Effect: Reduce the length of a plant's roots by .1n inches. Mana returned by channeling: .5T where T = mana cost per second.*

Right now, a single cast would allow Joe to cut back roots by an inch and a half, but by channeling, he could quickly destroy a root system. Not to mention, after ten seconds, the mana cost would be effectively halved. He was excited to try it out! He started walking around the area, and it didn't take him too long to find some bristly weeds—the kind that look like dandelion leaves, but instead of little yellow flowers, they had *spikes.* Joe knew from his experience getting these out of his lawn that they had deep roots, so they would make for a perfect test.

"Wither Plant!" Joe demanded, channeling his mana through his staff. A corkscrew of black water fountained from his staff, sinking into the plant and vanishing. If he didn't see the mana flowing through the air and his reserves dipping, he would think that there was no effect. About ten seconds later, the plant was showing no signs of motion or faltering, and Joe was getting suspicious. There was no mana coming back into him. That either meant that he was casting the spell wrong, or the plant had no roots any longer.

He poked the plant with his staff, and the entire thing moved. "Oh, well, there we go. No roots. Strange that there wasn't any notice... but I suppose I can always just keep an eye on the mana return."

Joe walked around and removed four more of the small plants, only stopping when he got a notification.

Wither Plant (Beginner VI). Woo, are you usually this fast or are just extra excited about this spell?

"That was *fast.*" Joe looked at his hands, then around, trying to come up with an explanation for the rapid advancement. His eyes landed on the Pathfinder's Hall not far from him, and his eyes lit up. "*Right!* I gain skills at four times the regular speed, and the building boosts that even *further!* Is our guild going to get overpowered?"

Enticing visions of his guild becoming a major superpower filled his thoughts, and he had to shake them off. He kept working at his skill but over the next few hours was only able to get it up to Beginner eight. He shook his head at the thought, 'only' got to that after *learning* the spell this morning. He decided to change up his routine and went over to where the guild had set up a small training area. "Excuse me, I'm looking for strength and constitution characteristic training. You guys have anything for that?"

The guard looked familiar to Joe, but he couldn't place the face to a name. He had *very* good posture though, almost as though he saw a chiropractor... regularly... "You! Are you on *Jaxon's* team?"

"No idea what you mean!" Joe stammered nervously, backing away. "I'll come back!"

"Hey! Not so fast!" The guard let a half-smile show on his face. "I'm the only person running those courses right now, so if you want 'em here, you gotta come to me either way!"

Joe plastered a fake smile on his face. "Great, great! Can I get your name?"

"Jay. Come with me." Jay walked closer to a box, pointing at it with a wide grin. "Hop on in. Doing both at the same time requires two hours of effort at the first threshold. That where you are?"

"Yes, but only have me going for thirty minutes, please." Joe was going to continue, planning to explain *why* he wanted that, but Jay shook his head with a snort.

"You'll get nothing out of it," he warned, though there was a glint in his eyes. "It *is* painful, and you gotta keep at it."

"Thirty minutes," Joe resolutely reaffirmed.

"Fine by me. Strip to your skivvies." Jay pointed at the box. "You stand there holding this square shield up. I pour hot coals on top, and we keep slowly adding weight the entire time. What's your strength at?"

"Twenty-three. Constitution is at twenty-eight." Joe nervously got into the man-height box wearing only his game-equipped loincloth. One side of the box was empty, he assumed so that people could dash out if the training was too much for them.

Jay nodded. "All good. That means we use hotter coals but less of them."

Joe picked up a scorched, metal shield and got in position. Jay had grabbed a shovel and dumped the first load on Joe. "Time starts now!"

The handles were already *hot.* Not enough to burn him, but they were getting close. Hot ash drifted down with each shovelful that was added, as well as each time the wind blew even a *little.* In just a few minutes, he had painful welts popping up on his skin. If he couldn't heal himself at the end of this, he could tell that he would have already jumped out and away. Joe's perception was fifty-three, which was almost double the raw score of constitution as well as being an entire threshold higher. He. felt. *Everything.*

"Keep going!" Jay called down, *helping* Joe. He hadn't been expecting that. "It's only a *little* pain, and you look like someone who is getting unbalanced as a character! Only way to numb that pain again is to get expensive, otherwise impractical items... or boost your constitution! You keep running at perception, you won't be able to handle walking through *grass* too quickly!"

That took Joe right out of what he was doing and made him think about the repercussions for becoming too unbalanced. Where else was this going to play out? He knew that a higher constitution made people denser and heavier; would they get to a point that they couldn't lift themselves if they didn't also work on their strength? If people worked on strength and constitution but not dexterity, would they become like bodybuilders that had so much mass that they couldn't move properly? Joe shuddered as he thought about them hiring someone to wipe their butt for them because their arms couldn't bend that far.

"That's time! Move away!" Jay called to him, pulling Joe out of the spiral that his mind had gone down. Joe stepped out and angled the shield to let the coals fall into the box. Then he healed and Cleansed himself, reading the notification that had popped up.

Characteristic point training completed! +1 to Strength and Constitution! These stats cannot be increased further by any means other than system rewards for twenty-four hours game time.

"Now you see why I recommend staying." Jay shook his head at Joe. "That was a waste for you. You only had to keep at it for another hour and a half, and you would have gotten two points."

"Thanks, Jay. I appreciate you looking out for me." Joe grinned and started putting his clothes back on. "I'll keep at it!"

"Do that!" Jay called back as Joe waved over his shoulder. "Joe, I meant now!

"See you tomorrow!" Joe ignored the follow-up grumbles, choosing instead to focus on his current skill. Thanks to his spell efficiency, he could cast the spell for a total of eighteen seconds if he got no mana returned or twenty-six seconds at maximum mana return. That meant he could only cause a tree to lose about forty-six inches—or just under four feet—of roots. A quick search of the internet at the coffee shop— one of the only places to get internet without respawning—told him that roots can get twenty feet deep and thirty-five across. That was for standard, non-magical trees. He had a feeling that he would need to get this skill a *lot* higher.

"Then again, all I really *need* to do is reduce them far enough that the tree can't support itself," Joe mused as he cast his spell at a patch of brambles while sipping his coffee. "If the tree is attacking, swinging back and forth... hmm. Maybe I don't need to reduce the root to *zero* to win."

He kept at it, sipping his coffee and using his spell until he ran out of coffee. Then he just cast the spell until it started getting too dark to clearly see what he was aiming at. He went over to have dinner, then found a bed and crashed. When he got up, he looked at his skill gain with a cheerful expression.

Wither Plant (Apprentice V). Just how much do you hate plants to have gained nearly ten levels in this skill overnight?

"That's... thirteen seconds of casting, well, sixteen. And that makes... forty inches. Wait. Did the spell get weaker?" Joe looked at his mental math, and it had indeed gotten weaker. "What in the...? Did I make the spell wrong?"

Joe looked over the spell, but it was correctly made; he *knew* it was. "Huh. I guess... I need to get it to the student ranks to see what happens? At that point, if there is no change... I'll stop using the spell?"

Discouraged, he got up and took a few hours to tackle all of his characteristic training, starting with strength and constitution and moving on to his standard four-aspect training. Gaining a point in six characteristics was a heady feeling, and he decided he liked it.

"Oh nice, intelligence got to seventy-five!" Joe hopped up and went to find his team. They had anticipated him... no. *Jess.* He looked to the side, and there she was. She glanced away when their eyes met, but he could see the smirk on her face. "Ah... you guys?"

"Yup, ready to go." Alexis seemed to realize that he was caught off-guard and couldn't hide a smile either. "Jess told us that you were about done with your training for the day and that you were gonna want to go out again really soon."

"So, we got ready!" Jaxon chimed in.

Joe blew air out of his nose, a disgruntled chuckle. "Let's go kill some tree people. Jess! Give yourself a small raise, and if you say '*done*', we are going to go have a *talk*!"

Jess's mouth closed with an audible *click*. Joe glared at her suspiciously until he was through the door to the Pathfinder's Hall.

CHAPTER TWENTY-THREE

''Alright, shall we go over what we did wrong during the last trip?" Joe looked around, getting confusion in reply. It appeared that his attempt to emulate Tiona hadn't been as successful as he had hoped it would be. "Basically, I am looking for us to discuss our weak points and how we can improve after what happened last time."

"Ah think yer gonna haveta take the lead on this one." Bard shook his head at Joe's insistence on talking whenever there was silence. "Nah gon' display mah faults for all yah ta pick at."

"That's not at all what I..." Joe scratched at his neck as he tried to explain, "Fine, look. Here is what I failed at. I didn't have proper spells for what we faced, and I didn't adapt as quickly as I should have to the situation. I was negligent at night, too used to everything in the area being weaker than us, and it led to me dying. I am trying to fix that by using a new spell and will be far more wary."

"So, you just want us to talk about little things like that?" Jaxon cocked his head to the side and grinned. "That's easy! I plan to get hit less and hit other things more often!"

"You aren't–" Joe started to complain.

Alexis joined in, "Same here! More damage out, less coming in."

Joe was sputtering, and he fumbled his words a few times before noticing that his friends were chuckling and holding back full laughter. "Oh, ha ha, make fun of the guy trying to help you improve!"

"At this point, we can see the forest, Joe." Poppy wiped his eyes. "Ah, needed that. Anyway! I think we all tried to figure out a way to do better. Let's just go ahead and assume we are all adults and don't need to be spoon-fed? Sound good? I like it. Let's make like those trees and kill anything that comes too close."

Bard shook his head. "Ah feel sad tha' idioms are changing so much."

"Let's make like a tree and bark?" Jaxon tried, getting an eye roll from the Skald.

"Nah. Trying ta force it... is jus' sad."

The group walked into the forest and stuttered to a stop. Joe looked around, trying to figure out why he felt so out of place. He could tell that the others were feeling the same way. "Are we... did we come in at the same place as last time?"

"We *definitely* did," Alexis confirmed. "At least, we entered the forest at the same place. Unless this place had some drastic growth, this isn't the same area."

There were trees and rocks that had fungus, moss, and all sorts of different colors and plants in the understory. It was obvious that they were in a different part of the forest than the last time they had been here, but the question was *how?* Alexis ventured a guess, "You think that is going to be a recurring theme? That each time we enter here, we get a new location as our starting point?"

"It'd make sense," Bard rumbled, stroking his burgeoning beard. "A defense mechanism for the forest? Make it so tha' people with no reason ta be here get turned about, make 'em wanna leave?"

"Make them want to *leaf?*" Jaxon watched Bard in anticipation of a good reaction.

Bard cupped his face in his hands. "I shoulda jus' left well enough alone, huh?"

"That may be the *root* of the problem, yes."

"Either way, we don't know if the monsters in the area are going to be the same as the last time that we entered, so keep a close eye on your surroundings," Joe cut into the conversation. They all went silent as a crash echoed through the area, though they started moving a little faster. "Let's try and find some... shelter. Crud."

A strange, sinister sound came from in front of them as what Joe had thought was a flowering bush *stood up* and turned to look at them. It was some kind of... animal? It was green and had all sorts of vines and leaves woven on it, like a new kind of fur. There were roses dotting the entire creature, which looked like a cross between a wolf, tiger, and compost pile. It *smelled* like a compost pile as well, which they noticed as the wind shifted.

"Joe, you have a new spell, you said?" Alexis quietly asked, trying not to draw too much attention. "Wanna show us how it works?"

"Not gonna be too useful on this." Joe's words seemed to be the catalyst for change, and the creature lunged at them. Its acceleration was far faster than a creature the size of a car should be able to manage, and the group didn't have time to scatter. Joe reflexively dual cast Shadow Spike, and the beast rammed into the spikes at full speed, stopping it from slamming into the humans. A deep rumble sounded, and the beast twisted off the spikes. A clear fluid poured out of the disconcertingly shallow wounds, likely this creature's blood.

The melee members of the group took advantage of the six-legged creature's forcible pause, darting in and landing blows that would have ended the fight against creatures they were used to fighting. Sadly, all they managed was to enrage the creature, which reared back on its hind legs and lashed out with the front four. Jaxon dodged one, only to be hit by the slightly-varied angle of the next. The other two fighters took their hits, grunted as they were forced back, and charged in to retaliate.

"Hits like a train!" Poppy called as he slashed twice to the side, leaped back, and activated a skill. "*Fuori misura!*"

The distance he had created was crossed in a blur, his body darting forward without him taking a step. The move seemed to fully ignore physics. Poppy plunged his rapier into the creature's shoulder, grabbing and squeezing a ball near his rapier's pommel. He took another hit and rolled with it, using the momentum to get away. "Joe, need healing! I took a hundred and seventy-four damage each hit!"

"Gah!" Joe washed a Mend at him, then his teammates for good measure. He cast another at the Duelist, wincing as he lost nearly a third of his maximum mana by using that spell four times. Luckily, his spell efficiency allowed him fifty-five percent off the mana cost, or he'd be half drained already, and combat had just started!

"Did you use that poison I gave you?" Alexis called at Poppy even as twin bolts thudded into the huge creature. She worked to reload as she got an answer.

"Yeah, sorry to say, I used *most* of it with that attack!" Poppy dodged a swipe that nearly took his head off and returned with a deep stab into the creature's head. "This is more plant than beast, looks like no brain! Gonna need to hack it to pieces!"

A powerful chop severed a leg, and Bard grunted. "Way ahead o' yah. *He~e~ere we go again, double speed for moves again!*"

The melee attackers were suddenly moving at a *much* faster pace and easily dodged the next few attacks while landing their own far easier. Joe cast Wither at one of the roses on the creature, and after two seconds, the flower fell off the beast. The creature staggered around drunkenly for a moment, then howled and redoubled its ferocious attacks at the group. Joe decided it was time to lead. "Weak spot found! Take out the roses!"

"On it!" Jaxon flipped over a thorn-coated paw, then jammed his finger into the center of a rose. A long spike stabbed out of his glove, and the flower started to bleed like a normal human would. "Seems effective! One... two seconds and the flower died after being stabbed!"

Alexis called, "Creature seems to be moving slower!"

"Can confirm!" Poppy slashed with his rapier, and two flowerheads drifted sadly to the ground.

The Beast snarled and pounced at Alexis, pinning the startled ranged fighter and taking her to the ground. It tore into her, and the others mercilessly assaulted the beast as Alexis screamed in pain. Just as the beast finally died, Alexis did as well, brutally torn open even though they had done all they could to prevent it.

*Exp gained: 777 (777 * Rosebeast x1)*

Bard pushed the huge mass of rotting vegetation off Alexis and shakily reached down to touch her mangled face. "Tha's a nasty way ta go."

"I got this, Bard." Joe took a deep breath and started circulating mana. He went through the motions and pushed a palm at Alexis. As he cast Resurrection, a portal appeared above her body. Alexis stepped out of it as her corpse melted like snow on a hot day.

"Ugh." She shook herself as she looked at the mess she had come back to. "That sucked. Also, do you guys have any idea how bad you smell right now? Joe, Cleanse them. I think they are coated in some kind of lure. We won't get fifty feet if they go into the forest smelling like that. It's... pheromones of some kind. Stupid Rosebeast. I died to an angry *flower.*"

"I'm glad you were able to get *clover* your death, Alexis. You really *rose* above it." Joe grinned as he cast Cleanse on the people that had been in close proximity to the Rosebeast. "You're so impressive. You *grow*, girl!"

"I'll shoot you," Alexis warned him.

"Sorry, you're just my best *bud*, but you're right, Alexis. Let's get going. Petal to the metal." Joe flinched as a bolt bounced off his Exquisite Shell. "Oopsie *daisy*. Peony for your thoughts?"

"How do you have all these ready?" Alexis narrowed her eyes fractionally. "Did you waste time thinking up puns when we were all getting ready for this?"

"Totally not!" Joe denied, possibly *too* quickly. He decided to leaf the forest puns alone for now as well. "Shall we continue?"

The group started moving again, keeping an eye on the verdant and deadly area. First angry trees, now murderous shrubbery? There was no telling what would attack them next. They defeated a few small, mutated foxes soon after, but in total, they only gained six hundred experience by the time they were forced to stop for the night. Unlike Joe, the others had standard vision at night, and it was too dangerous to continue.

As Joe lay on his new bedroll, he looked over his stats to see what had changed. To his disgruntlement, his progress had slowed dramatically.

Name: Joe '*Tatum's Chosen Legend*' Class: Mage (Actual: Rituarchitect)
Profession: Tenured Scholar (Actual: Arcanologist)
Character Level: 15 Exp: 124,813 Exp to next level: 11,187
Rituarchitect Level: 2 Exp: 2,390 Exp to next level: 610

Hit Points: 250/250
Mana: 937.5/937.5
Mana regen: 27.5/sec (Base 25.01/sec increased by gear)
Stamina: 225/225
Stamina regen: 5.64/sec

Characteristic: Raw score (Modifier)

Strength: 25 (1.25)
Dexterity: 34 (1.34)
Constitution: 30 (1.30)
Intelligence: 75 (2.25)
Wisdom: 69 (2.19)
Charisma: 26 (1.26)
Perception: 54 (2.04)
Luck: 30 (1.30)
Karmic Luck: +6

"That death set me *way* back," he muttered almost too quietly for himself to hear. "At least I only lose experience and not stats. Ick. I lost all the progress from clearing the entire salt mine. Stats are looking good though..."

"Joe, I think something is coming," Bard called in a low tone. Instantly, the group grabbed their weapons and prepared themselves. A silhouette stepped out of the forest slowly and resolved into a huge Wolfman Warrior.

"Peace offered. Conversation requested."

Jaxon stepped forward and snarled what sounded like a garbled threat. The others tightened their grips on weapons, knowing that this wouldn't end well. To their utter shock, the Wolfman's ears perked up, and his tail shifted in a soft 'happy wag'. "Pain power man! Ha! The O'Baba will be pleased! Come, come. You stay here, you die to the spores."

Jaxon convinced the others to follow, so the Wolfman waited for them to break camp, and the confused humans followed after him into the darkness.

CHAPTER TWENTY-FOUR

The Wolfman Warrior stopped them after an hour of stumbling through the dark. Frankly, Joe had no idea how they had managed not to be attacked by all the things that were going bump in the night—or screeching into the night; that was more common.

"I bring you this far on honor of Pain Power man. Sleep is safe for the night, at the least." The Warrior was towering over them even though he was badly hunched. "But here... here I need strongest vow from each of you. Swear you will bring no harm to those where I bring you. That you not show this place to anyone, not breathe *word*."

"We could never find our way back to here anyway," Poppy smarmily responded, obviously grumpy after the sudden shift in sleep schedules. There was no reply to his sass, so he reluctantly agreed, "*Fine*, I won't tell anyone where your secret base is."

The others also agreed to protect the secrets of the Wolfmen, so he nodded and walked off again. Another half hour tromping through the lush forest, and they looked up to see the tips of a dozen arrows pointed at them from the trees. Joe grabbed the shadows around them, tossing them into the air. The group was blanketed in a thick, cloying, shadowy mist that even Joe couldn't see through. "An *ambush*?"

"Hold! All!" The Warrior then literally barked something at the Wolfmen Scouts that had lost sight of their targets and were starting to panic. The arrows came down, the Warrior growling at a few who still hesitated. "They swore strong vow to do no harm. We pass. The O'Baba waits. Humans, this is just perimeter guard."

Joe and the others were standing in a defensive posture even as the black mist boiled away. When everyone was calm, the group carefully followed the Warrior into the camp. The foliage was at a density that didn't allow for much in the way of scouting out the area, but that was probably the intent when living in such a dangerous area. The party winced as a large square of blazing light appeared, but their eyes adjusted quickly and they realized that a door was open in front of them.

Jaxon skipped through, leaving both the humans and Wolfmen slack-jawed as he got to the wizened, old Wolfman crone that was sitting near the fire and swept her up into a hug before poking her all over while snarling at her. Joe and company got ready to head to respawn but then heard chuffing laughter from the elderly leader. "Hello, friends of Jaxon. I see that you have not been able to housetrain him yet."

"It's an ongoing and thankless task," Joe managed to reply. Something flicked past his ear, nicking his throat and drawing blood. Joe reacted instantly, and a Shadow Spike skewered the... he picked up a fresh-blood stained origami paper crane. "What just...?"

O'Baba gestured and snarled, and a robed form was slapped out of the room by an invisible power. Joe saw what looked like an armful of books go tumbling with whoever that was, then turned back to O'Baba with a questioning look. She sighed and sat down. "Of course he was unable to resist. I am sorry. I allowed you to be attacked by one of mine when you are here as a guest. I will make reparations for the damage caused."

Joe was going to speak, but Jaxon darted over and put a hand on his mouth. "Don't insult her debt. Also, they make the *best* cured ham, if you get to choose the form of repayment."

"I... Humans are so strange." O'Baba shook herself. "If I may be so bold, why are you here? You are too weak for this area; your kind should barely be testing the edges of the Mad Forest."

"Is that what you call it? Interesting," Joe commented as he tried to find a proper way to phrase his next words. "My people are on the verge of starvation. After the battle, millions more humans arrived. At this rate, many will die. Even more will work to strip the land of all things of use and will eat the trees if it comes down to it. I found an ancient text that listed this area as a place that Elves once lived in, and it said that they had access to nearly unlimited food. We came here to find anything that might help us."

The O'Baba sat on her wooden chair, tapping a long claw on to the arm of it. "You know... I have a vested interest in ensuring that humans do *not* do too well. There is bad blood between us. Our King is slain, our people shattered, but... I do remember a time when my own people starved. If you think we are animalistic *now*... hmmm. I will help you, and here is why."

She stood and walked over to Joe, looking him directly in the eyes as she approached. Her irises were a deep, swirling red, just as he knew that his eyes swirled with a lesser amount of blue and black—the signature of concentrated mana in a body. "Our people have a rule. Only family may touch another without causing pain. In this way, we train ourselves to become hardy, to ignore the pain. Do you know what happens when someone is in pain or *fears* pain... Human Joe?"

"They tend to lash out, swear to get revenge later, or collapse into a puddle?" Joe replied with a fair bit of humor, trying to diffuse the tense environment.

"This is true." The powerful Shaman nodded. "So, as a small act of petty revenge... I am going to help you get what you want."

"I don't understand." The humans all looked at each other and offered up shrugs.

"Nothing leads to weakness like a fat society who do not need to struggle to attain what they need. If I give you all the food you need, I may not need to do *anything* when the time comes for our ascendancy. Your own people will simply move out of our way. They will move out of fear of *losing* what they have for free. You might think on this, swearing you won't use the ability you have, but when the first human starves to death in front of you... you'll give in." O'Baba turned away and sat in her chair again.

"Now. This is still information that is worth much. You will personally benefit and soar to great heights among your people. So, I need you to do something for us first." O'Baba had returned to being a smiling, old crone, and looking at her now, Joe would never think that she was the one that had made him sweat bullets moments ago. "I need you to clear out a temple in the area. There is an infestation that I would rather not lose people to clear. *You* can always return, so it shouldn't be that much of an issue."

"Offering a... quest?" This was something that Joe could get behind. "Could I bypass this as amends for whoever it was that just attacked me?"

O'Baba returned with a chilly stare. "The compensation I am offering is to *not* have to reach 'Friend' status with The People before I ever offer you a quest personally. Is this not enough?"

"You make a good point." Joe swallowed and tried not to smile. Showing his teeth seemed like a bad idea right now. "Let me guess, the temple is at the center of the forest, and we need to slay whatever is controlling all the imps and expanding the forest so much?"

"No." O'Baba snorted. "You are barely able to survive at the edges of the forest, and even then only by attacking strays that are away from their packs. You want to go into a level thirty raid zone? That would require a much more... *grand* reward than simple growth houses. Certainly not something either of us are ready for."

"Oh."

"We will guide you to the northmost site, which is too close to us for comfort." O'Baba gestured at a door next to them. "Go rest. You will need to be in the best shape possible to survive tomorrow."

"Can we see the greenhouses before we agree to this quest?" Joe stopped her from dismissing them. "I know that you would not be offering something you don't have; I just want to see what it is that we are getting out of the arrangement."

"Sleep now," O'Baba ordered with a bite in her voice. "In the morning, we will venture to the production area, and you will find what you came looking for."

Joe looked at his team, who were swaying on their feet. They needed sleep, and there was plenty of time to find answers when they had clear minds. Joe reluctantly agreed, and they were shown to a set of surprisingly comfortable, extra-large beds. "Well, at least this is really nice. You guys think I made the right call here?"

He looked around but found that his team was already asleep. An unnatural tugging pulled at him, and Joe succumbed to the embrace of Morpheus as well.

CHAPTER TWENTY-FIVE

"Awaken, humans." Joe's eyes snapped open, and he was *perfectly* awake. Awake like when a foghorn went off near your ear, without the pain or flinching.

"What did you do to us?" Poppy snarled as he launched out of bed. "How did you get around sending us to our spawn room when you knocked us out?"

The Wolfman that would be their guide for the remainder of the day snorted through his elongated snout and declined to answer. There was something shifty afoot, but they wouldn't be finding out from this Scout. The Wolfman gestured for them to come along, and the confused and somewhat salty humans followed him. Joe scratched at his side, then Cleansed himself and his team. No need to remain salty when he was a walking shower.

"I bring. You see. You take quest." The Scout didn't seem to have the same linguistic range as the others that the group had interacted with, but after a moment, he was having a conversation with Jaxon in the Wolfman tongue as they walked.

"What happened while we were all doing our own thing?" Joe asked the others, getting nods of understanding as they watched Jaxon lash out and pound on the Wolfman for ten seconds. Then again *strangely*, the Wolfman stood tall and handed over a bag of something. Jaxon looked inside, nodded, and the walk continued. "Jaxon, what is..."

"Cured ham."

Joe had no words, but luckily, they arrived at their destination only a moment later. The only way that he knew they *were* there was the glass sparkling in the sun. The building itself was clear glass, and Joe could see that the place was *stuffed* with greenery. They walked into the building, and it was like going from having a stuffed nose to being able to smell *everything*. The Scout with them started sneezing and even had to cover his snout after a short while. The air was *potent* with flavor and rich aromas. Joe's stomach growled, and he wasn't alone. From what they could see, there was enough food to feed dozens of people for weeks, and this was just the entrance of the building.

"Is greenhouse. Many functions. You see? Good." The Scout waved them backward, and they were forced out of the building. "To The O'Baba."

Passing through the door again seemed to pull away all the scents that they had been marinating in only moments ago. It must be a function of the building, and Joe was *itching* to make a blueprint and create his own version. He had only been able to see a small area in the greenhouse, but it seemed to be *massive* on a scale that he was having trouble understanding. Such a huge building shouldn't be able to exist in hiding, but then again... it hadn't seemed that huge from the outside. Perhaps there were some tricks to it like the spatial magic of the Mage's college? That was the only thing that Joe could think of. Was this another Artifact building? Higher? Would he even be able to build it elsewhere even *if* he had the blueprint?

His thoughts were tumultuous as he walked, and he was on full autopilot mode until they arrived back to O'Baba. She saw his faraway gaze and nodded. "You have questions. I have a few answers. Not too many until you complete my task. Then you may ask about the building as much as you like."

"Fair enough." Joe took a steadying breath and looked her in the eye. "Does that building use spatial magic? What tier is it?"

"Yes, it is larger than it should be. It is classified as a 'Special Unique'." O'Baba showed teeth. "You wonder why the ranking is so low for such a potent building, I can see. The high cost to create it, and the... downsides that come with the building lower the perceived value. Not everything can be the best in the world, *Architect of Artifacts*."

Joe flinched but decided that it was foolish of him to think that the current leader of a nation wouldn't have a way to look at his titles at the very least. "Well, that's good. I don't have the resources I'd need to make a bunch of Artifacts or better. Can you tell me more about the greenhouse?"

"No, I don't think I will," came the disappointing answer. "Just know that there are downsides, large issues with the building, that reduce the rarity to where it is. You'll get your food, but you are still going to need to devote yourself or others to *securing* the food. Let's talk about the need The People have."

"Please." Joe looked to his team, getting affirmative responses from them as well. They all knew how this 'game' worked. Nothing for free, but rewards were *enforced* to a scary degree.

"There is an infestation of humans in a temple near us." O'Baba waited for a reaction, and her eyes twinkled approvingly as Joe said nothing. "To be fair, they are not like you and yours. They are... wrong. Broken. Their minds are in a different way, but they are dangerous, in a way that you will simply need to learn for yourself. Telling you, well. Just observe them for a short while before you decide to charge in. You'll see."

"Do we only have one chance at this? If we die, it could be that we never find our way back to you," Poppy stated the obvious, and O'Baba's ears flattened.

A hulking Warrior stepped forward threateningly. "*Silence!* You have not earned the right to speak in the O'Baba's presence!"

"Where I come from, we do not conform to a *caste* system. I have every right to talk to *anyone* I care to." Poppy's words were as pointed as his rapier. "Joe alone does not speak for all of us. He is leader by virtue of his position, but he has made it clear that he wants and values our input. Understand that our cultures differ *greatly*."

"Your *mother* differs greatly." The Warrior snarled at him, but the O'Baba made a whistling sound; the Warrior reluctantly stepped back.

O'Baba looked at Poppy with her ears remaining flat. "Swordsman, did you not just tell him to *understand* that our cultures differ? Perhaps you should look into your own actions before telling another to take heed of your own. Let me tell you something, swordsman. I smell youngling on you. You have a child, yes?"

Poppy reached for the hilt of his weapon. "If you even *try* to threaten my family, I will hunt you all to extinction no matter how long it takes."

O'Baba once more whistled down the bristling guards. "As you can see, we are rather on edge here. Your attitude is not conducive to good relations. Tell me, swordsman, do you know why we have come to this terrible place, this forest full of death and gloom? The last respite for our people? Do you know what it means to become a shattered race? I think only your Jaxon has seen the true danger of becoming as such."

Joe had no idea what to do to calm the mounting tensions. He looked around at the group helplessly, his gaze eventually landing on Jaxon. The Chiropractor seemed confused and stepped forward to say as much. "Hello! I *do* enjoy being included, but I have to admit that I have no idea what's going on. What do you mean?"

"Jaxon, you met me for the first time as someone was hunting us in a forest. Did you not wonder *why* I, the *greatest Shaman* of The People, was scurrying away instead of standing to decimate the attacking humans?" O'Baba stared at the stressed face Jaxon was pulling and tilted her head to the side. "Do you remember how you found us?"

"Of course!" Jaxon brightened instantly. "I heard someone running away from me, so I skipped after them to see what was the matter! It was just one of your pups, so I tried to leave, but you got attacked."

"Correct, Jaxon." The O'Baba turned to Poppy with hard eyes. "As you put it so threateningly, a Shattered race can go *extinct*. Have you seen other children out and about? No? Just the protected area? It sure is *hard* to make a race go extinct when the children are *safe*, don't you think?"

Poppy paled as he made the connection that O'Baba was drawing for him. "Now, you see. I was taking our *future* to this location, to a place so dangerous that the armies of your Kingdom cannot easily find us. *Forgive* us, that we are on *edge* around a group that has a vested interest in slaying or enslaving us. Perhaps you prove to us that you are a good people instead of hurling insults and threats because you were forced to get a good night's rest?"

Poppy hung his head in shame, nodding slightly to show that he had understood the issue. O'Baba looked back to Joe. "Now. Let's get back to the quest."

Quest alert! The Cult of the Burning Mind. The O'Baba has told you of an area that is too dangerous to leave alone. An infestation of 'not right' humans have taken control of a place of power in the Forest of Chlorophyll Chaos and are expanding their influence in the area. Defeat them, ensure they cannot challenge the Wolfmen, and you shall have your reward.

Reward: +1,000 reputation with The People. +10,000 experience. Blueprint for 'Evergrowth Greenhouse'. Failure: The place of power remains in control of the Cult for two weeks. -1,000 reputation with The People. Lose chance at gaining blueprint. Caution! Minimum recommendation for this quest is level 25! Accept? Yes/No

"Yikes." Joe shared the information with his team, and all of them paled as he had. This was a quest designed for people ten levels above *Joe*. Not all of them were even level fifteen yet, and frankly, this was outside of their range. They shook their heads, and Joe turned to O'Baba to refuse the quest as politely as possible.

"I will gift you a beacon that will allow you to get here consistently whenever you enter the forest," O'Baba spoke before Joe could. "I will tell you right now, refusing the quest is the same as failing it in my eyes. You will not be allowed to return here peacefully."

Joe bit his words off and reluctantly accepted the quest. O'Baba nodded once and gestured at the door. "Show them the path, as many times as it is needed. Bring them here when they want to return. Show them the respect we would give those on a quest to join The People. Good luck, team of Joe. I know I ask too much, but this is what is needed."

CHAPTER TWENTY-SIX

An odd sight graced the forest that morning. Two Wolfman Scouts slowly and carefully picked their way through the forest, and a few feet behind them trailed a party of their racial enemy, humans. Now, no one was around to see this odd sight, and the Scouts went out of their way to make sure that remained the case. The enemies here were far too powerful for two standard Scouts, but they used their enhanced senses to great effect in avoiding conflict and choosing the best path forward.

As The O'Baba had mentioned, the place of power was nearby. After only an hour of creeping through the woods, huge, gray, stone walls appeared between the trees. If they had been walking at a normal pace in a straight line, it would have likely only taken fifteen minutes or so to arrive. The walls themselves seemed to be pulsing with a faint light, and just as the group arrived, they found why this place was considered so dangerous. The Scouts brought them to a tree, and after carefully ensuring that the tree wasn't an Ent, the group was helped up to an overwatch position.

"This is a *cathedral!*" Joe's voice was *almost* too loud, and in an instant, a poisoned arrow was at this throat. He wasn't overly concerned, as he had maximized his Exquisite Shell, but he was somewhat embarrassed over his outburst and quieted down. The wait stretched, ten minutes. Fifteen. Thirty. Then the front doors swung open, and a formation of people marched out. They were all humming the same tune, and it was *catchy*. Joe, still embarrassed over his previous outburst, stopped himself just before joining in but noted with horror that everyone else *including* the Scouts were humming along at a much lower decibel.

"Guys! Stop it!" Joe demanded, taking their attention and getting glared at. Then they noticed that they were humming, and Joe was *pretty* sure they tried to stop. But they *didn't.*

The walls of the building flashed more brightly, and a roar from the forest directly challenged the light and music show. The understory began to wave as a creature moved toward the formation of maybe two hundred people, and the humming began to reach a crescendo. A Rosebeast burst from the leafy ferns that coated the ground, and after a moment to orient itself, it charged directly at the huge group of unarmed people.

Joe wasn't sure what he was expecting, but it wasn't the Rosebeast tearing the group apart with ease. The level twenty-ish beast hit the second ranks of the formation with a spray of blood... which came from the first ranks. Then the people piled on the Rosebeast, all of them still smiling and humming. Alexis nudged Joe and whispered, "Average level of those people is *five.* I don't see anyone above seven."

"What in the abyss?" Joe looked back at the fight, the *slaughter,* just as the Rosebeast shook itself and sent a wave of thorns flying from the vines that encircled its body. Another dozen humans fell to the thorns and poison, but the wave of bodies started to cover the Rosebeast, punching, kicking, and biting between smiles. The two hundred were reduced to one hundred. Fifty. Twenty. Five. Two. Then the Rosebeast finally fell, the last of its roses torn away.

The two remaining humans began to glow with golden light, hyper leveling from the experience of killing such a powerful creature and only splitting it between two people. Joe had no doubt that they gained bonuses, skill levels, and all sorts of goodies for fighting barehanded and unarmored. The two people stood, resumed humming, and returned to the cathedral.

As much as Joe wanted to discuss what he had just seen with his group, he knew that they were currently here to learn about the fighters and the challenges that they would need to face. The doors swung open, and a few people stood waiting for the returning fighters. From what Joe could see, the open area was full of people. He had no idea how so many low-leveled people had gotten here, but he had a sinking suspicion that just *perhaps* some of them had thought they were going off to become farmers.

"Intrusive Scan," Joe muttered when he saw a musclebound, glowing figure welcoming back the survivors. He held the contact for three second before the figure became aware of his scan and slammed the doors to block the hostile, intrusive information gathering. That was fine with Joe, as the information he had already gained was enough to make him wince.

Brayden_W, Hierophant of the Burning Mind.

Highest stat: Intelligence

Ongoing effects: Burning Mind. Unification. Mana-well Shielding. Empowered by Many. Enemy of the Forest. Hypnotism Aura. Amphitheater Amplification. Arcane Double Damage...

The list of active effects continued for another two lines, but they had vanished before Joe got a chance to read them when the Hierophant slammed the door. "Yikes. This is... yeah, this is going to be really hard, you guys. Listen to some of these effects that guy has."

As Joe explained the names of the effects, the expressions around him turned defeated. To Joe's delight, he got a notification as soon as he stopped speaking.

Skill increase: Intrusive Scan (Novice IV). Hey. You shouldn't have been able to scan him. Just saying. He *critically failed at blocking it. Big ol' boost because of that. Tootles!*

Weird message aside, Joe was happy to see some progress on the skill even if he didn't know what would happen as it got stronger. Maybe people would be less likely to notice it happening? Bard interrupted his thoughts, "Ya think tha' hypno-aura is why we were humming tha' garbage tune?"

"Likely, and the way the wall is pulsing with light is probably from the effect of the 'Amphitheater Amplification'. I bet the building is boosting his ability," Alexis stated after a moment. "Joe, have you ever gotten bonuses from being in a temple or anything?"

Joe was taken off guard by the sudden shift in conversation but couldn't think of a proper answer. "You know what? I bet I *would* if I ever spent any time in one. Usually, I'm on the go way too much to accumulate bonuses, but I know a lot of clerics tend to stay in one place. There has to be a reason. I'll try it out sometime."

"Right, I think we are going to need a plan of attack," Poppy spoke out to the others. They agreed and started *very quietly* discussing their options. Twenty minutes later, they had narrowed it down to a pretty standard distraction snatch-and-grab.

"I think that if we can take over the building, that is, convert it to Tatum, we will be able to take away the majority of the active effects that the Hierophant is getting." Joe was not entirely *sure* of his plan, but it was their best option right now. "Plus, we would get a few of the temple guardian-golem things. For the life of me, I can't remember what they are called right now. Oh, *Juggernauts!* I have a major issue with this plan, though. There is *no* way that I have enough mana to convert this place on my own. A roadside *shrine* drains me dry right now."

"What if we were all joining you?" Alexis asked him.

"No, think about it." Joe shook his head sharply. "We need someone defending us, and the only way that we are able to get here is to go to the Wolfmen. We can't exactly bring other people with us to do a proper raid, right?"

"Good." Bard harrumphed. "Didn't relish the idea of being a battery, anyway. Not what I signed up for."

"Wait! A battery!" Joe's eyes sparkled, and he opened his mouth to say more. Right then, the walls of the building flashed again, and the doors began to creak open. Joe shut his mouth but indicated that they would talk later. The humming started up, and soon, the scene from before played out. Two hundred people walked out, a Beast charged, and the two sides fought.

"None of the survivors from the last group are here," Alexis pointed out. Joe hadn't even thought to look for them. "Back to the highest level being seven."

This time, combat ended very differently. All of the humans were wiped out, and the Beast advanced on the building. The doors opened again, and Alexis pointed out two people in the crowd of about fifty that exited. "There's our survivors."

Still, the group was unarmed, but now, the average level was twelve, and the Beast was weakened. A dozen humans died, but the rest shared the experience and grew stronger. Then they reentered the building, and the doors closed again. The Scout with them spoke in a harsh whisper, "It is time to leave. Every two hours, they flood out of the place of power and seek anything in the area. They are *thorough*."

They descended from the tree and made their way to the edge of the forest. Originally, they were going to go back into the Wolfman area, but the team had convinced the Wolfmen that they needed access to many things that weren't available in the current area. After the slow walk to the exit, one of the Scouts passed Joe a small object that fit on his wrist like a watch. The Scout spoke then, staring at Joe with hard, deadly eyes, "This will bring your party to our area *if* you return. I do not want to let you go, but The O'Baba has spoken. Do not..."

The other Scout gripped his partner's arm and pulled him into the woods, where they vanished. Joe started walking, knowing that if they were in the same situation... well, he might not listen to someone else. He'd fight *anyone* that might hurt his family. It was late evening when they got to the small shrine on the side of the dirt road, but from there, a single step pulled the entire team all the way back to the Pathfinder's Hall at the low cost of the majority of their mana and stamina.

As much as they all wanted to relax and come down from the constant stress of being in such a deadly area, the two-week time limit was nagging at all of them. Joe took a moment to fully explain the rest of his thought process for the attempt they would make on the place of power.

"Guys, I found an... I'm not sure if it's an enchantment or spell. Whatever. It converts a Core into a Mana Battery. I need someone to go out and find the highest-grade Core they can find, use the guild if needed. You know what? Make Jess do that. Ah... I'll talk to her about the tasks we need completed actually, just so that I can answer any questions right away." Joe paused, thinking about what he should say.

"Right, so. Here is the plan. Please, *please* tell me if you come up with a better idea." Joe looked around, meeting all their eyes. "This is what I need each of you to do."

CHAPTER TWENTY-SEVEN

"Alrighty, Jess-a-mundo!" Joe's enthusiasm bounced harmlessly off the iron defenses of Jess's single-track focus. "I have a few *really* important tasks for you. I need a couple Cores for testing purposes and one that is the most powerful that you can find. Use the guild for this if you can. They promised to fund our operation."

"Can do." Jess whisked a note into a small notebook. Joe nodded approvingly; people were starting to take note when he spoke.

"Great. Next, I need an update on finances, both for myself and for my party members. I don't know what they are getting paid or what *I'm* getting paid, and that needs to be fixed. What else..." Joe snapped his fingers. "Interviews. I need to hire a few people who have high mana pools. I don't care what level they are, but I can offer them pay, a class, housing, and stuff. They can keep their day jobs; I'll just need them at various times. Put them on retainer."

"You're just going to trust that I'll pick out the right people?" Jess seemed surprised.

"Yes, but also no," Joe decided to clarify. "They'll apply with you, but after you give the initial okay, I'll do a second interview and see if we mesh. There will be a huge benefit to working with me, but there is often a lot of pain and failure. I need people that will only care about the great benefits. Most of the people I need right now are going to be part of my Ritualist Coven, but check around for people hoping to be clerics; I'm pretty sure I can get them that class too."

"What are you going to be doing while I do this?" Jess already seemed resigned to being overworked. Poor gal. "Where will you be?"

"Only place you'll be able to get to me is at the coffee shop. At all other times, I'm gonna be a little... hidden." Joe replied evasively. "One last thing, I need a way to capture, hold, and transport a high-level, captured, Rare beast. See if that's doable?"

"Mmm-hmm." Jess looked at him with a twitching eyebrow. "Anything *else*?"

"Not so much. You get the class you were after?" Joe's personal question seemed to disarm her.

"Oh. Yes. It took a bit, but... I'm training up some pertinent skills right now. Even found a class trainer, though he keeps pretending to be a ranger."

"Gonna give me a hint?"

"Not a chance."

"Excellent. I'm off to *achieve* the *improbable!*" Joe pointed into the air and marched off, getting a laugh at his antics. Good. No need to be unapproachable! Joe only had a few days to make his goals come to life. Every member of their party had their tasks, and frankly, Joe felt that his personal requirements were quite a lot harder. The reason he hadn't delved into the mana battery book thus far was that there was a *lot* of misinformation in it.

He needed to compile the correct information, tinker with areas about *why* the creator of the process seemed to think this was important, and then turn the spell into a useful process. From there... well, there was plenty to do from there. This was one of the final steps needed in capturing the building. They needed a distraction, and they needed a way to take down the Hierophant. Joe knew that last chunk might be the actual difficult portion of this quest. The enemy was smart, and Joe had no real understanding of his capabilities. Joe hadn't even *recognized* some of those active effects.

Entering the lower, hidden area of the Pathfinder's Hall, Joe was fully secluded for the first time in days. It elicited a feeling of both relief and a longing for companionship. Maybe he would hire a bard to play music for him while he worked. Nah. None of the instruments here would work for making EDM or the various video game music he listened to in order to help him focus. A lute wasn't going to be able to beat silence.

Joe got over to his desk and rifled through it until he found the Mana Battery manual. He took a deep breath and resigned himself to wasting a *lot* of gold on paper in the next few days. As planned, he started with compiling, he made sure that all the correct information among the various pages all went on a fresh sheet with plenty of space for more info to be added around it. The book was thick in comparison to most spell manuals, and as the info came together, Joe realized that his initial hunch about this was correct; this was an enchantment. He wasn't sure if everything was going to translate into a usable form, but all he could do at this point was try.

Surprisingly, the information that was useless was the explanation of *why* the enchantment worked. That had some impact on the spell diagram that was in the book, making a few of the lines go from golden to a gray coloration. They weren't *black*–which indicated completely false–so it was likely that the lines would work in a limited fashion. To be included in the Mage's College at all, the enchantment must have worked at *least* once.

"You know what this means?" Joe scribbled at his paper excitedly. "I bet this diagram works perfectly on a certain type and shape of Core but not on all of them. That would make it succeed in some cases, and *maybe* work on others, but I bet they would be... unstable..."

At that moment, Joe remembered the Archmage of the College. He had tried to use an unstable Core to destroy the city when it was obvious that he was going to lose. Was this the spell book he had used to create it? If Joe failed to enchant a Core properly... would it detonate and take a chunk of his surroundings with him? In that case, it would be better to do this off-site like a nuclear test. While he could potentially make a potent weapon... how did someone stabilize a Core that was going out of control? Better not risk it.

"Let me see. This going here should work on trash or damaged Cores, but the higher density of power in other types would make this wobbly line go haywire, leading to an explosion." Joe started picking apart that section of the diagram, poking and reshaping. "If I treat this portion as an open-ended equation, I should be able to compensate for higher-tier power throughput. The downside, obviously, is that there will be a loss in efficiency. I'm going to lose some of the potential, but I don't know at this point if it is one percent or eighty."

Joe cracked his neck and pulled out a fresh paper. His increased intelligence score was showing its usefulness; making spell diagrams was essentially a combination of discrete mathematics, calculus, and trigonometry. The difficulty was an order of magnitude more difficult to him than making a ritual, which was similar to using a programming language. Hard, yes. Of course. But creating a spell diagram was more similar to determining the breadboard layout of a CPU but first proving it with math so that you didn't blow up a facility.

Though he was unsure what an intelligence score of seventy-five translated into in terms of IQ, the modifier of two-point-two-five told him that he was currently two and a quarter times as smart as the pre-Eternium Earth average. Joe smiled as he worked down the list of variables, angles, and power flow diagrams that would have made him run screaming when he first joined the game... and made alterations that *fixed* some of the issues. Still astonishing to him.

He frowned as he made a line that wobbled and glared at his hand. Oh? It seemed that his hand was shaking. Low blood sugar? Must be it. Joe checked the time and realized that he had barely moved in fourteen hours. That needed to stop happening! He set down his quill with a sigh and walked to the surface. He needed food and a nap, but there had been an unexpected gain from his work.

Complicated work success! Intelligence +1!

Skill increase: Ritual Magic (Journeyman VIII).

Training the body to withstand hunger, thirst, and ignore the need for sleep and bathroom breaks is unpleasant, but your outstanding focus can pull you through! Constitution +2!

"That's insane!" Joe looked at it again, and he had indeed gained *three* stat points just by working at this issue. He decided right there that he was going to have to reevaluate every step of this process to make sure it was done correctly. Perhaps he was *still* not treating this with the actual danger level it represented.

You have made three choices within eight hours that averted disaster! Wisdom +1!

Make that four stat points. Joe swallowed on a dry throat, then cast Cleanse to hydrate up. Were enchantments *really* so deadly and difficult? He should check in with Terra to see what she was getting out of her experience. She was trying to become an enchanter, right?

Joe entered the mess hall, finding that it now had a pavilion over it instead of being an open-air picnic area. There was the guild food area as well as an entrepreneur who had opened a small restaurant. It was about the same size as a food truck and seemed to be doing well—if the number of people in line was any indication. Joe hoped they could stay in business as food shortages started to hit.

He swallowed the tasteless standard fare that the guild was offering members, realizing why there were so many people uninterested in it—but it was filling and nutritious, and everything was secondary to coffee anyway. Joe looked up as Mike walked over, a gleam reflecting off his glasses. "Joe! There you are! I was hoping that I might get your assistance on a few construction projects."

"Hi, Mike! I was hoping to exchange contribution points for useful items! Whatcha got?" Joe enthusiastically stood and reached out a hand for a fist bump.

Mike stuttered to a stop and looked pained. "We, ah, we're still working on setting up a contribution shop..."

"Oh, no problem." Joe grinned wickedly, "Let's talk about getting a few more buildings up better and faster than *anyone else* could do!"

"Ugh. Yes, let's talk," Mike replied sourly, knowing he had been played. "Look, I'm gonna be straight with you. For some reason, the barracks you made is just... *better* than the ones we have been making. Better bonuses when in use, higher quality sleep... just better."

"I have a title. Any construction of a new structure will boost the building's overall statistics and potential boosts by ten percent." Joe nodded as Mike realized the potential of such a title. "Got it from setting up that beast."

Mike followed Joe's thumb to see the towering egg-structure of the Pathfinder's Hall. "I see. Well... please help us out. We need a whole lot of work done. We need houses, barracks, walls, storage facilities, sanitation, baths, sewage... everything. If we can make all of this with the bonuses that you provide, we will be able to make a stable base, turn it into a town, and get the town to rank one a lot faster than we could otherwise."

"Rank one?" This was the first Joe had heard about town rankings.

Mike nodded and started to explain, "We get certain bonuses as a guild for having a town under our control. While we own the land around us, we can't do too much to make use of it. Ranking up helps with that and allows us to petition for new and better building blueprints from the Kingdom's Architect and Carpenter Guilds. No point in having a granary if we don't have grain fields, right? No point in a sewer system without points of collection like buildings or restrooms. We are stuck with latrines and such, which lowers morale over time."

"I see."

"Listen. We can't do too much, but... how about this." Mike took a deep breath. "I know that you don't want to run a guild, but the amount of work you've already done to help us to this point has not gone unnoticed. If you can help us get to town level five, forgoing other rewards, we'll give you a new position."

"I'm listening..."

"At level five, we will have the option to choose which direction our guild grows. We decided that at that point, we will upgrade our guild into a Sect. This will change around the structure—a *lot*—and open up a new position. There will be ten spots for a 'Guild Elder'. You get a say in the direction the guild grows if you want it, more pay, direct sponsorship of projects from the guild, and straight up a ton of respect. You will also be able to add or remove people from our guild—Sect at that point—so long as another Elder doesn't contest the choice."

"Interesting," Joe muttered, thinking on the decision. "Better me than someone I don't trust, and this would go a long way to clearing the air from when I quit the guild. Alright, Mike. Deal. I can't do this all day every day, so make a choice about which buildings you need, and I'll try to do one a day."

"Deal."

CHAPTER TWENTY-EIGHT

Guild Quest accepted: The making of an Elder. You have agreed to forgo short-term rewards in order to gain a long-term position. Help the guild by building enough buildings that the town can reach town level five. Current town level: 0/5. Reward: position of an Elder when the Noble Wanderer's Guild becomes a Sect. Failure: No reward.

Joe looked over the quest again as he got out of bed. He was glad that he had made the deal, but he was still somewhat leery of agreeing to work now for a *possible* reward later. It was like an artist being asked to work for 'exposure'. People *die* of exposure! Still, the reward was contained in a quest, so they would need to cough up the position when it was available. Otherwise, who knew what could happen? Bleh. It felt like a Monday when he had a regular job. He woke up with a bunch of time-restricted tasks that he needed to get done or lose a bunch of potential forward or upward momentum.

Shuddering at the parallel he was drawing, Joe got up and got in line for coffee. He was once again greeted as 'Elbow', and it took a lot of effort *not* to drop a shadow-formed anvil on the barista's head like a cartoon character. As he was eating his meager breakfast and drinking his cooling coffee, Jess walked over to him with a handful of people trailing behind her. "Hey, Joe! Got some hopefuls for you. These guys want to create those area-of-effect spells you make."

"Thanks, Jess!" Joe gestured at the table. "Sit down all. Let's talk. I want to know why you want to join up, we will talk about expectations, and then we'll go do a trial run."

He finished his coffee as the others spoke and had soon narrowed what he considered to be the *actual* candidates to three participants. As far as he could tell, everyone else wanted either to unlock their mana or to use his questionable fame to get ahead in the guild. Joe could understand the first, but the second was just confusing. He wasn't concerned, as people who were just trying to get ahead were going to get scared off *real* quick during this next part.

"Let's get to it, then!" Joe stood, and the others joined him as he walked. "Listen, if you think you really want this, great, but we are going to see if you *actually* want it *right now*. We're going to go build a building, and we shall see if you stick around. Also, I gotta tell you, mana unlocks automatically for everyone at level ten. If you can't stand pain, you might just want to wait until then to get it. Doing it this way is effective, but... yup."

No one left, and in fact, they had gained a person. Didn't bother Joe at all, but he *did* wonder what the new guy thought was going on. They met up with Mike and were directed to a pile of resources. Joe had stayed awake late into the morning to convert the blueprint he was given into a ritual, and it was time to make it happen. He only needed to add in a few more details. Joe cheerfully pulled out his survey grid and tinkered with it for a few moments. After a few false starts, he managed to create the grid over the area the storage building was scheduled to be built.

"Neat." Joe looked at the soft light that created a box over the area. "Is this in the correct spot?"

Mike had an administrative person run over and check the boundaries, and Joe had to make some small adjustments. When the spot was approved, Joe touched the wand-like Survey Grid to his ritual diagram, and the positional information was automatically added. Then the laser grid shifted from a box into a translucent blue outline of what the building would look like when finished. Mike grinned at the Rituarchitect, throwing his hands into the air. "Fine! I admit it! That's super cool! What is this, some kind of illusion magic?"

"Probably?" Joe started collecting blood from the people who wanted to participate, giving hard looks at the ones who seemed squeamish. "Look, guys. This is the *easiest* part of doing what I do. You haven't had to create, troubleshoot, or design any of this. If this is too much to ask, you can leave now with no hard feelings. You physically *can't* leave during the building process."

None of the eight left, so Joe shrugged and collected blood. "Mike, looks like I'll need you on this again. No idea what the mana pool is gonna look like for a few people here."

Mike paled and looked around wildly. "No, I'm just here to make sure–"

"Mike."

"Ugh, is this why Aten keeps sending *me* to do this?" Mike complained as his finger was pricked and a drop of blood landed in the silver chalice. "Because he knows he'll be used as a battery if he comes? I bet it is. Next time, *I'm* sending a proxy, too."

"I'm working on solving this issue," Joe breezily told Mike as he positioned the man on the southwest balanced position. "All set. Listen up, everyone! For those of you who are here to unlock mana, this'll work, but you'll still need to learn mana-based skills or spells. Those of you looking for a class, this is what it is like *every* time. It isn't easier as you rank up. Think on that. For anyone who came along for fun... please *do* come back."

Joe activated the ritual, and the ritual circle blazed to life. Energy flowed from the lines Joe had drawn on a chalkboard, encircling the group and lifting them into the air.

Then those same lines reached into each person, drawing at their innate mana supply to keep the ritual running. The components needed for the ritual crumbled into dust and were sucked away by the swirling vortex of power, and the construction materials began to move. In just over a minute, the storehouse was completed, and the group returned to the ground.

Three people were coated in vomit; two were unconscious. The other three were pale and sweating, staring at Joe with wide eyes as they collapsed to the ground. Joe himself had already gone to the ground, knowing before he started that he was going to be drained to the last drop a few times during the process. "And that, *ugh*, is why I need a few more people that can do this on a regular basis. I can't run these on my own anymore."

"How long have you been making these?" one of the people—a watery-eyed lady—questioned him sharply.

"Since I joined Eternium," Joe told her bluntly. "I've gained skills and such that make it easier to handle, at least physically, but I've died several times while either designing or activating these rituals."

"Why in the *world* would anyone take a class devoted to this sort of thing?" A man shuddered as he sat up, having recovered consciousness while they talked.

"Easy." Joe pointed at the completed building. "A day of designing and refining the ritual, one minute of total suck, ten minutes of recovery... and a permanent building. Not all rituals make permanent things like this one does, but there are a ton of *really* cool things that I can make and automate."

Over the next short while, people wandered away. It was expected, so Joe tried not to take it too personally. He just sat there and looked at his gain of a hundred class experience, wondering if that was the standard for Uncommon-ranked buildings. Probably. He *did* hope that he'd gain more for more *impressive* buildings. Joe stood up and looked around, surprised to see that there were four people still standing with him. "Hello...? Are you guys wanting to...?"

"I want in," the watery-eyed lady told him. The other three agreed, the third being the straggler they had picked up on the way over.

Joe looked at that guy, and he shrugged. "I got a basic Warrior Mage class, but I couldn't afford to take the classes. Even with the discount, I'm still broke. This seems like a viable way to move up, and I hear that you'll be paying to do this in the future? I can take the pain of mana drain, and every other door seems to be closed to me until I make money. I'll go to an entry-level position, at least I'll *have* a job."

"Fair enough." Joe looked at the others, hope blooming in his chest. Starting with four people was four more than he had expected to have. "Just so you all know, making progress in this class is both difficult and expensive. Both in terms of time and money. I'll pay you for all the help you give me, yes, but your personal projects are on your own."

There wasn't any argument from the others, so Joe simply smiled. "Excellent. Well, I am the *only* class trainer for the Ritualist class, so come with me, and we'll get started."

Achievement earned: Start a Coven. You have become the leader of a group of magic users, convinced them to follow you, and are the only class trainer. Nice work! Are they there because you convinced them or because there are no other options? Does it matter? Charisma +5! (1+1 per initial Coven member). +5 to skill: Speech.

Skill increase: Speech (Novice VIII). Explaining the downfalls truthfully and still having people follow you is the best way to use this skill. Don't follow the route of politicians in the past, and this skill will have you commanding the masses in no time!

Joe felt his body shifting in minor ways. He blinked as he read over the notification; that was the largest single gain to just charisma that he had gained... ever. It was also nice to see his neglected Speech skill getting some love. Joe walked with the others to the Pathfinder's Hall and brought them into a secluded section. He touched the wall and connected to the various options. He opened the Ritualist class to these four people and watched as they *accepted* the class.

Their eyes bugged out as they went over the benefits, and they looked at Joe for confirmation of what they were seeing. "Yes, there are great benefits. Don't share that with other people because this is a class that most people *aren't* going to get. You four showed something special today. Going forward, people are going to really need to *work*—and work *hard*—to be considered for this. Consider this a hidden class, because it *is*. Let this be your advantage, and..."

Joe confirmed something and looked at the others with hard eyes. "Just so you know, I *can* remove this class at any time. I won't ever use that ability without needing to do so, but don't think I'll let you get away with doing terrible things. Now. With that said, if you'd like to come see what I am working on, get access to a few rituals, or just see the secret of this building... come with me. I have an enchantment to work on."

CHAPTER TWENTY-NINE

It had been four *long* days, and Joe was still in the process of working out the kinks in the Mana Battery enchantment, but the quality of his work area had increased tremendously. There were other people around, and all of them had unique ideas and plans for what they wanted to get done. Joe had offered his cleaned-up copy of 'Rituals for Dummies' as a training guide, promising to let them see his other books when they were ready. That was the first time he actually felt like a class trainer—denying higher-leveled abilities until someone was 'ready' for them.

Joe was currently staring at the workable version of the Mana Battery. There were still issues, but it would work. He might lose out on some of the potential power that could be stored, but he was nearly out of time. Not to mention, he needed to get this into ritual form. He completed the diagram, watching as the papers shuddered slightly. There was no mana in there, and this wasn't something someone could just read and learn like a scroll, but still, the papers struggled to contain the magical truths contained on them. A spell—or in this case, *enchantment*—diagram was still a rewriting of reality on a small scale.

Item created: Leaflet of Enchanting (Mana Battery). This leaflet contains step-by-step instructions for turning a Core into a Mana Battery. This process has not yet been perfected, leading to a loss of potential mana. By inscribing this diagram on to a Core, you will be able to store (4*potential Core experience) mana into the new, rechargeable, Battery.

Skill increase: Spellbinding (Apprentice II). Wrangling the universe and convincing it to stay on paper is always an impressive feat!

Skill increase: Words of Power (Written) (Apprentice 0).
Not all powerful words are scrolls, but they all help to make
them! Congratulations! You have reached the Apprentice ranks
for this skill! You are less likely to set yourself on fire! Not from a
boost, just because you are getting better at dodging your
mistakes!

Skill increase: Ritual Magic (Expert 0). Your ability to
create, maintain, and change rituals much more efficiently has
reached the ranks of an Expert! You are now able to create
Expert-Ranked rituals without too much fear of them exploding!
Congratulations! You have maximized the amount that you can
reduce the mana and component cost! Current bonus: 75%
reduction. (25% from Ritual Magic + 50% from class bonus!)

"Hold up... did that rank up just take away all the extra
benefits of increasing my skill level?" Joe was about to grumble
more when information on Expert-ranked rituals began
appearing in his mind. He knew they were just the fundamentals
of the Expert ranks, but it was fair to say that these rituals were...
on another level. "Hee. I'm freaking hilarious."

"This... hmm." Joe looked at the leaflet and waffled on
the next step. He desperately wanted to perfect the enchantment,
but he was on a dangerous time limit. After promising himself
that he would eventually make it happen, he moved on to
creating a ritual for this same process. The new Ritualists would
come in every once in a while to watch as he made careful
adjustments, but they all eventually left. During a break, the man
that had joined because it was his best option asked Joe what he
was doing.

"First off, Taka, right? Great. I am taking a spell and
turning it into a ritual." Joe watched as Taka looked over Joe's
hodgepodge of work with a frown. "What was your class before
this again?"

"Takacomic. Yes, please call me Taka. I was a Warrior Mage cross classer trying to create a Magic Gunslinger class. I like guns, and I kinda miss them here." Taka told him after a moment, "That ritual looks like my old programs written in C. But... it's strange."

"Yup. Turns out the universe is actually cobbled together with Python." Joe and Taka chuckled at the reference, and Joe's eyes shone as he realized that his new... Coven member? He'd need to give them a designation soon. Anyway, *Taka* seemed to understand programming, which had been a hobby that Joe had considered turning into a job back on earth. "I think you are going to like this class, Taka."

"Good. I get distracted pretty easy, but all this stuff is so intricate that I can just *stare* at it, ya know?"

Joe got back to it, not needing to leave since he now had minions that he could send out for food and coffee. They even got quests from him when he asked for it, gaining minor amounts of experience and money that came out of his bank account. Nifty. Another day passed before Joe put the final touches on his ritual, and he looked unhappily at the final result.

Ritual created: Ritual of Enchanting (Mana Battery) (Expert). This ritual creates a mana battery at half the efficiency of creating the enchantment directly. In return, after activation, the ritual no longer needs mana input, becoming self-sustaining. Simply place a Core into the ritual, and it will be converted in [potential experience] seconds. Components needed for ritual activation...

Joe stopped reading, rubbing at his tired eyes. It made *sense*, he supposed. If he could easily replace Enchanters, the class would become useless. "Grr. This means that a low-grade Core will only give me a thousand mana to use. Not only that, but... this ritual is Expert-ranked. I *am* an expert, but this is still going to be on the edge of what I can create."

"Got used to talking to yourself while working?" Taka kindly asked, making Joe flinch away and reflexively cast Cleanse on the man. As Taka sputtered, Joe blinked at him and looked around. The room had everyone working in it. That is, all the new Coven members.

"Yeesh. I think I need to boost my perception." Joe looked at a soaked Taka. "Sorry about that, but it's a lot like a shower... if that helps."

"Right, whatever. What's the big deal about Expert-ranked rituals?" Taka asked as he wiped off his face.

"I'll show you." Joe sent his intent into the room, and the floor began to lift until there were four rings clearly showing. The fourth, on the outer edge, was only seven feet in diameter. "This is the basic setup of an Expert ritual, four rings that turn in alternating directions. Both sides of the rings, top and bottom, need to have the proper diagram. The rings, while turning, will lift into the air and move like a gyroscope. There will be a massive input of mana required, and if I get it wrong at the start, the entire thing will explode like a thermite bomb. If it gets all the way to activation and *then* something goes wrong, we could wipe out the entire town."

Silence swept over the area, and Joe was glad to see them all taking his words seriously. "We are playing with mana concentrations that the College sees as weapons. That's *before* the effect we are after is in place."

"*Celestial Feces*," one of the others whispered.

"I just don't know how I'm going to make this ritual in only a few days," Joe fretfully muttered.

"You control this room, right?" Taka looked at Joe sidelong. "Can't you make it on those rings?"

"*Yes*, but again. One mistake? Boom." Joe wiggled his hands to mimic an explosion, and another of his new Coven members spoke up.

"Right, right, but why not make two sets of the rings and emboss the top of one and the bottom of the other in the pattern you need? Then pour molten metal or something over it and press them together? Use the room to make a mold, then take your new rings out somewhere else and activate the ritual?" The watery-eyed woman really liked to talk with her hands, but right now, Joe didn't care even a little; in fact, he might have kissed her if she wasn't across the room.

"That's *brilliant.*" Joe started making preparations right away, and in his mind, he even had a plan for how he was going to do it. It remained to be seen if he *could*, but... "Alright! I'm heading out, I'll be back as soon as I can!"

Joe ran up to the temple and teleported to Ardania. He appeared on *top* of someone, and even with the sudden added weight, they didn't stumble. That was how dense the press of people were. Joe looked around and realized that he was crowd surfing along with hundreds of other people. It seemed like the overpopulation issues were getting worse, *far worse*, instead of better. At least this way people would *live*, he supposed. He felt bad doing it, but he stood up and started hopping from person to person as a method for crossing to the merchant area.

By the time he got there, Joe was exhausted and getting sick of the rancid smell of unwashed bodies. Sometimes literally; he had seen several corpses in the crowd, people that had died either by being crushed in the press or attacked by someone else, and it had made him both ill and glad for his Exquisite Shell. As he got close to 'Masterwork Metals', his face became grim. It seemed that people had finally stopped caring if the area was well-guarded or not, this place was stuffed as well. Joe pushed his way to the door of the shop and got in, closing the heavy wood before people started getting shoved in.

"Customers *only!*" the smith bellowed as the door slammed shut. Joe looked down and noticed blood on the floor. *Fresh* blood. Apparently, people had been testing the area for greater elbow room.

"Hey there! Remember me? Please?" Joe's smile was strained, but the smith put down the huge hammer he had been readying. "I need to buy several buckets of molten metal to pour into molded stone. Is that something that you can make happen?"

The Smith grunted and looked Joe up and down. "I hope you aren't planning to pour it on some *one*. Nasty way to go, that. What sort of item are you making? How resilient do you need the metal to be? Is it going to be used to channel magic at all?"

"Making components for a magic spell," Joe confessed without worrying about the smith's reaction. "Big disks of metal. Expert-ranked item."

"Huh." The smith pulled out a booklet. "Far as I know, anything channeling lots of mana needs Rare-ranked material in order to hold up at all. In bulk... liquid form... I can get you High Steel at fifty gold per ingot. About five ingots to a bucket crucible, in case you are wondering. How much will you need?"

Joe did the math for the area and thickness he needed and was told that he would need three buckets at a minimum. Joe got three buckets and one ingot extra just in case but first had the smith melt an iron ingot to liquid. Joe thrust his hips at the bucket crucible, making the smith sputter as a *sensitive* area almost touched the molten metal. Then the crucible vanished, and Joe waited until the smith said it *should* be cool enough to touch. Joe then made the liquid come out of his codpiece, appearing at the tip of his finger as a red-hot stream.

"Excellent, it stays molten for at least long enough that I should be able to put it to use." Joe gave the smith eight hundred gold worth of bank notes, wincing as he paid the equivalent of eight thousand dollars for three buckets full of metal. He *really* hoped this would work the way he had hypothesized. After another awkward and painful—for them—crowd hopping experience, he was back at the Pathfinder's Hall.

Following his notes, Joe created the details of the first—*smallest*—ring. Ensuring that the details were correct when translating from notes to physical object was always a crapshoot. He measured everything twice, but since it was no longer a *written* thing, instead of being an *item*, well... his skill to see a written object's 'correctness' didn't work anymore. He directed a thin stream of high steel over the ring, and as soon as it appeared even, he used his will to press the top ring down into the bottom. He kept the ring pressed down for fifteen minutes, unsure how long it would take to cool enough to remain stable.

After the time he allotted for it, he had portions of the room retract. What was left was a disk of still-hot High Steel. Joe inspected every inch of the inlay before he was satisfied, but when he was done... all he could do was smile. "Looks like we have a new way to create permanent ritual circles."

The cost was prohibitive, but... if this worked as he needed it to, it would be worth every copper.

CHAPTER THIRTY

"Tell me again why we are going back to the salt mines?" Poppy looked around at the *much* lower level people coming along and raised an eyebrow. "Also, why are *they* coming? Who are these people?"

"They're coming along to help us with the ritual that I need to complete. The one that will let me have enough raw mana that we can potentially complete that timed quest we have?" Joe was in a foul mood; he had been running himself ragged to make this happen in time, and Poppy had been complaining since he joined them because he had a hangover Joe was refusing to cure for him. "Unless you want to help power the ritual instead of them?"

"No, I'm just not sure you need a full party in a *cleared* area," Poppy grumbled a little more, but Joe just ignored him in favor of walking a little faster. "*Why* the salt mines?"

"Alright, new Coven members!" Joe spread a smile on his face with the ease of putting warm butter on toast. That charisma boost had really helped him hide his actual emotions, which he thought was a strange function. "We are almost in the testing location, and I want to let you know ahead of time that if we die, I'll make it up to you."

"Question!" Taka raised a hand. "Why the salt mines?"

"Good question, Taka!" Joe responded brightly. Poppy drew the first inch of his rapier at Joe's gleeful reply. "I remember a history lesson where salt mines were used as nuclear testing facilities, and I'm hoping that if this goes wrong, I'll be able to contain everything. Also, the guild hasn't been able to start mining here, so there is little chance of someone getting hurt or accidentally stumbling on to us."

The rest of the walk was completed in quiet concentration, and they reached the bottom of the salt mines within another fifteen minutes. Joe pulled out the rings, placing them in order and ensuring that they were properly aligned. The higher the rank of the ritual was, the more intricate the details on each ring became. Starting positions were important as well, since the sympathetic links connected to a space, not another ring. When it was as perfect as Joe could make it, he stepped out and started getting everyone into position.

"Now, here's the thing." Joe took a deep breath. "We should have a lot more people for this. A *lot* more, and more highly trained and skilled. We should be able to get away with this for *only* this ritual since we only need to supply mana to a certain point. Then the Core being converted should begin supplying the remaining mana. If it doesn't, we are going to die for sure. Let me explain something: novice rituals have a base cost of about two thousand mana. A good rule of thumb is that this increases by double for each rank."

"Of course, that is without *any* additional things added, creating only one, single, very *specific* function. That should tell you that as an Expert-ranked ritual, this has a base cost of two thousand doubled six times. Also known as *one hundred twenty-eight thousand* mana." Joe's words made the others blanch, and a few even looked around for an exit. "Hold on. There is more. My bonuses bring down mana cost by eighty-five percent and component cost by seventy-five percent, dropping the cost to nineteen thousand two hundred. My bonus spell stability brings the mana cost down even further, by fifty-five percent."

"So, the final mana cost is eight thousand six hundred and forty." The group was breathing easier at this point, and Joe's lips quirked up at the rapid changes. "Still, it is more than I can handle on my own, by far, but the five of us Coven members should be able to do it and maintain a nice, balanced positioning as well. Now, as far as I know, the ritual is still treated as having the original amount needed. I hope this explains why we are away from other people."

"Hey, I just got the skill Ritual Lore!" Taka announced, followed by the others—including Joe's actual party members— saying the same.

"Neat! I had to study rituals for a week to get that!" Joe motioned for everyone to get into position while he was setting out the components. He had two low-grade Cores for testing and one higher-grade for usage. He didn't know the actual names or rarity, as he had no way to appraise them. When everything was ready, he placed a low-grade Core in the center of the ritual, nodded, and took a deep breath. "*Formam mutatio!*"

A feeling like a static discharge *almost* made him stumble. Blue lightning arched from him to the Core, then out to each of the others taking part in the ritual. If the shock hadn't locked their muscles, there would have been people out of position right away. The first ring—which had the Core placed in the empty space at the center—lifted into the air. The Core lifted as well, even though nothing was touching it. Then the second ring began to move, then all of them.

As this was the first time Joe had done this ritual, he had no idea what to expect. Would there be odd flying like with the Pathfinder's Hall? No movement like Novice rituals? His question was answered as more lightning struck, somehow forcing the group to their knees instead of locking them in place. Then the ring slid out from under them. Joe almost panicked, but the ritual was continuing. This... was a part of the activation? Mana flooded out of him, and soon, his pool of nine hundred and fifty was approaching empty. He was okay with that, as his mana regenerated at about twenty-eight per second, and he could regen his entire mana pool in thirty-five seconds.

He was given twenty before the pull started on him again, and still, he didn't worry. If Joe *needed* to do so, between shocks, he would drink one of the three mana potions he had been able to 'requisition' from the guild for this project. By the time the draw switched away from him again, he had already contributed over sixteen hundred mana, a full quarter of what was needed. Joe gasped as his mana poured out of him. Unlike previous large draining situations, there was only exhaustion: no pain. Why was this different?

Then he remembered that his mana had suffused his body, no longer contained strictly in his center. Was that the secret? He didn't need to draw mana into his channels; they were *always* channeling? Interesting. The draw switched to him again, faster this time, and he realized that everyone else was only regening a tiny amount at once now. Lightning hit all of them at once, and the ritual did something Joe had never seen before. It started taking mana from all of them at once, not giving them a chance to individually regen. Uh-oh.

Two people went unconscious a few seconds later, then Taka, then... the ritual empowering completed. Joe stood a moment later, staring at the ankle-height, hovering rings. He watched as the other members either stood or *woke up* and stood. "Excellent, everyone. That didn't go exactly as expected, but as far as I know... not a single ritual works the same way as another. Even among some of the same type, well, I've seen lots of variance."

"So that's it? A light show, hovering disks, and knocking us out?" One them gestured at the rings in disgust.

Joe really needed to learn their names so that he could react more dramatically. "Not at all... Sport. I was simply waiting for everyone to wake up so I could do... this!"

You have created a ritual...

Joe skipped the text and mentally slapped 'yes' to get the ball rolling. The disks started to spin, slowly at first, then faster and faster. Then they moved higher and began to rotate on their axis. Soon, the accumulated mana of the Coven began to leech out of the dully-glowing rings and into the shining Core at the center of the ritual. The rings moved faster until it was like watching a flashlight through a fan. Wind was blowing away from the rings as they acted like fan blades, and Joe stood there with his robes fluttering. He lifted his arms, *really* feeling like he was a powerful mage at that moment.

Clang. After eight and a third minutes—or five hundred seconds—movement stopped in an instant. Even though there was nothing that the rings hit, the metal stopping created enough stress that they resounded like clashing swords. The High Steel that the rings were made of was *hot*, enough that they had been blowing superheated air. Joe was glad that the smith had told him he needed a certain quality of metal to channel mana, and he wondered how magical inks and paper managed to contain what they did if this was the result of *metal* creating the ritual.

When the rings were back to hovering at ankle height, Joe wrapped a ball of shadow around the Core at the center of the rings and pulled it to himself.

You have created an item! Mana Battery (Artificially Rare, actual Uncommon). This enchanted Core has been altered to contain and release mana! With the methods used to create it, this Core can hold up to 1,000 mana! It can be charged by either holding or wearing it. It can take mana directly, or you can set your mana regen to pour into the Battery. Stores mana at a rate of 10:1. Current charge: 0/1,000.

"That's a lot of odd information..." Joe poured a hundred mana into the battery, feeling disgruntled as the charge ticked up to '10/1,000'. "Ten mana only makes one mana stored? Ugh. At least I don't need to do it actively..."

Joe walked around to the Coven members and handed them each five gold. It didn't feel like much to him, but Jess had informed him that most quests paid *copper*. Not only that, but he, as a *highly ranked* guild officer in a *Noble* Guild, only brought in ten gold a day as salary. The Coven member's eyes lit up, and Joe realized that Jess was worth her weight in the gold he didn't need to pay out. He had no idea what was average at this point; his sense of scale totally blown out of the water.

Payment complete, Joe walked over to the cooled rings and looked over them. There weren't any signs of cracking or melting, but Joe wasn't foolish enough to think that was impossible. It was likely that this ritual had a usage limit, and he certainly didn't want to go overboard with greed. Still, he needed to convert the other Cores. He put the higher-rarity Core into the center, which had a potential experience load of fifteen hundred experience.

Joe had decided to use this Core next instead of the other small one, just to make sure that he had the best chance of keeping the rings usable. The conversion of this Core would take fifteen hundred seconds, or twenty-five minutes. Joe knew that moving parts had a high need for replacement, and... he stopped himself from getting too worried. Circular logic? Bad!

The rings lifted again and started to spin, and Joe watched them with pure excitement. Soon, they would be out a' quest-ing.

CHAPTER THIRTY-ONE

"Are we all ready to go?" Joe looked around, wondering how different everyone was in only a week. Did they have storage devices that they were bringing their gear with? Did their skills improve? Joe himself had been forgetting to go out and do his characteristic training. He thought of it as going to the gym, something he *should* do, but he kept finding other things to do. Oops.

"Let's do it!" Jaxon fist-pumped the air, and they started walking to the temple area of the Pathfinder's Hall.

"Joe?" A runner caught up to them as they were walking to the temple. The others groaned as Joe stopped to listen. "Lord Mike is requesting that you bring up another building before you go."

"He actually sent a proxy?" Joe chuckled and apologized to the others. "Where are we going? What is the building?"

"Another barracks, as far as I can tell." The runner wiped the sweat off his face and walked with Joe. "Mike gave me some information that he thought you would ask for."

"How high is his charisma? How predictable am I?" Joe muttered aloud.

"Ah... he didn't give me *that* information," the runner continued. "Lord Mike told me that it is going opposite to the first barracks, on the other side of the guildhall. There will be two more that go up, to put one in each cardinal direction. Then a wall around all that to create not only housing but a final fallback point if needed."

"Hmm. He really has me pegged." Joe could only shake his head. "Listen, can you go find Taka and... um... yeah... they are hanging out at the tavern right now. Were supposed to be off, but tell them I need a hand."

The runner ran off, and Joe walked to the guildhall, standing next to a pile of wood and nails. He used his grid to get the correct positioning and just finished everything up when his Coven members showed up. "Hey all, this should only take a minute or so. Sorry to bother you."

"All good," came the reply from the proven-to-be-resilient lady that had joined on.

"One more time, before we do this, can I get all your names? I'm *terrible* with names. Then tell me a little about yourselves," Joe admitted with a light blush. He got the stink eye, but they responded.

"Taka. We talked."

"Kirby," the lady told him. "I plan to be an evil overlord, but every time I try to be evil, it ends up helping a lot of people. Abyss, even my foreboding and clearly *evil* laugh! Instead of striking fear in the hearts of those unfortunate enough to cross my path, it *buffs* them! I'm getting frustrated, so I joined this group to see what I could do."

Joe stared at her for a moment, drawing out his words as he spoke, "R~r~right."

A man standing about six inches taller than Joe said, "Big_Mo. Also known as William. I'm a thief class and was looking to respec into Alchemist when I found you all. If I ever get a chance at race change, I want to be a Dark Elf. Drow. Whatever it's called."

"Hannah." Joe did a double take; brown robes were *really* unflattering. Good thing he had asked.

"Robert. I'm a ranger, but I got a fractured class. I'm actually a necromancer now, but I can only summon a single skeleton. Luckily, our new class absorbed both of those, and now, I can switch between them at will. It was an issue for a while."

"Can I call you 'Bob'?" Joe asked the last.

"No. I hate how many people are called Bob. *Bob* is everywhere. I'm *Robert*." He crossed his arms, and Joe decided not to push.

"Great." Joe got them into position, and just under a minute later, a barracks was fully built, complete with shingles. The others got an 'I owe you, so go bug Jess', as Joe wasn't carrying any money. When they all split ways, he rejoined his party at the temple. A moment later, they were a half-day walk from the forest of Chlorophyll Chaos.

Luckily, they had planned well, and even though they had a small interruption in the form of Joe having to help create a structure, they arrived at the forest by midafternoon. Joe put on the watch, the beacon, and crossed the border of the forest. It was instantly obvious that the device was functional; the territory beyond was familiar. A Wolfman Scout carefully came into view, not wanting to be attacked by the jumpy humans.

"You return. I lose bet." The Scout motioned for them to follow, and they walked through the deadly forest with relative ease. They paused at one point when a half dozen Imps flew through a clearing just ahead of them. They seemed to be *going* somewhere, not patrolling, and Joe really wondered what was different this week.

A short time later, the glowing walls of the quest area came into view. Joe looked at the Scout askance, but the wolfish features were uncaring. "Orders from The O'Baba. You no see our home unless quest completion. Listen. Cultists do one more fight, then next is two-hour mark, scouring area. Use brain."

The Scout pointed at a tree with a reddish mark on it, then went over and climbed into the safety of the canopy. This would be their exit if they needed it. Good to know. Joe looked at his team. "Are we all set with our plan?"

"I did what I was supposed to do," Alexis stated, and the others nodded as well. Joe carefully handed Jaxon a taglock with an assigned 'Gravedigger's Requiem' ritual created on it to be used as a last resort if things went poorly. Joe only had a containment ritual assigned to the taglock on his staff and was really feeling the pinch of not doing more research on combat rituals. Ah well.

"Okay, then. As soon as this round of combat ends, we'll get in place. Great timing, actually." Joe's team got into place in a tree just as humming started to reach their ears. As one, even though the party started to hum along, they stuffed their ears with earplugs. The world was muffled, and the humming stopped coming from Joe's team. He was pretty sure. He *did* have earplugs in.

The walls of the building flashed, and Joe felt a rumble in his chest as something nearby roared. A new creature charged out of the forest, some kind of three-limbed gorilla. It had a sunflower growing out of its head, but that was all the information Joe could glean. Alexis tapped his arm and waved at the formation of humans, then held up nine fingers.

Did that mean that the average level of people down there was *nine* now? Joe thought about it, and it *did* make sense. Still, that meant that they were going to have a harder time than they originally thought. The gorilla thing hit the ranks at that point, and they hit back. Still, they held no weapons, and the majority of them were slaughtered. It seemed that, similar to the Rosebeast, the flower was this creature's weak point. A few humans were able to climb up and beat on the sunflower as their people fell like rain around them.

Falling to the ground, the gorilla joined the fallen after seven and a half minutes of combat. There was only one survivor, a human who had his arms torn off just before the creature fell. He leveled, and leveled... too bad leveling didn't restore health. The door swung open, and a bolt of green fire raced out and blew off the man's head. Effective. *Cruel* but effective. The man would be back, but this *did* allow his pain to end.

As the door shut, Joe jumped from his position on the tree and ran toward the building. He first zipped over to the gorilla and dipped his hand in an open wound, then raced toward the door. He had planned to use his own blood, but this would be *much* more dangerous. The moment of truth approached: there were no windows on this side of the building, but would there be a way for the people inside to detect him?

Joe stopped before getting too close, pulling out a prepared Predator's Territory ritual, rubbing the gorilla blood on it, and officially starting their plan. This ritual had been altered slightly, boosting the range of the 'predator claims this spot' feeling to the maximum. He was nervous about this process, and using this blood *might* be overkill. The gorilla had been level twenty-one according to the info he got while activating the ritual, which meant that anything that came to challenge this area would be at least level *forty-two*.

Since O'Baba had mentioned that the center of the forest required a minimum of level thirty people to raid it, he assumed that there would be *something* that would react to this. Would it bother to show up? That was the real question.

The door to the building didn't open, and his head remained attached to his body, so Joe turned and ran. He got back to the tree, and the entire group retreated. Things were going to get hairy here one way or another. The Scout wasn't sure what they wanted, but Jaxon told him that they wanted to be away during the scouring; *that* he could understand.

They moved away for another five minutes before stopping. The Scout pulled out a rope and handed one end to Bard. Then the Wolfman climbed the huge tree and looped the rope on the lowest branch, fifteen feet above the ground. They clambered up and hid as well as possible. From here they could still see the flashing walls, and they settled in to wait. A short while later, they heard something even through their earplugs. *Humming.*

Joe could see a line of the cultists walking through the forest, and it seemed that the area they passed turned a slight shade of green. Not *forest* green, but radioactive green. He had no idea how they were doing that or what it could mean. Where was the humming coming from? It sounded close, and it was deep. Joe looked at his people, but they weren't showing any signs, and earplugs were in... he whipped his head around to see the Scout starting to stand on the branch. Green sparks were flickering around his eyes, and he took a step toward the line, falling right out of the tree.

The nearest cultists converged on the fallen Wolfman, smiling as they got closer. The Scout was alternating between humming and whimpering, unable to stand with his broken body. If he had been thinking, there would be no way such a fall would hurt him. Too bad he had basically belly flopped. Cultists were now surrounding the Scout, and one started to reach for him with a green-fire-coated hand. Just as he was about to do... *something*, all of the cultist's heads snapped to be facing the place of power they had come from.

Joe looked as well, but in that direction, the only thing he could see was a wall of dust. The cultists took off at a run, leaving the Scout behind and taking the odd glow with them.

Joe's team shimmied down the tree, removed their earplugs, and Joe inspected the Wolfman's eyes. He was *sure* he had seen green sparks, but right now, the eyes were only filled with pain. "I'm going to heal you, don't worry. Jaxon, align his bones."

Squee!

Joe stared at Jaxon. "What was that?"

"Nothing." Jaxon started gently but efficiently moving bones around. Joe followed along after him with healing spells, and in only a moment, the Wolfman was as good as new.

The Scout snarled as he shook off his wet fur. "You wish for thanks? I would not be here were it not for you!"

Joe watched the Scout stalk away and climb a new tree, this time using his rope to secure himself in place. The humans started jogging toward the battle near the structure, soon finding themselves witnessing a legendary clash. A treant, likely one of the bosses of the forest area—possibly even Trent the Treant, who had killed them—was slamming branches, vines, roots, and occasionally *other* trees on to the humans it was fighting. Hundreds of people had poured out of the cathedral, and to Joe, it seemed like there was no end to the wave of flesh battling the vegetation.

"That place had to be as packed full of people as Ardania is," Joe whispered to the others. There was no *need* to whisper; between the clashing of the treant and the now-chanting swarm of hundreds, Joe could almost not hear himself think. The plan was in motion, and they raced into the now-empty cathedral.

A bright green glow tinted everything they could see, and Joe was nervous at first. Then it vanished, and he realized that the glow had come from a spray of fire. Outside. Like lightning, the blaze had washed away all other color with the sheer amount of light it produced. He felt sweat break out on his face as the temperature of the air increased by at least ten degrees. "*Celestial Feces*, I'm glad that isn't us."

The building was different on the inside than Joe had expected. He had thought there would be an open room, perhaps pews or bleachers. Instead, the room sunk down to a bowl, then up into an almost Mayan temple, complete with the altar at the top for human sacrifice. They ran down, then started climbing the huge stone slabs that made up the stairs. Here Joe cheated. While the others climbed, he would *jump* to the next one, over and over until he needed to rest.

Getting to this point in the room took a solid five minutes for him, but the battle was still raging outside if the sounds, heat, and creeping dust were any indication. On the last three layers, Joe had to move carefully to ensure he didn't slip on the still-smiling bodies of people that had been sacrificed here. When he stood atop the altar, he noticed that there was a hole in the slab of stone. A quick glance into it left Joe shaken. Something down there was *moving*.

"*Not* a fan of horror movies." Joe held down his bile, placed his hand on the altar, and starting the process of capturing the building for his own deity. Instead of the place rippling and flowing like all the other times he had done something similar, here it almost seemed like the building was... fighting back. That was *also* the moment that the clashing outside paused, followed by one last *massive* crash. Then cheering... and the sound of many feet rushing toward the building. Uh oh.

CHAPTER THIRTY-TWO

The top slab of the building was covered in a gold and white glow, and all the bodies, blood, and ick that had been there had vanished. Actually, it seemed that the absorption of those bodies had sped up the process a small amount, which made Joe nervous. He had been warned before that Tatum could easily be pushed into the role of an 'evil' deity, and he certainly didn't want to be the cause of that. Was that what all the sacrifices were about? Boosting the range and power of this place?

Boom. The doors slammed open, and green-eyed, smiling people began flooding into the area. Joe called on his team to distract them as long as possible. "I need time!"

"We've got this, Joe!" Alexis fired an arrow at the entrance, hitting a barrel that Joe didn't remember seeing. With a *whamp*, the barrel detonated and the contents turned into a thick smoke. Any bodies that emerged from the smoke were just that: bodies. "Found a way to turn the venom from Sheila the scorpion into an aerosol. Painful way to die, but at least they're still smiling."

Bard swallowed hard and showed a shaky smile. By now, the top three slabs were golden, but Joe was running low on mana. He pulled out the smallest of the Batteries he had made and placed it on the altar.

Would you like to use this as a source of mana to convert the altar? There is a 50% chance of the battery being destroyed in the process. Yes / No.

"Yes, even though that is just *typical*." Joe snarled. Instantly he felt relief as the mana drain switched over to the Battery. He had spent time to fill all three, and to his delight, the largest one had only taken about seventeen minutes of his mana regen to fully charge. The mana drain didn't seem to go any faster, but now, all the bodies and blood had been converted as well... meaning that the process was slowing.

As the first Battery drained to empty, Joe used his personal mana until it ran out, then placed another battery down. A green fireball flashed into the entrance, and the resulting explosion and shockwave nearly destroyed Joe's position. He would have gone flying but was instead slammed into the altar hard enough to see a large dip in his Exquisite Shell. "*Guys!*"

"We're alive, Joe!" Bard bellowed up at him. "Thar' gettin' in, though!"

Murder could be seen on the faces of the cultists. Behind the smiles, beyond the chanting... rage. Pure, unadulterated *hatred.* If they had been able to bring ranged weapons to bear, Joe knew things would have gotten grizzly in a hurry. Luckily, they were still only humans, unarmed and unarmored humans at that. Still, Joe had seen what they could do as a swarm. "Be careful, everyone!"

"How about you *focus?*" Poppy called up, just as the first of the smiling humans pulled themselves on to his ledge. His rapier poked out in rapid thrusts, each strike a critical and deadly hit since the first part of each person to pop up was their head.

The humans were realizing that their attempts to scale where a person was standing were futile, so they began to swarm around and up the altar. Jaxon started to shine here, and for a long moment, everyone paused as the sound of a pair of triumphant T-rex heads showed their pleasure. Then sharp teeth met unprotected flesh, and everyone began moving once more.

Joe made a mental note to look into getting hands like that; he was sure he could if he tried hard enough.

Alexis was having a harder time as people closed in on her. Her bolts were deadly but took a long time to reload. She revealed a new trick as people tried to dog pile her, tossing down a canister that acted as a smoke grenade. There was an effect similar to what she had done at the door but on a much smaller scale. It seemed that this smoke wasn't instantly deadly, but nonetheless, the humans impacted by it started to collapse.

Bard was chanting his own song while swinging his axes, and Joe could practically *see* him gaining skill levels as his Counter Song allowed the group to resist the hypnotic reverb of the chanting people. Now the entire Mayan-style portion of the cathedral was glowing gold and white, and as the color touched the floor... it spread like spilled wine. Whatever had been resisting the conversion had been defeated, and now the conversion was going apace!

Joe coughed, sucking wind as his mana bottomed out. He slapped the last, largest Mana Battery on the altar and selected yes. "Three thousand more mana, hope that does it."

"*Enough* of this!" A glowing orb appeared before Bard, detonating and slamming the man into the wall behind him... also ending his Counter Song. Paul The Hierophant had joined the battle. "How *dare* you defile these sacred walls!"

"Your... maw has baws, and..." Alexis coughed out at the man as the last of her smoke cleared away.

Poppy interrupted her, "Let's let Bard use the Scottish insults. Hey! Feces face! How about you leave now before we turn you into the cheese of the Swiss!"

"That's Swiss cheese," Jaxon told the Duelist.

"I'm Italian. I don't care." Poppy pulled his rapier out of another face and pointed it at the Hierophant. "Bring it. I think we can take you on."

"There is *no* need for that." The Hierophant sighed indulgently. "Listen, I am just trying to ensure that humans have a place in the coming world! I've been working *so* hard to get as many converts as possible, and you come in here trying to take all of my hard work away? Why don't we just talk about this?"

Poppy swished his weapon and snarled, "You make a valid point! Why *don't* we discuss this? I... huh."

"Yeah! Let's hear this nice Hierophant out!" Jaxon called as his fists tore another chunk of meat out of a cultist.

"What are you guys *saying*?" Alexis seemed confused. "Of course we would hear what the Hierophant had to say! It's in his name! *Hear*-ophant."

"That was fast." Joe was crouched behind the altar, hoping that a fireball wouldn't find him. "Gonna need to boost that Counter Song, maybe have a backup in the future."

The conversion was still going, but only a third of the mana had been used by the Battery. This was the first time that Joe had ever hoped he could sink power into something *faster*. He intentionally had the altar drain him dry, giving as much as he could before letting the drain go back to the Battery.

"As for you, cleric, don't you think we should *chat*?" the Hierophant called. Joe felt the power in the words, likely *Words of Power: Spoken* or something similar boosting his other abilities. Joe didn't resist the compulsion to stand up. "Ah, there you are. Come, stand away from there. Let us *discuss*."

Joe found his feet moving and knew he *could* stop thanks to his Mental Manipulation Resistance skill, but he allowed himself to be 'controlled' so that he could get into a better position to resist when needed. The next words of the

Hierophant almost made Joe give himself away, though, "Look at that! A familiar face! Why would you be resisting this when it was *you* who opened the doorway, you who created the path for our Lord to be free? Speak."

"I don't understand." Joe was watching the Hierophant, doing his best not to look at the gold coloration that was still progressing. Either the other man didn't see it or didn't care; Joe wasn't going to risk calling attention to the fact.

"I'm *hurt*!" The Hierophant pulled a face. "We were in a party, deep in the bowels of prison together, were we not? You freed a spark of The Burning Mind and allowed me to capture it. I thank you, but I still cannot allow you to have this place. Come, we shall discuss more deeply, and soon, you will realize the error of your ways."

Joe took a step forward and realized with horror that he no longer had the option to resist. A smile was on his face, but screaming was in his mind. It seemed the Hierophant's ability to hypnotize became stronger over time—perhaps the longer you listened—and a fifteen percent resistance was no longer enough. The party started walking to the Hierophant, uncaring of the damage they took falling off the ledges. Joe took less damage thanks to his Jump skill, but his Exquisite Shell still broke by the last few falls, and he snapped his nose after reaching the ground.

"Hi there." The Hierophant had a beatific smile on his face, and he had somehow coated his hand in green fire. "Let's seal up my control, shall we? I want you to come back no matter *how* often you die!"

None of them had paid attention to the conversion happening at this point, but all the bodies that had fallen in the structure during sacrifice or combat had vanished. With a flash of light, the structure *shifted*. In the same moment, vibrancy fell away from the Hierophant as nearly a dozen buffs he had been steeped in failed at the same time.

Place of Power captured! Cathedral captured! A portion of all divine energy accumulated here has been shifted to your deity! All benefits granted by this area have been removed from others! Soak in the power and commune with your deity to gain stackable buffs!

Quest updated: Paying a Great Debt. You have taken control of a Cathedral that has had no official *deity to take the accumulated divine energy! This* particular *cathedral also sits upon a place of power, a nexus of interwoven ley lines. It generates triple the amount of energy as a standard Temple (Grand). Current debt paid: 1,014,700/13,000,000.*

"How? *How!*" the Hierophant shrieked, wild-eyed with fury. He looked around, seeing no one at the altar. Then he noticed an unnatural glow at the top of the deforming altar. "Some kind of power device? Is that a *thing* here?"

The green fire flared up on his hand, far less dense than before, and he reached toward Joe. "I can always re-convert this place, but you've cost me *weeks* of work! Better finish this quickly."

CHAPTER THIRTY-THREE

"*Ah don' like ye, ye don' like me! Let's keep our slop ta ourselves!*" The first chord of Bard's Counter Song gave Joe exactly the boost he needed in order to break the hypnotism. In a flash, the Rituarchitect twisted his staff to block the green-glowing hand. Then he *jumped* backward, pumping stamina into escaping.

Bard was standing on the collapsing altar, blood flowing freely from a wound on the back of his head. His song was as off-key as usual, but to Joe, it was the sweetest thing he had ever heard. Joe started calling out right away, "Alexis, obscure! Poppy, armpit! Jaxon! His spine is too straight!"

"Oh *no!*" Jaxon had both hands facing the Hierophant, and he was reaching forward with a dangerous glint in his eye. "Spines need *proper curvature!*"

Poppy's rapier was speeding toward the armpit that the Hierophant had left unguarded with his attempt at doing *something* to Joe, and Alexis slapped a vial on the ground from a quick access bandolier she wore as a belt. Oily smoke covered the area in an instant but vanished in a shockwave of green flame that exploded in a nova around the Hierophant.

"Do you think I am so *easily* brought low?" His words shook the air with power and fury. Everyone close to him, including the double handful of remaining cultists, were sent flying. Most of them were even on fire, so Joe sent out a wash of his group healing spell to give his stricken allies a boost. "I am the Hierophant of the Burning Mind! You are *worms!*"

Joe *jumped* to the side as the place he had been standing was incinerated by a continuous burst of flame. The Hierophant was seething, his eyes narrow. "It is too early, but you have forced this. Never forget that it was *your* actions that released Gameover upon Eternium!"

"What in the *abyss* is he on about?" Poppy called as he skewered a smiling cultist. There weren't too many left at this point, maybe a hundred, but they were the most highly-leveled of the cultists.

"Not a clue!" Alexis threw a vial in a high arc at the Hierophant, and as he reached up to swat it aside, she whipped another at him. The first broke as soon as it was touched, and the second shattered on the man. The gases that poured out of the two interacted, and somehow formed into a tight column that encompassed the Hierophant before sinking into him. "That'll give him something to write home about!"

As the cult leader got away from the strange creation, his skin started to welt. He sent two palm-shaped flames at her, one of them landing on her thigh and lighting her on fire. The sheer force of the impact caused an audible **snap** as her bone cleanly broke. Alexis dropped, and the Hierophant went to finish her but screamed and started furiously itching at his skin and coughing.

"*Ah*, geez, ow!" Alexis sucked in a breath and shouted at the others, "Nasty itching powder! His whole body is going to tear at his concentration, and he's gonna get interrupted during spell casting!"

Those words were her last for now, as a geyser of flame hot enough to cause the marble floor to bubble and pop sent her to respawn. The Hierophant sneered, "Not enough to keep *you* alive."

Humming began to increase in intensity as the remaining cultists tried to overpower the party, and Poppy was taken to the ground. He rolled back up and put a dagger in his off-hand to help deal with the large number of people charging him. Bard had joined the fight as well and was easily able to overcome the hypnotic tones now that their opponents were no longer being amplified by the building. He was using the cultists as cover, a very *weak* shield since the Hierophant had no trouble roasting his people to get at them.

Still, it slowed the attacks and made them inaccurate. This kept Bard alive, and he used his remaining time to the fullest. His axes were whipping back and forth, taking down an unarmored cultist with each swing. Joe hadn't been idle through this, and sprays of acid and Shadow Spikes were alternating from him every few seconds. Then every cultist stopped moving, simultaneously releasing a groan and dropping to the floor.

"What just happened?" Joe looked sharply to the Hierophant, who was staring at Jaxon with hatred.

"That. *hurt.*" The Hierophant backhanded Jaxon, the simple strike moving too fast for Joe to see. Somehow, Jaxon managed to dodge the majority of the blow, but his arm was torn off by the force the strike contained, and he was sent spinning across the room with blood flying away from his amputated limb. "I don't care about converting you anymore. You lost your chance."

Joe made the connection right then. The cultists falling, looking withered but still alive. The sudden physical boost of an obviously magical nature, on to a person Joe was *certain* was an actual human from earth. That meant... this was a *guild* or at least acted like one. The Hierophant was a guild leader, and he had just pulled all the stats from his people.

Even though Joe had realized this, it didn't matter. The Hierophant blurred across the room, stomping down on Jaxon and popping his head like a grape that had been squeezed too hard. Then he incinerated Poppy and the cultists surrounding him. In an instant, he was a hundred feet away and had grabbed and tossed Bard into the wall. "Better make sure he's gone this time."

Joe felt like he was moving in slow motion as the Hierophant was zipping around. Joe channeled Acid Spray, and the potent liquid destroyed the cultists on the floor with practically the first drop. No wonder why, their constitution had been reduced to 'one'. He jumped into the air as high as he could, swinging his staff in a wide arc. The Hierophant was coming after him now but was visibly slowing as the people he was draining stats from died. At this point, if there was a handful of living cultists remaining, Joe would have been shocked.

Now breathing heavily as he ran at Joe, the Hierophant sent a fireball upward at the falling man. There was little power behind it, comparatively, but the explosion still made Joe lose control and fall to the floor in a tangled, bleeding heap.

Health: 160/270. Might want to get a shield up!

The Hierophant tackled Joe as he tried to get to his feet, and Joe lost another ten health as his head bounced off the floor. The Hierophant was still far stronger than Joe, thanks to whatever boost he was still getting from living cultists. He pummeled Joe, his fists still covered in welts and now blood. "You think this has been *easy*? You think I'm just going to let you pop off to respawn somewhere and come back to hunt me again? You're *mine*, and you're going to be working for *me*!"

Joe was able to cast Mend on himself as the Hierophant monologued, and seeing Joe return to full health seemed to make his opponent fly into a rage. Flames sprouted on his fists as he concentrated, and Joe retaliated by ballooning his mana out into an Exquisite Shell. As a fist came down, Joe's protection solidified and flames cascaded around him.

The Hierophant obviously didn't like that; he screeched and started slapping Joe's face over and over. Each strike blocked Joe's vision as flames pooled around him and a palm was stopped mere centimeters from his face. Joe was struggling, trying to cast any spell he could, but the Hierophant grabbed his staff, ripping it from Joe's hands and tossing it to the side.

"This is the most boring battle I've ever been in!" Joe yelled at the Hierophant. "You can't hurt me, I can't hurt you, and we are rolling around on the ground like a couple kids having a fistfight!"

"I'd be happy to *talk it out.*" The hypnotic words bounced off Joe's Mental Manipulation Resistance, no longer being amplified by hundreds of people and a place of power. "Just *lower your shield,* and we'll become best friends!"

Through all of this, flaming flurries of fists were flashing in Joe's face. The Rituarchitect decided to mess with this jerk a little. "Yes... lower my *shields...*"

Hearing the words, the Hierophant paused in confusion. Joe took that chance to Acid Spray him in the face. The cult leader screamed and rolled away, the acid causing many of the welts on his face to burst. The pain of the itching gas and acid combined made the man *howl* as he rolled around on the ground, and Joe realized that all his bonus constitution must be gone at this point if he was feeling this poorly.

"Something you either forgot or just don't understand, *Hierophant,* is that when you have an actual deity... well, there are bonuses for capturing a powerful cathedral like this. The divine energy? The mana? It has somewhere to *go.*"

The North Cathedral of Chlorophyll Chaos has gained protectors! Six Divine Juggernauts have spawned within the cathedral!

You have earned a reward from the continuous quest: Reclamation of the lost. After claiming a Cathedral and Place of

Power for Tatum, you have been blessed! You have gained: +5 Intelligence. Temporary buff: Mana Node.

Mana Node: so long as you stand in this cathedral, all spells cost 25% of their normal mana cost. Mana regenerates at triple speed. Lasts 1 hour.

"Six? Even the Grand Ritual Hall only got four... though I guess that was only a mid-sized temple?" He looked over at the Juggernauts that had appeared, really glad that they were on his side. Just like the others he had seen, these ones stood eight feet tall with matte black armor covered in shifting, glowing runes.

"Awaiting assignment," six exactly synchronous voices spoke.

"Grab him, make sure that he's completely helpless," Joe ordered them.

"Instituting helpless target mode." One of them moved forward, a huge naginata lifting into the air. The edge flashed a deep purple, and the Juggernaut dashed forward and took off the Hierophant's arms and legs in a smooth motion. The wounds cauterized instantly, and Joe winced as the man shrilly screamed. The Juggernaut grabbed the Hierophant's neck and squeezed just hard enough that he could breathe but couldn't speak.

"Not... not what I meant." Joe barely kept himself from puking. That had happened on his order, even if he hadn't wanted it done that way. He needed to be clearer. "Let him speak."

"Kill me, you coward," the man spoke around coughing.

"Aren't you the one who was all worried about *me* going out and coming back to kill you? I feel like you'd be *way* more dangerous to let go. You know, cause you have a cult of over a *thousand* brainwashed players? Nah, I just need to figure out what you were going to do to *me*."

"You'll find out right *now*." Paul The Hierophant still managed to smile despite his situation, and Joe was on guard right away. He jerked his head to the side. "You freed the Sliver without putting a leash on him. Now we *all* die."

Joe looked over, seeing that the structure in the center of the cathedral had finally bubbled away and into ooze. It had only lasted this long because it was *steeped* in decades of power and, more recently, a continuous supply of blood and life energies. The same blood that was used to contain... was also meant to strengthen and bind the horror that was now emerging from the pit it had been sealed within.

A name tag appeared above the creature as it pulled itself out of the place it had grown for decades. Bright red formed above its head, resolving into the largest health bar Joe had ever had the misfortune of seeing; it was like seeing a rainbow that stretched across the horizon.

Sliver of The Burning Mind: Gameover.

CHAPTER THIRTY-FOUR

Gameover: this Sliver is only a small portion of the unending hunger of The Burning Mind. Caution! Any Travelers eaten by this creature will have all their data deleted, a true game over. Use utmost caution! Each true death will strengthen Gameover, granting new and horrible abilities.

Joe looked up at the towering abomination, his mind having trouble processing what he was seeing. "What kind of sick game is this?"

Think octopus, at least in terms of the beak and multiple waving limbs. It didn't have the bulbous body, instead looking like a stretched trampoline with eight eyes, three mouths, and *teeth*. So many teeth. Oddly, all the teeth were flat like an herbivore's. Joe had been expecting sharp, pointy, scary teeth. Gameover looked like it had just got a set of braces off, and the dichotomy was just another thing that bothered him.

Uughh, it screamed; a deep and oddly manly scream like a weightlifter that had just completed his best set ever. Then it began to move, and its limbs slapped the floor as it barreled at the group. Joe was grabbed by a Juggernaut and tossed across the room. Five of the six Juggernauts attacked the creature as it came close, various weapons lashing out. Joe righted himself in the air, landing in a crouch thanks to his Aerial Acrobatic skill, which even ticked up a level from the usage.

Joe looked on in awe as the Juggernaut's danced around the floor-shattering spikes that were raining on to them. Blood poured like rain as Gameover took wounds that would leave any number of creatures paralyzed, drained, or dismembered. Still, the *thing's* health barely ticked down at all. The vast health bar even refilled when there was nothing actively hitting it, and Joe wondered how anyone was *ever* supposed to defeat this.

Then he remembered the creature's name: Gameover. If this was its *weakest* form, it was likely that no one was *supposed* to be able to beat this. A Juggernaut took a hit and detonated like a phosphorus bomb, all the fragments latching on to the being that had killed it and dealing a huge amount of damage over time. Gameover responded by lopping off that limb and focusing on landing strikes on the other Juggernauts. In moments, another fell, and Joe realized that he needed to figure out a way to help.

He scooted forward, dropping his staff and dual casting—then channeling—Acid Spray. Acid was supposed to be good at stopping regeneration, right? He controlled the streams as much as possible, trying to get acid *only* on Gameover. He was *mostly* successful, and the continuous damage started to prove its worth. Joe could keep this attack up nearly indefinitely thanks to the 'Mana Node' buff, so he tried to do exactly that.

Then another Juggernaut was smashed, and the battle started to turn against them quickly. A shard of floor hit Joe hard enough to break his Exquisite Shell and send him flying. He stared at the ceiling, blinking as the *Stunned!* debuff wore off. He started to sit up, but an odd sound made him flinch and look to the side. It was the Taglock that he had given Jaxon? He must have dropped it! Picking it up, a plan formed in Joe's mind. "I *really* hope this isn't stupid."

Skill increase: Magical Synesthesia (Novice III). Don't read, **_fight!_**

"Fair." The taglock went into his ring storage, and Joe took a deep breath to get himself ready. "Juggernauts! Distract it!"

He ran at Gameover, which was luckily focusing on the Juggernauts. Joe pumped every drop of mana he could manage into his Exquisite Shell, the Mana Node buff allowing him to create an overshield four times stronger than he had ever before managed. He smoothed and curved the front portion of the shield upward. As he reached the edge of the blood on the floor... he *jumped* forward and at an angle. He shot across the wet ground, his Shell acting as a toboggan.

Gameover saw him about to go under its body and started to move to crush him. The Juggernauts took Joe's orders very literally, however, and the one holding the Hierophant decided that a treat would be a good distraction. It threw the man at Gameover's maw, to the Hierophant's delight and terror. Seeing the flying body, Gameover paused and accepted the gift.

Both groups had made a terrible mistake.

Joe finished traversing the ground, leaving a clean path where he had been. He had stored *gallons* of blood inside his codpiece, and he didn't look back as he got to his feet. Joe got up and *ran*, ending up at the pit Gameover had crawled out of. Pulling out his taglock with the Ritual of Containment filling it, he poured on Gameover's blood and activated the ritual at the same time as tossing the needle into the hole.

The taglock landed at the bottom of the pit and formed into ritual circles. Joe looked back, expecting Gameover to drastically weaken. This ritual made the target lose health, mana, and stamina at an unbelievably fast rate when they were out of the containment. So, valid expectation. What he saw made him cringe. Essentially, he had only managed to *slow* Gameover's regeneration. Now some of the damage being done was at least sticking, but it really didn't matter.

Gameover's body was rippling, and a new growth appeared on its body: a perfect bone spearhead longer than Joe's body was tall. It aligned with the body of a Juggernaut, then launched out faster than the guardian could react. The bone went *through* the powerful creature, then retracted, pulling the huge body to its mouth. A harpoon? Joe looked at the two remaining Juggernauts and made a choice. He ran for it.

He got out of the door and was empowering every step with a *jump*. Mana, stamina, whatever it took... he needed to get *out* of there! He passed the tree where the Scout had secured himself and realized that he was running toward the Wolfmen Village. "Nope, nope, nope!"

Joe altered his course and sprinted away. He had no idea if Gameover could track him or would even *bother* to follow him, but somehow, he felt it *would*. Joe almost screamed as the Scout appeared beside him, running casually beside him. "What happened? Why are you fleeing as coward does?"

Joe declined to answer, the echoing rumble of the side of the cathedral crumbling being enough to stall any future questions. "Desert! Where?"

The Scout sniffed the air, not looking back even as trees behind them were smashed apart. That could be *anything*, after all. He altered their course, and the pair sprinted in a straight shot across the forest. They passed *multiple* creatures; Rosebeasts, Imps, Ents... it didn't matter. Soon, they had almost a dozen hostile monsters chasing them. Frankly, if they killed him, he wouldn't need to worry about Gameover for a few hours. Then again, if the beast got out and started eating farmers... Joe ran harder.

"Head start. Thirty-two constitution." Joe turned his head to the side and puked as he ran, something he hadn't done since his early days in the army. Gameover was faster than them, and if he slowed at all, the lead he had gained would be lost.

They burst from the tree line and started running across the sand. The monsters came to a screeching halt at the edge of the forest, roaring in triumph as they successfully defended their territory. Joe wasn't far enough away to miss the screams of pain and tearing meat that soon followed, and he almost felt bad about knowing that he had gained a few seconds thanks to them.

Only a couple hundred extra feet, sadly. Gameover destroyed the last of the vegetation between them and began lurching across the flat terrain. Joe had *really* been hoping that sand would be difficult for it but apparently *not*. Joe pulled his staff in front of him and poured blood on the attached taglock, activating the ritual and then storing his staff in order to run faster.

Heavy breathing and thudding, loping movements told Joe exactly where Gameover was in relation to him. The Scout looked over his shoulder, yelped a loud '*Nope*', and dropped to all fours. He *shot* off, which Joe understood... even if it left a sour taste in his mouth.

Then a new sound met his ears. A chiming, ringing sound. The ritual was activating! Joe chanced a glance backward, and *really* shouldn't have. Gameover loomed over him, and his harpoon was lined up with Joe. It launched forward as Joe turned to face the creature fully. He *jumped* back, falling to the ground.

The harpoon hit Exquisite Shell at an angle, and *skid* along the shaped surface. It glanced upward and started to retract just as the Shell fully shattered, the single glancing blow just *barely* blocked. Joe hit the ground, rolled a few times... and by the time he looked up, Gameover had vanished, sucked into the shifting ground. Gravedigger's Requiem had managed to pull Gameover down.

It wasn't over. Joe knew it, and the tremors coming from the ground a few minutes later was all the proof he needed. He staggered to his feet and started back toward the forest. He needed to get back to the Grand Ritual Hall and make enough rituals that Gameover would never see the light of day or even be able to move if it *did*. He was going to debuff that creature so much that it would glitch out of the world.

Joe had no faith that *anything* he did could kill that thing. He was sure that the reason it had been trapped and not *brutally eviscerated* was that no one from the past could manage it. He didn't think that he was ready to try where they had failed, so it was time to set contingencies.

The Scout arrived just as Joe got to the demolished trees. Without a word, especially not an *apology*, he led Joe to the cathedral. Joe walked into the already-healing building and looked around. The rubble had been absorbed, and even the floor was smooth again. Where the strange altar had stood, a large statue of a man holding a book in one hand was forming. The features were indistinct... *hidden*, Joe supposed. There was only *one* concerning factor.

Where he had created the containment ritual, the pit, a plume of energized air was flowing upward. The statue's other hand formed, creating a palm that sat at the top of the energy and absorbed it. Interesting. Then Joe started getting notifications.

You have created an energy source to empower your deity! The constant infusion of health, mana, and stamina is an exceedingly *corruptive influence. This energy could be used in* many *ways, but be warned! Only deities will be able to safely* use this energy source without fear of corruption and exceedingly harsh *penalties to karmic luck! This plume of*

*energy adds 2,000 divine energy to Tatum each day that it
remains active.*

*The Juggernauts guarding this temple have been
defeated! Time until respawn: 24 hours until the first one returns.*

*Quest complete: The Cult of the Burning Mind has been
defeated in this area. The Hierophant has been* permanently
*defeated, and you shall have your reward. Return to The
O'Baba to claim it. Reward: +1,000 reputation with The People.
+10,000 experience. Blueprint for 'Evergrowth Greenhouse'.*

*Quest alert! The Other Three. You have captured a
Place of Power in the Forest of Chlorophyll Chaos. There are
three more around the center, and each of them can give
interesting benefits. Capture all of them. Reward: Variable.
Failure: None. Recommended level: 30.*

"Hey." Joe motioned the Scout over. "I'll be back in a
day or so. Can you have someone meet me here?"

"Sure?" The Scout looked around, not seeing anywhere
Joe could go. The Rituarchitect didn't bother to explain himself
and began exploring the cathedral.

At the foot of the statue of Tatum, he found the fast
travel point and added it to the others. An option appeared that
he had never seen before.

*This is the bind point for 1,498 people with an opposing
alignment. Would you like to remove this as a respawn point for
them? They will appear in another location upon respawn. Yes /
No.*

Joe selected 'yes', then accessed the fast travel point and
vanished from the forest.

Chapter Thirty-Five

"Joe... you look *rough*." Alexis had respawned eighteen hours after Joe had returned to the guild. He had spent the time forming four Gravedigger's Requiem's and five more containment rituals. He had activated all of the first and was holding off on the second. "What happened? I see that we are looking at a quest that's ready to be completed?"

"It was... *horrible*, Alexis." Joe waited until the others were all with him before recounting the entire story. "...and I've spent the last few hours dropping that *thing* into the deepest, darkest hole that I could make. At this point, it *should* be two and a half miles down and encased in stone. I have *no* doubt that it's gonna get out if I just leave it, so I am going to go and spread its health and such around until there is *nothing* left for it to use."

"Whoa. It was really *that* bad?" Poppy, oddly, was the one to offer Joe some comfort. "What can we do?"

Joe gestured at his Coven members, who were all collapsed on the table around him. "Get them fed and rested. Get Jess to pay them. I made an emergency quest, and they did a great job."

"Hey, at least you were right that this section of the game had plenty to keep us busy for a good long time! No one would have thought that there was a level thirty to fifty zone in the first area." Poppy grinned and slapped Joe on the face. "Get up! You survived. Now *drain* that thing."

"Good. Yes." Joe stood and walked to the Pathfinder's Hall and into the temple. He got close to the altar to Tatum and placed the disk he had formed on to the stone. "Tatum, get ready for more."

Joe dropped some blood on to the disk and activated the containment ritual. It started to glow, and Joe just stood there and watched it. This was made of High Steel and didn't need to move. It should last indefinitely, and the ritual itself was powered by the thing it contained. Soon, the ritual was draining Gameover of so much power that it began to spill over. Tatum's altar sucked the excess in, but small strands made their way to each of the other active altars.

Divine Energy boosted by +1,500 per day! Your relationship with all members of Tatum's Pantheon has increased by 500 points!

"C'mon, Tatum..." Joe watched the disk and was only satisfied when the altar sucked it in, and the disk vanished. "Good."

No one else was around to see where Joe had put the ritual, and he planned for that to be the norm. These suckers were getting as well-hidden and protected as possible. Heh. Suckers. Double meaning. He smirked as he left the temple.

When he rejoined his party, he remembered to Cleanse himself before he settled in for a coffee. He picked up the mug with shaky hands, sipping the hot ambrosia too fast. "Good, yeah. Set for now. Also, remember not to leave your blood anywhere. You can get targeted from a huge distance. Just saying."

"Gotta tell you, Joe." Alexis coughed into her hand. "Not liking the forest. Two deaths add up. We got no experience for all that."

"Right. We do have ten thousand coming in soon. Just need to drop off the quest." Joe stood, but the others stayed seated. "Did I mention that we have a fast travel point right to the cathedral? Fifteen-minute walk to fix our experience issue."

That got some smiles, and Joe decided to ponder some of the things that were on his mind. "All the cultists were *people*, and we don't get experience for PvP. Yeah, that quest *sucked*. Sorry guys. Honestly, we should get a *lot* more out of this than we are, and I feel terrible about it."

"No worries, Joe. How about we just go finish this and get back for dinner? Hopefully, we can start getting something more than wild game and oatmeal for every meal if you can get this building up and running." Jaxon was leading the way, and Joe noticed something *different* about how he was acting.

"Jaxon, did something change with you?" Joe asked him.

"No? Did some training while everyone was hanging out?"

"What... *kind* of training?"

"Stat training." Jaxon rolled his eyes. "Got all of my stats up, actually. I respawned *way* before them, and I was bored."

"Did you get above a threshold for anything?" Joe had to wait for the answer because at that point, they teleported and arrived at the cathedral. The huge distance took a huge toll on them, and they flopped to the floor gasping.

"Got to... *pant*... ten in charisma," Jaxon told them, looking around in confusion at their elated faces. "What?"

"He's *normal!*" Bard gave Jaxon a hug, getting an awkward squeeze in return.

They started walking, the Scout bringing them to The O'Baba right away. She was *very* pleased to see them. "I have heard such interesting stories. I am glad I did not know the danger you faced; I would have never sent you there. I would not have had a way to pay for the service."

Quest complete: The Cult of the Burning Mind. Reward: +1,000 reputation with The People. +10,000 experience. Blueprint for 'Evergrowth Greenhouse'.

"Nice." Joe blinked away the notification. "Just over a thousand experience to level sixteen."

Jaxon leveled up; he glowed golden and started wiggling his fingers cheerfully. "Drat. I lost some charisma. Forgot I do that when I level up now! Ah, well!"

"Such a *short* amount of time." A tear threatened to leak from Bard's eye, but he glared and somehow sucked the moisture back in.

"Here is blueprint for the greenhouse. I am sorry to say that it is not in the best of conditions." O'Baba looked at the paper wistfully. "It should be serviceable, though. I wish you only the best."

Joe looked at the tattered roll of paper. "I have another idea. Could I scan the building directly?"

"You have another way to gain a blueprint?" O'Baba's eyes filled with laughter. "A good thing I ensured you had a chaperone at all times, yes? Let us see what you can do."

They went to the greenhouse and waited as Joe made his preparations. "Link the blueprint... insert the Core..."

Joe activated the ritual Architect's Fury, and a holographic ritual circle erupted out and on to the building. It spun in place, slowly traversing the entire structure. Ten minutes passed, fifteen... at thirty, the ring swirled back to the blueprint, and a three-dimensional building plan appeared on the paper. "With this, our deal is complete."

You have captured a blueprint for a Special Rare building! Class experience +500!

"Ugh. Ten experience to class level three, *c'mon.*" Joe shook his head in annoyance.

O'Baba looked at what Joe was holding, and her ears perked forward with interest. "We may have to speak again sometime, Joe. For now, let me explain the downfalls of the building you intend to build."

She stepped into the building, leading the way past the front room they had been allowed to see. Around the corner were several Wolfman Warriors, fully armed and armored. "You see, Joe, in here... at a certain density of mana and vegetation, the food begins to fight back. You want a chop salad? Your lettuce wants chopped human. Your farmers will need to also be adept at fighting, eventually. There is a long time before that begins to happen."

"Now, the loot is always food, and it is *very* good food. But if you don't do enough to hold back the foliage, your greenhouse will evolve into a full-fledged dungeon. More food, yes, but more danger. At that point, it will also *always* be a dungeon unless you destroy the building." O'Baba looked at him. "It is made of glass. It breaks easily. That is the other *main* concern."

"I see." Joe was calm. This was even better than he had hoped for. "Thank you for your warning."

"I look forward to seeing your people become fat and slow." O'Baba grinned at him. "I look forward to the day you are all prey animals."

"Don't we all?" Joe's team was led out of the area, and soon, they had returned to the guild. Fast travel was amazing.

The next morning, Joe returned to his usual place at the coffee shop and settled in for a long break from fighting. He had earned a major reward, and he needed to figure out how to put it to good use. He started writing out a list of everything he needed, and it just kept growing and growing. Most of the components were pretty standard; they were just in quantities that were going to be difficult to acquire. Glass, metal for the frame, dirt, crushed stone, sand, loam... lots of variations of ground for things to grow in. The last minimum requirement needed was a Flawed Greater Core, which Joe had only ever seen once.

That was when he got it as a gift from the Royal Family as recompense for the Prince killing him. Every other Core he had used or seen was a 'lesser' Core, to the point that was what he thought of when he said 'Core'. Joe wasn't even sure where he could go to *get* a Greater Core. Maybe he could get the Prince to attack him again? Joe shook his head; that wasn't even funny, and he knew it. There were only so many things he could do without angering the kingdom, and he knew that getting close to—and antagonizing—the Crown Prince was not likely one of them.

Still, that begged the question... where to get one of these? Could he buy one? Find monsters that produced them? Couldn't hurt to ask around. Still, while he was searching, he could start getting the rest of the material. Maybe he could even figure out a way to upgrade this blueprint somewhat?

There were things that he couldn't go without, of course, but he could finally figure out if he had been imbuing glass for no good reason. Joe simply changed the list of materials by adding 'imbued' before glass. He hissed as the list turned black. "Son of a..."

"You know what you're doing wrong there, don't you?" The valley-girl voice almost caused Joe to start throwing acid around, but luckily, there were hand motions needed when he wasn't holding his staff.

Joe turned and looked at the now-purple haired Enchanter. "Hi there, Terra. What brings you to my neck of the woods?"

"Oh, you know. Day off." Terra sighed dramatically, throwing her hand over her face. "I get one at least *once* a month. Almost have my first enchantment learned, too. Gonna be able to make armor that doubles health when it is a full set."

"Nice." Joe pointed at his paper. "Since you were snooping, what did you mean?"

"Hmm?" Terra pointed at the blueprint. "You're trying to substitute imbued material for the regular version, right? Looks like you know it wouldn't work, but maybe you just had gas?"

Joe glared, so she just shrugged and continued, "Look here. Your glass is connected to the frame, which means that the frame will play a role in controlling and channeling whatever mana is running through the place. It looks like you have High Steel as the frame—for one, ouch, your wallet—but that also can't handle constant and consistent channeling without heating up. Since this is a... greenhouse, right? Yeah, that would make the interior too hot. All your plants would die."

He looked at the blueprint and realized that she was right. "How did you see that at a glance? I've been at this since breakfast."

"What, do you think enchanters can just *enchant?* We need to know where to put the enchantment, every bit of what the material it is made of, and even what time of the year is best for each individual enchantment." Terra smirked at him. "I already have Magical Material Lore in the Apprentice ranks. That's almost *all* I've been doing. Memorizing."

"Would you mind telling me what I should be using for a substitute for these materials, then?" Joe chuckled as she pulled a face. "Alright, I get it. I think you're *wrong* about all those variables with enchanting, but otherwise, good information to have. I'll figure it out somehow."

"Sure, you'll just pull it out of your butt somehow, huh?" Terra eyed him critically. "What do you mean about the variables? I'm training directly with a *Master* Enchanter."

"Oh, you know." Joe pulled out a Mana Battery and tossed it to her. "I have my ways, like making open-ended enchantment patterns that don't *seem* to have any requirements like what you're talking about."

Terra stared at the Battery with wide eyes. "Joe. You... how? Only Masters have something like this. Apparently, the enchantment for these is so dangerous that you need to be a Master before the College even *considers* making one for you!"

"Really? *Odd,* I can make one like that in about eight minutes." Joe pulled out the larger one with a capacity of three thousand mana storage. "*This* one takes almost half an hour, though."

CHAPTER THIRTY-SIX

"Well, *that* wasn't what I was expecting." Joe looked at the list of material that they had come up with. "I would have never guessed that a *lower* quality metal would work perfectly. Heck, even a blacksmith told me it wouldn't work."

"Typically, it wouldn't have, but this is why you go to an enchanter when making magic, not a smith." Terra pointed at the frame of the building. "Usually, the frame would be more important in making sure that the glass stayed together. It's fragile and all that, but since the glass *wraps around* the frame, the imbued glass will be able to remain unbreakable to most standard attacks. Then the frame's ability to *ground* excess mana without heating becomes more important than supporting it. Too heavy for armor and weapons, but common usage in stationary enchantments. Hence, don't ask a smith."

Joe grinned as he did the math on the cost difference of using iron with a silver core instead of using High Steel; he didn't even *want* to think about what he would have needed if he went higher up the rare metal chart. "I think you just saved me about a thousand platinum."

"More like ten thousand," Terra smugly informed him. "Your building grows and only by feeding it more material to grow *around.*"

"Frightening." Joe handed over his small Mana Battery. "This is for you."

"Excuse *you*. Pretty sure I'm taking the big one." Her arms went on her hips just before she made a 'gimme' motion.

"So, you're going back with something only *Master* Mages have, and you want one with *triple* the capacity as them?

I feel like that's going to be a bad idea," Joe told her equally smugly.

"Not *triple*." She seemed to realize she wasn't taking the larger one, and her arms dropped. "Looks like however you did this, this one only has half the capacity of my Master's. The big one only holds about a thousand more."

"Huh." Joe looked at the sky. "That's true. Doing this by hand would give a better result, hmm? Ah well, I can mass produce them, so it doesn't matter as much to me. Although... if we worked together on the diagram, maybe we could figure out a perfect solution, and there wouldn't be any loss."

"You have an enchant template? Did you make it somehow?"

"More like reverse engineered, then improved upon." Joe shook his head and got back to work. "Making a totally new spell diagram is *way* harder. Someday, not now though."

Joe looked at the last component, the Flawed Greater Core, trying to put together the last pieces of the puzzle. "How about this? What happens if we use a better or worse Core?"

"Worse? Nothing." Terra stopped him before he got too excited. "*Actually* nothing. The building becomes a house made of glass with really expensive walls. That level of Core is needed to power all the functions. If you use a *better* Core, either the building will function faster than before, or it will overfill with mana and break down or destroy itself. You'd need to check all the materials again to make sure that they can handle the throughput, and the cost will likely rise exponentially."

"Now... this *might* increase the rarity of the building, perhaps even becoming a new or unique structure, but, just a thought, do you *want* to make that happen?" Terra shook her head. "Pretty sure you want to feed people in a hurry. Progress is great, but a stable foundation is the key to success."

"Woo, the College has been doing a number on *you*, huh?" Joe grinned as she stuck a tongue out at him. "That's more like it! Thanks, Terra. Feel free to bring enchantment diagrams over, and I'll see if I can help you improve them."

"You want me to bring along thousand-year-old, unchanging secret documents to you... so you can *improve* them." Terra shook her head. "You're either going to get me killed or promoted."

"A sign of good faith then." Joe pulled out the leaflet he had made for Mana Batteries and held it in the air. "Promise me that this stays between us only. At least unless I give you permission to share."

"Sure? What is it?" Terra took the leaflet and looked through it, her eyes going wide. "You... how did you compensate for the aetheric... oh, I see. That's smart. How did you know to... Joe, *seriously*! Do you even *know* what this is?"

"Mana Battery enchantment."

"No! Well, *literally*, yes." Terra smacked the table. "Joe, if this is usable and so *stable*... even with the power loss, this is a revolutionary way to do all sorts of things! Slot one of these into a staff or wand, and you have a way to cast spells outside of your ability. Into armor, and a warrior has a mana shield! Into buildings, and you could create the equivalent of artillery or defensive systems! You think you can improve this *more*?"

"Yes, because when you were going over it, I had no idea what I was doing in ways of standardization. You said 'aetheric' something and not a clue. I'm doing this all with magical and mathematical proofs." Joe shrugged when she looked ready to throw things at him. Luckily, she didn't want to let the papers go. "If I had someone who knew the quick conversions, the proper tools, we could make this process *way* more efficient."

"Triple or more, potentially." Terra took a deep breath and handed back the paper. "I can't take that; the temptation would be too much. Can I talk to my Master about this?"

"Sure, because I'm keeping the template. It's as good as holding a patent." Joe knew that there was no way someone else was going to be able to easily replicate this, or they would have in the last hundreds of years. Cleric-Mage-Ritualist-Occultist combo for the win!

A ritual you created has been activated! Deactivate? Yes / No.

Oh, so that was how that function would work at a distance? Joe hadn't known what it would look like. There was only *one* ritual of his that was out in the wild right now, and he had given it to Jess to reduce the cost of hunters trapping a rare animal for him. Delegation for the win! He really hoped that they had used the ritual intentionally; it was single use, after all.

"Joe? Hello? You there?" Terra poked him in the ribs.

"Gah! Clip your nails, Wolverine!" Joe rubbed at his side. "Sorry, got a notification about a quest I have in progress right now. Where were we?"

"Let me see... I am leaving after popping in to randomly help you with a project you had," Terra indifferently informed him.

"Right, you *totally* don't seek me out because you know I am always tinkering around with magical stuff, and you want dibs on the cool stuff I find and make. All *my* benefit. How's that enchanted elevator diagram keeping you?"

Terra blushed, and Joe knew that he was on the mark. "So, we use each other for personal gain. At least we *both* benefit, right?"

"You don't have a *quest* to get info from me, do you?" Joe jokingly questioned. Terra *fully* flushed, and his mouth dropped open. "From *who*? You little *spy!*"

"Oh, stop. Nothing like *that.*" Terra turned and walked away, refusing his follow-up questions.

"Now I know why she kept looking for me." Joe was somewhat disappointed, but he tried not to be. She was fun to be around, no matter how annoying she was. Looked like he would need to make sure she always stayed at arm's length; even if he had been playing around calling her a spy, he still lost a lot of trust with her just now. She was feeding someone information on him, and no matter how innocent it *might* be...

Joe decided to set aside his concerns for now. He pulled out a square foot of glass and started to pour mana into it. He glanced at the amount of glass he would need to imbue to create the initial structure and tried not to get frustrated. That was a *lot* of glass. It was going to be a long couple of days. Joe glanced at his status sheet and had an idea.

Name: Joe '*Tatum's Chosen Legend*' Class: Mage (Actual: Rituarchitect)
Profession: Tenured Scholar (Actual: Arcanologist)
Character Level: 15 Exp: 134,813 Exp to next level: 1,187
Rituarchitect Level: 2 Exp: 2,990 Exp to next level: 10
Hit Points: 270/270
Mana: 1,012.5/1,012.5
Mana regen: 27.9/sec (Base 25.37/sec increased by gear)
Stamina: 235/235
Stamina regen: 5.64/sec

Characteristic: Raw score (Modifier)

Strength: 25 (1.25)
Dexterity: 34 (1.34)
Constitution: 32 (1.32)
Intelligence: 81 (2.31)
Wisdom: 70 (2.2)
Charisma: 31 (1.31)
Perception: 54 (2.04)
Luck: 30 (1.30)
Karmic Luck: +1

His idea was simple and fairly straightforward. If he could get his intelligence up to the next threshold—one hundred—his mana pool would likely boost a large amount. That would let him use all of his abilities better and more frequently. There would also likely be benefits that he was unaware of. Joe needed nineteen points, which meant almost a month of just characteristic training. Viable, and he would use that as a supplement, but what he really needed to do was work on complicated things.

He decided to follow a simple regiment. Start the day with coffee, do his characteristic training for the guaranteed point, a few hours of imbuing glass, tinker with spell diagrams, and start producing scrolls and enchantment diagrams. The varied and difficult work would likely boost his intelligence, and Joe hoped to find the threshold in under a week.

"Excuse me, Joe?" Joe looked at the messenger as he continued, "I have a building request for you from Lord Mike?"

"Barracks again?" Joe got a nod in return. "Sounds good. Can you go round up the same people as last time?"

"I... we haven't met before." Joe did a double take, and sure enough, he didn't know this guy.

"*Ahem*. Sorry, the uniform and all..." Joe sputtered to a stop and gave the information on the people he needed. From there, he walked over to the guild hall and started the preparations. "How are they getting all this building material? Seriously, I couldn't buy a *plank* from Ardania."

After setting up the holographic building, he waited. After ten minutes, no one showed up. Joe didn't see anyone, and he was tired of waiting. "Time to see if I can use these in a ritual."

He placed the Mana Batteries to form a triangle with him and activated the ritual. If this didn't work, this was going to be a bad time. Joe lifted into the air smoothly, as did the Mana Batteries—to his great relief. That gave him a total of five thousand mana to use at the outset of the ritual, excellent. With his regeneration, he'd be able to do this entire ritual on his own now.

The drain switched from him to the Mana Batteries, and as they drained down, the building was slotted together. Nails went smoothly into wood, the frame had walls placed along it, and overall, the building came together nicely. As Joe was being set on the ground, the smaller of the Mana Batteries popped and fell to the ground as a powder. "*Feces!*"

At least the larger one held together, but was that luck or due to the higher quality? Joe hated that he didn't know. He cursed as the ritual diagram for the barracks went up in flames, turning into ash in an instant. Ah, right. This was the third time he had used it, and it must have had the durability reduced to nothing. Well... at least all the barracks since the very first he made would have shingles.

Class experience +100!

Class Level up! You are now a level three Rituarchitect!
New ritual learned: Raze.

CHAPTER THIRTY-SEVEN

Raze (Expert): the second major ritual granted to a Rituarchitect; this ritual allows the user to convert a previously built building into the resources used during construction. Not all resources will be reclaimed, as the wear and tear on the resources will be fixed using the material, but all resources reclaimed will be in perfect condition. Perfect for gentrification! Time to Raze target structure is dependent upon rarity, complexity of the structure, and how well-built target structure is. Using a higher-quality Core in this ritual increases the amount of material available for reclamation and the speed of destruction! This ritual can be interrupted by the destruction of the item containing the ritual circle. Components needed...

Joe grabbed his head as information was *crammed* in. This was like learning four years of architecture... and engineering... and sapping all in the same day. "*Ow!* What! This is... *so* much information!"

"An Expert-ranked ritual to tear down a building? *Really?* Why is that so much harder than scanning a building or just smashing it?" Joe looked over the information in his head, as easy to access as seeing a file on a computer and saw what he was missing. "Oh... it repairs all the material reclaimed? Okay... not a huge fan of not knowing how fast this process would go, but it *is* good to know that a better Core means more stuff and faster process."

"It's already getting dark? How long was I out? Hope this ritual at least piles everything *neatly*," he grumbled as he got to his feet. Joe was coated in dust and sweat, and his Coven *still* hadn't shown up. He grabbed his Mana Battery and walked into the guildhall, nearly colliding with Aten, who was sprinting toward him.

"Joe! Emergency!" Aten picked Joe up and sprinted away, carrying Joe with no apparent effort. He kept running, almost getting to the salt mine before stopping and putting Joe on his feet in a clearing. "I really don't like how easy it is to abduct you, Joe. You need to protect yourself."

"You think *I* liked that?" Joe sputtered, face red from Aten's unfair words. "If you were an enemy, you would be chunks of meat by now!"

"Joe!" Mike stepped into the clearing, the suddenness of his arrival getting him a Shadow Spike in the leg. "*Ow!* What the heck, man?"

"Sorry!" Joe healed him with a wave, then glared at him. "Startling people who are in combat all the time is a *bad idea*, Mike."

"Sheesh." Mike looked at the hole in his pants and visibly calmed himself. "Listen, Joe. We have an informant from the Architect's Guild. At great personal risk to themselves and a huge amount of money from us, we are getting a tier-two building. We need you to do your thing and make a copy. If this isn't back by morning, people are going to come looking for it."

"What's the building?" Joe looked at the two of them. "The fact that you're not answering the question is making me oddly nervous."

"We don't *know*, alright?" Aten stomped his foot, making a crater and *also* making Joe wonder about his actual age. "The informant only told us that it was guaranteed to be beneficial. Just so you know, once we build it and people *know* we built it, they are going to be pretty mad."

"Why build it, then?" Joe looked at the other two. "Tell me!"

"The builders have a pretty serious rule." Aten snarled. "If you build a building above the tier of your town, they won't allow you to work with them. Ever. Only *they* are allowed to build more than tier zero buildings. Anything ranked Common or above? *They* build it. Total monopoly. Even the King can't force the issue since their failsafe makes sure the blueprints they have would be destroyed if they hit the button."

"Then there would be *no* one who could make them." Joe nodded in acceptance. "So... we are out, my bad. Will they come after us?"

"Nah, the Kingdom has a 'fair use' law now." Mike chuckled at that. "Apparently, it is in place thanks to your work with the Archmage. All Mages were Nobles, and the Nobles get a vote on certain laws. Now, anyone who makes something has the legal right to use or make it if it's legal to have and use. No more forced joining of Guilds or Colleges to cast spells and such."

"That's *awesome!*" Joe high-fived Aten.

Aten nodded. "Yes, but what we are doing right now is *definitely* illegal, corporate espionage and all that. But! Here's the thing: if we build this, there is nothing they can do about it anymore. So, can you make this ours in time?"

"Probably." Joe looked back at the Pathfinder's Hall towering above the tree line, the beacon at the top outshining any star in the sky. "Would have been a lot easier back at my *desk*. Where all my materials for *making blueprints* are."

"Him?" Yet another voice reached Joe's ears, but at least this time, he wasn't the only one to jump. "That's your 'wunderkind'? Are you sure about this?"

Joe only needed a single glance to realize that he knew this person. She was the guild representative that had denied him all building materials. "Oh, hey! Good to see you again. I hope that in the future we can have lots of positive interactions."

She stared at Joe, then glared at Aten. "Did he just threaten me? Are you trying to blackmail me? I'll leave *right now* if this is–"

"Nothing like that!" Aten assured her, pulling a huge sack of clinking coins apparently out of thin air. "He's *just* an idiot."

"Here." She pulled a tube off her back and handed it to Joe. "You have four hours since it'll take me an hour to get back to Ardania and I need to sneak this back in. If you are late, at all, I'll be telling my boss about the 'thief' who broke in. He's *bald*."

"Joe, hold tight!" Aten picked Joe up and started running. "Where is your gear?"

"Hall!" Joe shouted over the wind and pounding feet. Aten veered slightly, blowing past the guards and dropping Joe when they got indoors. "Follow me, Aten!"

"Where are we going?" Aten looked around the huge, open space. "I've seen everything here. There's no office."

Joe smirked at Aten as he led him to a small booth. "You *really* haven't, Aten."

The door closed behind them, and the wall started to warp and open. A ramp leading downward appeared, and the Guild Commander gave Joe a *look*. "This goes *where*?"

"My office!" Joe laughed outright at the frustrated look on Aten's face. "Time's wasting. Let's go!"

They got to the true core of the building a moment later: the Grand Ritual Hall. Aten was sent to sit in the corner while Joe started doing the preparation work for converting the blueprint into a ritual. "Alright, let's see what we have here... tier two building, also known as an *Uncommon* building. You know that the barracks I've made are tier two, right? Moving past that: seriously, pick a nomenclature system, Ardanians!"

"What is it? The building? Anything good?" Aten had a lot of hope in his voice, and Joe could understand why. That bag he had handed over was full of *gold* coins, and he had no information otherwise.

"Looks like... oh neat." Joe started drawing out the plans with a pencil, his enhanced intelligence allowing him to come along and scrape away mistakes with a nearly autonomous razor made of solidified shadows.

"Joe!"

"Let me work, Aten! Oh. Right, it's the plans for a gatehouse." Joe kept moving along.

"Gatehouse...?" Aten sounded crushed.

"Gatehouse. Thing you put in a wall around a city," Joe told him absentmindedly. "Since this is an Uncommon building, it also includes the plans for the wall it fits into, all sorts of crenellations, defenses, and a drawbridge. Everything we need to have in order to make a full defensive wall around our town."

Aten *whooped*, jumping in the air and breaking out into dance. Luckily, Joe was *far* too deep into his work to notice. There would have been screenshots for *everyone* otherwise. An hour passed as Joe finished the ritual rings, and just after that point, he put the finishing touches on a four-ringed Student ritual. "Frame, construction, details, magic. Good... gold all over... wait."

He looked closer at the fourth ring, then made a tiny shadow that picked away a slightly out-of-place mark. Then the pattern shimmered a beautiful gold, and Joe nodded with a relieved expression. "Now for the ink..."

Infused ink was poured into an orb of shadow magic, and that was fitted to his quill to act as an ink hopper. Joe couldn't risk making uneven lines, and he was really missing ball-point pens right now. With a steady hand, he followed along all the pencil that he had put down, using his control of shadows to form rails for the nib of his quill to fit between. The use of his shadow magic in all aspects of this process allowed the finished process to have machine-like exactness but also stunted the growth of his drawing skill. He didn't care at all.

As the ink dried, he followed along after his work and looked for anywhere the ink had run. Tiny shadow razors removed those spots before they could dry fully, and he sat back to look down at the completed diagram. "Okay... the hard part is done."

"You're done?" Aten looked at the rings—specifically the headache-inducing detail Joe had placed on the rings—and reeled back. "What is *that?*"

"Oh, right! I suppose you've never seen the ritual circles themselves, just the holographic energy representations of them." Joe pointed at the various rings and spoke, glad for the break. "This portion allows me to create a sympathetic link to a blueprint. This activates the ritual. Here lets me add people to the setup. This—"

Joe talked for a minute, and Aten's face got more and more bleak. "Joe, you do this every single time, to cast *one* ritual? So, a mage just chucks a fireball, and you'd need like... two hours to make the same effect?"

"Well... if I wanted to cast the fireball as a ritual, yes." Joe reached for the blueprint and pulled it in close.

"You're using infused ink, paper, and quills?" Aten looked at everything Joe was using, then behind him at a shelf with neatly labeled and explained reagents. He flipped back to looking at Joe as he pulled out a standard Core, also known as an Uncommon Lesser Core. "Geez, man. That's... overkill, isn't it?"

"Bare minimum actually. Hey, at least you know what you're paying for when you reimburse me later." Joe put the Core in the center of the ritual circles, then touched the blueprint to the Core. The blueprint glowed brightly, the Core dimmed, and Joe grunted as he impressed mana into the process. The Core crumbled, finally on its last use, and Joe made sure that Aten saw. He was running low on Cores and could really go for a guild-sponsored refill.

When the glow dimmed, Aten leaned in and gasped at the holographic building sitting in the center of the ritual circles. It matched perfectly. He pulled open the blueprint and saw that there was nothing on it to indicate any changes. "Joe, you glorious... how many of these rituals can you set up? If I can get you into their vault for an hour, how many...?"

He trailed off, seeing Joe shaking his head. "Each ritual is custom-made for the building when I pull it from a blueprint. It's actually harder than just scanning a building. Look here. This part says 'wall, wall opening'. Sure, it's written in trigonometry, but that's what it says. No shortcuts like that."

Aten rubbed his well-trimmed beard. "I see. Well... I'll get this back to... hmmm."

The Guild Commander walked up the ramp, and as he stepped into the building above... the way down vanished. "Fine then, Joe. Keep your secrets."

***

None of them saw when, just over an hour later, the person who had 'stolen' the plans returned to Ardania. She walked up to the leader of the Architect's Guild and handed over the plans to the wall, as well as the gold she had been given. "They fell for it."

"Good work." He pushed the gold back to her. "When they are tried for treason, we will finally have someone to point at and say, 'See? Bad idea to go behind our back and do this yourself. You never know when you might accidentally build *treason* against the Kingdom'."

CHAPTER THIRTY-EIGHT

"I'm doing a lot of things recently for *maybe* rewards in the future," Joe contemplated quietly as he worked to pump mana into his glass. It was more of a 'constant pressure' thing, so he took the time to look over his gains from last night and this morning.

Skill increase: Solidified Shadows (Apprentice IX). Oooh. One rank away from the Student ranks! What will happen? Something good? Nothing at all?

Skill increase: Spellbinding (Apprentice IV). Making magical documents comes in all shapes and sizes. You've been making lots of them! Good job. You know there is a whole world full of people to meet, right?

Of course, the most exciting one for him was the increase of his Ritual Magic to Expert one. Knowing that there was no way to increase it other than study and practice made each earned rank feel just... *so* invigorating. It was also thanks to this skill that he had been able to create the ritual so quickly last night. While it had felt like he was doing each step at the same pace, the Journeyman bonus he had gained allowed him to create Student-ranked rituals thirty percent faster.

He wanted to study that effect in closer detail, as there had to be *some* kind of logical reason for why it happened. Did he physically move faster when making rituals? Some kind of perception boost? Haste? Either way, he wasn't aware of it when it was happening. Joe shrugged and looked at his stat gains, pleased with what he was seeing. He had stuck with his plans today and had gained a point in everything except luck and charisma. Good start to the day.

Done patting himself on the back for a single-day-streak, he turned back to his glass. He kept pumping mana into it, then holding it in place as the mana fused with the grain of the glass, enhancing and increasing durability. Joe looked at his Magical Material Creation skill, hoping that force of will alone would bring it up another point. The glass finished, dropping to the table with a very non-glass-sounding *thunk*.

"What does increasing the density of the mana matrix do?" Joe growled at his skill. "Make it absorb faster? Absorb more? Both?"

Joe started again, adding the infused glass to his ring and having a new chunk appear on the table. As he surrounded the glass, something in his mind *clicked*. Perhaps it was the fact that he had gained more intelligence, wisdom, or that his mind was always looking for a way to automate things, but... what he was doing with his mana was a *lot* like what he did when making his Exquisite Shell.

This time, instead of making the mana form as a bubble and holding it there, he stretched his Exquisite Shell into shape around the glass and pumped mana into the space left behind. He wasn't sure if this would work, but it was worth a shot! When the glass brightened, he knew it had been a success. Though... it was different than usual.

Item created: Natural Imbued Glass. You have found _ERROR_ You have created a type of glass that has absorbed wild mana or a type of mana with an aspect of suppression resistance or wildness. This glass allows mana to flow through it much easier than imbued glass made using a matrix while retaining the damage-resistant properties.

Skill upgrade available: 'Magical Material Creation' will change into 'Natural Magical Material Creation'. This type of material creation does not allow for the choice of mana matrix used, instead making the material gain whatever property best fits. This can result in anything from incredible to incredibly dangerous results. Accept? Yes / No.

Joe was concerned but knew that he could always go re-learn the original skill if this gave him issues. He chose 'yes' and watched as his skill changed.

Skill gained: Natural Magical Material Creation (Beginner I). 50-1n% chance for skill use to create a material dangerous to the creator where n = skill level. 1% chance for material created to increase in rarity upon completion. This is a skill usually reserved for NATURE, *Mr. Error Generator.*

Title upgraded: Baldy II. No facial hair either. You have eyebrows and eyelashes left, but don't push it. -50% chance to successfully hide when in sunlight.

Joe touched the small beard he had been trying to grow, catching falling hair. He looked at the tufts in his hand and sighed. "Is this really my fault? I'm sorry that people haven't been very experimental here in the last few centuries, but this seems to be intentionally pushing down creativity."

I can be petty if I want to be. Baldy III: the loss of chest hair.

"Hey!" Joe started to itch as hair trickled down his shirt. "Is that a curse or are you making movie titles?"

No other message came, and Joe decided against antagonizing the world AI any further. He Cleansed himself to remove the itching, took a few deep breaths, and got back to work. There was a thirty-nine percent chance of making something harmful, but... no other choice right now. At the Expert rank, there would be no more harmful stuff, which made sense. Ah well.

Joe made four chunks of natural imbued glass before he got his first... failure. He sat there, staring at the glass in his hands. His mind was blank, his body shaking. Joe was fully terrified. He had no idea how long he sat there before someone tapped him on the shoulder and he dropped the glass. It shattered on the table, and the effect it had on him was broken.

"You... okay there, mate?" A big dude was standing well away from Joe, looking at him awkwardly.

"I was under a fear effect. Thanks for breaking me out of that." Joe went to stand, and the man pushed him down.

"At least that's explained, but... stay seated. Ya made a lil' mess there." Joe was patted on the arm, and the man moved off. Joe looked down at his wet robe, flushed, and Cleansed himself.

"Yup, harmful material." Joe suddenly liked his new skill a *lot* less, no matter that his other glass had been formed almost three times faster than before. No way around it than to get good, though. He made a deal with a server that was walking around. If Joe started acting oddly, the server would knock the glass out of his hands. The server, in turn, would get a nice tip.

Joe started again, and as soon as the glass was completed, he started to laugh. "Yes! I am the *best*! I can't believe how amazing I am at *everything*! Look at this glass! *Look at it*! Muhuhaha!"

The glass shattered as it hit the table. Somehow, the failures didn't have the resilience of the correctly-made versions. Joe thanked the server, who glanced at the broken glass and shook his head. Five more glass sheets were made before it happened again, but this time, Joe thought he was someone across the room and threw the glass at him, thinking the other was an imposter.

"Whooo, *boy*." Joe took out a fresh chunk and nervously wrapped it again. "Next failure means done for the day."

One... two... twelve success in a row. On the thirteenth, something changed, and Joe prepared himself for the worst.

Item upgraded! Random attribute assigned. Item created: Natural Imbued Glass of Fertility. This glass exudes fertility. All plants and animals in the area of effect will produce offspring 21% more quickly!

"Well..." Joe looked at the glass with interest but also concern. "Let's make sure this gets into the greenhouse? How big is the area of effect?"

He continued, getting twelve more done before suddenly shouting to the others in the area, "Gather around, gather around! I am here to tell you the tale of Zed the Bard and his great influence on another world!"

Smack Joe's glass broke, and the server pointed into the distance. "Get out."

"Fair enough." Joe stood and went to work on his other projects. He continued this way for the next four days, training and perfecting a ritual of Feather Fall in the evenings. Four more points in six stats, and closing in on a thousand one-foot-by-one-foot glass sheets.

He looked at the changes that five days of hard training had netted him, pleased with the results.

Natural Magical Material Creation (Beginner VIII). Grinding, huh? Still an impressive speed, but I suppose you're actually earning it this time instead of your deity sneaking you boosts.

Ritual Magic (Expert II). Fancy stuff.

Exquisite Shell (Beginner II). Interesting choices were made in learning to make new shapes with this. Some bald disrespect for the craft, some might say.

Cleanse (Student II). You've really been making a mess of yourself recently. You realize that usage determines boosts... right?

New ritual created: Feather Fall. What falls faster, a ton of feathers or a one-ton anvil. The anvil, less wind resistance. That won't matter to you though because, with this active, you can survive three falls that would otherwise deal at least half your remaining health!

Difficult issues solved! Intelligence +1!

Joe had gotten that last message four times, netting an additional four intelligence over the grinding session. "Woo! Got to ninety int!"

"Congrats!" Jess was sitting across from him, and this was the first Joe had noticed her. "Listen, a few things. You've totally ignored your team for the last five days, so they went off to do their own thing. Also, you still need to pay them if they aren't doing anything. Aten was looking for you for an update on the food situation and wanted you to know that they have gathered all the soils and miscellaneous stuff that you've requested. In that sense, good call on a week of downtime."

"What would I do without you, Jess?"

"Likely hire someone who costs more and does less," Jess deadpanned, handing over a clipboard. "This is the invoice for the trappers you sent out. They are here and want payment. I checked, and they came through, but you might not like it. Still gotta pay them. Still no word for sure on the Greater Core you need, but a 'Terra' told me that she *might* be able to make that happen. 'For *money*'. She laughed at me as she said that last part, so I hope it means something to you."

"Only a couple weeks on the payroll and you are invaluable." Joe smiled at the table. "I should have everything I need for the greenhouse by tonight except the Core. Tell Aten that, and ask if they've got a plan on where to put it. Also, any news on other building requirements?"

"Nothing else." Jess told him where to find the trappers, and he went over after buying her a coffee. The trappers were almost exclusively rogue-type characters, and they seemed leery about standing near the small cage they had. "Everything okay?"

"Gonna need a bonus on this one, sorry to say," the leader of the small group told Joe bluntly. "Three of us died, and we've been hearing stories about groups vanishing after catching really rare creatures."

"Sounds familiar." Joe sighed and paid twenty percent more than the previously-agreed rate. He wanted to work with them in the future, so it was important to make good impressions now. When they had the gold in hand, they nodded at the tarp-covered cage and walked away.

Joe got close and threw off the cover. Staring at the creature contained by bars and ritual magic, he rubbed his eyebrows and had to find somewhere to sit.

"Seriously? A squirrel?"

CHAPTER THIRTY-NINE

Joe had pressed the button that the colorful Jester had given him and waited next to the cage the entire night. He wasn't sure how else to reach the Zoo's... assassin. It was very, *very* strange that a Zoo had a trained killer. Joe continued to create glass, and he made sure to remain awake the entire time. Unless he was in a totally safe location, there was no chance that he was going to sleep after *summoning* a *Jester Assassin* that was after him.

So, he sat across from the squirrel, back to the wall, and made imbued glass. The process sped up each time he gained a skill level and also reduced the odds of him making an odd failure. He had also taken to holding the glass precariously to drop and smash the failures before they messed with him too much. This did cause a few mishaps with dropping regular glass, but it was worth it in his opinion.

Natural Magical Material Creation (Apprentice 0). No extra boost for you at this rank.

As he made his thousandth successful glass square, Joe broke through to the next tier. He hopped to his feet, flush with success. A voice caught him off-guard, "Here I thought that my entrance was undetectable. We should discuss my lack of stealth in the future so I can improve."

The multi-colored robes the man wore were still garish and distracting, but somehow, Joe hadn't seen him before he spoke. Joe nodded at the man, then waved at the cage. "As agreed, one Rare monster."

"Interesting." The assassin looked at the cage. "*Very* interesting. I have no idea how you managed to contain this creature in simple bars of iron. Creeping Death Squirrels tend to be rather... *difficult* to contain. I will admit, I thought that I would be getting the most basic of rarity from you. You have cleared your record with us, and here is a small token of our appreciation and hopefully a visual reminder to bring such creatures to us instead of a... *pet store.*"

Quest complete: Too Many Zoos! You have proven to The Zoo that you aren't trying to compete with them! Reward: Kill order rescinded. Small non-combat pet (Coffee Elemental).

Brown liquid flowed up Joe's arm like a snake, resolving into a small creature that smiled at him with huge, brown eyes. It spoke in a tiny, high-pitched voice, "*Drink me?*"

"Later for sure, but not right now." The Elemental flowed down and into his ring.

"Ah, that's your storage device, hmm?" The assassin leered at him. "Good to know. Now, as I was pleasantly pleased by the work you did here... this is a little something from me."

Item gained: Backstage Pass. This pass will get you into the 'underground zoo'. Attend at your own risk, and make sure you are dressed your best!

"If you want to see your little friend here in action, come tonight. This little guy... I know *exactly* who to set this against." The assassin patted the cage and vanished, cage and all.

Joe looked at the pass and the empty room, deciding to take this chance to go to sleep instead of making any rash choices. After waking up and drinking an *amazing* coffee in bed, he decided that it might be for the best to go and see what was going on. The location for the zoo was marked on the pass, and it turned out to be in Ardania. *In* the city proper, which was somewhat confusing to Joe. The city was huge, yes, but a full zoo was in the walled area?

He popped over to Ardania and went to get some new, fancier clothes. Buying a full set of a dark blue, Noble-style suit, he decided to pay a visit to his mother. It had been a while, and the flashing notification of a completed quest was rather enticing. She must have taken over *Odds and Ends*, then.

"Joe!" She ran over to give him a hug when he got through the door. The place was filled with people, and everything was neatly organized and arranged. His ritual was still in effect, then. "So good to see you! We have so much to talk about!"

They sat and talked while checking people out, eventually getting around to the quest that he was turning in. "Oh, good! I was wondering what it was that Old Minya left for you. Go to the back room, use this key on the chest. Oh, I can't wait to see what you got from her!"

Joe walked back, and sure enough, a chest was built into the wall. He placed the blue key into the blue hole and twisted.

Item gained: Grimoire of Annihilation (Artifact). This is the personal journal of an ancient Waritualist. This book becomes soul bound on use, only accessible to one person until their true death. After binding, the bound creature now has access to many dark rituals that were forbidden... even in their time. Decide before binding if you want access to these rituals, as the knowledge of them will forever tempt you. Accept? Yes / No.

Joe looked at the blank, black cover, shocked that the old lady had something like this in her possession. He knew that there were things out there like this, and he *also* knew that there were times that using them would cause people to fear and hunt you. He didn't want to go down dark paths like the ritualists of old... but his current rituals were almost entirely utility. Joe *did* need attack spells, and... it looked like these would fit the bill.

He pressed 'yes', and the clasp around the dark book sheared off. The book opened, the first page turned, and Joe saw an index of the rituals contained within.

Ritual of the Insomniac Stalker. This ritual requires two targets, the first creature will target the second. The first creature will no longer receive the benefits of sleeping beyond the absolute minimum to maintain health. Instead, that creature now has an intense animosity for the second target. They will know the direction and distance to the target at all times. When the first target encounters the second target, they must attack the target unless able to resist the compulsion. They must resist every minute the target is in sight, which will grow harder over time. This effect lasts until one of the two targets die. Requirements: blood-stained pillow...

Ritual of Sacrificial Regeneration. Choose up to four willing creatures, including the target. Whenever the creatures take damage, the target will heal for one half of the health lost by the creatures. Effects last until target falls asleep. Requirements: the fresh-shed blood of a creature with...

Ritual of the Hidden Shield. Choose up to five willing creatures and a type of damage (see requirements for examples). All but one of the creatures now have resistance to chosen damage, but the final one will have 2x vulnerability to chosen damage, where x = number of protected creatures. This effect lasts for seven days or until death. Requirements: for heat damage protection...

Ritual of the Ghostly Army. You create a one-hundred-foot-high and a half-mile-long wall of dense fog which appears to have a screaming face in the center. The fog moves at the marching speed of an army and will dissipate after one full day.

All sight is reduced to a five-foot range, and all sounds are wildly distorted. Requirements: a small lake...

Ritual of the Lonely Tree. The caster can summon and plant a seed of the Lonely Tree. This tree will mature over a period of six weeks and will slowly kill all vegetation in a fifty-mile radius. Once mature, the tree will live for one month and will cast the area spell 'Salt the Earth' before turning to ash. If 'Salt the Earth' is cast, nothing will grow in the impacted area for seven years. Requirements: a willing sacrifice...

Ritual of Argus. Choose up to five willing creatures, including yourself. Upon ritual completion, an eye spawns on the back of your head. Each creature included in the ritual has dark vision, cannot be ambushed, and can see invisible things. The main target of this ritual will also be able to mystically observe anyone attempting to see the target through mystic means. This lasts for 7 days or until dispelled by the caster. Requirements: 2x Eyeballs of your own race...

Ritual of Dark Reach. Choose a target. Chosen target's attack range will increase by five meters when making a physical attack. Requirements: the leftmost finger of the target...

Joe looked over the rituals quickly. They seemed much more targeted at large-scale conflicts than at individual fighting prowess, but Joe supposed that made sense for a Waritualist's book. Still, the requirements for the rituals seemed... hefty. He could see how people would look at the preparation for these and see an evil wizard, and that was only for the *first* needed component shown by the index. All the others were contained on the requirements page of the rituals. Plus... all of these were optimized.

That meant that these were the most effective ways to cast the ritual, and anything else would produce failures. Joe could see why there was a warning when opening this, as he could see great applications for the rituals, but... did he want to cast them? *Could* he? That was another concern. Two of them were Master rituals, and the others were high-level Expert-ranked.

The ritual of the Lonely Tree, a Master ritual, could be really useful for clearing out the forest of Chlorophyll Chaos, but did he want to make a fifty-mile *radius* barren desert for a minimum of seven years? This was obviously a siege technique, a potent one, but it seemed likely to backfire. Either way, Joe wasn't going to be using them *now*, so he packed up his book and went out to see his mother. They visited for a short while longer before Joe decided that it was time to get going if he were going to make it to the Zoo.

Pushing through the crowd, Joe walked for an hour and a half—almost clear across the city—before getting to the outer edge of the Zoo. He read the gilded sign, not sure how to feel about being there, "Grand Zoo of Ardania. Entrance by invitation only."

Joe looked around, seeing that he was in a bad part of town. He had seen this earlier but didn't really think much of it. Now, the golden gate and such stood out in such stark contrast that he wasn't sure he wanted people knowing that he was going in there. It felt like asking to be robbed when he left. Still... he was already here, dressed too nice for the area, and was running out of time.

He pulled out his pass, and the gates swung open to allow him entrance.

CHAPTER FORTY

"Welcome, good sir!"

As soon as the gate closed behind Joe, a man in full clown attire stepped out to meet him. He honked his nose and did a cartwheel, arriving inches from Joe's face. "Are we here to peruse the menagerie? See the lost splendor of the lost civilizations? Sample the delicacies of a thousand–"

The clown stopped dead, staring at the rich black-and-gold of Joe's pass. "I... am so sorry, sir. I had no idea. Please forgive my ignorance. It is not often that new people are allowed *backstage*. One moment."

A butler came out of the doorway a moment after the clown had entered. Whereas the clown had been energetic, fun, and slightly creepy... this man was geared to be fully regal and subservient. Joe only noticed it was the same person when he spoke. "Again, my deepest apologies. Please allow me to show you the *backstage* area."

Two people came out of another nearby area, pulling a small yet luxurious passenger cart that was stocked with cool drinks and fresh fruits. Joe was motioned toward it, and frankly, he had been walking for a good long time, so he got on. The butler walked beside the cart as the two others pulled it along the roads of the Zoo. "If there is anything you would like to see as we proceed, please allow me the opportunity to make that happen for you."

"Ah... of course." Joe took a grape and bit down, his eyes going wide as juice flooded his mouth. That was the best grape he had ever tasted, and there was an entire bunch of them!

The butler saw his expression. "I see Sir has found the Floodwater Grapes! This is a *Rare* fruit exclusive to the city and a gift from the Floodwater family. I *do* hope they are to your liking."

"Very much so." When he knew no one was looking, he 'wiped his mouth', actually storing the seeds in his storage ring. This would be a great addition to the greenhouse when it was operational. Joe was taken past various sparkling enclosures and was treated to the sight of interesting and beautiful creatures as they passed. Unlike other zoos that he had seen on earth, here the creature was always clearly and easily viewable, which must have been accomplished via some form of magic.

"We are arriving at the backstage area. Please hold on tightly, as there may be some discomfort otherwise." The butler seemed to tap the air, and a familiar sight greeted Joe. There was a sudden, shining pillar of white light, and the view *changed*.

They had just teleported somewhere! The butler and two people pulling the cart were panting and had obviously somehow incurred all the cost of long-range transportation without impacting Joe at all! He needed to learn how to do that. "Sir, we have arrived."

Joe looked up and saw an impressively gargantuan coliseum. There was a train of small carts being pulled to it, and Joe surreptitiously checked his surroundings. Beautiful plant arrangements lined the entire path and obscured vision of everything besides the path and the towering building, though Joe could see stars and the last edges of the sun setting behind the building. It was still late afternoon where they had come from... where *was* he?

"Would Sir allow me to go over the rules of the Bloodsport Arena?" The butler looked to Joe, who simply nodded. No one wanted to admit ignorance. "Excellent! The arena stands as a testament to when our great city was first founded, and the entire world was embroiled in war. Here, our greatest warriors can train and pay homage to their baser needs! In the classic man versus environment scenario. Our chosen fighters compete with the creatures of the wild."

"This allows them the chance to gain fame, following, and great rewards!" The butler's eyes were shining, and he was obviously buying into his own pitch. "When a contestant defeats a monster, they are allowed to purchase the goods attained at a lower rate than the audience, or they can take the difference as gold when the onlookers purchase the goods."

"Now, you are fully allowed to discuss the amazing things you see in the Zoo, but the arena is... special. I am certain that you understand the negative connotations of being on the bad side of the Zoo." The butler looked pointedly at the pass Joe was still holding, "There is nothing here that is strictly legal, but this is also the favored entertainment of the Nobility. I'd recommend not discussing it with others, and any attempts to bring the guard against us can only end in failure, as there is a special transport system in place."

Joe thought over what he was being told, firmly believing that he had made an error in judgment coming here. Something was going to go wrong, and he was going to be blamed for it and have people hunting him again. A cynical outlook, yes, but also looking more and more likely to him. They were approaching the extra-wide doors, and as they passed through them, Joe got a notification.

Welcome to the Bloodsport Arena! All damage done here by sentient creatures against another sentient creature will halt when reaching 'one'. This allows blood but as a sport! When fighting non-sentient creatures, there are 50:50 odds that the creature will drop their best loot upon death, but the sentient falling in combat to a creature means returning to the beginning of the previous level. Fight strong, fight deadly, fight smart!

"I see..." Joe considered the words of the message. If he was reading this correctly, this building would be making a *massive* profit. Fifty percent odds of the best loot? The best loot Joe could think of was Cores. Was this a Core mill? Or did it mean loot boxes and natural stuff?

Either way, there was a roaring coming from the building, and it wasn't an animal. There was combat in progress, and the crowd was loving it. A rumbling announcer's voice reached Joe, "Looks like that's *all!* The newcomer has defeated the rock troll! Somehow, a thousand cuts managed to overcome the resistance and regeneration sung about in legends! Let's hear it for *Sam*–"

"Excuse me, Sir!" The butler gestured to the side. "Your seat is this way, and if you hurry, you may be able to bid on the items from the most recent battle."

There was a chance that Joe could get some rare Troll's Blood, a component for the *Ritual of Sacrificial Regeneration* that he had recently gained. Joe nodded and followed along. He was handed a paddle with a number on it and shown to a small, square box that seemed to be the primary seating method in the arena. There was no stadium seating, no bleachers or standing room: only small, private booths.

"I will be here if you need anything, sir." The butler seemed to be a package deal with the ticket. Neat. "Your ticket can be exchanged for up to five hundred gold worth of goods, but if you do not spend at least a thousand gold during your trip, you will lose your chance to attend again without another personal invitation."

No wonder this place could manage to afford individual attendees and make this place invitation only. A minimum tab of a thousand gold to come back? Joe was going to scoff at the idea until the Troll was harvested and the available goods were announced. "Looks like we had good luck here today, good people! Not only did we have the standard drops of crafting materials, our collection group has just informed us that there was a special drop! They are authenticating the item now..."

A minute later, the announcer came back with excitement causing his voice to tremor, "We have had the item appraised, and our new fighter has declined to purchase the item himself! Are we all ready?"

The crowd cheered, but the announcer hadn't been waiting. "As you all know, while everything is valued against the standard rarity scale, most professions have their own scale as well. What we have here is an alchemical drink, which ranges from a potion at the least to a concoction at the *Mythical* rarity. This item has been found to be an Ichor of Troll Aspect!"

Silence reigned as the announcer clarified, "This means that we have an *Artifact*-rarity drink to offer tonight! This Ichor will increase both strength and constitution by twenty points *permanently* while giving a week-long boost that will double regeneration of both health and stamina. There is a minor side effect of loss of balance that will clear up thirty minutes after drinking, but minor means just that: minor. We will start the bidding at thirty platinum!"

Joe paled at the cost. There was a one-hundred conversion between coins, which meant that the starting bid was three thousand gold. That would be about thirty thousand dollars when the game first got going. No wonder whoever was down there didn't jump at the chance to buy this, but they were going to make a good chunk of change anyway. He watched as the price climbed, stalling out at fifty platinum. That was half the amount that he had gained from killing the Archmage and freeing the mages from being slaves after hundreds of years.

Sickening that people could just casually toss that much money around. He was closing in on a total of twelve hundred platinum in his bank—if he converted everything up—but there was no way he was giving up one twenty-fourth of his total wealth for a boost like this. When the bidding came around for Troll's blood, he was able to get five servings for a hundred gold each—or five platinum—and that *still* made him ill. The Butler, on the other hand, nodded approvingly.

Just a short time later, the next battle started. It seemed that this was where all the creatures that weren't better used as menagerie members ended up. In the short amount of time that the next three battles took, Joe saw enough money pass through here that he could have bought a hundred miles of land from the Kingdom. The announcer came back, and this time, Joe's ears perked up.

A hulking man walked on to the field. "Hunter of the most *dangerous* game, this paladin of a deity has spent his last few weeks taking down his opposition, and tonight, he wanted to show us all his skills once more!"

"We have a treat *tonight*, everyone! We were recently gifted a rare and deadly creature that will debut against one of the fan favorites!" The crowd hooted as the man blazed with violent, purple light, leaving the ground around him looking like someone had attacked it with a chainsaw. "As his opponent, we have a *Creeping Death Squirrel!*"

Once again, the crowd reacted, but this time, it was in horror. People stood to leave, but the magnified voice cut them off. "Don't worry, we have trained professionals standing by that will be able to return the beast to its cage if something happens, and besides, the safest place is the arena!"

Muttering filled the air, but the show went on nonetheless. A small door opened, and all eyes turned to watch the platform the squirrel was trapped on appear in the area. It was remaining in one spot or really close to it. Joe could tell from here that the confinement ritual hadn't been tampered with, and it seemed that they were setting this fight up to make the paladin look good.

"I wonder if I should do anything here?" Joe wondered *very* softly. Near inaudibly, really.

Query (Pray) success! You have been given a divine answer to your question. Message from Tatum:

'Absolutely, *you should.*'

CHAPTER FORTY-ONE

"Well, that's clear enough for me." Joe watched as the paladin charged at the platform in a blaze of purple light. Joe waited, and just before he brought down his gargantuan, two-handed claymore on the creature...

Do you want to deactivate Ritual of containment targeting creature: Creeping Death Squirrel? Caution, this will fully deactivate the ritual. To reactivate the effect, the ritual must be completed again. Yes / No.

Joe hit 'yes'. *Clang*. Had he been too late? Cheers filled the air, and though the paladin seemed confused, he raised his arms in victory. He started walking toward the exit but was met with the grim visage of a butler on the other side of a *closed* gate. The arena was not allowing him to exit, which could mean only one thing: his opponent was still alive.

The Paladin blazed with light, coating himself in protection as he walked around. There was no sign of the squirrel, and he eventually looked up at the crowd and shrugged. The man coughed, and blood came from his mouth. He spat on to his hand, and somehow, Joe's balcony view zoomed in so he could see what was happening. A mouthful of teeth was in his hand, but only for a moment, as they transformed into acorns a moment later.

As the Paladin ran around looking for something to fight, more and more of his body fell apart. Only a minute after the start of his degradation, his body collapsed into a pile of acorns. The squirrel appeared on top of the pile and picked up a nut, adorably nibbling on it.

"Ohh, that's going to *hurt!*" the announcer told the crowd. "We know that he had just reached level twenty, dropping to the start of level nineteen is going to be *rough*! Well, time to move on!"

A bubble appeared around the squirrel, and it appeared to freeze in place. "We'll bring this little guy back sometime soon. Make sure you come back often so you don't miss when it is finally defeated!"

Reward gained from continuous quest: No, I'm right! You gain 100 reputation points from your deity and 1000 divine energy for your deity!

"Must have been an indirect attack on him?" Joe grinned as he watched the next round of combat begin. That was an unexpected boost, and he had even managed to drop the guy a full level. A regular fight couldn't do that, as PvP caused no experience loss. No wonder Tatum had reached out when Joe 'used' his daily query-prayer. It was nice to see that he was still watching.

Skill increase: Query (Pray) (Novice II). About time you used this skill again. Weren't you told to focus on the skills you had?

Joe looked at that message—a *friendly* message—and knew that the last part must have come from Tatum. Joe was so lost in thought that he completely missed the next battle and only perked up when he heard the announcer talking about what would be for sale. "From this Variant Winged Terror, we were able to retrieve an Uncommon Greater Core! The bidding will start at five platinum and increase from there!"

Joe knew he needed to get this, and he also knew that showing too much enthusiasm would cause these filthy-rich people to make it impossible for him to do so. So, he waited as the bid slowly climbed, peaking at seven platinum. This might be a more common item than he was expecting if it was only going for this much. Joe raised his paddle, and his room flashed.

That was the signal that he was bidding, and he continued until he got the Core for nine platinum.

Yikes. Well... the flawed version had given him five thousand experience. How much would an Uncommon be worth? The butler gently coughed and handed Joe the Core as it dropped out of a chute. "Here is a return ticket, Sir. As you have spent the required minimum, you are welcome to return again."

You have gained an item: Uncommon Greater Core. Would you like to convert this into experience? Experience value: 10,000. Yes / No.

Joe slapped 'no' and stored the Core in his ring to get the temptation out of the way. He pulled bank notes out of his codpiece and stacked them on the table next to him. When he looked over again, the butler had left change for the remainder. "Keep that as a bonus for doing such an excellent job."

"My thanks, Sir." Joe watched the other fights, but there was nothing else that demanded his attention. Anything else that he would have wanted was at a price that he simply couldn't manage to make happen. The evening started to wind down, and Joe was given a *spectacular* meal as the fights ended and a light and firework show began. He shook his head; those were all spells, not fireworks. Still, by the time Joe was full, the show wasn't even close to being over.

He was finally ushered out of the room and brought back to Ardania via the person-drawn cart. A strange night but very interesting. Joe had really thought that he was going to have a bad time, but the arena had been interesting. It was a gladiator pit, yes, but it doubled as an amazing auction hall as well. He was looking forward to his next visit, though he wasn't as excited to spend more money. The fourteen platinum spent this evening translated into fourteen *thousand* dollars. For six small items.

Still... he had a great time and got a few much-needed items. For that alone, the night was worth it. As he arrived in Ardania, he was surprised to find himself in the main square. Transport from the arena to the nice part of town? That was handy. Joe accessed his own travel system and appeared a moment later in the guild's town. As he walked out of the temple, two messengers caught him.

"Mr. Joe? Message from Lord Mike!" The first was cut off by Joe's rapid-fire question.

"Does he *ask* you to call him that?"

"Ha!" The second messenger laughed, and the first flushed. "He totally hates it. That's why we do it. Message from Aten, this one takes priority."

"Go ahead then." Joe motioned at the second.

"Aten says that they have what they need for the wall around the guild area proper. Something about how it was easier to get rock hard than processed wood?" The messenger had a smug grin on his face, and it didn't take long to figure out why.

"*Seriously?*" The first messenger took a swing at the other. "I had *the same* message. Why didn't you just tell me we were supposed to say the same thing?"

"Hey, I didn't want to wait around all *alone!*" The messengers walked off, so Joe ignored them and went off to do his own thing. It appeared that he would be raising more than one building today.

"Wonder if... hey!" Joe called out to the messengers before they got too far away. "Tell Aten that I'll get to that in the morning! It's late, and I want to sleep!"

"Okay!"

Joe didn't want to keep running off to do stressful things as he arrived back from *other* stressful things. He found a bed and lay there thinking about the amazing things that he could do with a Greater Core converted into a Mana Battery. He would need to upgrade the material making the ritual circles before he attempted it with something like this, as a *ten thousand* second conversion process meant almost three hours of spinning ritual circles. His current version would melt to slag well before the process completed.

When he drifted off, he didn't even realize it. When Joe woke up, it was to the amazing smell of potent coffee waving under his nose. His coffee elemental was bubbling happily, and as he opened his eyes... the tiny voice came into his ears.

"*Drink me! I'm delicious!*"

"You sure are, little dude." Joe opened his mouth and allowed the coffee to pour in. Bliss. Total bliss. Much reduced, the elemental poured itself back into Joe's ring to recover. Now it was time to gather his people and make the magic happen. Joe went about his schedule, taking three hours to get his stats to increase. All but luck, karmic luck, and charisma once again. Too bad there hadn't been a potion for sale last night to boost his intelligence. He might have gone for it.

During this time, he had messengers going to Aten, Mike, and all his Coven and party members. Today was going to hurt in terms of mana expenditure. Finally caught up in what he felt he needed to do, Joe started toward the guild hall area.

Aten had decided that it was going to be much more important for them to have a food source in the most highly-protected area of the guild than to have yet *another* spare housing space. To that end, the space originally set out for the final blocky barracks was allocated to the greenhouse. Right now, there were huge piles of dirt and the like that were around the area, to the point it looked like the guild was building a berm around their back area. Today's activities would fix that.

First, Joe needed to deal with some minor inconveniences. "Hi, Aten, quick thing?"

"What's up, Joe?" Aten looked over and saw that Joe had a certain look on his face. "You did something that is going to cost me money, didn't you?"

"I got a Greater Core that will work. It's stronger than strictly needed, but I double checked and it is still within tolerances. In fact, it will make the building stronger, faster." Joe looked at Aten straight on, preparing himself for what he felt needed to be said. "It cost nine platinum to get this. Not only that, but I infused *all* of the one thousand required glass chunks after buying them myself."

"You want us to pay you for them, then?" Aten rolled his eyes, a touch of resentment appearing. "I can make it happen–"

"No, Aten. I'm saying that I want to make sure that I am more tightly tied to the guild." Joe maintained his stare. "I need a promise from you that the guild will always have my back. I'm not going to make a power play, you know that better than most, and Mike has promised that I'd be an 'Elder'. I just want to make sure that I am always going to be welcome and respected by not only you but the guild as well."

"I'm putting a *lot* of myself into what I am doing here, more than you've heard yet. My team almost got *deleted* for these plans, and I need you to know that we are risking our *actual* life for the guild. Permanent deletion qualifies as an actual threat to *all* of us now that this has become our world." Joe was trying not to get emotional, but he needed Aten to realize what was on the line here. "We've had problems in the past, and I want those behind us. I'm committed to the guild now, and I just want the same in return."

Aten didn't break eye contact, still nodding heavily. "Joe, you are my *friend*. I *swear* that we'll do right by you and your team. I swear it as a friend and as the Guild Commander."

Guild Commander Aten has made an oath to take your side when you are actually in the right! This is a binding promise and will result in negative repercussions if broken! Not very cool of you to have your friends make this sort of promise, though.

"Good enough for me. Let's make some magic!" Joe cleared his throat and changed the subject; sharing emotional moments was uncomfortable. Out came the ritual blueprint of the building, and Joe worked with the city planner to get everything set up in the correct spot. This was going to be an interesting addition to the area, as the greenhouse would be shaped like a curved, seven-pointed star when built. There was only one entrance and exit, which would make it easy to control what went in and out but make it harder to protect the building itself.

Joe glanced at the people showing up and decided that it was time to get everyone involved. "Alright, we are going to need as many people as we can possibly get on this one. High powered building, high-powered magic needed. Or just a *lot* of it."

CHAPTER FORTY-TWO

"How many people do you think we need, Joe?" Mike pulled out a clipboard, quill in place to write out a requisition order.

"At least another three dozen. The cost is a combination of Rare and Special at the Expert rank, one hundred ninety-two thousand minus–" Joe was going to explain more, but Aten cut him off.

"I'll handle it, throw me into the ritual." Aten stepped forward, and Mike looked at him with concern.

"Are you sure? That's a once-a-week skill!" Mike's words failed to sway Aten. "That's supposed to be the last line of defense–"

"It's a skill that needs only *one* more use before ranking up." Aten dismissively waved away Mike's concerns. "Is everything else ready?"

"Just need your blood, a scale from a green Wyvern for coloration, and... and the placement of Jelly Slime to increase the building's self-healing goes in this slot. I'll physically place this specialty glass after, but a thousand chunks of Imbued Glass goes here..." Joe was moving around the illusion of the seven-pointed-star building and leaving nodes of reagents and stabilizing goo's where the ritual dictated.

Aten, following along with Joe, listened to the mumbled words and paled. Items kept appearing wherever Joe went, and some of the things he casually placed had a value no less than the glass he had supplied. Joe knew that Aten was listening and watching and took his time so that he could really showcase his sincerity in maintaining good guild relations. Eventually, there was only one last item that Joe had and was hesitating to add.

"This is optional..." Joe waffled back-and-forth, debating over the benefit of using this here. "I do only have *ten...*"

"What is it? What does it do?" Aten quietly inquired, leaning in closely to see what Joe was debating about.

"Condensed Ectoplasm." Joe held up the barely substantial component, letting the misty, mysterious nature showcase itself. "If I added it in, there is a chance that the building just *ignores* certain physical attacks. The Imbued Glass will make it hard to damage in the first place, but with this added, there is a thirty percent chance that a physical attack does *nothing* to the building itself."

"Really?" Aten leaned in to observe it more closely. "One item can have such a drastic effect?"

"Oh, absolutely." Joe made his choice, and he placed the Condensed Ectoplasm next to the iridescent Core. "Alright, if I'm gonna be all in, I need to be *all* in. Let's hurry and get this done. A thief would have an *amazing* time here right now. He could *buy* a town with all this. A crap town, but still."

Joe and Aten stood just a few feet apart, the Coven spaced equally around them. "Alright, everyone ready? Aten? Don't use your stat-absorbing skill too soon. It still only lasts for a minute, correct?"

"One minute and *six seconds* now," Aten told him proudly.

"Gotcha, wait until I say go, okay?" Aten nodded, and Joe continued the setup. "Starting in three, two, one... *Nos pascat: nos pascat: nos pascere!*"

With the first few phrases of the ritual out of the way, mana began to flow like a river. First, the outer members of the Coven were coated in mana; then it stretched between them. The energy started to change form, becoming blue chains that then reached out and wrapped around Joe and Aten. Shackles formed on ankles, wrists, and necks. As the third circle lit up, the group was pulled into the air like marionettes, and by the fourth circle, they were rotating in a strange dance.

"Is this supposed to happen?" Aten managed to shout.

"Different..." one of the new Ritualists shouted as he spun in place like a ballerina, "every... time!"

"Good work remembering that, Hannah! Aten, pretty sure the chains are a reminder of what I did to get the Condensed Ectoplasm!" Joe barked between chants. "It seems that the reagents used impact the ritual and are a small throwback to your experiences!"

Skill increase: Ritual Lore (Apprentice II). Learning while doing! Dangerous, yet effective!

Skill increase: Teaching (Beginner 0). You can teach in many situations! People you are teaching now have a chance to start with an additional 2% of your skill level when learning a skill from you!

The notifications took Joe off guard, and his control nearly slipped. He pulled himself together but not before wasting fifty mana by missing his cue. With a motion and a wave of power, the rings began gyrating. Illusions of ritual circles were covering the area, and it seemed that a black hole was forming in the center. Not due to a lack of light but because the land around the area seemed to be ignoring gravity and collecting into a single point.

Dirt, loam, sand, compost... all the things that had been collected over the last ten days began lifting and swirling. Soon, nearly ten metric tons of earth was in the air above the guild hall in a giant ball. The next stage of the process began, and Joe spat blood as his mana was pulled on *sharply*. Splitting apart into seven identical shapes, the land was hidden behind flying, now-green glass. "Aten, do it!"

Aten closed his eyes for a moment and began to *swell*. Not in physical size but the aura of danger that always lightly coated him. Mana exploded out of him, mostly captured by the ritual. Some went to waste, as he was intentionally pouring out everything he could for the full minute that his skill lasted. Joe wasn't immune from the effects of the guild-draining skill; he felt all of his stats get reduced to their closest threshold.

He struggled to maintain control of the ritual, holding on just *barely*, like holding a heavy-yet-fragile glass as you were spun in a circle. Actually, *exactly* like that. The final stage of the ritual began, and Aten was still going strong. The last time Joe had seen this, Aten had managed to get all of his stats to around two hundred. That would put his mana capacity at twenty-five hundred and his regen at a fifty a second. The glow faded as Aten's skill ended, and Joe's attributes returned to normal.

The last of the needed mana was added just as Joe felt his ear get torn off. He screamed, seeing a massive ballista bolt *missing* him as the ritual spun him away. Unfortunately, Aten was spun *into* place and took the tree-sized bolt in the chest. "*Urk.*"

You have created an Evergrowth Greenhouse! This building provides a necessary service; it allows for the production of food! You are also able to grow herbs and other plants within, but be cautious! When the mana density of the building reaches a certain point, it will grow. After the first growth cycle, Weeds will begin to spawn. If the weed problem is ignored for too long, this building will revert to a dungeon. This will increase output of all cultivated goods by up to 1000% but increase the danger of taking them by the same amount!

To grow, the building will require the same resources that it was given to be created. Upon reaching the first growth, the Evergrowth Greenhouse will begin to absorb from the ground in the surrounding areas, functionally acting as a sewage system. If there are not enough 'deposits' in the area, plant growth may be stunted as resources are pulled from the area.

You have created a Special Rare Structure, as this building is no longer Unique to this world! Congratulations! All stats and bonuses for this building have been increased by 10% thanks to your title 'Architect of Artifacts'. Building durability: 211,200/211,200 (Original value: 193,000) Mana: 0/35,200 (Original value: 32,000) Special: 33% chance to ignore physical damage. (Original value: 30%)

"Aten!" Joe struggled against the mana chains that were dissipating, and they vanished into motes of light which were sucked into the shining new building. Aten's body was still dancing, the chains twirling him in place. Joe pulled on his foot, and the man collapsed to the ground. He was already dead, and Joe was starting to get woozy.

Then he saw the glistening tip of the ballista and realized that he had likely been poisoned. "Cleanse!"

He washed out his ear hole, then had the water delve into his body. A moment later, poison washed out of the wound, making his ear look like a black-blood spigot. "Mike, where are you?"

"Working on coordinating the effort to find who did this!" Mike called over, his hands flying around keyboards that only he could see. A moment later, Joe received a guild-wide quest.

Emergency Guild Quest: A Perfect Ten. The Guild Commander has been brutally attacked! A ballista bolt took him through the chest in the middle of the Guild's town! Find who did this, bring us their head, name, and group affiliation! Reward: 5,000 gold, promotion or accolades depending on position.

"A perfect ten? Really?" Joe looked over at Mike.

"I make the quest, not the name," Mike informed him with a growl. "Feces, Aten is really the best person to deal with all this."

"Gimme a moment here. I'm pretty sure we are the same level. Abyss, I might be *higher* level than him by now." Joe took a breath and started doing what looked like tai-chi movements. Ten seconds passed before, "*Resurrection!*"

Skill increase: Resurrection (Novice III). Bring three people back to reach the next rank! People seem to die all around you. This skill should be a breeze to rank up!

Aten stepped out of the portal just as his corpse vanished, and the gooey sensation and ick vanished from his boot a moment later as his previous body faded. "Anyone see what happened there?"

Guild Quest updated: Feed the people! The building is in place! When it can sustain a population of at least 10,000 people, you will get the reward!

"Someone tried to kill Joe, pretty sure," Mike called over. "I think they were trying to see what would happen when he was killed during a big ritual."

Joe blanched at the thought. "Well... there wouldn't be much town left. There would be an instant release of the equivalent of a hundred ninety-two thousand mana. Boom. Big boom."

"Are there any... protections we can put in place to avoid something like that in the future?" Aten calmly inquired, even as Mike sat down hard. "You know what? Let's go ahead and get that wall up right now. Mike, get the guild on high alert. I feel like this isn't the end of whatever people are sending our way. Also, start pulling enough from the treasury that we can get a full wall around the entire town by the end of the week and start hiring for guard positions. I'm seeing this as an act of war, and as we get better things..."

He gestured at the vibrant-yet-empty greenhouse next to them. "Well, I doubt people will be *less* likely to attack us."

CHAPTER FORTY-THREE

"Ten minutes before the wall goes up!" Messengers were shouting the announcements throughout the town, which had every guild member ready for action. There would be no repeat of the near-disaster from that morning. The Guild was ready.

"Who comes for the Wanderers?" the message changed suddenly, and the few buildings in the area shook at the reply.

"*The Strongest! The Best! We kill all the rest!*"

"I think it's time, Joe." Aten looked at the Rituarchitect, who was furiously writing out various formula changes. "You have a working version?"

Instead of answering, Joe barked over at his Coven, "Kirby, where is that tri-fold array design? I need it *yesterday!* Big_Mo! Do you or do you *not* have the final calculation for the angular momentum of the drawbridge? Tolerance is three percent!"

"Yes, Joe!" Kirby's harried response came.

"Big_Mo!"

"Math is harder when getting *yelled* at!" Big_mo shouted back. "Done! Check it!"

Joe looked at the equation for a bare instant. "Two percent off, go to the third decimal on step three next time! Kirby, add a sine curve right... here, and we'll have a sympathetic link that can accommodate the power shift!"

"Why is all this not ready?" Aten looked at the robed figures helplessly.

"It *was*. We made slight adjustments," Joe didn't even look up from his paper as he launched a reply back. "Adding in some Troll Blood. It'll boost durability and add in a self-repair function. We're going all out here; hold tight, Commander!"

"Three minutes!" the words echoed over the area, and Joe nodded at the group.

"Done! Validated, get in position!" The Coven members scattered to stand in a pentagram with Joe at the northmost point. "Need seven volunteers!"

Seven people, including a reluctant Aten and Mike, got into the non-cardinal positions Joe indicated. "Get ready. Remember to breathe! Wall is going up in ninety seconds."

As the messengers counted down from ten, Joe started the ritual. It was going to be really neat to have an effect happening right at the same time as hitting zero, and showmanship was something everyone enjoyed. As the messengers hit zero, a ball of light jumped into the sky and started following the holographic path that Joe's Survey Grid had set up. Where the ball passed, a completed wall was left behind.

Joe and the others had been left on the ground to awkwardly stare at each other. This was... new. Every once in a while, someone would cry out as their mana was drained, but since they were all just... *hanging out*, this made things even more awkward. For some reason, the mana drain was invisible this time around, making the process... cringy.

"Ah~h!"

"Ooh!" A person spasmed and fell to his knees.

"Yah!"

"*Ouchie*!" Joe coughed and tried to pretend that someone else had said that. The wall was forming around the area with a sound like approaching thunder, leaving them in shadow as the stones mortared themselves together. There was very little in the way of overexertion; the large number of people was easily able to compensate for the mana draw needed by the wall.

"And..." Joe watched as the ritual faded in his eyes, "done!"

"Good work, everyone," Aten called to the assembled people, who started to cheer. "This marks a new point of safety for our people! I know we have been having trouble sometimes, but no longer are we sleeping in unprotected areas! Now the guild has a way to point outward and tell people that we can protect our own, and soon, we can feed them all!"

People began to cheer as Aten, the face of the guild, continued to speak. In the background, Mike was moving around the area and reassigning people. By the time Aten stopped talking, there were guards patrolling the new wall.

Guild alert! The Guild's Town has reached town level one! You have earned the right to appear on the map! Your leader is selecting a name for the town now... name accepted! Welcome to 'Wanderer's Argosy'.

Aten was looking around proudly, waiting for people to be excited about the title. Joe was really happy when someone *else* was the first to speak up. "Uhm. Aten, what does that mean?"

"Seriously?" Aten looked crestfallen. "It... Argosy means 'a rich supply'. So here it means either that the Wanderers have a rich supply or that there is a rich supply *of* Wanderers!"

Guild vote started: Petition to change name to 'Towny McTownface'. Yes / No.

"What? That's a *thing*?" Aten called as the green bar next to 'Yes' rapidly filled up. "Who made that a thing? *Voting*?"

Guild vote completed: Petition to change name to 'Towny McTownface' has passed! Welcome to Towny McTownface!

Joe pretended that he hadn't voted, but he *definitely* had. His lips were twitching, and not a single person met Aten's eyes. The Guild Commander was glaring at *everyone*. "I hate you all."

That got the entire group to start laughing, and soon, even Aten had to either join in or make things worse. They laughed, and Mike announced a small feast to celebrate the achievement. It was an actual achievement, with the guild being the first to *raise* a town to level one. Others had started with a more *improved* town, but they missed out on the bonus. All it gave them was an improved reputation with Ardania, but it was still great for the guild.

A *very* small feast was eaten, and Joe finally did some relaxing. He checked his notifications and saw that he had gained twelve hundred combined class experience for the greenhouse and the wall. He smiled happily; there was something about being surrounded by a huge, *thick* wall that let you relax more fully.

Joe ate with the group, then joined a small expedition into the Evergrowth Greenhouse so that he could teach people the functions. Only Aten, Mike, and a few other non-combat squad leaders that were going to be in charge of taking care of plants and harvesting food were allowed to go in.

"How does this work, Joe?" Aten poked the dirt as they got to the third room, as there was still no plants or instructions of any kind.

Joe looked over at the guild leader in surprise. "Ah... standard greenhouse rules apply? Plant seeds in those rows, water comes from there, and harvest when ripe?"

"Fin! Come here." Aten introduced another guy to Joe. "This is Fin, our guild's head Herbalist. He's a Druid and has been working tirelessly to keep us fed until now. He got a promotion for his work until now, so he's gonna be running the show in here."

"Only reward for hard work is more work, right?" Fin quipped, then shook Joe's hand and motioned for him to continue.

Pulling out a small bag of seeds he had collected for this exact purpose, Joe walked to the planter rows. A corn kernel was in his hand, but a red glow appeared when he got close to the dirt. "Looks like this area isn't good for corn. Let's try... potatoes? Yep! There we go. Looks like french fries are back on the menu! Figure out a beef supply next, and we are going to have a good time."

The group watched the soil for a minute, and in that amount of time, a tiny sprout popped out of the dirt. Joe was watching the building menu and noticed the minor amount of mana accumulated by the building trickle back to zero. "Neat, looks like the building uses its mana to grow things. It's out, so that's all for now. I'll plant the rest of these and join you guys? Aten? A word?"

"Nice to meet you in person, Joe!" Fin waved as he walked off.

"Nice guy." While the others excitedly chattered and left, Joe pulled out another seed and started walking around.

The fifth star-annex showed that it would accept the seed, which was great because Aten was getting antsy. "What are you up to, Joe?"

"This seed is from a grape plant that I swiped when I attended a... Noble event. Pretty sure it is the main export of a Noble family, and I doubt that they'd be happy I have it. Just so you know... so be careful with who you let know about them."

Aten grinned at Joe. "You sly dog."

"I'm good at keeping things *hidden*." Joe grinned as he planted the other seeds; then he looked Aten dead in the eyes and pulled out a special plate of glass. There was a slot for things on all of the side paneling, and when Joe placed the item, it closed and locked. "Natural Imbued Glass of Fertility. Makes any plants in the area of effect produce offspring about a fifth faster. We'll have a crop of grapes in no time."

"I'll look for some discrete people who want to make wine for a living." Aten winked at Joe. "By the way, you've really proven yourself to me, and I was trying to think of how to show my appreciation after our conversation. When we make a Sect, you are going to be First Elder. Third in command; basically, the Prime Minister of our group. Sound like a plan?"

Guild Quest updated: The making of an Elder. Reward increased: position of First Elder when the Noble Wanderer's Guild becomes a Sect. Failure: No reward.

Joe was shocked, though quite pleased with this outcome. "Aten, thanks, man. I'll make sure to keep the amazing things coming."

"Never had a doubt." Aten fist-bumped Joe, and they left the building; the two only taking a few minutes to plant the rest of the seeds Joe had brought along. There weren't many, as Joe only had a small selection for testing purposes. The guild had a larger shipment coming in, actually having made a deal to buy some of the stock from the Golden Greens Guild that Joe had made friends with. Apparently, Teddy had found a large store of plants that had gone to seed, and she wanted to sell them before they rotted. Joe was glad that the conversion to Tatum had benefited them so quickly.

Leaving Aten to his own devices, Joe went off to get a drink. The guild had subsidized the pub for the evening, setting the prices extra-low in celebration. He had just started taking a sip of his first drink when a well-dressed man covered by a *perfectly ordinary* over-cloak sat across from him. "You *really* screwed up this time, Traveler."

Joe couldn't see the man's face, but his bearing was familiar. "Do I know you? Or how I messed up?"

"Kind of and not likely. In that order." The man looked up, and all of a sudden, Joe felt a sharp pressure on his forehead. Pressure in the *exact* spot that the King had pressed a small object into his skin to grant him a skill. The fact that the item was reacting could only mean one thing.

This man was Royalty.

CHAPTER FORTY-FOUR

"I am actually here to warn a member of my *Extended Family* about a plot against him." The unknown man seemed to be taking his time, enjoying watching Joe squirm. It was obvious that he was here out of obligation, not true care. "But first, I am wondering why you seem *so* familiar."

Joe looked at the man in puzzlement, but the man's words made it click for him. This was the Prince. "Oh. Ah. I'm not sure you'd like to know, Your Maj–"

Hist. The man made a sharp gesture, and Joe stopped talking. "None of that here, please. Just tell me. I *swear* I won't hold it against you."

"Deal." Joe swallowed, knowing that this was a bad idea nonetheless. "You wouldn't happen to remember a jail cell, perhaps a healer that was punched to death?"

The man was silent. Joe sent a wave of water at a man near them who was stumbling from drinking too much, and a moment later, the man in question was sober. "I... see. Well. I never thought I'd get to do this in person. Can I see your weapon?"

He pulled out a small item and touched it to Joe's staff. "Superb. I'm going to send you something from me soon. My parents told me that they 'fixed' the issue, but I remain very unsettled over the entire affair. Thank you for my life, Joe. What I'll do here in no way makes up for you saving my life and me taking yours, but I hope it is a small start."

"There is a plot against you, Joe," the Prince informed him seriously. "Not you *personally*, but Travelers in general. As you return to life, there becomes a need to force you into acting a certain way without threats of your death. What has happened thus far is that most guilds and such have made it impossible to gain their skills and abilities without giving them some commitment to work for them in return; that is, joining them."

"Now, most of these groups caved when the Mage's College opened, as a good portion of the pressure was coming from the Nobility. Actually, The Accords." The Prince paused as Joe raised a hand.

"Also my doing."

"...Right." Now the Prince had a different look in his eyes than when he had started the conversation. Arrogance had shifted to concern, to friendship, to near-awe. "I see what my father likes about you. Listen. Here is where the issue lies. This wall you just built. Does it look familiar at all?"

"Not really?" Joe stared into the distance and tried to figure out the issue. "I've got nothing."

"You built a tier-two version of the tier-five wall that surrounds Ardania." The fact was stated bluntly, but Joe still didn't understand the issue.

"The fair-use law should prevent any issues, shouldn't it?" Joe breathed, trying to figure out what was wrong.

"Not from violations of national security," the Prince told him grimly. "If others can see this wall, study it, and find the flaws... our Kingdom could be toppled far easier than we would ever expect. Blueprints for this structure are stored in the vault of the Architect's Guild, and your guild will be on the hook. Not for theft: for *espionage*. Not for building a wall: for exposing a national secret. *Treason.* Your reputation cannot protect you. Your standing means nothing against this charge."

Joe swallowed on a dry throat and wet his lips. "What can I do?"

"That's up to you, but the Royal Guard got a tip about the wall being built. Likely as it was happening, since you are all being watched so closely. The Crown has issued a quest to seek the truth of the matter, and the Royal Guard will arrive in force tomorrow. If the wall is erect, which it is, this guild will be disbanded. The leaders will be jailed. All buildings owned by the guild... will be seized and turned over as thanks to the person who informed the Crown: the leader of the Architect's Guild."

Joe felt his stomach sink. "They would take the buildings *I* made?"

"As a reward, yes," the Prince confirmed, looking around carefully and pulling his robe tighter. "I need to leave soon. If you make it through this, we will have a quest for you to complete in return for the warning."

"Wait!" Joe stopped him as he stood to leave. "What if the Guard gets here and the wall is *not* here?"

"Oh...?" The Prince smiled. "Then I did my job well, and the person who made a false claim to the King would be jailed and also forced to pay reparations to the wronged party *and* the Kingdom."

Joe nodded, and the Prince resumed walking away. Joe stepped outside just after him, but in that time, the Prince had vanished. "Need to learn how to do that. *Messenger~r~r!*"

His shout echoed around the area, and he kept shouting until someone showed up. "Go get Aten. Tell him it's an emergency! Tell him third stall from the left, look for the big guy."

"You got it!"

Joe took off running for the Grand Ritual Hall, opening a passage to it and leaving it open. He pulled a Juggernaut from door duty and had him make sure only Aten was allowed access. There was no time to waste; Joe had a ritual to design. It was time to learn how to Raze.

Ink was splattering as Joe worked, but he cared not one whit. He simply had his shadows come along behind him and grab the waste. "Calibration... this can be used on any structure, but knowing the blueprint ahead of time will allow for faster destruction and more resources reclaimed. I know the blueprint, but should I work on that or just get to Razing?"

"Joe, what's happening? What's the emergency?" Aten came running into the room, a fluffy robe and boxers being the only thing he was wearing.

"I need to take down the wall," Joe told him, unable to look away from the ink. "*Drat!* I messed up."

He restarted, his quill flying across the page and leaving behind complex differential equations that were so small that they looked like straight lines. Aten was trying to figure out what Joe was saying. "Joe! Explain!"

"*Treason!* The wall was a *setup!*" Joe garbled the explanation as he slowed his furious scribbling. He was getting near the part he messed up last time. "Ring one complete! Ring two, go! Aten, if the wall is here in the morning, the Royal Guard will disband the guild, throw all leaders in prison, and hand over the buildings to the Architect's Guild! Figure out ways to stall them, make sure no one tries to stop me, get me the two most powerful Cores the guild has, *now!*"

Aten didn't ask any follow-ups, showcasing his trust in Joe far more than his words ever could. He took off at a run, returning half an hour later as Joe completed the second ring. "Here, Cores! I have people going out to drop trees across the road, set knockout traps, and anything else they can think of. What else do you need?"

"I need *fifty-seven people* to get with me and balance this ritual," Joe told him. Just start spacing them out in sets of prime numbers. Two, three, five, seven, eleven, thirteen, seventeen. I'll be at the center with the most mana-stuffed mage you can find, and the rest are going to make this thing *zip*. *Everyone else* needs to be making sure that we aren't attacked."

"You got it." Aten waited a moment longer, but nothing else was said. He ran off, still in his robe. Joe nodded belatedly, his mind back on the ritual in front of him.

"Good." He pocketed the Cores, then continued working. The next ring took an hour to create. The fourth and final took two. It was now three in the morning, and Joe was exhausted. There was no way he was going to stop, so he got his Coffee Elemental to whip up a fresh batch of caffeine for him.

Ritual ready to be used, Joe ran out to the main area, leaving the Pathfinder's Hall and locking it behind him. The Juggernauts were given orders to slay anyone that tried to force the door, and he made sure that they would be as *vindictive* as possible to anyone attacking the temple. There might be someone who was legally granted his toys, but they would need to walk through an *ocean of blood* to get them.

Joe hurried out to the same area he had been in for the *creation* of the wall, assuming that the others were thinking they needed to be in the same spot to take it down. Incorrect but beneficial to finding where people were waiting. Where *was* everyone? This was... wasn't Aten supposed to be on top of things? Then Joe found the first unconscious body. "What in the...?"

He felt the people's necks; still alive. What was going on? "*Cleanse*!

Skill level too low!

Joe stared at the notification mutely. He had never run into something that he couldn't even *start* to cure. Sure, the water had gone into the person, but Joe hadn't been able to use it to find anything! To him, it seemed that there was nothing wrong with the bodies on the ground. "How did they get *everyone*?"

There had to be *someone* around that was awake, and Joe was determined to find them and exact revenge... no. Never mind. He was going to continue with the *plan*. Seeking out whoever had done this was a fool's errand, more likely to get him killed than to get revenge. If he was killed, there was no *way* that the wall was coming down in time. Joe hefted Aten on to his shoulders when he found him and trudged back to the Pathfinder's Hall. This way, he would have an indication of when people were waking up. He felt good carrying Aten, strength-wise at least.

Name: Joe '*Tatum's Chosen Legend*' Class: Mage (Actual: Rituarchitect)
Profession: Tenured Scholar (Actual: Arcanologist)
Character Level: 15 Exp: 134,813 Exp to next level: 1,187
Rituarchitect Level: 3 Exp: 4,390 Exp to next level: 1,610
Hit Points: 330/330
Mana: 1,137.5/1,137.5
Mana regen: 30.3/sec (Base 27.55/sec increased by gear)
Stamina: 183/295
Stamina regen: 5.67/sec

Characteristic: Raw score (Modifier)

Strength: 31 (1.31)
Dexterity: 40 (1.40)
Constitution: 38 (1.38)
Intelligence: 91 (2.41)
Wisdom: 76 (2.26)

Charisma: 31 (1.31)

Perception: 60 (2.10)

Luck: 30 (1.30)

Karmic Luck: +1

His stamina was draining rapidly from lugging Aten around, but it was needed. Back to his current predicament; it was more than likely that the guild had been knocked out so that the Architects would be sure that they were *all* arrested and collected. Joe just had no idea *how* they did it.

Was it the beer? If so, why hadn't he been affected? Actually, no. He knew that Aten didn't drink in public, and there was no way *everyone* from the crafters to the guards *on duty* were drinking. Must be a spell or an item of some kind that could hit the entire group. Was he missed because he was underground? Were the slow-down efforts in place to give him more time? A magical effect would at least explain why Cleanse did nothing.

Since everyone was unconscious, Joe decided to alter the Raze ritual using the blueprints for the wall. Why not? When that was done and there was still no sign of change in Aten, Joe started to get worried. There was another way... but he was reluctant to use it. Still... he took a deep breath and went to the walled-in guild area. He got near the base of the guild hall and looked up.

He needed to get up there, and he had no idea if there were ladders around. Joe was about to *jump* when something in his mind tickled him. Didn't he have a quest? Might as well get working on that. He took a look at the nearly forgotten quest and set Jumplomancer as his 'public' class.

Quest updated: Playing your fake role III. As a Jumplomancer, your job is to create confusion, avoid attacks,

and demonstrate amazing ability beyond the dreams of another!
Avoid pursuit three times by jumping to an improbable location
and escaping unseen. 0/3. Dodge ten attacks by jumping out of
the way. 0/10. Jump through the _ERROR_ Finish destroying a
structure while in mid-air. 0/1. Reward: Variable.

Did... did that quest get altered as it was being assigned?
How? Who? He didn't have time for this! Joe crouched down
and put all of his thirty-one points of strength behind jumping.
Now, being thirty percent stronger than an average human on
earth didn't translate to being able to jump fifteen feet up.

Luckily, he had a Master-rank zero Jump skill to make
up for it.

CHAPTER FORTY-FIVE

Joe caught the edge of the roof and pulled himself up. "Ugh, *yeah*! Third time's the charm, baby!"

He had needed a running start, as the first jump had proven to him. The second ended with him *just* missing the edge, but the third time had been as perfectly done as possible. Joe wasted no time, walking up the roof and getting to the center. He pulled metal ritual rings out of his codpiece and positioned them as well as possible on the slightly sloped roof.

"I really hope Aten understands if this all goes to feces." Joe pulled out one of the Cores that Aten had given him and looked it over. It was a high-grade Lesser Core and could be converted to thirty-five hundred experience. Trying not to resist *too* much, he placed it into the center of the ritual and stood back. As the ritual started to spin up, he looked around the area and at the slowly brightening sky.

It was already five in the morning, and this ritual would run for just over fifty-eight minutes. He waited in place for a few of those minutes, letting the hot air blowing from the spinning rings wash over him. Either he would gain a Core that let him run the Raze ritual by himself, or the rings would melt down and explode in a terrible storm of uncontained mana. If the latter happened, he hoped that his current position would allow the walls to be reduced to rubble.

All the other buildings could be rebuilt, even if it was unfortunate. The Pathfinder's Hall, however, couldn't be replaced. Not for *decades* if the requirements were any indication. Joe would rather burn *everything else* to the ground than hand that over. While he waited, he pulled out his diagrams and started creating a second Raze ritual. He wouldn't get it done soon—certainly not by the end of this conversion process—but he managed the first ring and half of the second. When the ritual completed, Joe was a little surprised that he was alive.

Frankly, he had thought that he would blink and be in his respawn room at some point. As the rings *clanged* to a stop, they screeched and warped. The white-hot metal collapsed, forming four rings of molten metal on the roof of the building. Joe winced; if the process had lasted much longer, that would have meant outcome number two happening. As it was...

Joe formed a cup around the new Mana Battery, pulled it away from the superheated goop, and set it to start charging. It was now six in the morning, and a full charge of seven thousand mana was going to take... he did the math and gulped. Nearly four hours. That meant that he could *start* the process at ten o'clock—wait!

That was wrong. His math was wrong! He redid the conversion of one to ten for storage. Also, he had done the original conversion to *seconds*, not minutes. He could put in one hundred fourteen mana right away, and... it would take thirty-eight and a half *minutes* to fill it with mana regeneration only!

He really needed to stop doing panic-math; it always made him freak out. Mana began flowing, and the Mana Battery started glowing. Six twenty. Six thirty. Six *forty*! The battery stopped taking a charge, and Joe dropped it into position. He had spent the time between the start of the charge and now getting everything else in position. Taking a few deep breaths, he waited for his mana to return to full... and started to Raze the wall.

"*Evacuate usque ad terram!*" he intoned, and the ground started to light up around him in four concentric circles. Oddly, the outer three lifted off and merged into a single ring that spun at the wall like an out-of-control tire on the highway. The circular energy hit the rock and sunk into it, expanding out and looking exactly like the ritual Architect's Fury engulfing the wall. There was one *key* difference, however.

Stone began crumbling into rubble, then floating into the air and vanishing. Joe had used the other high-grade Lesser Core Aten had given him for this ritual, so the destruction should be moving apace. However, there was a pile of stone, wood, and all sorts of minor items being neatly stacked around the ritual site. Destruction was *slower* than *building* the structure in the first place! By a *lot.*

Another difference was that this ritual allowed people to walk away from it. Joe hadn't understood why that was an important part of things, but he did now. This ritual was going to take at least an hour to fully perform. He walked away cautiously, and to his surprise, the brightly glowing ritual circle followed him. Another circle stayed under the Mana Battery he had added to the ritual, so he grabbed that and threw it on the roof. No point in letting someone find that and smash it or something. Plus, would it work if he placed it in his storage? Not something to test.

Now... now, he needed to find some way to slow down the Royal Guard. Joe looked around at all the people who were unconscious, wanting to put them in more comfortable positions but knowing that they had a better shot at being 'comfortable' if they had a home to wake up to. How was he going to make this happen? His mana was effectively at zero, but luckily, the draw on him was fairly minimal per second. A benefit of a slow-moving ritual, no doubt. Joe had no spells that were free to use, and he had no rituals set up. That was going to change in the future; he was going to start carrying a *binder* of active rituals.

Where could he find poison? Did the guild have any large barrels of dangerous reagents laying around that he could dump on the road? Joe was wracking his brain for anything that he could use to stall the Royal Guard, but he was *so* tired! So... *tired*. That... how long had the guards been awake and moving? Joe looked over at the small food cart that had set up shop in the mess area and formulated a desperate plan.

He loaded up some supplies and started pulling the small food cart. It was made to either be pulled by a person or small creature like a donkey and rolled really easily. Still, this sucker was *heavy*. His plan wouldn't have worked if he needed to carry anything in the cart, and Joe *really* hoped that the pile of goods he had tossed out wouldn't get him into too much trouble.

Joe strained and pulled, eventually getting out of town and on to a slight downhill slope on the road toward Ardania. It took a solid ten minutes of hauling, but he got to the charred tree line. He kept going, getting about a five-unencumbered-minute walk into the trees. Far enough that a casual stroll wouldn't let people see the wall that was still being torn down. Joe didn't need the morning light to see by, but he was glad for it anyway. The brightening morning hid the glowing ritual circle around his feet.

"Mate, I need you to get out here and start smelling up the area. You have a name... no. 'Mate' works well then. Coffee Mate. Hee... I'm *so* tired..." Joe pulled his Coffee Elemental out of his ring and had it sit on the counter. He pulled out one of the small Mana Batteries he had remaining and channeled Cleanse using it and his staff. He needed to look into getting a socketed weapon so he could do this more easily in the future; Terra's offhand comment about socketed weapons and armor was really sticking with him right now.

Once the pot was full of *utterly* clean water, Joe dumped coffee grounds that he had stolen into the pot and started swirling it. The smell of coffee started to pervade the area as the massive pot of coffee joined in with the Elemental's natural scent. Good. Joe used his *basically* free ability to shape shadows, creating a fine mesh over the top of the pot with a large plunger. Boom. Instant French Press.

The sound of horses walking started filtering into the area, and Joe added a final touch, solidifying shadows on to the cart to spell out 'Free Coffee'. Not a moment too soon, as the first people started to emerge from around the bend. To Joe's surprise, there were only five Royal Guardsmen and three other people, including the woman who had sold the guild the blueprint in the first place. Now it made sense how they had been tattled on so swiftly.

"Good morning!" Joe called cheerfully as they got into earshot for unenhanced humans, which none of them were. "Care to pause a moment and have a fresh cup of coffee? Free for loyal servants of the Kingdom, of course!"

There was no verbal response for a long moment, but all the horses slowed. The apparent leader of the Royal Guard looked at the others and nodded. They swung off their horses and approached. "You know that it would be High Treason for you to poison a member of the Royal Guard, do you not?"

"I would *never!*" Joe managed to look properly aghast. "M'Lord, please take a good look at me. Particularly *here.*"

The Royal Guardsman looked at Joe's forehead, and his tired eyes widened fractionally. "Extended Family to the Royal Family! Please, forgive my caution. We would be glad of a small respite; we are on an *unhappy* mission that arrived suddenly."

"*Must* we pause so close to our destination?" This came from a disgruntled man still sitting on his horse. "We are not a quarter hour from the *Wanderer's* Guild. In fact...! *Him!* This is the man who committed the treason that we have brought to light!"

"Ah, you are this 'Joe' that has been causing such a ruckus?" The guard looked Joe up and down. "Of course you are. Bribery will not allow you to escape justice."

"What*ever* are you talking about?" Joe looked around the people and saw glee dawn on the Architects. The guards looked pained, but the leader spoke up again.

"I see. I had forgotten that you all were not informed of the charges." He took a deep breath. "The Wanderer's Guild has been accused of Treason against the crown for building a small-scale version of a national secret: the Wall of Ardania. Again, bribery will not help in this matter."

Joe slowly poured the coffee from the pot into a serving carafe, nodding slightly as the aroma filled the area even more. "Huh. That doesn't seem like something we'd do. What happens if they *lied* to the Kingdom about this matter? You have travel mugs, or shall I grab a few from the cart here?"

The Architect Leader looked panicked for a moment and made a *shooing* motion at the other two. They charged off down the road, earning a glare from the Guard Captain. He spoke loudly at the Architect Leader, "Don't think that I will not report your joy in causing others pain."

"I am simply wanting to get a read on the situation," the Architect Leader deflected disingenuously.

"*Surely* a treasonous wall that was built... when? Some unspecified time in the past? It would be there no matter if you waited five minutes to finish the best coffee in a hundred miles?" Joe shook his head at the 'poor manners' being displayed. "You would *think* that a man who had the respect of the *King* would be of at least *slight* interest in maintaining good relations with."

The others took a moment to parse that sentence, and the Architect smiled and came over for a cup. "I would *love*

some coffee, if you don't mind. Interesting *pet* you have there...
it seems we *do* have a few things in common."

Joe wasn't sure what the man meant, at least until he saw
a flash of a gold-and-black backstage pass from the Grand Zoo.
Ah, so that is where they got whatever was used to knock out his
guild. Good to know. As the guards finished their coffee, the
other riders returned with darkly jubilant looks on their faces.
This didn't escape the notice of the Royal Guard, and he set his
cup down with a heavy sigh.

"I am afraid that I will need to ask you to come with
me." The cart was connected to a horse, and they started
walking toward Towny McTownface.

Class experience +250!

Joe felt his mana start to trickle in—no longer devoted to
a ritual—and he glanced at his feet. No glow. No ritual circle.
Great timing.

Chapter Forty-Six

There were three people sputtering obscenities as the group got close to town. A few buildings, knocked over trees, damaged landscape... but no wall even *closely* resembling what was around Ardania.

"Something... the matter?" Joe hid his grin and sniped at the others as they started converging together on their horses, "Where is this wall supposed to be?"

The Royal Guard spread out to surround everyone but continued moving at a brisk pace toward the town. They left no openings that someone could use to dart away, and their glistening weapons and caffeine-enhanced stare left the group without hope of escape. A walk to glory was over, and the Architects knew it to be true. The Royal Guard was just happy to have the Guild Leader, sub-leader, and main assistant in hand already and not hiding behind heavy defenses. Next on the docket for the three was an attempt at damage control.

"Who reported this to me?" The Guild Leader barked at his subordinates. "I was told in no *uncertain terms–*"

"Don't even *try* it!" the assistant hissed at him. "This was *all you* from the start, and there's no way I'm taking the fall for this!"

"You're both–"

"*Each* of you has confirmed treason, and *all* of you will be on the hook for lying to the Crown if there is no wall," the Guard Captain lazily mentioned. The pace never slowed.

"*You!* How did you do this?" The Guild Leader pointed a shaky finger at Joe. "The wall was *there* less than *fifteen* minutes ago!"

"I'm *sure* I have no idea what you mean," Joe stated blandly. "As you were present to see, I was with these fine gentlemen for the last long while."

They looked amongst themselves, at a loss. The assistant hissed, "Who could have helped them? Did the Zoo set us up?"

"*Silence!*" the Guild Leader snarled. Too late.

"Why would my guild have needed help with something? What does the *Zoo* have to do with anything?" Joe's voice was *extra*-loud, just to be sure he was clearly heard.

"You know as well as I do that your guild can't do *anything* right now!" once more, the assistant opened her mouth and stated something she *shouldn't* know.

Joe turned and looked at her dead-on. "Did you three *do* something to my guild? When we get there... are we going to see them attacked or some foul play?"

She paled, and her mouth worked like a fish on land as she tried to explain herself. The Royal Guard kicked the sides of the horses, breaking into a trot. Something sinister was at work here. They rode into town and came across the first of the sprawled bodies. The Guard Captain was on the ground in a flash, feeling for a pulse. "Alive but nearing death from exposure, at least a second-tier debuff of 'chilled'."

He waved various powders under the nose, poked the man with a dagger, but nothing got a reaction. "Sleep of the Dead? No... who would waste such a potent weapon on such a small area?"

The captive Architects were squirming. "If someone is using such a thing, perhaps it would be better to come back another time?"

"No need. The people will awaken twelve hours after inhalation, and almost all items of this nature are single-use and have a very short time to affect people," one of the guards firmly stated. They rode to the Guild Hall area and looked around. "What is *that*?"

"Oh, a greenhouse!" Joe told him casually. "We plan to begin producing food for ourselves and the Kingdom as soon as possible!"

"What is all this?" The Captain waved a hand at neatly stacked rows of stone, wood, metal, and a small vial that Joe cheerfully tossed in his ring. It was good to have his Troll Blood back.

"Looks like the guild was planning on putting together some more buildings when we were able, but from the look of things, whatever this *will be* could take *weeks* to put together!" Joe nodded sagely at his own words.

"This is..." The Architect Guild Leader looked around, and his eyes lit up. "This is the material needed to build the wall!"

"Oh?" Joe looked at it doubtfully. "I guess *I* wouldn't know! I mean, if this wall is so secret... who really *does* know? Surely there are other buildings that can be made out of stone? Is having *rocks* and *wood* treason now?"

"Of course not." The Guard Captain motioned at the Architects, who were dragged to the ground and bound. "I will be bringing you all back to the Kingdom... eventually. I would like a rest after being dragged out of bed for a *false* claim! At least we have evidence of your attack on a guild in good standing."

When the Architects were secured, the guards helped Joe collect people and get them into safe, warm locations. Joe pulled out some food, more coffee, and even used Cleanse to hydrate the guards before sending them on their way. They promised that he would hear from them soon.

Joe looked around the empty area, not sure what to do while waiting for people to wake up. "Well... wall. Can't use the Kingdom's, for obvious reasons."

His eyes turned to the forty-foot-tall, black, twisted stone wall that had been formed by the area turning into a punishment dungeon. Only one section of the wall had been left standing after the massive blast during the battle with the Wolfmen, but... "I wonder."

By one o'clock, he had created an Architect's Fury ritual and scanned the section of wall. To his great excitement, the blueprint that formed was the full wall that had originally been in place around town. Joe started making adjustments to the formulas, tinkering with it until three in the afternoon when Aten suddenly jumped to his feet and looked around in confusion. Whew! Joe had been about to give up and go get some sleep.

"Joe...? What... the wall! We need to– what *time* is it? I fell *asleep*?" he shouted in fear and turned to run.

"Aten! We're good!" Joe shouted at the wide-eyed man. "I took care of everything."

"What? Then... the wall?" Aten looked into the distance, looking through his status screen. "We're still a tier-one town, though? The wall is gone? You're sure?"

"Yup."

"How are we a tier-one town then? Did you make a bathhouse? Cistern? Sewers? Warehouse-restaurant combo?" Aten may have continued, but Joe stopped him.

"Greenhouse doubles as a sewer system—not sure how, but it does," Joe told him easily. "Just needs some time to grow, and it'll cover the entire town."

"It... then we really need a wall..." Aten's head was spinning; too much had happened, and he had been *asleep*!

"Working on it." Joe waved at the sprawled documents. "We were attacked with some kind of sleep spell or something, just so you know. Not your fault, *everyone* was knocked out. Well. Not me. I was underground, and I *think* this place has a separate air supply? That or I should really get some plants down here."

Aten didn't know what else to say, so they walked out into the main area and were swarmed with people. "Aten! The wall! It's *gone!*"

"We were attacked!"

"Someone raided my food cart!"

"Oh, that last one was me." Joe flushed, and Aten sighed. "Mind taking care of that for me? It was the only way to save the guild. Stole a lot of coffee grounds from the coffee shop too."

"Yeah, sure, fine," Aten grumpily muttered. "Coffee was the key to success my *butt*. You're lucky you are so integral to our success."

"Aren't I though?" Joe preened, breaking into a chuckle. A messenger ran up at that moment, just as the area began *really* getting going. People were rather upset at losing a day of grinding because of sleep.

"Message for you, Joe. It... it has the Royal seal on it, and I was *ordered* to give it to you today if you were 'still around'?"

"Thanks." Joe took the letter, knowing that it was likely from the Prince. He *had* mentioned that his help didn't come freely. Joe stepped into a secluded area and opened the letter with a grim expression.

Joe, it is good that you have managed to foil this plot, but *I also know that the 'false charges' were actually true. No*

matter how you got the plans, you had them. That means
someone else might as well, and the Kingdom could be in
danger. In exchange for your freedom and to maintain a clean
record, I am assigning you a quest. It will appear as soon as you
read this message. I have transferred twenty platinum to your
bank account to be used for this task only. *Best of luck.*
   From Her Majesty, Queen Marie the Battle Tyrant.
   P.S. I finally found out what they were doing.

   [Mandatory] Quest alert: Black to Purple. Queen Marie
has learned that the Grand Zoo of Ardania is a front for a Black
Market and possibly the headquarters of a non-sanctioned
Assassin's Guild. There is a unique building that has been
observed by informants, but there is no known way to reach this
area without assistance from the Zoo itself. Find the building,
and either 1) Create a blueprint for the Kingdom to use. 2)
Secure a way to and from the location without outside assistance.
3) Destroy the building.
   Rewards: Dependent upon number of objectives
completed. 1) Record remains clean, this issue goes away. 2) Act
of Nobility recorded. 3) All other rewards, plus use of the
building's blueprint for your guild.

   "Well... this creates a lot of questions for me." Joe sighed
and watched as the parchment lit on fire and burned itself. "Was
the 'failure' just implied? There wasn't a fail condition. How
much does she know about my abilities? I guess I kinda fell out
of secrecy mode, huh? Lastly... I wonder if I can get all of those
rewards?"
   Joe didn't want to waste any time. Frankly, he wanted a
long nap and a bubble bath. Right now, he was supposed to be
enjoying the fruits of his hard work, not getting another difficult

task out of the gates. Still... this *was* a chance to go back to the Zoo and get a whole bunch of great things done in one fell swoop, *and* he had the Kingdom bankrolling it.

One last thing was making him hesitate. "What does it mean that the Zoo is a *non-sanctioned* Assassin's Guild?"

CHAPTER FORTY-SEVEN

"How is everyone doing?" Joe wearily posed the question to his current Coven members. Six hours of sleep just wasn't enough after a day like that. "It's been all emergencies and instant need on my end. I think you've all more than earned some training if you want it. Anyone?"

Joe was pleased by the reply; *everyone* had a project they were working on. As a reward for the past few days, he unlocked some of the most minor features of the room, allowing them to make the stone morph into the shapes they needed for ritual circles. He retained full control, of course, but they all got a small section to work in.

For the next few hours, he helped everyone with their projects. Joe winced at first when he saw what people were trying to pack into *Novice* rituals, but he remembered that he had tried the same thing when he was at that rank. He helped them iron out issues, create interesting effects, and essentially, just helped them learn.

Skill increase: Teaching (Beginner I). Woo! Look at you, stepping into your role as a class trainer. You were going to get a bonus when you started the Coven, but I figured that all your bonuses to increased skill level were enough already.

Joe did his best to ignore the extra-snarky messages, and soon, his minions had energized rituals just waiting for a target. When they seemed done, Joe cleared his throat and dramatically threw out his arms. Four circles appeared in the center of the room, and he informed them that he was going to be in a very dangerous area soon. He wanted some safeguards in place, and they were going to hopefully help with that.

"Only thing, this is an Expert-ranked ritual. I'll see you all in a few hours. Take a break, nap, whatever." Joe dismissed the others, and he just *knew* that they were going off to put their new rituals to good-ish use. He was especially interested in seeing what Big_Mo would do. Joe tried to think what the man would use a blood *collection* ritual for but... failed.

Flipping open his notes, Joe tried to figure out what sort of ritual he was going to need in the Zoo. What he *really* wanted was a summoning or teleportation ritual, but if wishes were fishes the whole world would stink of rotting fish. He had nothing even resembling that and had no idea where to start. So, he turned to the rituals he currently had and got to work picking through them.

There were only two valid options: Stasis or Ghostly Army. Even then, the point was to escape. The Ritual of Stasis might protect him for a short while, but the Ghostly Army would make a massive distraction. Mind made up, Joe got to work on the ritual. Instead of the four rings made by the room being used for the ritual, they formed into a seat, a back support, a desk, and a footrest. Was he using the Grand Ritual Hall as intended? Probably no. Could anyone call him on it? Also no.

Joe pulled out a new bottle of ink that Jess had purchased for him, but before he tried to turn it into Imbued Ink, he pulled out a glass bottle and started working with that one. He had made the mistake in the past of letting the ink remain in a standard glass bottle while he altered it, and his self-repairing robe was still working to get rid of the stain from when the glass exploded. He held the glass gingerly as his skill got to work, and in a few minutes, he had created a 'Natural Imbued Glass Bottle'. Good. He poured the ink into the bottle and started massaging mana into the liquid. Then he saw something that he had never noticed during previous failures. The ink flashed *red* for a bare instant.

Item altered: Natural Reversal Ink. Anything written by this ink must be written in reverse-mirrored form or be completely useless and unintelligible. Caution! Keep out of the reach of children.

This... this was mocking him; Joe was certain of it. Even though it was considered a failure, he decided to keep the ink. Maybe it would come in handy someday to write something backward. He created another imbued bottle and tried again with the ink. This time it flashed gold, and he got excited. He held up the bottle, looking at the ink within.

Item altered: Natural Fire-Resistant Ink. Anything written by this ink will withstand fire up to the Expert-ranks.

"Cool... but *only* the ink is fire-resistant? Good to have... I guess?" Joe tried a third time, creating a standard Natural Imbued Bottle and standard Imbued Ink. Then he was finally able to get started on the *actual* work he needed to complete. Six hours later, Joe stumbled out of the area and began the hunt for food. The ritual had been far more complex than he had expected, easily a mid-late Expert ritual.

He had messed up twice so badly that he needed to restart *entirely* and had needed to heal as his material turned into a fiery ball of released mana. This was a turning point for him, as until this moment, he hadn't realized how different the difficulty could be even within the same tier of ritual. Joe hadn't even gotten a rank in his skill level, though he felt that he had to be getting close at this point.

Joe chewed numbly on a salad, not really thinking about his nutritional needs until the flavor hit him. Rabbit food! Why was it so *tasty*? Why was he eating *salad*? He bit into a cucumber and moaned. What was this? So *good!* He looked around and saw a sign:

All vegetables are now locally grown! Sign up now to gain daily gather quests that you don't need to travel for! Special farmer-related classes available upon request.

"Already? It's been a day at best." Joe saw someone swagger into the area with an armload of cabbages, only to be accidentally knocked over by a bald young adult and two people sprinting after him.

"My *cabbages!*" The man dropped to the ground to collect them before they were smashed.

Joe took a sip of water and shook his head. "That was rude."

"There he is!" Kirby's voice made Joe's ears twitch, and he looked over to see his Coven walking over. "Joe, you shut the tunnel. We couldn't get in."

"Ah. Here..." Joe opened his permissions and gave Hannah permissions to allow entrance to the area. "Hannah can get you all in now. Be discrete please. Only Aten and my party members know about that area."

"You ready for us, or should we go do other things?" Big_Mo was *covered* in blood, and it took Joe a moment to figure out how to respond.

"You... want that blood off of you?" Joe waited only for the start of a nod before Cleansing him. Much better. "Yes, I'm almost ready, but I need a few reagents that I don't normally carry, and then we need to go find a lake. I'll pop over to Ardania and come back shortly."

"Sounds good." Taka nodded at the salad bar that had been set up. "We are just about to have dinner. If you're back in an hour, we'll be here."

It was nice to see that the five of them had become close. Then again, they had a diverse enough setup currently that they were likely a party. Joe nodded, trying not to feel jealous over them having commonalities at such a low level. He was already on his second party, and even so, he had no idea where all of them were. Their training and off-hours were just too different.

Joe went to the temple, then to Ardania. It was time to bite the bullet and go to the place he wanted to go the *least*. Jake the Alchemist. For the *life* of him, Joe couldn't remember the shop's name; Jake the creepy man had taken point in Joe's memory of that place. The crowds in the town square were far less dense, which made Joe both happy and morose—happy that his travel was easier, sad because there was no way that eight *billion* people had shown up here. There was a good chance that only about ten percent of humanity had come through what must have been an apocalypse.

His mind *slid* away from that subject, and only his Mental Manipulation Resistance allowed him to realize that it was happening. Joe didn't fight it; this was something he'd rather *not* think about. Still, it made him realize why people weren't freaking out or having more severe reactions to being trapped here or losing people out on Earth. They were getting over it *really* fast. Artificially fast.

Still, he couldn't argue with the results. He hurried to Jake's shop and pulled out the laundry list of things he needed for the first time, things he needed restocked, and finally, things he *wanted* to have so that he could make alterations to current ideas. Jake went over it, making marks in certain areas.

Jake handed the paper back to Joe. "A star means I can get it in a few days, a number shows how many weeks I would need to get it, and a frowny-face means I can't get it at all. Everything else I have on hand."

Joe read over the list and arched a brow. "You're usually so well stocked."

"Busy times, even if it is for one of the most interesting specimens to come through my shop." Jake leered at Joe, trying to hold back his excitement. "You know, the population density is still so high that a wave of zombies would *devastate* the city. Or! Oh, I have a parasitic mushroom that sends people into a rage...!"

"Please stop trying to use me to spark off an extinction event." Joe's mouth was really dry. Jake had a way of making Joe tense.

"Oh, I don't want that! I am just looking at your reaction to see how... *into* it you are," Jake promised him rather insincerely. His fidgeting body was starting to really make Joe nauseous.

"About the things you *do* have in stock...?"

"Oh, sure, sure." Jake started dancing around the shop, packaging things into neat, little bags made of some kind of waxed paper. "The only difficulty is going to be the Water Core. Specialized affinity Cores are created naturally, and this makes them expensive. Of course, there is an alchemical process to making it happen, but all this does is boost the cost of a Core further."

"Naturally?" Joe thought of his skill and wondered if that would work.

As in, spending multiple years growing within certain creatures. Creatures that live in areas which have a single natural affinity at least seventy percent higher than other energies. An example: in an ocean, where there is far more water affinity than fire affinity." Jake nodded sadly. "Not something easily replicated, as trying to force mana into a Core without an Enchantment tends toward..."

He put his hands together and mimicked an explosion. "Point being, I have natural and alchemical versions. Natural is going to be better overall, but that costs the most. Alchemical *should work* but sometimes may interfere with the intended reaction."

"Natural, please," Joe replied, getting a nod and an invoice all in one. He took a deep breath and left a stack of banknotes on the counter. He was waved off by Jake and started toward the town square. "I needed the items. I was low on everything. *Eighty thousand dollars?* No, no. Just... eighty *platinum*. Small, tiny coins that have no intrinsic value. Yes."

Joe teleported back to Towny McTownface and collected his Coven. It was time to find a lake.

CHAPTER FORTY-EIGHT

"This is going to be the perfect place, guaranteed," Jess told Joe as the group stopped at the swampy morass that lay just to the east of the guild's area. "There is a lake's worth of water, and the guild made a quest to clear out the bugs in this area. They are huge and deadly, and they keep killing off the livestock that we are trying to raise. One stone, many birds."

"Good work, Jess." Joe paused and looked over at her. "Everything else working out well? Need anything from me?"

"If you aren't opposed, I'm going to collect samples from the area when we are done here. I could use... certain things for my class." Jess once again avoided the subject of what her class actually *was*.

"Fine by me." Joe called over to the meandering Coven members, "Y'all! Ready to make this happen?"

He pulled out the three-foot by four-foot paper that he had made this ritual on and was actually *impressed* by how small he had managed to make it. The level of detail had been so high that he had expected to need to use the Ritual Hall to make full-sized rings. Cheating shadow-eraser for the win! He placed one of his Mana Batteries in place as well, not wanting there to be any power requirement issues. This had the added effect of balancing the circle, making a prime number of seven 'participants'.

"*Ego similis ad aquam. Eam continet testudines!*" As soon as the ritual activated, things went crazy. All the liquid water within ten square meters evaporated at the same time, and all the water that rushed to replace it met the same fate when passing the boundary. This reduced visibility to *nothing* for everyone in the area, and the instant cloud started whirling around them as the ritual circle absorbed it for future use.

Multiple sounds started filling the area: rushing water, fish flopping around on suddenly dry land, and the drone of insects as their habitat was disturbed on such a massive scale. Joe couldn't see what was out there; he could barely see his hand in front of his face. Still, he was *concerned* about what would be waiting for them when this was all over.

Grunts, animalistic screams, and furious buzzing started reaching his ears, increasing in volume as the ritual continued. Soon, the sound of rushing water turned into *sloshing* water as the ritual finished up, and the unnatural fog vanished into the circles as suddenly as it had appeared. Everyone looked around to see what had been happening, and Joe's eyes alighted on a familiar figure.

"Joe! Joe, is that *you?*" Jaxon was standing a few meters away, his hands shifting from T-rex heads into regular hands, and he was bleeding from multiple weeping wounds and covered in various forms of ick. "It *is!* Joe, you came for me! I've been lost in this swamp for *days!* Thank goodness! I was getting so worried that I'd need to go to respawn to get home, and then you came and drained the whole area just so I could find my way back!"

There were *piles* of insect corpses around Jaxon, most of them with at least one bite out of them. Joe could only swallow as Jaxon stumbled toward him, and before anything else, he used Cleanse to not only clean him up but get rid of the various disease and infection debuffs that he had gained in the last few days. Then he healed him and gave the no-longer-feverish Jaxon a hug. "Glad you're okay, buddy."

"I need new clothes." Jaxon looked at his ragged gear and stumbled along as Joe led them home. "I deserve so many contribution points. So many *bugs*."

Joe grimaced at the mention of the contribution points. As far as he could tell: still a useless currency. After depositing Jaxon in a barracks with a large meal, Joe checked that he had an empowered Raze as well as an Architect's Fury ritual ready. Since they were charged and ready, a simple thought would get the process moving. It was time to get to the Zoo.

He laughed at the grim thought he was having. He was pretty sure those words were usually said with cheerfulness, faked or otherwise. Joe went to Ardania, stopped at the bank, and restocked his ring with bank notes, then started his walk across the city. He was wearing his fancy clothes again and starting earlier in the day than he had last time. Joe paused to refresh himself before entering the Zoo, a quick Cleanse bringing him to full alertness and spotlessness.

This time, there was a butler that greeted him. No hint of clowns or the feared Jesters, which Joe had come to realize were the Zoo-kept Assassins. "Welcome back, Sir!"

"Thank you." Joe showed his pass, and once again, the handcart was pulled out for him to ride in. It didn't move, and he soon found out why.

"One moment, please forgive my impertinence." the butler looked so distressed that Joe could only look on in concern. "It has come to our attention that you may have smuggled out a Rare seed the last time you were here and that you may be attending the Zoo today with less than the best of intentions."

"What—"

"If I may, Sir," the Butler cut Joe off smoothly. "There is no proof that you took the seeds, none at all! In fact, all of our concerns will be allayed if you would be so kind as to allow me to hold your storage ring while you attend today. I *swear* that we will return it to you, without *ever* looking into it, but... to attend, you will need to do so."

"What about my bank notes and such?" Joe looked at the distressed butler. "How will I buy anything?"

"If you will show them to me, I will vouch for your ability to purchase anything up to the amount disclosed." The butler waited as Joe pulled out fifty platinum worth of notes, and his eyes widened fractionally. "I see that our Zoo has made an... *impression* on you."

"Yes..." Joe looked into the distance, feeling the need to feign the manner of Nobility. "Before now, even a *positive* one."

"I *am* sorry for the inconvenience, Sir." The butler put the ring into a pocket, and the cart began moving. "The Floodwater family noticed that there had been a small batch of fruit that went out with seeds, and even though they are unlikely to grow anywhere but their specialized vineyards, the family became slightly... feisty."

"Why would they allow out fruit with seeds if this were such an issue?" Joe avoided the subject of why the Zoo might think he was there with bad intentions. He knew why. They knew why. He simply didn't know *how* they knew that he was there to cause damage, as only the Royal Family likely knew about his quest. Perhaps they simply thought the Architect's Guild had ratted them out for supplying them with a knockout weapon?

"I'm told it was an error that has been rectified." The butler paused, "As far as I know, only *one* harvesting crew was slain over the issue. A very lenient punishment, but they *are* known to be softies like that."

The cart traveled through the menagerie of interesting creatures, but Joe didn't bother to look around. Looks like he might have made another powerful enemy. At least, if the news about the seeds got out. Joe had no doubt that the seeds would thrive in the environment he had planted them in. Oh well. At this point, he would just add that family to the list that wanted his head.

There was a stutter in the air as the cart and group arrived at the Bloodsport Arena, and Joe watched as spells exploded in the air to announce another day of bouts and black market sales. The cart moved much more slowly this time, as the path to the arena was filled with other, *very* well-dressed people. Joe suddenly realized that wearing his fancy clothes twice in a row was likely a sign of not being well-off, and he tried to decide if he cared or not. Nah.

A short while later, Joe was in the arena and in his plush chaise lounge. The door closed, and soon, only the butler and Joe were in the room together. "Anything I can get for you, Sir? Might I suggest the barrel-cut Filet Minion this evening?"

"Filet *Mignon?*"

"No, this is a type of meat from Minions, the creatures that work to protect the Boss creature of various dungeons. Succulent."

Joe couldn't think of anything to say, so he simply nodded and waited for the first fight to begin. His food came, as well as a full bar on a trolley. Joe arched a knowing brow at the butler. Apparently, they had extra service for people that were known to spend large amounts of money. "Trying to get me tipsy?"

"Never!" The butler politely lied. "Can I get you anything that would pair well with the Minion?"

"I am doing well for now." Joe ate his steak, and about halfway through... the fighting began. Joe had several issues that he needed to attempt to balance while everything was going on. He needed to ensure that he was paying enough attention to the fighting that the butler would pay less attention to *him*, he needed to get his ritual into a good location for activation and *activate* it, and he needed to pay enough attention to the *butler* so that he would know when to make his move. Oh, and he needed to buy anything he thought he would need. Keeping an eye on deals. Yes.

The fighting began in earnest, and Joe motioned for a drink, which was happily obliged. Joe took a sip, and a slew of notifications appeared, various buffs and debuffs. He held the drink in his lap and made sure to keep it less than two inches from his codpiece. For every sip he took, two-to-three times that amount was siphoned into storage.

If anything, the butler seemed pleased to see Joe drinking so much of the expensive drink. When the first items he wanted to purchase came up for sale, Joe made sure to slightly overpay for them. He could see the man starting to relax in the corner of his eye, so Joe made the Architect's Fury ritual appear under his own shoe.

Everything was ready to be activated, so Joe covered the paper in shadow and sent it silently sliding across the floor. It went up and behind a tapestry; then Joe solidified the shadow, creating what he hoped would look like a natural backing to the woven artwork. There was no reaction from the butler, so Joe ordered another drink in celebration.

One down, one to go.

CHAPTER FORTY-NINE

An auction came up that Joe was actually interested in. He had secured the second ritual to the wall on the arena-side wall of his balcony, again coated in a solid yet thin section of shadow. There should be no indication of where the ritual was activating from, for *either* of the rituals he had in place. To the butler's *great* distress, Joe cast Cleanse on himself and removed all the debuffs associated with drinking.

Joe was pleased to find that the *good* aspects remained, and he got to some serious—if more frugal than the butler expected—bidding on items and materials. It was only halfway through the night, and Joe had already burned through the twenty Platinum that he had been given by the Queen. The bidding on the most recent item ended, and the announcer stopped everything for an intermission.

Standing and stretching, Joe asked to be led to the bathroom while the announcer was describing the amazing show that they had planned for the break. Seeing an opportunity, Joe reached through his connected shadows and activated Architect's Fury just as they left the room. No one was inside to see the rings bloom out and sink into the stone, but everyone watching the interior of the arena was able to see when they expanded and bloomed around the building.

There were shouts at first, then clapping as the light was mistaken for part of the show. Joe looked around to see if anyone had seen where the rings came from. The butler, keeping an eye on Joe, assumed that the glancing was to see what was going on. This was lucky for Joe, as he soon discovered after returning from relieving himself. There was a person seated on his lounge, a person that Joe recognized from the palace.

When he spoke, even his voice was familiar; he was the announcer at this event.

"Joe." The Ringleader, Robert, was watching Joe *very* closely. What was more frightening was the group of brightly dressed *Jesters* that were fanned out behind him. "What did you do to my arena?"

"Ringleader." Joe bobbed his head at the man. "I am *quite* sure I don't know what you are talking about."

"Take a look, Joe." The Ringleader gestured at the balcony. "What is that light that is shining in the area?"

Joe stepped closer, intentionally leaving his back open. "Is... are you talking about your intermission light show?"

He turned to look at Robert, catching the barest flicks coming from his butler's hands. Sign language? Robert's eyes once more rested on Joe. "I *do* hope you don't try to do something foolhardy. I have been keeping an eye on all of the things you have been buying, and each of them is a potent component for various powerful spellcraft. Items that have a very *small* chance of appearing in the world. In fact, the Tigerlily Titillation you won recently has less than a one in *ten thousand* drop rate."

"I... I'm sorry to say that I am not sure what you are accusing me of?" Joe looked around at the silent people in the room. "Are you *not* happy that I have purchased what I did? I certainly don't want to cause offense. I came here *because* I knew how rare the items were, and I came prepared to buy...?"

Robert's eyes flicked to the side, and Joe saw the butler sign 'fifty' and another that must have meant 'platinum'. Seriously, how *rude*. Joe kept his mouth shut and simply waited. When he turned back to fully face the Ringmaster, all of the creepy Jesters were gone. He hated that people could do that around him.

"As far as I can tell... you have done nothing wrong." Robert stood and looked Joe dead in the eye. "However, you will be under close observation for the remainder of your stay. We will assess at the end whether you are invited back."

"I can only hope that I am. As you stated, another place to find all this doesn't exist elsewhere," Joe replied coolly. Now he was going to buy *everything* that he could, just to make his innocence appear realistic. He should have *really* brought less money.

"Hmm." Robert stalked out of the room, turning back just as the ritual finished and the lights vanished. "I do *wonder* what that was. Have a *pleasant* evening, Mr. Joe."

"You as well." Joe sat down, intentionally not looking at the dangerous man who was likely in charge of a large group of assassins. This night was not going as smoothly as he wanted it to, in some respects, but it was going far smoother than he had *expected*.

He stood from the couch, sighing as the door closed. He started walking around and looking at the various tapestries in the room, touching a few of them and getting *very* close to others. "Butler, *you* don't think that I've been doing anything wrong, do you?"

"Sir, of course not! I've been here with you–" Whatever he was going to say was interrupted as a swarm of Jesters barged into the room, grabbed all the tapestries from the wall, and inspected them before leaving. They took the art with them.

"I...! I shan't touch anything else!" Joe kept a stricken, faintly enraged expression on his face at all times as he sat down stiffly and waited for the fighting to continue.

Skill gained: Acting (Novice VII). You are really *bad at acting, but somehow, that fact is helping you right now, leading to a high initial skill level. +1n% chance for your acting to be taken as you intend it to be taken, where n = skill level.*

A new skill! How long had it been since he got one? Only a few days, actually. Still, he seemed to be getting fewer recently. Then again, he had been branching out less as well. The fights resumed, with the creatures winning the next three battles in a row. This meant no auction, but that was fine with Joe.

The next few hours passed swiftly, and Joe dutifully purchased goods and items. Then... then something appeared that he *really* wanted.

"Ladies and Gentlemen!" the announcer, the Ringleader, spoke to the crowd. "We have just gained a new item, an *Injection*! For those of you in the know, this is a *Legendary-*ranked potion, one rank below a *Concoction*! Now, this Injection has been appraised to provide a *fifteen-*point boost to intelligence!"

There were appreciative murmurs from the crowd, but the next words stopped them. "This particular injection does have a few side-effects that may seem unpleasant, but a day or two of seclusion is no matter for such a distinguished crowd! Firstly, the injection creates in the user a nearly irrepressible urge to hug whoever or whatever they see. This will last a full day and isn't *normally* an issue."

A pause. "The other side effect is a twelve-hour-long loss of bowel control. As I am sure you all realize, this *particular* combination has unfortunate possible repercussions. We will start the bidding at ten platinum."

Joe couldn't believe what he was hearing. So *what* if there was a messy consequence? Why was no one bidding? ...Noble Pride! Yes! Everyone knew that whoever bought this would have no bowel control, and *so would everyone else!* Joe bid on the Injection and waited.

Every time someone else bid on it, the price only raised a small increment. Joe waited until the Ringleader started to count down and raised the bid. He was given a *Legendary* potion for just under sixteen platinum. Joe couldn't even believe that had just happened. The small bottle arrived in his room, and Joe shook his head.

"Well, butler, I think we are done here. Can you call for my cart? With this, I am out of money, and we are nearing the end of the evening anyway." Joe held the bottle and pretended to try and put it in his ring. "Oh right, can't store this. Well, I'd hate to lose it... better drink it then."

He popped the top and swallowed the small mouthful that was in it even as the butler tried to stop him. "Sir! I... you could have gotten your ring back..."

The cart stopped in front of the room, and Joe sat down in it. This made the butler wince as he put the ring on Joe's hand, but the potion hadn't taken effect yet. When it did, the effect was instant.

Intelligence +15! You have gained a debuff: Seep and Squeeze! For 24 hours, the urge to hug things and people around you becomes nearly unbearable! You have no bowel control for 12 hours! Anything in there? Let's find out!

"I don't... feel so well." Joe stated as his stomach released an ominous rumble. Then his eyes rolled up into his head, and he collapsed on the cart. The butler hissed in annoyance.

"Go, *go!* Ugh!"

Joe thrashed twice, and his eyes re-opened. They held a new clarity, and the world around him seemed *so* much easier to understand. He had reached the next threshold of intelligence. As the cart started to move, a shadow snaked out of the cart and into the room he had just vacated, connecting to a dark patch on the other side of his balcony. The shadows became firm, and as the cart was hurried out of the building... a dark line followed them.

CHAPTER FIFTY

Joe pretended to be unconscious, and his stomach continued to rumble and twitch violently. To pass the time as they moved, he looked at his updated stat page.

Name: Joe '*Tatum's Chosen Legend*' Class: Jumplomancer (Actual: Rituarchitect)
Profession: Tenured Scholar (Actual: Arcanologist)
Character Level: 15 Exp: 134,813 Exp to next level: 1,187
Rituarchitect Level: 3 Exp: 4,640 Exp to next level: 1,360
Hit Points: 330/330
Mana: 1,590/1,590
Mana regen: 30.3/sec (Base 27.55/sec increased by gear)
Stamina: 295/295
Stamina regen: 5.67/sec

Characteristic: Raw score (Modifier)

Strength: 31 (1.31)
Dexterity: 40 (1.40)
Constitution: 38 (1.38)
Intelligence: 106 (3.06)
Wisdom: 76 (2.26)
Charisma: 31 (1.31)
Perception: 60 (2.10)
Luck: 30 (1.30)
Karmic Luck: 0

The first thing he saw was the 'three' in his intelligence modifier. If he went with the direct translation, that is, the average IQ being one-ten back on earth, did this mean that he would have an IQ of three-thirty-six point six? His brain was on *fire*, and his thoughts were zipping along at a rapid pace. Now, he didn't *feel* smarter, but he was able to clearly think about multiple things concurrently and process them at the same time.

This was going to help his spellcasting *tremendously*, he could already tell. Now... they were getting near the exit. It was time to make his move. Joe lurched into a seated position, "Oh, *lordy*! I need... I need a *bush* right now!"

"Sir, we are just about to teleport. No one is allowed to be in this area on foot," the butler ground out through clenched teeth.

"Well, alright. I guess I'll just... sit in this as it comes." A wet sound could be heard, and Joe started to sit.

"*No!* Off, off, *off!*" The butler yanked Joe out of the cart and shoved him to the edge of the path they were on. As Joe stepped past the bush, he realized that only the path had ornamental plants along it; otherwise, the area was fully empty; just bare stone.

"Oh...?" Joe hiked up his robe and let everything flow naturally. Time to work; no one was going to come bother him when he was making sounds like *this*. He pulled out his large Mana Battery and gave it a kiss, then did the same with the smaller one he had. He Cleansed himself and stood straight, holding both Cores in the air.

He looked over at the arena, watching as the closing ceremony began. Spells, light show... he sent a pulse of mana along the shadowy path. His hope was rewarded an instant later.

Would you like to activate the ritual 'Raze' on Bloodsport Arena? Yes / No.

"Ye~*ee*~ess," Joe grunted as a powerful spasm made him clench. He managed to stay upright, and a blue ritual circle appeared under him as well as under the Mana Batteries. For an instant, he was holding twin blue orbs of power as a ritual sprang into existence across the rocky plain. "See you, buddies."

Joe dropped one of the objects right behind him, into a bush, where it landed with a faint *splash*. Hoo-boy. He tossed the other as hard as he could and pulled a huge tube out of his codpiece. The shouting was starting as people around the area saw the active ritual. There was no way he could claim ignorance when the circle shining at his feet matched the one on the arena. "Activate ritual of the Ghostly Army."

The scroll he was holding vanished, and Joe flinched. No effect? He needed to–

Whump

A fog bank a hundred feet tall and half a mile long sprang into existence so quickly that it displaced the air and made soft thunder. One of the effects of the fog was that it distorted sound, so Joe felt like he had once again entered a new world. This was a world of dim light, poor vision, and soft, cloying motions in the air. Joe knew what he needed to do, though. He kept his hand on the bushes and started to walk. He followed the foliage, walking slowly until it started to curve out and away.

"This has gotta be the teleportation landing point," Joe spoke aloud and, even so, couldn't hear the words clearly. There were a... *few* things he was able to hear, however. There was a low, muted buzz that seemed to come from everywhere, a *deep* humming that was coming from somewhere near him, and high-pitched trills that seemed to be moving around.

"Magical Synesthesia?" Joe took a step forward, following a moving trill. When it was *right* in front of him, a man appeared. No... a *Jester*! The man saw him at the same moment, and a curved dagger flicked out at Joe.

He *jumped* to the side and started pulling mana into a thin Exquisite Shell. Oddly, the Jester didn't follow him, and Joe got a notification.

Quest updated: Playing your fake role III. Avoid pursuit three times by jumping to an improbable location and escaping unseen. 1/3. Dodge ten attacks by jumping out of the way. 1/10. Finish destroying a structure while in mid-air. 0/1.

Joe got the message: don't follow the trilling noises. It appeared that meant that there were... perhaps enchanted weapons? The low buzz was moving away, and Joe had to assume that was the ritual, as it was *everywhere* and moving at the pace of a marching army. What was the deep hum, then? Hopefully, what he was looking for.

He crawled along the ground, leaving a dark trail for different reasons than earlier. Joe was just glad that he couldn't *hear* anything from back there. *Feeling* it was bad enough. His fingers started to feel regular lines on the ground, and he brought his face close enough that he could see them. Enchantment-style runes and lines! He could only hear a mass of sound and decided that it was time to use the last four skill points that he had been holding on to.

Skill increased: Magical Synesthesia (Novice VII). You can hear magic in the middle of a sound-distorting ritual, but you can't even listen to your body right now. You are very strange.

Yes! He could make out individual noises now, just barely. Joe followed the deep hum, working hard to distinguish various lesser sounds mixed into the magical mental noise. Hah. A sense that worked even through his rituals. Something to remember.

"That... that one is familiar." Joe followed a small sound, and when he found it, he was overjoyed to realize that it was the *exact* sound that he heard in altars and various waypoints. All of this—the *huge* enchantment that acted as a landing pad—was all so that the Zoo could replicate the same ability the fast travel system had? Joe pricked his finger and touched it to the *exact* spot that the sound was emanating from.

You have wrested control of an area enchantment from the previous owner! They have been notified of their loss! Current functions of area: teleport to Grand Zoo of Ardania, teleport to Ardania Main Square. Current people allowed to use this enchantment: Joe.

Joe looked toward the Bloodsport Arena. It was really too bad that he couldn't collect the building material or at least see what was happening over there. Still... this *was* an area filled with assassins. Angry, vengeful, clown-like assassins who were in the process of losing their base. Probably better to get going. Joe stood up and formed a black barrel made of shadow. He made the bottom thin and pulled his staff out of his ring. To hold off his other current need, he got close and wrapped himself around his creation. Big hug for shadow barrel.

"*Acid Spray!*" Joe channeled the spell, and after twenty seconds, the barrel was half-full and hissing. He gripped the shadows with his mind and took one last look toward the arena. The mist was thinning, which made him realize how exposed he was, but... it also let him see the sky. All the stars and such but somehow much closer than usual. "It's a projection? *We're underground!*"

Now it made sense why this place was nearly impossible to find. Joe looked at the enchantment at his feet and even recognized it. This was a massive version of the elevator enchantment he had once bribed Terra with! That meant... that meant they were *under* Ardania! But how far?

"You!" A Jester appeared out of the thinning mist. "Who are you? What are you doing?"

"Just watering my barrel," Joe replied easily, continuing to channel acid. "Don't mind me."

"Stop what you are doing this *instant*, and come with us! You are in a cart-restricted area. If you do *anything* besides follow my instructions, we will cut you down!"

"I'm so *sorry*. I had no idea." Joe continued filling the barrel.

Skill increase: Acting (Novice IX).

Skill increase: Channeling (Beginner V).

"Come with me!"

"Nah." When Joe replied, the other Jesters surrounding the area attacked. Joe focused his mind and *jumped*. He vanished in a flash of light, and the blades *clanged* together in the air where he had stood. The dark barrel wavered for a moment, then the bottom disintegrated, followed by the rest of it. Potent acid washed over the etchings and lines of the elevator enchantment. The acid combined with a bonus five percent armor penetration managed to score and pit the strong enchantment so badly that it was unrecognizable within moments. In under *ten* seconds, the enchantment sputtered, flashed, and failed.

Just like that, an Assassin's Guild, a black market, and a collapsing arena full of Nobility and wealthy lawbreakers were trapped in the depths below Ardania.

EPILOGUE

Twelve hours after fleeing for his life from the Bloodsport Arena, Joe sat in the waiting room of the palace. He had jumped in place for as long as he could while the ritual circle remained around his feet, and he had gotten lucky enough to be in midair as the ritual finished. Then he had waited until the... *first* effect of the Injection had worn off, but he was still in an extra-huggy mood and so was trying not to push himself to see the King just yet. Cleanse had been a constant companion, but there had still been... mishaps on the way here.

Joe shook off the thought and looked over the notifications he had gained. While he had the ability to go into the throne room if he pushed it, there was no need to rush. Better to wait until they were ready for him. He decided to look over the messages that had appeared over the last few hours, alternatively wincing and smiling.

You have a characteristic that is two thresholds above others! Look at the full listing of debuffs that this places upon you here*.

You have reached a hundred points in intelligence! Mana becomes more plentiful for you, and each point of intelligence is now worth fifteen points instead of twelve point five!

An area enchantment you control has been destroyed! Outgoing teleportation functionality damaged beyond repair.

Your reputation with the Grand Zoo of Ardania has decreased by 10,000! New reputation: -11,300 (Blood Feud). All members of this faction will attempt to kill you on sight!

Quest updated: Playing your fake role III. Avoid pursuit three times by jumping to an improbable location and escaping unseen. 1/3. Dodge ten attacks by jumping out of the way. 1/10. Finish destroying a structure while in mid-air. 1/1.

Class experience +500!

The positive messages made him happy, but Joe had serious misgivings about each of the *negative* ones. He took a deep breath and started with the listing of debuffs. Reading over it, he deflated and realized that this must be the way the game punished unbalanced characters and that he would need to start putting in more effort to increase his stats.

Intelligence is two thresholds above charisma! Debuff added: Hammerwords. Does this dress make my butt look big? 'Yes. Go Up a size. It does not fit.' Effect: Blunt objectivity at the cost of some subtleness. Usually all of it. 5% Chance to decrease reputation by a full rank during conversation.

Intelligence is two thresholds above constitution! Debuff added: Not a chance. No, I'm not doing it. That's going to be terrible for me. Get someone else or actually pay attention so we can do this smartly. Effect: When planning something, there is a 5% chance that you will realize that it is a terrible idea beyond redemption.

Intelligence is two thresholds above dexterity! Debuff added: Risk Assessment. Based on my knowledge of candelabras and swing ropes... you are an idiot, and I'm not doing this. Effect: 10% chance of not making dexterous decisions when there might be an easier option.

Intelligence is two thresholds above luck! Debuff added: I Know Better! Little Joey would soon learn that he did <u>not</u>, in fact, know better. Effect: 1% chance to make a <u>terrible</u> decision.

Intelligence is two thresholds above strength! Debuff added: Calculation Drain. Overthinking so much that you've determined that while you can hit and do damage, you missed your chance to do so. Less chance of making an attack, rather than missing one. Effect: -10% speed of action decision.

"Yeesh." Joe looked over the various things that he had going against him right now and gulped. "Right... I need to get everything under the threshold of fifty above it before I get wisdom to one hundred. I bet that would add a whole *slew* of additional debuffs."

Wisdom +1!

"Ahh! My stats are trying to kill me!" Joe yelped, jumping to his feet. At that moment, the door to the waiting room opened, and a Royal Guard stepped in.

"They are ready for you."

No other words were spoken on the subject, and none were needed. The guard looked down at Joe, somehow managing to tolerate the arms that were wrapped around his waist. "Sorry, I have a debuff on that makes me want to hug."

"I knew there was a reason they sent *me* in." The huge guard sighed and listened intently. Indeed, he could hear light snickering. "Resist it. Shape up. The Royal Court are waiting."

Joe pulled back, somehow managing to resist the compulsion. "I'm good. Let's go."

They walked into the throne room, which had as many people as when Joe was here on trial. The place was *packed*. Joe was guided to the open dais, and the guard pulled him along to make sure he didn't stop and hug everyone. By being held in place, he managed to look at the Royal couple without charging at them for a hug. That just... wouldn't go well.

"Joe, Tatum's Chosen Legend." The King's voice rocked the room, leaving everyone slightly dazed. "You were given a mission by the Crown to infiltrate a dark cesspool of danger and villainy. In doing so, you may have provided a great service to the Kingdom."

Quest complete: Black to Purple. After finding the unique building, you managed to 1) Create a blueprint for the Kingdom to use. 2) Destroy the building. But failed to 3) Secure a way to and from the location without outside assistance.

Rewards: Two objectives completed. Rewards: 1) Record remains clean, previous wrongdoing expunged. 2) Act of Nobility recorded.

"Tell us what happened in as much detail as you are able," the King ordered. Joe launched into his story, and as he spoke, the tension in the room mounted, reaching dangerous levels. "I see... you say that this place was constantly frequented by the Nobility? Interesting. Also, you failed to secure a way to and from the location but *did* manage to make the trip one-way. In so doing, you may have managed to capture even *more* lawbreakers. Interesting indeed."

"We will be doing a full accounting," the Queen spoke into the still air. "All members of the Nobility above the age of minority are to present themselves before us within twenty-four hours... or be stripped of their title, hereditary inheritance, and be declared criminals until such a time as they have paid their debt to the Kingdom."

The room shook from all the angry voices that spoke out against this proclamation. The Royals let the commotion continue for a moment, then the King stood. Just like that, everyone was forced into stillness. "I see. So, *none* of you are confident that your heirs are *not* trapped in a pit full of *unsanctioned assassins*? In a tax-evading black market that has been preventing the *Kingdom* from gaining rare and *necessary* resources?

"How about this? If any *are* certain your people are innocent, feel free to join me when I send everyone else away. For everyone else, a *fifth* of your estates will be taken by the Kingdom to make up for lost taxation through a black market. If you agree now, your heirs will not be charged or *worse* when the area below is reclaimed."

A Noblewoman stood and spoke against the pressure, "Your Majesty! You would beggar us all, punish us for the deeds of the few? For what our children *might* be doing?"

"Yes," the King and Queen responded in synch.

The King nodded at Queen Marie, and she stood with a wave of stifling power that made the others choke on their words. "It seems that you have *forgotten* what *your* position is... and what *our* role is. The King and I *lifted* you into the positions you currently occupy. We *allowed* you to stand as equals amongst yourselves; we were *not* forced to do so. As you did not *earn* your positions, it seems your greed overcame you. You forgot *why* we exist. Perhaps you found that the power your title granted you was your *right*. You are very wrong."

The King stepped forward to stand alongside her, and the stifling effect multiplied. "Others would *gladly* stand to take your place, and you will decide *now* if it is time for you to vanish... so as not to cause us issue going forward and into troubled times. A Noble house that calmly allows the Kingdom to be cheated is no friend to us. A *replacement* for your positions can *always* be found."

Joe was doing his utmost not to move or draw attention. No need for people to remember who brought attention to this issue. The King finished with a growl that made glass crack, "You are all dismissed. The locations that allow for entry into the 'backstage' of the 'Zoo' are now under heavy guard, and anyone attempting to enter the area will be seen as a felon by the Crown. You have ten minutes to choose your path into the future. Believe in the innocence of your heirs and let them take the fall if they survive, or forfeit a fifth of your holdings *now.*"

"Another thing," Queen Marie caught everyone off guard with her words. "We now hold firm with a person's right to work their craft. We now find that all monopolies and agreements forcing people to work for them to be against the law and null. Guild systems, Colleges, and Unions have been grabbing power that is not theirs to hold. All people are freed of their obligations. This will be put into law tonight and, by the morning, will be in effect. Prepare yourselves. The change we have longed for is here. Let's hope we all survive it."

Joe was pulled into a side room, and he gave the King a hug. King Henry looked at him with some discomfort. "That's strange, but... it has been some time since I've gotten a hug. I needed that."

"You have been awarded recognition for an act of Nobility, Joe," Queen Marie stated as the silence stretched. "If we manage to gain the needed material to build this arena, are you willing to build it for us?"

"Of course!" Joe responded instantly.

"But... I haven't even offered a reward to you yet." The Queen looked at him with concern, which turned into a smile as he shrugged. "You act with more honor than many of our own Nobles. Can I ask *why* you work so hard when there might not be personal gain in it?"

"What can I say to that? Thank my mother for that." Joe bowed before looking up with a cheeky grin. "After all..."

"Just like the Arena, I was *Razed* right."

AFTERWORD

Thank you for reading and I hope you enjoyed Raze! The Completionist Chronicles has been so much fun to write that I have a fun surprise for you: I've collaborated with James Hunter, author of Viridian Gate Online and Rogue Dungeon, to bring you a new series within this world. Wolfman Warlock: Bibliomancer will be out September 17th!

Could you do me a favor? James and I are making a run at bestseller lists so it would mean so much to me if you could pick it up in advance of release. To whet your appetite, I've included a sneak peek at the end of this book so enjoy the read following the appendix and then purchase it at Books2Read.com/Bibliomancer. Thank you for being amazing and for your continued support!

Help us be New York Times or USA Today bestsellers! Pick up Bibliomancer today!

About Dakota Krout

I live in a 'pretty much Canada' Minnesota city with my wife and daughter. I started writing The Divine Dungeon series because I enjoy reading and wanted to create a world all my own. To my surprise and great pleasure, I found like-minded people who enjoy the contents of my mind. Publishing my stories has been an incredible blessing thus far, and I hope to keep you entertained for years to come!

Connect with Dakota:
Patreon.com/DakotaKrout
Facebook.com/TheDivineDungeon
Twitter.com/DakotaKrout

About Mountaindale Press

Dakota and Danielle Krout, a husband and wife team, strive to create as well as publish excellent fantasy and science fiction novels. Self-publishing *The Divine Dungeon: Dungeon Born* in 2016 transformed their careers from Dakota's military and programming background and Danielle's Ph.D. in pharmacology to President and CEO, respectively, of a small press. Their goal is to share their success with other authors and provide captivating fiction to readers with the purpose of solidifying Mountaindale Press as the place 'Where Fantasy Transforms Reality.'

Connect with Mountaindale Press:
MountaindalePress.com
Facebook.com/MountaindalePress
Twitter.com/_Mountaindale
Instagram.com/MountaindalePress
Krout@MountaindalePress.com

Mountaindale Press Titles

GameLit and LitRPG

The Divine Dungeon Series
By: Dakota Krout

A Touch of Power Series
By: Jay Boyce

Red Mage: Advent
By: Xander Boyce

Ether Collapse: Equalize
By: Ryan DeBruyn

Axe Druid Series
By: Christopher Johns

Skeleton in Space: Histaff
By: Andries Louws

Pixel Dust: Party Hard
By: David Petrie

APPENDIX

NOTABLE CHARACTERS

Alexis – Joe's second-in-command for his current team, Alexis is an Aromatic Artificer. By making poisons and weapons and using them to great effect, she has proven her worth time and again.

Aten – The Commander of 'The Wanderer's' Noble Guild.

Bard – Bard holds the position of a tank in Joe's current team. Contrary to his name, Bard is a Skald. Instead of staying in a well-protected position and playing songs, Bard is on the frontlines of any engagement chanting and swinging his axes.

Boris – The head librarian and the local leader of the Scholars profession.

CAL – Certified Altruistic Lexicon, the AI that controls Eternium.

Guard Captain Blas – Blas has proven himself to be an honorable man and is now dating Joe's mother. Joe has decided to keep a closer eye on this situation.

Jake – An Alchemist who has set up shop in the city, this man has deranged tastes and a mysterious interest in seeing random acts of violence.

Jaxon – An Acupuncturist and Chiropractor in real life, Jaxon came into the game to try out new methods of healing. Is it his fault that everyone is so... brittle? Playing the game as a Monk, Jaxon uses his talents to deadly effect.

Joey (Joe) Nelson – The main character of our story, Joe is a Ritualist who has specialized into a 'Rituarchitect' class. By supplying the material and power, he can grow a building with ease. His contributions in the future will need to be significant for the human race to survive.

Mike – Vice Guild leader of The Wanderer's Guild, Mike is ex-military specialized in logistics.

O'Baba – With the death of the Wolfman Warlord, O'Baba is the leader of the Wolfman race. She is the most powerful spellcaster of her people, and will do anything to ensure their survival.

Poppy – Papadopoulos Whisperfoot is a Duelist who wears eye-catching clothes and wields a rapier. Able to take down heavily-armored foes with ease, Poppy is an invaluable member of Joe's current team.

Tatum (Hidden god) – The deity of hidden and forbidden knowledge.

Terra – An overly exuberant enchanter in Joe's guild.

Sir Bearington – The Mayor of a small town that Joe's guild chose as a base of operations. Sir Bearington is an honorable man... and an unbearable foe if angered.

FINAL STATS

Name: Joe *'Tatum's Chosen Legend'* Class: Jumplomancer (Actual: Rituarchitect)
Profession: Tenured Scholar (Actual: Arcanologist)
Character Level: 15 Exp: 134,813 Exp to next level: 1,187
Rituarchitect Level: 3 Exp: 4,640 Exp to next level: 1,360
Hit Points: 330/330
Mana: 1,590/1,590
Mana regen: 30.3/sec (Base 27.55/sec increased by gear)
Stamina: 295/295
Stamina regen: 5.67/sec

Characteristic: Raw score (Modifier)

Strength: 31 (1.31)
Dexterity: 40 (1.40)
Constitution: 38 (1.38)
Intelligence: 106 (3.06)
Wisdom: 77 (2.27)
Charisma: 31 (1.31)
Perception: 60 (2.10)
Luck: 30 (1.30)
Karmic Luck: 0

SKILL LIST

Acid Spray (Beginner II)

Acting (Novice VII)

Aerial Acrobatics (Beginner I)

Channeling (Beginner V)

Cleanse (Student II)

Coalescence (Student 0)

Drawing (Novice VI)

Dual casting (Novice III)

Effortless (Darkness) Shaping (Legendary) (Apprentice VII)

Exquisite Shell. (Beginner 0)

Group Heal (Apprentice VI)

Herbalism (Novice VI)

Hidden Sense (Beginner VII)

Intrusive Scan (Novice IV)

Jump around (Master 0)

Jump Master (0)

Lay on hands. (Apprentice IV)

Magical Synesthesia (Novice VII)

Mana manipulation (Student 0)

Medic (Novice I)

Mend (Student III)

Mental Manipulation Resistance (Novice V)

Natural Magical Material Creation (Apprentice 0)

Query (Pray) (Novice II)

Reading. (Apprentice I)

Resurrection (Novice III)

Ritual Lore (Apprentice II)

Ritual Magic (Expert I)

Solidified Shadows (Mythical). (Apprentice IX)

Speech (Novice VII)

Spellbinding (Apprentice IV)

Staff mastery (Novice I)

Teaching (Beginner II)

Wither Plant (Apprentice V)

Words of Power (Written) (Apprentice 0)

SNEAK PEEK

Wolfman Warlock: Bibliomancer
A Completionist Chronicles Series

A sharp *knock-knock-knock* on the door pulled Sam from his hazy thoughts of far off places.

"Yeah, come on in," he pushed himself upright so that he was sitting on the edge of the mattress with his legs trailing over the edge, his shoes brushing the brown carpet.

His dad poked his head in, a knowing grin on his weathered face. "You got a minute, champ?" He was grasping the door and his fingers were drumming restlessly against the white-painted wood.

"Yeah, of course."

"Just wanted to stop in and make sure you're okay. I know this," he waved toward the door as he pushed his way in, closing the it softly behind him with a *click* "isn't really your whole thing. The party stuff, I mean. I also caught you taking to that brain-dead bunch in the backyard."

The older man grimaced and ran a hand through his short-cropped hair, which was a perpetual holdover from his Marine Corps days. "They're not bad kids, but I swear to all that is holy that there's not a living brain cell between the whole lot of them. And it's not their fault—their parents have to own most of the responsibility for their current status as leeches. But good lord, I've never seen a more spoiled or entitled group of people in my life."

Sam shrugged helplessly, trying not to agree *too* readily. "They're not all bad."

"No, definitely not," his dad replied, shaking his head, "wasn't trying to say that. I just know you don't really, you know, fit in very well with that bunch. You never really have. Frankly, there are few things in my life that I'm prouder of then the fact that you *don't* fit in with those knuckleheads. Your mom and me, we always worried about that. We were afraid you'd just coast along, but you going to college? Knocking it right out of the park like that? Well, I think that's one fear I won't have to worry about anymore. You did good, kid."

Sam blushed and looked away. "Thanks. Still, it's really gonna be good to get away and see some of the world. I mean Berkley was cool, sure, but a lot of it was the *same* if that makes sense. Like the scenery changed, but it was the same people I've been around my entire life. The same kind of environment in a lot of ways, and I can't wait to get out of here for a while."

His father glanced down, shuffling on nervous feet. "Yeah. About that. Your mother and I have been thinking. Talking a little..."

The man faltered, clearly searching for the right words. "Look, the thing is, I know you had your heart set on Europe, but we've been thinking it might not be such a good idea."

Sam's stomach lurched and dropped, worry rising up into the back of his throat. "*Seriously?*"

His father finally looked up, lips pressed into a thin line. "It's complicated. We had another idea, but it's a little hard to explain. It would probably be easier if I just showed you. But to do that, we'll need to take a ride. Don't suppose you want to blow this popsicle stand early?"

"If you stop speaking in clichés from the eighties, I mean..." Feeling a numb sort of detachment, Sam stood and followed his dad out of the house, not even bothering to say goodbye to the party guests.

***

The drive over from the house was a tense, uneasy thing. Sam worked furiously to get his dad to divulge some details, *any* details, about what was going on. Where they were going, and especially *why*. Normally his dad couldn't keep a secret to save his life, but all of a suddenly he was about as talkative as a brick wall and just as revealing. They lived in Orange County, but on the outskirts of the city, a handful of miles from San Clemente. His dad wouldn't let them know where they were going, but they were headed north toward Anaheim, crawling through the traffic on I-5.

Sam couldn't even begin to fathom what ominous thing might wait them in Anaheim.

He crawled through every memory, every conversation he'd had with his parents over the past few months, and came up with absolutely nothing that made sense. Then—because he had nothing better to do since his Dad was giving him the silent treatment—he thought back to the news. Had there been some sort of terror attack recently over in Europe? Something that might've convinced his parents not to send him on his backpacking expedition? Rumors of war? An outbreak of Swine flu? There was tension overseas, but then there was *always* tension overseas. Honestly, he couldn't think of anything that fit.

Eventually, he just settled back into the leather passenger seat of the Beamer, flicked on the tunes, and resigned himself for whatever was in store.

After another twenty minutes, they pulled off the five, weaving through the wide city streets before turning into nondescript office park with a manned guard shack and a formidable gate. Other than the presence of the guard—a beefy guy who looked like he ate nails and punks for breakfast—the complex beyond could've belonged in just about any city in America. The office building was four stories tall, boxy and white, with rows and rows of reflective windows. To Sam, it seemed like the kind of place someone might go to get their taxes done. What business could they possibly have in a place like this?

He squinted as the guard at the shack pressed a button, opening the gate and waving them through with a thick-fingered hand. As the car lurched into motion, Sam could finally make out the signage on the building. In bold letters, tattooed across the white stucco was the name of the company: *Elon's Electronics, a Division of Space-Y.* Sam, of course, had heard of Space-Y, which was a subsidiary company run by President Musk. He couldn't even fathom the idea that there was *anyone* who hadn't heard of Space-Y and its brilliant but eccentric founder.

But... none of this was adding up inside his head.

The more pieces of the puzzle he found, the more bizarre the picture became. The only thing his mind could come up with was that his parents had decided to launch him into space. Which was an insane conclusion, obviously, but every other scenario seemed equally absurd. He had to admit, though, getting launched into space sounded pretty fun.

His dad pulled the Beamer into a wide space, marked off with fresh white paint that had a sign reading *Reserved for VIP Customers.* The next spot over was also occupied... by his mother's car—a sleek Audi in slate gray. Or at least it was a car *exactly* like his mother's car, though Sam supposed it could possibly belong to someone else. He'd never bothered to learn the license plate number, and there were no other distinguishing marks, no bummer stickers or decals. But what were the odds?

"Come on," his dad said as he killed the engine. Now the old man was clearly suppressing a smile. Something tremendously unorthodox was going on here, but Sam was starting to get the feeling that it wasn't bad. Not necessarily. Sam got out of the car, the locks chirping softly as he closed the door, and headed up a short concrete walk, which ended at a set of mirrored-glass doors, which showed his reflection but nothing beyond. His dad pulled open the door, and gestured toward the yawning opening with one hand. "After you, kid."

Sam headed toward the uninviting entryway, apprehension mounting with every step. He wasn't even remotely ready for when his mom popped out from behind a planter in the office lobby, yelling 'surprise' as she waved her hands frantically in the air. There were more balloons decorating the office interior, but thankfully the place was devoid of the rest of the party guests—all of them must've been abandoned back at the house, which was fine by Sam but still shocking given his mother's normal attitude about guests.

"Surprise, *surprise*, surprise, sweetie-pie!" his mom squeed, nearly dancing across the floor toward him in sheer excitement. "And this time, it's for *real!*"

The entryway door swung shut with a *whoosh* and his dad ambled up beside him, clapping a callused hand—a working man's hand, despite the money—down on Sam's shoulder. He wasn't even *trying* to hide exactly how pleased with himself he was.

"I almost lost it," he beamed at Sam's mom. "You should've seen his face when I told him there was a problem with the trip—poor kid looked like I planted a knife in his guts. I almost spilled the beans right there. But I'm glad I held out. Totally worth it. Look at his face! Still confused. So good."

Sam raised his hands, head spinning like a merry-go-round. "Okay. Will someone please tell me what in the *heck* is going on?"

"We're sending you to space! *Oof*." His dad grunted as a pointy finger jabbed him in the ribs.

"We are *not*. And this is your *real* surprise," his mom replied, folding her hands together. "I knew *someone* may have let the cat out of the bag about the first party, so I decided to throw two parties."

She shot a sideways glance at Sam's dad, then waggled her eyebrows at Sam. "A false party to throw you off the scent; but this is the one I knew you'd actually like."

She stepped to one side and motioned toward a counter at the far side of the lobby. Behind the desk was a smiling receptionist of maybe thirty, wearing a neat white suit, her red hair tied up in a tight bun at the back of her head. On the wall, behind the service counter was a sleek chrome sign, the lines sharp and precise, which simply said: *Eternium.*

The cogs inside Sam's head slowly clanked to life, the mystery resolving itself slowly but surely. Eternium was the brand new ultra-deep dive MMO that released... *today*. No way. No *way!* The whole internet had been buzzing with speculation. Speculation Sam had largely ignored since: *one*, he was working through finals and *two*, rumor was the earliest version of the game cost an arm and a leg. He'd watched the video trailers, of course, he didn't know anyone who hadn't, but he never thought he'd have a chance to play. At least not in the first round of gamers.

"Yep," his dad's grin somehow—almost impossibly—growing even wider. "Your mom and I, we knew you had your heart set on that trip. But then a buddy of mine mentioned that this game was coming out, and knowing you, well..."

He shrugged. "Well, we thought maybe it would be better than backpacking around Europe. It just seemed so perfect. I mean, the game launches today. On the day you were due home. The slots were going so *fast* though, so we had to make an executive decision. Didn't even have time to talk to you about it."

The man sheepishly paused, rubbing the back of his neck with one hand. "We just pulled the trigger and went for it."

"And," his mom broke in, "you'll actually get an even *longer* break than you thought! Wendy, here—who is just lovely, by the way—was explaining to your father and I about something called *Time Dilation*. Sounds very complicated and fancy. I'm still not entirely sure how it's supposed to work, but from the sound of things a three-month trip inside Eternium will feel like six months to you."

She faltered for a beat, searching his face for any sign of a reaction. Sam was quiet. Still. She winced and wiggled uncertainly, before finishing weakly "I... *we* hope you don't hate it."

Sam rushed her without a word, throwing his arms out and pulling her in against him. He'd grown a lot since leaving for college, putting on half a foot in height and nearly fifty pounds, most of it muscle, and his mother seemed smaller than she ever had before. A frail and fragile thing, but still he hugged her tight. "I *love* it, mom."

It took a moment, but he finally ended up releasing her. Sam turned and almost tackled his dad. "This is the best gift *ever*! I think you guys might know me even better than I know myself."

It was true. Despite the fact that Sam's dad had been a football star in high school, he'd never pushed for Sam do the sports thing, especially not when it became clear that he'd rather be gaming with his friends online. In middle school, both of his parents had even signed up for World of Alphastorm Accounts so they could 'game together as a family'—his mom's words. They were both *terrible*. His dad just couldn't seem to get a handle on the controls and his mom spent most of her time running into corners, then accidentally blowing herself up with a fireball, but they'd tried.

He could see the visible relief on his mom's face as she sighed deeply. "Oh good. I'm so glad you like it, honey. I was a little worried that maybe you'd outgrown these games, but your father assured me this would be better than anything else we could give you."

"Welcome, Sam," the woman behind the counter said, standing. She smiled, her teeth white and unnaturally even. "We are so pleased to have you with us, and as one of the first people to ever play Eternium—and in a DIVE pod, no less—you're in for a world of fun. If you're ready to go, we're all set up and waiting for you. Your parents filled out most of the paperwork already, so we'll just need to have you sign some forms, get a blood draw and a few vitals. But then, your adventure awaits."

BIBLIOMANCER
COMING SEPTEMBER 17TH!

James and I are making a run at bestseller lists so it would mean so much to me if you could pick it up in advance of release. You can find it at Books2Read.com/Bibliomancer. Thank you for being amazing and for your continued support!

Made in the USA
San Bernardino, CA
02 August 2019